Dear Reader,

Double Your Reading Pleasure (the unofficial Duets motto) can only begin to describe the fantastic books we have for you this month.

Kristin Gabriel, popular with Love & Laughter readers, will charm you with a woman who has too many fiancés in *Annie, Get Your Groom*. Then Jennifer Drew writes a You Tarzan, Me Jane story set in the corporate wilderness! Readers of Yours Truly books will recognize the fresh and exciting talent that is Jennifer Drew and we welcome her into Harlequin Duets with *Taming Luke*.

Jacqueline Diamond returns with the hilarious *The Bride Wore Gym Shoes*. Need I really say more?—except the heroine's friend predicts she is going to marry the most unsuitable, although delectable, man.

We're thrilled that Tracy South is back with her second book, *Maddie's Millionaire*. If you like eccentric characters and a story filled with charm, this is the novel for you.

I hope you're enjoying our books. Feel free to write to us!

Malle Vallik

Malle Vallik
Senior Editor
Harlequin Duets
Harlequin Books
225 Duncan Mill Road
Don Mills, Ontario
M3B 3K9 Canada

"I'm looking for a bridegroom."

Cole's reaction wasn't quite what Annie expected. He shook his head. "You're wasting your time. I'm a happily single man."

Great! First she lost her purse, then her bridegroom and now the only P.I. in Denver even willing to talk to her was obviously insane. She sniffed and wished she had enough money to buy cold medicine.

Cole handed her a tissue. "There are more conventional ways to snare a man. Have you tried the personal ads?"

"I'm not that desperate. I just want to find *my* bridegroom. The man who asked me to be his wife."

It took him a while to digest her words. "You mean...you don't want to marry me?"

He frowned and began scribbling in his notepad. "A missing person case. This is great. Can you give me a description?"

"Not really. The picture was in black-and-white."

His pen stilled as he turned his gaze to her. "Picture?"

"I've never actually seen him in person," she explained. "I'm a mail-order bride."

Taming Luke

Maybe she was sleepwalking.

Jane Grant rubbed her eyes. She wasn't hallucinating. Her always unpredictable boss, Rupert Cox, had added a statue of a Greek god to the company's fountain.

The water god was perfect. Even from a distance she saw the power in the arms raised to clutch his head, and the chiseled grace of the naked torso. If only real men looked like that!

The statue moved.

Jane realized she was staring at a real live man— taking a shower in Rupert Cox's prized fountain!

The man turned, saw her and walked slowly in her direction, as naked as a man could be without getting arrested. To call the scrap of cloth clinging wetly to his body a loincloth was being generous.

He came closer.

Things like this didn't happen to Jane Grant, twenty-six-year-old office worker. Her life was mundane with a capital *M*. She backed away. She wasn't the kind of girl who splashed around in fountains with nearly naked men.

How she wished she was!

HARLEQUIN DUETS

ISBN 0-373-44073-1

ANNIE, GET YOUR GROOM
Copyright © 1999 by Kristin Eckhardt

TAMING LUKE
Copyright © 1999 by Pamela Hanson and Barbara Andrews

This edition published by arrangement with Harlequin Books S.A.

® and TM are trademarks of the publisher. Trademarks indicated with ® are registered in the United States Patent and Trademark Office, the Canadian Trade Marks Office and in other countries.

Look us up on-line at: http://www.romance.net

Printed in U.S.A.

KRISTIN GABRIEL

Annie, Get Your Groom

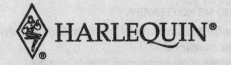

HARLEQUIN®

TORONTO • NEW YORK • LONDON
AMSTERDAM • PARIS • SYDNEY • HAMBURG
STOCKHOLM • ATHENS • TOKYO • MILAN • MADRID
PRAGUE • WARSAW • BUDAPEST • AUCKLAND

Do you ever feel like just getting away from it all? I love to travel, and one of my favorite vacation spots is Colorado. Only, my visits there haven't always been full of rest and relaxation. One time I had to be treated for an allergic reaction. Another time I suffered heat stroke. Then there was that embarrassing incident on the ski lift....

But I'm not going to let a few mishaps scare me away from those majestic Rocky Mountains. I'll just take out a good traveler's insurance policy before I cross the state border again.

When my heroine, Annie Bonacci, arrives in Colorado, she doesn't believe her life can possibly get any worse. I had so much fun proving her wrong!

—Kristin Gabriel

Books by Kristin Gabriel
HARLEQUIN LOVE & LAUGHTER
40—BULLETS OVER BOISE
56—MONDAY MAN
62—SEND ME NO FLOWERS

Don't miss Kristin Gabriel's trilogy Café Romeo in Duets in summer 2000!

To my son Matthew.

Thanks for the idea!

Prologue

ANNIE BONACCI wasn't going to panic yet. Worry? Maybe. Hyperventilate? Probably. But panic? Not an option. That is, until she found herself dangling out the fourth story window of her Newark apartment building.

"I really have to find a better way to make a living," she muttered, her fingers gripping the peeling edge of the windowsill. "I need a change of scenery. A new start. A forty-foot ladder."

She peered into the inky shadows of the narrow alley below. Forty feet might be an optimistic estimate. But Annie was a born optimist, a thirty-one-year-old Jersey girl with her life completely under control.

That's what got her into this mess in the first place.

Her short red dress rode up her hips, exposing more of her body to the brisk March wind. But it was the squall inside her apartment that chilled her. The screech of a stray cat in the alley sounded tame compared to the furious oaths she heard through the window.

She tightened her precarious grip until her pasty white knuckles shone in the moonlight. Her bare toes clung to the small crevices in the cold brick wall. Jumping was out of the question. So was waiting for help to arrive. The only person who knew about her predicament was laid up in the St. James Hospital with a compound leg fracture, several broken ribs and a severe concussion. All courtesy of her uninvited guests.

She could hear them rampaging through her apartment—them being hired thugs who wouldn't stop until they found her. She'd managed to evade them for the past two days, but they'd finally tracked her down. It was time to find a better hiding place.

But first she had to find a way off this ledge.

The bedroom door slammed open, the sound ripping through the open window like a gunshot. The hairs on the back of her neck prickled, and her palms grew sweaty. So much for hoping the cannoli she'd set out on the kitchen table would distract them.

Time to make her move.

She eyed the rusty drainpipe on her left. It looked like it could barely support the shriveled ivy vine clinging to it, much less her one hundred and thirty pounds. She took a deep breath and closed her eyes.

Think thin.

She reached out one hand, closing it around the broad pipe. Then she lifted one foot and perched it against a steel bracket. She winced as the thin metal cut into her toes. The drainpipe creaked as she wrapped her other hand around it and finally let go of her toehold on the brick.

Then she fell.

The rough metal scraped her hands as she slid down the pipe. She inhaled the sharp tang of rust and the heavy aroma of cooked cabbage from Mrs. Moynihan's third-story window. Her bare thighs braced against the pipe in an effort to slow her descent, the friction burning her skin.

Unfortunately, the drainpipe ended shortly before her feet hit the ground. She dropped like a rock onto the hastily stuffed duffel bag she'd tossed out the window only a few moments before.

Annie took a deep breath. "Just another day in the life of an investigative journalist." She slowly picked herself up off the ground, her knees wobbly as she surveyed the raw patches of skin along her body. Careening down a drainpipe in the dead of night wasn't quite as painless as she'd imagined.

But it was necessary.

Just like leaving New Jersey was necessary now. And she knew just where to go. She had a one-way ticket to Denver, Colorado, and enough adrenaline to run to the Newark International Airport. But with only an hour until her plane took off, she'd better take her chances with a taxi.

Annie unzipped her duffel bag, drew out a wrinkled trench coat, then frowned at the pair of three-inch heels she'd frantically stuffed into the bag. Shoes better suited for a tango than a getaway.

But at least they weren't made of cement.

She slung them on her sore feet, consoled by the one thought that kept echoing in her head.

It could only get better from here.

1

IT WAS crunch time.

Cole Rafferty took a deep, calming breath, willing himself to forget about the most recent trouble in his life and focus his concentration. It all came down to this moment. He needed to make it count.

The muscles in his shoulders tensed as he took careful aim. Then he raised his arm in the air and fired.

The wadded paper ball sailed toward the plastic basketball hoop hanging off the office door. If he sunk this shot his team would win the state...no, the national...no, the *world* championship. He raised his fist in a victory salute just as the door flew open, knocking the ball off target. It missed the hoop entirely and fell soundlessly onto the plush beige carpet.

"Interference!" he cried to the matronly woman filling the doorway.

Ethel Markowitz bent down, her mustard-yellow polyester pantsuit straining at the seams as she retrieved the paper ball off the floor. "It looks like trash to me."

"Give me my ball back, Ethel. I've got a game to play."

She crumpled the paper ball in her hand and executed a bank shot into the wastebasket. "That net thing hanging on the door looks very unprofessional. It collects dust up there, too. Perhaps I should take it down for a good cleaning."

He moved behind his massive mahogany desk. "Don't mess with my net again, Ethel," he warned, seating himself in the padded leather chair. "And we've already discussed this. P.I. work is grueling, not to mention stressful." He leaned back in his chair, crossing his ankles as he propped his stocking feet on the desk. "Shooting hoops helps me relax."

"If you relax any more, I'll have to start checking your pulse."

He smiled. "Spoken like a devoted secretary."

She peered at him over her bifocals. "Your father certainly thought so. I worked for him for thirty-five wonderful years. And he never put his feet up on the desk."

"That's because he lived in fear of you, Ethel. I, on the other hand, know you're a doll."

She sniffed. "Raggedy Ann is a doll. I am a sixty-two-year-old spinster who wears orthopedic shoes. Got it, Mr. Rafferty?"

He grinned. "Got it…doll."

She retaliated by pulling a pink memo pad from her pocket.

He groaned. "Don't tell me there are more messages."

Her olive green eyes gleamed with malicious pleasure. "Only three this time."

He slumped in his chair. "I don't want to hear them."

She chose to ignore his wishes and began to recite the messages aloud. "Miss Abigail Collins collects edible underwear and inquired about your favorite flavor. Penny Biggs wants you to meet her parents—as soon

as she finds the key to the attic. And someone named
Rita is planning, and I quote, *a bitchin' honeymoon
sure to freak you out,* thanks to the helpful suggestions
of her friends in Cell block D.''

"Dad really did it this time," he muttered, accustomed to Ethel's matter-of-factness manner. The
woman was unflappable.

She would also defend Rex Rafferty to the death.
"Only because he's a devoted father who has your best
interests at heart. Do you know how he slaved composing that advertisement? How hopeful he is that
you'll finally settle down and give him some grandchildren?''

"Do you suppose if I got a hamster he'd bond with
it, instead?''

Her pale lips tightened into a thin line.

"That's a joke, Ethel," he said, lowering his feet to
the floor.

"I do not get paid to frolic during office hours, Mr.
Rafferty.''

"You don't get paid to type up personal ads, either.''

She didn't actually blush, but the flicker in her eyes
told him he'd nailed her. She'd been an accomplice in
his father's latest fiasco.

Ever since his retirement a year ago, Rex Rafferty
had devoted his free time to interfering in his son's
life. He'd signed Cole up for a singles ceramics class.
Given him books with dating tips for his birthday. And
just last week, he'd placed a personal ad in the *Denver
Post* proclaiming Cole's desperate search for romance.
Which had, thus far, netted one hundred and thirty-two
breathless responses.

And not all of them from women.

Cole pinched the bridge of his nose with his fingertips. If he didn't love his old man so much he'd kill him. That personal ad was only the tip of the iceberg.

And he was the *Titanic*.

He glared at Ethel. "Did you have to include my name and number in the ad? Especially since you put in that line about my *playing around*. Do you know how that sounds?"

"Horseplay is one of your shortcomings, Mr. Rafferty." She looked pointedly at the basketball hoop. "You're thirty-four years old, and I think the least you could do is make an effort to find a nice, decent girl. Now I do have a niece—"

He cleared his throat before she could go any further. One matchmaker in his life was bad enough. Besides, he had more important things to do than discuss his marital status. Like finish his basketball game.

Gathering some loose forms scattered across his desk, he briskly tapped them together. "I'd love to hear all about her, but I've got work to do." He picked up a ballpoint pen, clicked it and then studiously pored over the paper in front of him.

"Five across is *conundrum*," she informed him. "Shall I tell the woman waiting outside that you're too busy to see her?"

He looked up from his crossword puzzle. "Woman? What woman? This isn't some fruitcake who read that personal ad, is it?"

"No. I believe she's a potential client."

"A client? A real client?"

Ethel arched a brow. "Were you expecting an imaginary one?"

He began clearing the top of his cluttered desk. "Why didn't you tell me sooner?" Then he looked at her, a fleet of paper airplanes clutched in one hand. "You're not teasing me, are you, Ethel?"

"I'm not that desperate for entertainment."

He crammed the paper airplanes into an oversize bottom drawer and wiped the Oreo cookie crumbs off his desk pad with one quick swipe. "Send her in. No, wait a minute. Let me put my shoes on first."

"You wore shoes to work today?"

"You really need to work on that sarcasm problem of yours, Ethel. It's very unprofessional." He grinned as she turned smartly on her rubber heels and strode out the door.

A case. A real case. Maybe. He told himself not to get his hopes up. Rafferty Investigations didn't exactly attract exciting cases. His father had handed the business over with the stipulation that Cole keep its high standards. Which meant no divorce work. No undercover surveillance. No blatant advertising. Just a discreet listing in the yellow pages and a fee high enough to attract only wealthy, discriminating clients.

By the time Cole realized what he'd agreed to, it was too late. Rafferty Investigations was one of the most successful, solid and boring detective agencies in Denver. Several companies kept him on hefty retainer as a security consultant. Occasionally he investigated a questionable insurance claim or handled employee background checks.

But most of the time he sat in his office, bored and restless, trying to figure out a way to leave Rafferty Investigations for more intriguing work without breaking his father's heart.

Then there was Ethel, who was as much a part of Rafferty Investigations as his P.I. license on the wall. She stood sentinel outside his inner sanctum, making

certain no unworthy or exciting cases ever crossed the
threshold. Even if he could persuade his father to
loosen the guidelines so he could take on some meatier
cases, he could never convince Ethel to lower her standards.

Or retire.

He sighed, sifting through his desk drawer for a tie.
If this woman got past Ethel she must not have anything too juicy for him to tackle. Probably another society dame accusing her maid of pilfering the family
silver. He'd spent two weeks last December in search
of a missing ladle that finally turned up in a pawnshop,
hocked by the family's youngest son to pay his gambling debts. Still, that case had earned him a generous
fee and several scintillating dates with the not-so-
innocent maid.

So maybe his job did have *some* perks.

It just didn't have any challenges. Cole liked challenges. In fact, he lived for them. That's why he'd
worked his way up to detective in the Westview, Ohio,
police force before leaving to take over the family business.

Now the only challenge he faced was holding on to
his bachelorhood before he found himself trapped in a
boring, predictable marriage. Just like he was trapped
in his boring, predictable job.

The door clicked, and Cole looked up to see Ethel
usher in his potential new client.

She wasn't boring.

And she certainly wasn't predictable.

Dressed in a long black trench coat and sporting a
black beret atop a riot of ebony curls, she inched her
big dark sunglasses down a notch to peer at him with
bewildered violet-blue eyes. Her generous mouth

turned down in a frown. "Who are you supposed to be?"

"I'M SUPPOSED TO BE Cole Rafferty," he replied with a wry smile, "but I'm flexible."

Annie wondered if her life could possibly get any worse. First she's run out of Newark. Then her purse is stolen at the Denver Airport, along with all her cash and her credit cards. And now...this.

Even through her sunglasses she could see the man seated behind the desk looked nothing like the distinguished, silver-haired gentleman in the portrait hanging in the outer office. This version looked much younger. Definitely taller. Broader, too, especially at the shoulders.

Damn. She didn't want this version. She wanted the older, fatherly version. White hair and wrinkles. The kind that patted you on the head and told you not to worry. Not this guy, with his mouthwatering muscles and brown bedroom eyes. The kind she fell for every time. The kind that always led to trouble.

He rose out of his chair. "And you are?"

"Having a really rotten day." She sighed. "I wanted the other guy."

"What other guy?"

She motioned toward the outer office. "The one in the picture. Is he available?"

Cole shook his head. "He's retired. I guess that means you're stuck with me, Miss... I'm sorry, I didn't catch your name."

"I'm Annie," she blurted, then mentally kicked herself for almost blowing her cover. Almost screwing up. Again. This is what guys like Cole Rafferty did to her.

This was the reason she'd sworn off men until she figured out why she always picked the wrong ones.

"Just Annie?" he asked.

"Annie...Jones," she said, seating herself in a leather chair. Annie Jones. Perfect. It had a nice, generic ring to it. She tried to ignore the prickly sensation on the back of her neck, the one that warned her of impending doom and occasionally of a head cold. Just what she needed on top of everything else—nasal congestion.

"Annie Jones," he repeated, resuming his seat. "Your accent...I can't quite place it."

Great. Two hundred dollars' worth of diction classes down the drain. You can take the girl out of Jersey, but you obviously can't take Jersey out of the girl.

"A speech impediment," she said, improvising. "I don't like to talk about it."

"Of course not," Ethel interjected from the doorway with a disapproving glance at her boss. "I'm certain Mr. Rafferty didn't mean to make you uncomfortable. He's usually not so insensitive."

"Thank you, Ethel," he said dryly. "You can return to your cauldron now. I'll handle it from here."

His secretary sniffed, then walked out of the office, closing the door behind her.

Annie looked up to find him studying her with appraising brown eyes. A warm, rich brown, like melted chocolate. She could lose herself in those eyes. Annie shook off that unsettling thought. *As if I need to get lost again.*

Maybe if she hadn't gotten lost on her way from airport to the Regency Hotel yesterday she wouldn't have missed her appointment. Maybe this entire trip to Colorado was all a bad dream. Maybe she'd wake up to find herself back in her apartment in Newark, safe and sound. Surrounded by the comforting familiarity of smog and sirens and overflowing Dumpsters.

Annie resisted the urge to pinch herself. Her nightmare had only begun. And it was all too real. Newark wasn't safe for her anymore.

Not since she'd double-crossed Quinn Vega.

Nowhere might be safe for me now. She closed her eyes to shut out that unwelcome thought. Two thousand miles might not be far enough to escape Vega, but it was a good start. All she had to do was stick to her plan and hope her bad luck hadn't followed her to Colorado.

When she opened her eyes, she found Cole Rafferty watching her, his long fingers steepled under his solid, square chin. The slight bend in his nose combined with the strong angle of his jaw added to his rugged good looks. If he was as smart as he was handsome she was in big trouble. Especially since she really needed him to fall for the tale she was about to spin.

Annie grew fidgety under his silent scrutiny, uncertain how to proceed. She'd never gotten this far with the others and didn't want to blow it.

"I'll take your case," he announced before she could even begin her story.

She blinked behind her sunglasses. "What?"

"Your case. That is why you're here, isn't it?"

It couldn't be this easy. "Yes, but I... You haven't even heard it yet. You may not be interested."

He leaned forward. "I'm definitely interested, Miss Jones. Intrigued, actually. Why the trench coat and shades? Are you being followed? Threatened? Stalked?"

He seemed so enthusiastic about the possibilities that

she almost hated to disappoint him. She removed her sunglasses and folded them in her lap. "You'll really take my case?"

"With a little shuffling, I should be able to squeeze it into my schedule." He leaned back in his chair. "Now tell me all about it. And remember that anything you say will be confidential."

He looked sincere, but she wasn't about to take any chances. The less this man knew, the better. Besides, she was more than capable of handling the situation. At least, that's what she kept telling herself.

"You don't know how much this means to me, Mr. Rafferty. I've been so anxious—"

"Call me Cole."

"Cole." His name rolled easily off her tongue, and he rewarded her with a devastating smile. Annie looked away for a moment to regain her equilibrium. "I can't tell you how relieved I am. I didn't think I'd ever find anyone to assist me. You're the sixth private investigator I've contacted today."

His smile faded. "Sixth?"

"You're the last name on the list. My last hope."

"All of them turned you down?"

"Flat. Most of them wouldn't even let me through the door. Until you."

"I'm an equal opportunity employee," he quipped. "But maybe you should tell me what I'm getting into."

"It's not complicated," she began, "although it might sound a little bizarre."

"I like bizarre."

Then he was going to love this. Annie's fingers tightened around her sunglasses. "I'm looking for a bridegroom."

His reaction wasn't quite what she expected. The pen

dropped out of his hand and onto the floor. He closed his eyes and fell back in the chair with a muttered curse. Rubbing his temples with his fingertips, he finally said, "My father sent you here, didn't he?"

"What?"

"This is a setup," he exclaimed, his eyes open and accusing. "And Ethel was in on it. I should have guessed. I knew this was too good to be true."

"I don't know what you're talking about."

A wry smile tipped one corner of his mouth. "You're wasting your time, Miss Jones. I'm a happily single man. So you can take your big blue eyes and your killer smile and your Mata Hari act right on out of here. Go pick on some other poor, unsuspecting bachelor. I'm not falling for it. Or you."

Annie watched him warily as he shook his head and whistled low.

"You really had me going there for a while," Cole said. "Tell Dad I almost bought it."

"Are you on medication?"

He sighed. "Not yet. Although I'm starting to believe my father and Ethel are conspiring to drive me crazy." He looked at her. "Not that I'm paranoid, or anything. I'm just your typical guy, working at a dead-end job, living in a three-story Victorian money pit and dodging desperate single women."

"I think you may have misunderstood—"

He held up a hand to ward off her explanation. "Then that makes two of us. I'm sorry, but I'm just not interested, Miss Jones. Thanks for stopping by."

Great. First she loses her purse, then her bridegroom. And now the only P.I. in Denver even willing to talk to her was obviously insane.

What else could possibly go wrong? Her throat tickled. Her eyes misted. Her nose itched. She sniffed and wished she had enough money to buy cold medicine.

Cole leaned across his desk to hand her a tissue. "Please don't take this so hard. There are more conventional ways to snare a man. Have you tried the personal ads?"

She sniffed again since it seemed to soften him up. "Oh, please, I'm not that desperate. I just want to find my bridegroom. The man who asked me to be his wife."

"Asked you?"

No wonder she didn't have to wait in line to see him. For a private investigator, he wasn't exactly bright. At least now he sounded lucid. "Yes, of course he asked me. Actually, it was a very poetic proposal."

It took him a while to digest her words. "You mean you don't want to marry me?"

Cole Rafferty might be attractive in a primitive, earthy, virile sort of way. He did have great bone structure and those warm brown eyes edged with thick, dark lashes. But that huge ego of his must send women screaming in the opposite direction.

"No," she replied briskly. "Whatever gave you that idea?"

He raked his fingers through his close-cropped sable hair. "It's a long story. My life's been a little crazy lately."

"I know the feeling."

"Let's start all over," he said, retrieving his pen off the floor. "Tell me how I can help."

She reached for another tissue. "Find my bridegroom. We were supposed to meet at the Regency Hotel last night. But my plane arrived late, then my purse was snatched...."

"Wait a minute," he said, cutting her off. "Someone stole your purse?"

She nodded. "At the airport terminal. So I didn't have any money for a cab. I had to hitchhike to the hotel—"

He sat up. "You hitchhiked? At night? In Denver?"

"What choice did I have?" She shrugged. "Besides, hitchhiking isn't as dangerous as people believe."

"Says who?"

"Me," she blurted, before biting her tongue once again. She didn't want to give Cole Rafferty any hints about her, which included her occupation as a journalist. "I mean, I read a story about it in a magazine. It was very well researched." Annie had written that story after dating a man who had hitchhiked his way across the United States five times. Unfortunately, he'd financed his trips by forging checks. He still occasionally sent her birthday cards from Sing-Sing.

"Okay," Cole said, giving her a long, searching look. "So after your purse was stolen, you hitchhiked to the Regency Hotel. Then what happened?"

"Nothing," she exclaimed. "That's the problem. My fiancé never showed up. He's missing."

Cole began scribbling in his notepad. "A missing person case. This is great. What's your fiancé's name?"

She leaned forward in her chair. Now they were getting somewhere. "Roy. Roy Halsey."

"Age?"

"Thirty-seven."

"Occupation?"

"He's a rancher."

He scribbled the information. "Can you give me a description?"

"Not really. The picture was in black and white."

His pen stilled as he turned his gaze to her. "Picture?"

"I've never actually seen him in person," she explained.

"You're kidding."

She tipped her chin. "Roy and I have corresponded for the last four months and have a lot in common. I'm sure we'll be very happy together."

He stared at her. "You mean you've never actually met this guy? He stood you up and you still want to marry him? Are you nuts?"

"Of course not. I'm a mail-order bride."

COLE DIDN'T KNOW whether to laugh or throw her out of his office. She couldn't be serious. Marriage was a huge gamble even when the couple knew each other inside out. The odds must really nose-dive when the bride and groom needed name tags.

But she looked incredibly serious. Not to mention just plain incredible. Those violet-blue eyes kept drawing his gaze. And the few times he did manage to look away, he found himself fantasizing about the curves concealed beneath her trench coat. Or watching her full, pink lips move when she talked. Why would a woman as appealing as Annie Jones resort to finding a man through the mail?

But then, why would one hundred and thirty-two people respond to an advertisement that read, *Aging bachelor seeks fertile mate. Enjoys playing around. Not as bad as some you've dated.*

Desperation obviously made people act in mysterious ways.

"So you really want me to track this guy down?"

he asked, still struggling with the notion of matrimony by mail.

"Yes. I thought he might be a nice addition to the wedding ceremony."

Cole tapped his pen against the desk pad. "What if he's changed his mind?"

"That's impossible. He probably thinks I stood him up. Now I don't know how to get in touch with him. I'm stuck here in a strange city with no money, no credit cards...." Her voice trailed off as she bit down hard on her lower lip.

Cole handed her another tissue. "Miss Jones, I'm sure it has occurred to you that Mr. Halsey might have gotten cold feet. Or at least had second thoughts."

"What are you saying?"

"That marriage is a big step. Perhaps he met some-one else."

She shook her head. "He sent for me. That's why I want to hire you. I need you to find my bridegroom. Today."

"What's the rush? I think you should take your time. Make sure he's a decent guy."

She leaned forward. "I don't have time for that. I've come all this way...."

"So you're from out of town?"

She hesitated. "New...England."

"You traveled almost two thousand miles to marry a complete stranger? If you want my opinion, Miss Jones, that sounds more than desperate. It sounds crazy."

"I didn't ask for your opinion."

"Well, maybe you should. Or the opinion of a good shrink. Maybe this Halsey character knows one. He could be an inmate at a mental hospital. Or a state prison. That could explain why he stood you up."

She waved away that possibility. "He's not an inmate. He's here...somewhere. We just have to find him."

"We?"

"You did promise to help me, didn't you, Mr. Rafferty?"

He shook his head. "I'm not sure finding this guy is in your best interest. Maybe you're better off without him."

She shook her head. "If I don't find Roy then I can't..."

"Can't what?"

She met his stare, and he saw a flicker of indecision in her eyes. "Can't...be a bride. I've dreamed of this moment for a very long time."

It sounded like his worst nightmare. How long would it take before his father came across a catalog entitled *Brides to Go* or *Wives Unlimited* and placed an order? Cole could just see it. He'd arrive home one evening to find his very own mail-order bride, adorned in a white lace wedding dress and matching veil, sitting on his doorstep.

"Cole?" Annie's voice made him blink and then focus once again on reality. The reality of an attractive woman in his office dressed like a spy in a B movie. Hell-bent on finding some stranger she'd picked up through the postal service. *Something doesn't make sense.*

"Are you interested or not?" she asked, her voice strained.

He watched her long, slender fingers twist nervously

together in her lap. Her teeth nibbled her lower lip. Shadows clouded her too-blue eyes.

Cole's rusty instincts finally kicked in. She was lying to him. Or at least not telling him the whole truth. The only question was why? Whatever the reason, he'd bet his P.I. license that Miss Jones wanted something from Roy Halsey.

And it wasn't a wedding ring.

"I'm definitely interested," he replied, barely concealing the smile that tugged at his mouth. After the recent chaos his father had caused in his life, Annie Jones—if that was her real name—was just what he needed.

A challenge. At last.

HE'D FALLEN for it.

Annie leaned back against the gray vinyl passenger seat of Cole's Chevy Blazer for the short ride to the Regency Hotel. She hadn't lost her touch, despite the chaos of the past few days. That story had gotten her kicked out of five P.I. offices before she'd landed at Rafferty Investigations.

Of course, that same cynicism had compelled her to begin researching an article on contemporary mail-order brides six months ago. She'd flooded the post office with responses to all the long-distance singles ads she could find. As a freelance reporter she was always looking for the unusual angle, the twist of fate that made for a profitable story.

Her own twist of fate was a sudden marriage proposal from one of her bachelor pen pals. Roy Halsey, a man with the writing style of a hokey cowpoke and the timing of a knight in shining armor. His invitation for a premarital visit to his ranch nestled deep in the Rocky Mountains was an offer she couldn't resist.

It was the perfect hiding place.

Quinn Vega and his band of mercenary men would never find her in such an isolated spot. Especially if they were still ransacking her apartment in search of Vega's private journal. She'd endured five long months of his obnoxious company to get her hands on it. That journal contained enough details of his extensive money-laundering business to put him away for a very long time. She'd verified her facts and found enough proof to write the story of the century. Unfortunately, she'd also learned about the unlucky fate of the women in Vega's life. His old girlfriends didn't fade away, they floated facedown in the Hudson River.

Annie sighed. Boy, did she know how to pick 'em or what? It had started with her very first date in high school. Obviously the star quarterback had forgotten she was the editor of the school newspaper when he took her out for pizza and boasted about the team's gambling ring. Then, in college, she had dated a history professor who sold grades for cold, hard cash. He was followed by Julio, the compulsive shoplifter, and Eugene, the illegal assault weapons enthusiast. They'd all made terrific stories and terrible boyfriends.

By the time she'd literally fallen into Quinn's lap while snapping an action shot at a Nets game, she should have known better than to hope he was Mr. Right. Despite his dark good looks and easy charm, she'd soon learned he was Mr. Wrong. They'd been dating for a month when she discovered he was a dangerous man with suspected links to organized crime. If that wasn't bad enough, she'd also uncovered evidence of his possible involvement in several brutal beatings and two mysterious disappearances. But instead of running for her life, she'd decided to stay undercover as his girlfriend to get the story.

Big mistake.

Annie stared out the window at the snowcapped Rocky Mountains. They were so majestic and beautiful. So unfamiliar. How did she ever end up here? Colorado was certainly different from Jersey.

Maybe Roy would be different, too. She'd never dated a cowboy before. They weren't exactly thick in Newark. Then again, she'd traveled enough to know men were pretty much the same everywhere. At least the ones she'd met.

What was it about her? Did she have some kind of internal radar that drew these guys to her? Some kind of invisible aura that made her the perfect target for every jerk out there? She couldn't take a man at face value anymore, no matter how handsome the face.

From now on she had a new motto—assume the worst.

She glanced at Cole, wondering what terrible vices lurked beneath that handsome exterior. Did he deal drugs? Wear women's lingerie? Watch *The Three Stooges?*

"So how exactly did you and Roy meet?" Cole asked, his wrist resting atop the steering wheel.

She watched the play of muscles in his forearm as he maneuvered a curve in the road. "I already told you, we haven't met. Yet."

"I meant how did the two of you start corresponding? Did Halsey find you in cyberspace? Is this one of those internet love connections?"

"Actually I came across him in a singles magazine called *Mountain Men.* He looked sweet."

He rolled his eyes. "Definitely the basis for a lasting relationship. Haven't you ever heard the old saying you can't judge a book by its cover?"

"If I wanted a book I'd go to the library," she quipped. "I want a husband. But it is too bad you can't scan the available men that way. Check them out for a few weeks, see what they're like between the covers, then return them."

"You can do that," he said. "It's called dating. You should try it sometime."

"I don't think my fiancé would approve."

He snorted. "Your fiancé. You don't even know the guy. He could be a serial killer, luring unsuspecting women to his isolated ranch. Or a pervert. Or a...disco fanatic."

"Now that would be scary," she said, laughing for the first time in two days.

"Hey, I'm half-serious here," he continued. "You could end up at the mercy of some loony tune just for the sake of a marriage license. It's just plain nuts. Is this the result of some kind of midlife crisis?"

Her mouth dropped open. "I'm only thirty-one!"

"Exactly my point. Your clock is ticking, isn't it?"

Annie resisted the urge to jump out of a moving vehicle. "My clock?"

"You know, that biological thing women are always worried about. The ticking is getting louder by the minute."

"You must be hearing things. Probably the result of too much heavy thinking."

He smiled. "I've already got it all figured out. You're marrying Cowboy Roy because you want a baby. Just admit it."

She held up both hands. "Okay, you've got me. My ovaries are holding me hostage. I've got forty-eight hours to deliver the sperm or I'm a dead woman."

"Very funny. But I'm right, aren't I?"

She rolled her eyes. "If this is an example of your detective skills, then I'm in big trouble."

"It's called deductive reasoning. And you're just upset because I figured it all out."

She folded her arms across her chest. "Well, what

if I told you, Mr. Private Eye, that I'm actually some mob boss's moll and I'm on the run because I squealed to the cops?''

''Is that the best you can come up with?''

She took a deep breath. Was she nuts? Letting the truth slip out just because she enjoyed bantering with him. Just because she wanted to confide in someone so badly her mouth hurt from keeping it shut. When would she ever learn? She should have kept her mouth shut three days ago instead of confiding in that cop. The one on Vega's payroll.

''You're right,'' she said lightly. ''I can be a lot more creative. I'm really an alien from the planet Borca, sent here to seek out intelligent life on Earth. So far I haven't found any.''

One corner of Cole's mouth tipped up in a grin as he slid a long, lingering glance down her body that made her toes tingle. ''I must say, you look pretty good for an alien.''

''Flattery, Mr. Rafferty,'' she quipped, her cheeks warm, ''will get you vaporized.''

THE RIDE to the Regency Hotel didn't elicit any more information for Cole than that strange briefing in his office. Annie Jones provided more questions than answers. She was definitely an enigma. One moment sultry and mysterious, the next, calmly planning to wed a stranger with a cool efficiency that terrified him.

He glanced over to see her gazing out the passenger window, scanning the busy Denver streets as if she expected to spot her errant groom at any second.

Fat chance. Unless they came across a panicky man with a return-to-sender stamp clutched in his sweaty hand.

Roy Halsey. The name sounded harmless enough. But what about the man himself? And why send two thousand miles for a wife? Colorado, as Cole knew from recent experience, had plenty of eager, eligible women.

He turned in at the hotel parking lot and pulled up next to the valet booth. The warm afternoon sun made him shed his jacket before climbing out of the car. He tossed his keys to the young female valet, a slim blonde wearing a nose ring and bright purple lipstick.

"By the way, I'll cover tips and other incidental expenses until the case is over," he told Annie, as they walked toward the hotel entrance. "But I'm sure Ethel explained all that when she collected your deposit."

Annie shook her head. "Actually, she never got around to collecting a deposit." She smiled at the doorman and swept into the hotel, leaving Cole in her wake.

He slowed down long enough to admire the curve of her trim ankles peeking out beneath the trench coat. Roy Halsey was one lucky man. Or doomed man, depending on how you looked at it. Condemned to a life sentence with a woman he'd never even met.

But what a woman.

Cole knew he should interview the doorman, but his curiosity got the better of him. "What do you mean, she didn't take a deposit?" he asked, catching up with her in the spacious, well-appointed lobby. Pink marble floors and furniture upholstered in soft ivory suede made it obvious the hotel catered to wealthy clientele. "Why not?"

"My purse was stolen, remember? Besides, Ethel was too busy telling me about you."

"What about me?"

Annie turned to face him. "Your secretary told me

you're the most pigheaded man she's ever met. And that once you're on a case, you'll stop at nothing to solve it."

"I think pigheaded might be a little extreme."

"I'm sure she meant it as a compliment. She also said you were noble, self-sacrificing, a loyal companion."

"Now I sound like a Saint Bernard."

Her gaze slid downward. "And that you have a birthmark shaped like a teddy bear on your backside."

Leave it to Ethel to spill all his secrets. "It's not a teddy bear. It's more like a grizzly, and it's higher up. A lot higher up."

"Fascinating," she murmured, and then raised her gaze to meet his. "I'm glad I found you, Cole. All those other private investigators cared about was collecting their fee."

He blinked. "Excuse me?"

"Don't worry, I'm planning to pay you," she assured him. "Eventually. But at the moment I've got no cash, no credit cards, not even any traveler's checks. I explained it all to Ethel. She was so understanding."

And so underhanded. Ethel never let a client through the door without a full financial commitment. He smelled a rat—wearing orthopedic shoes. But he could handle his secretary later. First he needed to find Annie a husband. "We can discuss my fee another time. The most important thing right now is solving this case."

"Good. I think we should start with—"

He cut her off mid-sentence. "I'll interview the hotel personnel and find out if Halsey made an appearance."

"But I already—"

"Please," he interrupted with an indulgent smile, "I'm the professional here. Let me handle this."

Cole left her standing next to a huge potted palm and headed for the front desk. She might chafe at his take-charge manner now, but she'd thank him for it later. A few clients always tried to participate in solving their case. Whether from a yearning for adventure or a false sense of control, it only made his job harder. He never should have brought her along with him in the first place.

Waiting in line at the concierge desk, he glanced over his shoulder at Annie, hoping she'd gotten the message. But instead of following his directions, she'd obviously decided to send a message of her own.

Frowning, he watched her remove her sunglasses and then her trench coat. An obscenely short red cocktail dress clung to revealing curves in all the right places. It also showed off her long, slender legs to perfection.

"May I help you, sir?" he heard the clerk ask. "Sir?"

Cole was unable to look away from his client. "Yeah. I'm looking for a man named Halsey."

"First name, sir?"

Cole licked his dry lips. "What?"

"The first name, sir."

Cole watched Annie take off her beret, then sweep her fingers through the thick mass of curls tumbling over her shoulders. "Uh, Roy. Roy Halsey."

"Is he a guest here, sir?"

Ignoring the clerk, Cole swore softly under his breath and strode toward his client. "What do you think you're doing?"

She stood next to a glass-topped coffee table, her toes propped on its edge, one dainty foot arched as she massaged her insole. "I've been wearing this outfit for over eighteen hours. I'm hot and sticky, and these shoes are pure torture."

He folded his arms across his chest. "Right. It couldn't be that you were hoping good old Roy might show up and collect his mail once he got a good look at the package."

Her mouth dropped open. "Of course not."

"Yeah, and I suppose where you come from that dress is considered sportswear."

She looked down in dismay. "What's wrong with my dress?"

"Not a thing if you're applying for a position on a street corner."

"Look, I realize this isn't exactly your typical traveling outfit. I left home in somewhat of a hurry so I didn't have time to change." She tipped up her chin. "Besides, red is Roy's favorite color."

"Why doesn't that make me feel better?" He placed his hands on her shoulders and propelled her three steps backward. "Just wait here like a good little client until I come back." Cole shot a disconcerted glance around the room. "And don't take off anything else. People are staring."

She glanced at the pimply-faced teenager seated in the wing chair next to her. His long, straggly brown hair moved in rhythm to the music blasting out of his headphones. He waggled his hairy eyebrows at Annie while giving her an enthusiastic thumbs-up.

She turned to Cole and sighed. "How did I ever get into this mess?"

"By trusting the wrong guy. Rule number one for mail-order brides—trust no one." He smiled. "Except me."

She took a step closer to him. "Can I really trust you, Cole?"

He looked into her violet eyes, fringed with thick, dark lashes, and became so entranced he forgot the question. Her lips parted slightly, like the petals of a pink rose.

"Can I, Cole?"

He blinked. "What?"

"Trust you?"

"Of course," he replied. "I'm a Saint Bernard, remember?" Why had he ever agreed to take this case? He'd wanted a challenge, not a woman who drove him to distraction. A woman full of contradictions. A woman he couldn't trust, no matter how good she looked in that skimpy dress. He turned on his heel and headed toward the front desk before the images crowding his brain erupted into a full-fledged fantasy.

"I believe you were inquiring about a Mr. Halsey," the clerk said as Cole approached him.

"That's right," he replied, forcing his mind firmly to business. "My client was supposed to meet him here."

The clerk pecked at his computer keyboard. "There's no one named Halsey registered at the hotel."

A feeling oddly like relief flowed through Cole's body.

"Let me check the message board." The clerk tapped a few more buttons, then his face creased with a satisfied smile. "Ah, perhaps this is it. A message from a Mr. Roy Halsey to a Miss Annie B., delivered only a short time ago. I assume this Annie B. is your client?"

Annie B? So she was lying to him. Or maybe she

was lying to Halsey. Although it was hard to believe she'd trust Halsey enough to marry him but not enough to give him her real last name. "Yes, that's her. If you'll print it out for me, I'll make sure she gets it."

The message was short and simple. Roy apologized for missing their appointment and wanted her to meet him at the hotel's front desk at eight o'clock this evening. Cole folded the message and put it in his breast pocket.

Case solved.

The only problem was he still had more questions than answers. By the time he returned from the fruitless interviews with the hotel staff, none of whom could remember taking Halsey's message, his frustration had reached the breaking point.

"Where is she?"

The hairy teenager was still slumped in the chair, oblivious to everything around him as he rocked to the beat blaring from his headset.

Cole reached down and pulled the earphones off his head. "I said, where is she?"

The teenager squinted at him. "Who?"

"The woman who's been sitting next to you for the last thirty minutes. Dark hair, blue eyes, red dress."

"Great knockers?"

Cole grimaced. "Yeah. That's the one."

He nodded. "The babe."

"So where'd she go?"

"She left, man."

Cole tried to keep his voice calm. "You mean she just got up and walked out of the hotel?"

"Nope. Some guy hauled her off about ten minutes ago. I haven't seen her since."

So MAYBE diamonds weren't a girl's best friend.

At least not the diamond engagement ring Quinn had given Annie. A flawless three-carat radiant-cut diamond set on a wide platinum band. A used diamond engagement ring, judging by the small nicks on it. He'd probably cut off the finger of one of his old girlfriends to get it back. She'd always hated that ring. But she never would've tried to hock it if she'd known it would cause this much trouble.

She shifted on the hard metal folding chair, looking for the first opportunity to make a run for it. Her three-inch heels would make her escape difficult. So would the gun slung low on the hip of the security guard next to the door. The same man who had dragged her from the hotel lobby into the hotel manager's office. He looked like a bulldog, with his pug nose and low, protruding brow. An angry bulldog, judging by the scowl on his craggy face when he caught her staring at him.

The office was small and cluttered with boxes and leafy green plants. A small window overlooked the three-tier fountain in front of the Regency Hotel. Classical music drifted softly from a speaker high on the wall, and the scents of Chanel No 5 and garlic mingled in the air. Since she knew the garlic emanated from the security guard, she concluded that the perfume must belong to the blond bombshell seated behind the desk.

She turned to face Ingrid Tate, the hotel manager according to the nameplate. The former Miss August according to the framed girlie magazine cover on the wall.

She was being held hostage by a Playboy bunny.

Something inside her snapped. She'd been living in fear for the last few days. But no more. It was time to take control of her life again. She had a plan. A good plan. Find Roy, let him whisk her away to his secluded ranch until Vega went to prison, then resume her regularly scheduled life.

Now if the newest man in her life would just come to the rescue. But Cole Rafferty was nowhere in sight.

This was so typical. A heel instead of a hero. He obviously didn't approve of his secretary waiving the deposit. Behind that slow smile and those deep brown eyes lay another unreliable male.

How many times did she have to learn not to count on anyone but herself? It was all up to her. And she wasn't about to let Miss August stand in her way.

"I think you've made a big mistake," Annie began.

"That's funny," Ingrid Tate said, without a hint of humor. "I was just about to tell you the same thing. We don't tolerate this kind of nonsense at the Regency Hotel." Ingrid narrowed her green eyes. "You've been hanging around the lobby on and off all day. Bruno thought you looked suspicious from the very start."

Bruno grunted from his post by the door.

At least they didn't know she'd spent last night on the chaise longue in the ladies' room. Or ordered room service from the telephone in stall number three. Somehow she knew the hotel manager wouldn't find that funny, either. Ingrid Tate might have big hair and an even bigger chest, but she was no dumb bunny. Intelligence gleamed in her green eyes, and impatience was pressing her lips into a thin line.

Annie lifted her chin. "I haven't done anything wrong."

Ingrid arched a finely tweezed brow. "Didn't you coerce a front desk clerk into hocking that diamond ring for you?"

"He offered. When I asked him where I could find

the nearest pawnshop, he told me his brother was in the business and he'd be willing to come down here and make me an offer.''

"At least you admit it. I can only hope you didn't steal that ring from one of the hotel guests.''

"I'm not admitting anything. And I didn't steal it. That ring was given to me by—'' she sputtered to a halt, unable to say Quinn's name. Not if she wanted to stay alive. "By my ex-fiancé. He's upset about our breakup and probably reported that ring stolen just to get even.''

Bruno snorted. "Give it up, lady. That rock is so hot it burned my hand.''

Annie bit her lip, annoyed at her own stupidity. Quinn dealt in stolen goods all the time. "This is just a simple misunderstanding. If you only knew what a really rotten week I've had....''

Ingrid rolled her eyes. "Spare me the sob story. I'm the one with the board of directors breathing down my neck.'' She motioned to the pile of papers cluttering her desk. "Do you think it's easy managing this hotel? I've got no free time. No social life.''

"And no reason not to turn you over to the police,'' Bruno concluded, with a nod to Ingrid. She reached for the telephone.

"Wait!'' Annie exclaimed.

Ingrid sat with one manicured finger poised to dial. "Can you give me any reason not to turn you in?''

Annie could think of several. The last thing she wanted was a police interrogation. A background check. Her name in the newspapers. Vega had connections everywhere. Maybe it was time to come up with a new plan.

The phone chirped, startling them both. Ingrid

picked up the receiver. "Yes, I see. Well, then, I suppose you'd better send him in."

Annie held her breath as the door opened, ready to make a run for it. Then she changed her mind.

Her hero had finally arrived.

COLE COULDN'T believe his eyes.

He'd had visions of Roy Halsey dragging Annie off by the hair, a brutish Neanderthal coming to claim his bride. He'd practically turned the Regency Hotel upside down searching for her, imagining her at the mercy of a sex fiend if not a possible psychopath.

Now here she sat in the hotel manager's office with every hair intact, shooting violet daggers at him and practically falling out of that damn dress.

He stopped short in front of her chair, ignoring the armed security guard by the door and the fluffy blonde behind the desk. "Where the hell have you been?"

Annie jumped to her feet, throwing her arms around his neck. "Darling! You came for me. I thought I'd never see you again."

Cole was momentarily distracted by the soft curves pressed against him. Did she just call him darling?

The blonde frowned. "I assume you know this man?"

Annie detached herself from him. "This is Cole Rafferty, my fiancé. The one I was telling you about. Darling, this is Ingrid Tate."

Ingrid gazed at him. "I believe you said he was your ex-fiancé."

Cole was still trying to catch up. He turned to Annie. "Your what?"

"My fiancé," she said, stepping purposefully on his foot to get his attention. "Please don't get angry. I've learned my lesson. You're the only man for me. I must have been crazy to even think of breaking off our engagement.''

"I do think you could use a good psychiatrist," he replied.

She grasped his hand in hers. "Maybe I'm just crazy in love."

The security guard snorted. "This is incredibly touching. But what about the cops?"

Cole blinked. "Cops?"

The guard moved in front of the door. "We called 'em earlier and told them about the ring she tried to hock. They said to detain her if she came back to claim the money."

"The diamond ring you reported stolen," Annie said, hinting.

The security guard stuck out his jaw. "They also said we might get a reward."

Cole looked at Annie, unable to imagine her stealing anything. Except possibly his sanity. Maybe it would be safer to put her behind bars. And throw away the key. "Care to explain?"

She squeezed his hand. "I know exactly what you're thinking."

"I really doubt it."

"Now, Cole, you know how much I love that ring. This is all a big misunderstanding. Why don't you just pay these nice people that reward and then we can go."

He couldn't believe his ears. "You want me to pay them?"

"I think a hundred dollars is reasonable," Ingrid replied, steepling her hands under her chin. "What do you think, Bruno?"

Bruno grunted his assent.

"A hundred dollars?" Cole exclaimed in disbelief.

"Each," Bruno added.

Cole shook his head. "I don't have that much on me. I've only got a fifty and a few odd bills."

Bruno scowled. "Then we're turning her in."

"Now let's not be so hasty," Ingrid said, leaning back in her chair as her green-eyed gaze flicked over Cole. "I'm sure Mr. Rafferty and I can come to an arrangement that satisfies us both."

"Then take the fifty and keep the ring as collateral," Bruno said.

"An excellent suggestion." Ingrid leaned forward, her slinky silk blouse gaping open far enough to hint at the black lace lingerie underneath. "Mr. Rafferty can bring the rest of the money this evening. We'll meet in the hotel lounge. Say around sevenish?"

He had two choices. He could call Annie's bluff and leave her to the mercy of the police. Or he could pay the first installment of this ridiculous bribe and finally get some answers.

He reached for his wallet.

"YOU OWE ME big-time, lady," Cole said, as he grabbed Annie's hand and barreled across the hotel lobby before Ingrid and her evil sidekick could change their minds.

"You told me you'd cover all the incidental expenses," Annie said, as they headed out the door.

Cole swung around to face her. "Bribes are not an incidental expense. And what you owe me are some answers. Two hundred dollars' worth."

She folded her arms. "I hired you, remember? I'm the one that gives the orders."

"You can't hire someone unless you actually pay

them. So far, I'm the only one doling out any cash here.''

Annie tipped up her chin. "Ethel said you didn't care about money.''

"Quoting Ethel will not get you on my good side.''

"I think she's sweet.''

He folded his arms. "We're not talking about Ethel right now. We're talking about you and this bad habit you seem to have of not paying for things. Like my services and that diamond ring.''

"I didn't steal that ring," she insisted, her big violet eyes focused squarely on him. "Honest.''

He didn't want to believe her. He shouldn't believe her, not after that convincing demonstration of her acting talents in the manager's office. But he did. And it only made him more curious about her and her phony story.

"Then I guess that means good old Roy is the thief. Great catch you got there, Annie. Maybe you two can flee to Mexico for your honeymoon.''

"Roy didn't give me that ring," she began, then her breath caught in her throat. "My honeymoon? Does this mean you found him?''

Cole hesitated. This was his chance. He could tell her about the message Roy had left and consider the case closed. If he had any sense, he'd do it. But he still wouldn't have any answers.

"Not yet," he finally replied.

"Not yet?" She closed her eyes and groaned. "Now what am I going to do? I was counting on the money from that ring to tide me over until I found Roy.'' She opened her eyes and scowled at him. "What have you been doing all this time?''

He looked at her in disbelief. "Saving your butt!

Where would you be if I hadn't arrived in time to play the part of your fiancé?"

"I suppose you have a point."

"Damn straight. You owe me. Now here's what I want you to do...." His voice trailed off as he saw Annie staring openmouthed at something over his shoulder. He turned to see his shiny black Chevy Blazer rolling up next to them.

"What is that?" she asked, pointing at his windshield.

"Just get in," he said, stifling a groan of irritation as he pushed her toward the passenger door. He made a wide arc around the valet, tossing her a small tip as he dove into the driver's side. He could barely see out the window. Dozens of purple lipstick kisses smudged the front windshield. The same shade of lipstick worn by the young valet.

"I don't think you should encourage her like that," Annie said, as the woman clasped the dollar bills to her chest with one hand and blew Cole a kiss with the other.

"I gave her a tip, not my phone number," he said, peeling out of the parking lot.

"I think she left you hers." Annie reached for the slip of paper attached to his visor.

"Throw it out the window."

"It *is* a phone number. And several rather graphic suggestions for your first date." She held up the note for him to see. "Isn't it cute the way she dotted all the *I*s with little hearts?"

"This is not funny," he said, his jaw clenched. The woman must have recognized his name from the car registration. Shouldn't a woman that age be reading bathroom stalls instead of the personal ads? Then dread filled him. What if she did read about him in a bathroom stall? What if his father had started infiltrating women's rest rooms?

"You're right. It's not funny," she agreed. "She looks about seventeen. How can you solve my case if you're in jail for corrupting a minor?"

"I can't go on like this," he muttered, rubbing one hand over his jaw. "What if she memorized my address off the car registration? What if she shows up at my house?"

"Maybe you'd better stock up on Barbies."

He scowled at her. "You are not helping. This has gotten totally out of hand. I need to do something drastic."

"You could always tell her you're gay."

"Not that drastic." He pulled into a convenience store parking lot and shifted into Park. Then he flipped on the windshield wipers.

"I think it's getting worse," she observed, as the thick purple lipstick smeared the entire windshield.

"It's getting a lot worse," he muttered. He turned to Annie and took a deep breath. "I've got a proposition for you."

3

"YOU WANT ME to marry you?" Annie placed her palm on her forehead. Maybe she had a fever. Sometimes high fevers caused hallucinations, didn't they? But her forehead felt cool to the touch. So maybe Cole Rafferty really did propose to her.

"I don't get it," she continued. "Didn't you just tell me, less than two hours ago, that you were a happily single man? That you spent your time avoiding desperate women?"

"That's true, but..."

"And now you're proposing?" She shook her head. "And I thought I was impulsive."

"I don't have any choice." He rubbed one hand over his jaw. "I don't really want to marry you. I don't want to marry anyone. That's the problem."

"And somehow I'm the solution?"

He nodded. "I'm a confirmed bachelor, but my dad is determined to find me a wife. His latest antics have finally pushed me over the edge."

"What exactly has he done?"

Cole sighed. "He placed a personal ad in the newspaper."

"Well, maybe he's just lonely."

"The ad wasn't for him. It was for me and my desperate search for romance."

"Uh-oh." Annie had done enough research on personal ads to know he'd probably been inundated with responses. It also explained the message left on his windshield. "Doesn't an engagement seem a little extreme?"

"I'm afraid there's no other way to get through to him. That's where you come in."

"As your fiancée?"

"Not just any fiancée. The fiancée from hell. A woman so incompatible, so wrong for me that he'll cringe at the thought of welcoming you into the family. In fact, I'm hoping he'll use all his spare time trying to get rid of you."

She rolled her eyes. "Gee, that sounds like fun for me."

"Naturally, when we break up, I'll be devastated." He grinned. "I'll need a long recovery period to get over you. It may take years. Or at least long enough to make Dad forget about matchmaking and find a new hobby."

"So what's in it for me?"

"Well, besides the pleasure of my company, you can stay at my place until I track down Roy. I'll supply food, clothing, anything you might need. And I'll handle your case for free."

She blinked. All her problems solved in an instant. Well, maybe not all her problems. Quinn still wanted her dead. But she did need somewhere to hide until Roy whisked her away to his mountain ranch. "Did you forget that I'm already engaged? What if I find my fiancé before you've accomplished your mission?"

He shrugged, not quite meeting her gaze. "That's a chance I'll have to take. Just think of me as fiancé number two in the meantime. You can practice on me."

Actually, he'd be fiancé number three. But who's counting? "It might work," she mused.

"It's the perfect plan."

She hesitated, not quite ready to commit to another engagement, even a phony one. "What exactly would I have to do?"

"Basically, make my life miserable. You know, just pretend we're married. Dad's a real old-fashioned guy, so the more liberal and kooky you are, the better."

She folded her arms. "Just in case I agree to this crazy plan of yours, I'd better warn you, I'm a little old-fashioned myself."

He arched a brow. "Which means?"

"Which means this so-called engagement is on my terms. No fringe benefits." She tipped her chin. "I don't believe in sex before marriage."

It was the same line she'd given Quinn Vega when he'd proposed. It hadn't made him rescind his offer, as she'd hoped, but at least it had kept him out of her bed.

Disappointment flickered across Cole's face. Or maybe it was relief. "That really is old-fashioned for this day and age."

She shrugged. "It's the way I was raised. I'm Catholic and Italian. A double-guilt whammy."

His eyes narrowed. "Italian? That's odd. Annie Jones doesn't sound very Italian."

Certainly not like her real name, Antonia Bonacci.

"I'm Italian on my mother's side," she said, improvising. "Her grandparents immigrated here from Milan. She's honeymooning there now with husband number six." That, at least, was the truth, and it comforted her to know her mother was out of Vega's reach.

He whistled low. "Six trips to the altar? Wow, she must know all the vows by heart."

"Actually, she makes up her own now to break the monotony," Annie said lightly, hiding her fear that she had the same bad luck with men as her mother. Maybe it was genetic.

He didn't say anything for two long beats, his gaze intent on her face. "Anything else I should know?"

As far as she was concerned, he already knew too much. She certainly didn't want to give him the opportunity to find any more holes in her story. "No. Why don't we just make up the rest of it as we go along?"

"So then it's a deal?" he asked, extending his hand.

Annie felt his large, warm hand close around her cold fingers. She knew as soon as he touched her that she was in big trouble.

"Deal," she answered.

"THERE'S A STRANGE WOMAN in your shower," Rex Rafferty announced as he walked into the kitchen.

Cole almost jumped out of his shoes. "Dad! Where did you come from?"

Rex hitched a thumb toward the ceiling. "Upstairs. I was fixing that plaster crack in the south bedroom when I heard the water running. When did you get home?"

Cole placed a saucepan on the stove, wondering what had possessed him to give his father a spare house key. "About ten minutes ago."

Rex sat at the table. "So who's the woman and why is she naked?"

Cole pulled a soup can out of the cupboard. "How do you know it's a woman up there? And more importantly, how do you know she's naked?"

Rex snorted. "I may have lost your mother over ten

years ago, but I can still recognize a naked woman when I see one. Even through a steamed-up shower door.''

"Dad, will you stop talking like Mom is dead. She's alive and well and living in New Mexico." Then the rest of Rex's words hit him. "Wait a minute. You went into the bathroom while Annie was in the shower?"

"I heard a suspicious noise and thought I should check it out," Rex said in his own defense. "It could have been a burglar. Just because I'm retired from the business doesn't mean I've lost all my skills."

"A burglar?" Cole exclaimed in disbelief. "Stealing what? Hot water?"

"So it wasn't a burglar," Rex admitted. "Since the lock on the door is broken, I just took a quick peek, then went right back out again. No harm done."

Cole gritted his teeth, torn between outrage that his father saw Annie naked and envy that his father saw Annie naked. Well, not exactly naked. But seeing her through a shower door was closer than Cole was ever likely to get. Stifling the urge to ask for details, he focused on his outrage. "Dad, that's an invasion of privacy. If you want to peek at naked women, then I suggest you go find one of your own."

Rex shook his head as he reached for the bowl of soup crackers on the table. "At my age? I'd rather concentrate on finding you a woman. Then maybe I can finally have some grandchildren to spoil."

"I've already found a woman."

The light in Rex's eyes almost made Cole feel guilty. But he steeled himself against backing down. Rex was out of control. The personal ad wasn't his only folly. Last week he'd bought fifteen boxes of cookies from a Girl Scout, then asked her if she had any single older sisters she could deliver for his son. And two weeks ago he'd ordered premium white oak from the lumberyard to build a baby cradle.

The man had to be stopped.

"You found a girl of your own?" Rex asked, a wide grin on his face. "You've finally fallen in love?"

"Her name is Annie," Cole said, avoiding the question. "Annie Jones."

"So how old is she? I couldn't tell much through the shower door. Although I must say she looked pretty good."

Cole reached for a glass of water. He'd been trying to convince himself he wouldn't notice an extra body in such a big house. Even a body like hers. But this shower conversation wasn't helping any. "She's thirty-one years old. Dark hair. Big blue-violet eyes. She's from back east somewhere.

"Thirty-one," Rex mused. "A little older than I'd hoped. Still, her biological clock is probably ticking pretty loud by now, so she'll want to start having my grandbabies right away."

"I wouldn't mention her clock to her if I were you. She seems to be a little sensitive about it."

"Annie," Rex said with a satisfied smile. "Annie Rafferty. Has a nice ring to it."

It gave Cole goose bumps. "Her name is Annie Jones."

Rex's smile faded. "She's not one of those women who's going to insist on keeping her maiden name, is she?"

"She could be," Cole said enthusiastically. "Or maybe she'll hyphenate it. Then all our kids will be known as those Jones-Rafferty brats."

Rex scowled, and Cole knew he'd hit a sore point.

Hyphenated names, women with tattoos and men with earrings set his father's teeth on edge. Rex still clung to the traditional roles for men and women, which made him a dinosaur in this age of equality between the sexes.

"You'll have to put a stop to any of that kind of nonsense, son. Otherwise, my grandkids won't know how to spell their name until the third grade."

"Oh, I don't have any control over her, Dad. She's totally independent. A woman of the nineties. I wanted to get married right away, but she insisted we live together first." He sighed as he popped a soup cracker in his mouth. "I'm just putty in her hands."

Rex raised a skeptical white brow. "If you're living together, then why isn't she sharing the master bedroom down here with you? Looks like she's encamped upstairs. The bed's all made up in the west bedroom, and her lacy red underwear is scattered across the floor."

Cole choked on the cracker. He grabbed a glass of water to wash it down just as Annie entered the kitchen.

"I can answer that," she said, sliding into a chair at the kitchen table. She was wrapped in his big blue terry cloth robe, looking all soft and warm and disheveled.

Rex's face lit up at the sight of her. "You must be Annie."

She extended her hand for him to shake. "And you must be Cole's father."

He rose to his feet. "Call me Rex."

"It's a pleasure to meet you, Rex."

"Believe me, young lady, the pleasure is all mine."

"Speaking of pleasure," she said as he sat beside

her. "I believe you were asking about our separate bed-rooms?"

The skin under Rex's gray whiskers grew pink. "It's probably none of my business."

"Nonsense," she exclaimed. "We're going to be a family soon. And a family shouldn't have any secrets from each other."

Rex smiled. "My sentiments exactly."

Cole poured the soup into the pan, waiting to hear her explanation.

"It's the infection," she began.

Soup spilled onto the stove top. Cole swore under his breath, then reached for a dish towel to wipe up the mess.

"Infection?" Rex echoed.

Annie held up one hand. "It's nothing for you to worry about, really. It comes and goes. But the doctor advises celibacy during the flare-ups. Cole said he doesn't care if I'm contagious because when we marry, he'll probably catch it sooner or later. But I say why double the pharmacy bill?"

Cole couldn't believe it. He'd created a monster. Still, from the stunned expression on his father's face, the plan was working beautifully. Soon he'd be begging his son to remain a bachelor.

"So how in the world... I mean, how did you two meet?" Rex asked, still staring at Annie.

"Ethel introduced us," she replied.

Rex blinked. "Ethel? My Ethel?"

"Oh, are you two involved?" She clapped a hand to her chest, breathing a big sigh of relief. "I can't tell you how happy I am to hear that. I thought maybe she wanted to dump Cole and was using me to soften the blow. You should see the way he looks at her."

"Looks at her?" Rex scowled at his son. "What's that supposed to mean?"

Annie smiled. "You know how it is, Rex. Two attractive single people working alone together, day after day. And some men find older women very appealing."

Rex turned to Cole. "What the hell is going on between you and Ethel? She's old enough to be your mother!"

Cole finally cleared his throat. "Absolutely nothing. The whole idea is ridiculous."

"I think we should believe him," Annie said. "I just hope he hasn't turned to me on the rebound. That's what happened with Vinnie."

"Vinnie?" Rex and Cole asked at the same time.

"My last boyfriend." She twirled a damp curl between her fingers. "A real two-timer. Of course, that knife wound has probably slowed him down a bit."

"He was stabbed?" Rex asked, his eyes wide.

Annie shrugged. "Hey, nobody ever proved I did it. And it really was just a superficial cut. Nothing to get excited about."

Cole set a soup bowl in front of Annie, barely resisting the urge to shove a piece of bread in her mouth. He wanted the fiancée from hell, but there was such a thing as overkill.

"Wish you could stay for dinner, Dad," he said, as he handed her a spoon. Then he moved toward the back door. "Annie just wanted something light to eat. She's really tired. And I've got an appointment to catch."

"That's right," she said, pulling a tissue out of her pocket. "You have a date with that woman tonight, don't you?"

Rex frowned at his son. "What's this about a date?"

"A meeting," Cole amended, with a warning glance at his faux fiancée.

"At least he says it's a meeting," she said, dabbing at her nose. "I guess my problems with Vinnie have made me a little insecure."

Rex cast a worried look at his son. "You'd never two-time Annie, would you, Cole?"

"It's all right, Rex," she said, gazing at Cole. "I trust him not to break my heart."

Cole turned toward the door, unnerved by the unexpected vulnerability in her eyes.

"Aren't you even going to kiss her goodbye?" Rex asked, obviously surprised at his son's apparent neglect of his fiancée. Rex might be a dinosaur, but he was a chivalrous dinosaur.

Cole hesitated, his hand on the doorknob. Damn. So much for a quick getaway. He took a deep breath. If they were madly in love, it was only natural that he'd kiss her goodbye. Rex might be eager to believe in an engagement, but he was no dummy. And they'd pushed the limits of credibility far enough for one day.

Annie must have realized it, too, because she met him halfway. He wrapped his arms around her waist at the same time she wound her arms around his neck and tilted her face.

"I might be contagious," she whispered.

"I'll take my chances."

The musky aroma of his aftershave mingled with her scent in the folds of his robe, making his heart thud against his ribs. Surely she could feel it pounding, pressed up so tightly against his chest. He could certainly feel every soft, curvy inch of her.

Better to get this kiss over and done with before he completely lost his senses. Cole lowered his head, catching her lips with his own. But what started as a simple, chaste kiss somehow didn't turn out that way. Her mouth parted at the touch of his tongue, allowing him to tenderly explore the warm depths within. Her arms tightened around his neck as a soft moan sounded deep in her throat.

He kissed her deeply. Hungrily. She tasted of minty toothpaste and spicy secrets. His mouth moved over hers with the reckless intensity of a starving man. Annie melted against him, meeting his heat and his passion.

Just when he hoped the kiss would never end, she pulled away from him, her breathing as ragged as his. He saw the color in her cheeks and the fast rise and fall of her chest. He took a step toward her before remembering they had an audience.

Cole turned to see if their kiss had satisfied his father. A kiss like that should satisfy any court in the country. It certainly must have convinced Rex, because sometime during that incredible interlude, he'd made a discreet exit.

So did Annie. When he turned to tell her they must have passed the test, he found himself standing all alone in his big, empty kitchen.

COLE HAD NEVER been so confused in his life.

Annie Jones, alias the fiancée from hell, was the most consummate actress he'd ever met. The lies dripped from her mouth like honey. Her mouth reminded him of honey. Sweet, moist and succulent. He closed his eyes, remembering the way she'd tasted, the way she'd felt in his arms, the incredible way she'd kissed him. She couldn't have been acting then.

Could she?

He plowed his fingers through his short hair. He never should have kissed her. Especially since she was engaged to someone else. Roy Halsey might still be a total stranger to her, but did that make their betrothal any less binding?

If Halsey really was her fiancé.

Cole couldn't shake the feeling that Annie was keeping something from him. A feeling supported not only by the implausibility of her story but by the shadows in her violet eyes.

He had to find out the truth. He had to know if he could trust his instincts or if her killer smile and that dynamite kiss had completely clouded his judgment.

"You're late," Ingrid said as he walked into the hotel lounge. She sat at the table nearest the door running a straw over her full, pouty lips.

"Sorry." Cole sat in the chair across from her. "Something came up."

She lean forward and whispered, "Did you bring the money?"

"Did you bring the ring?" he countered.

She looked furtively around the empty bar. "The money first."

He reached into his coat pocket, drawing out a hundred-dollar bill and a fifty. For one brief moment, he wondered if undercover vice cops would leap out from behind the bar. But nothing happened. Ingrid took the money, then handed him the ring. He blinked at the size of the diamond.

"It's been a pleasure doing business with you," she said, slipping the money into her handbag.

Cole slipped the ring into his pocket. "I've got another twenty for you if you'll answer a few of my questions."

"Make it fifty, and I'm all yours, Cole."

He drew another fifty out of his wallet, hoping he'd be able to solve this case before he had to declare bankruptcy. "It's about Annie."

Ingrid scowled. "Your fiancée?"

He nodded. "I'm worried about her. She's been acting a little...strange lately. Doing odd things."

"Like hocking her engagement ring?"

He nodded. "Is there anything she might have said to you this afternoon before I arrived in your office? Anything that seemed unusual?"

Ingrid pursed her lips. "Hmm. Actually she did make one rather odd comment."

His pulse quickened. "What?"

"Let me see, how did she put it?" Ingrid idly twirled her straw in her margarita, giving Cole the uneasy feeling that she was playing with him.

"Paraphrase," he prompted. "Just give me something to go on."

"Well, she kept muttering something about a car." Ingrid crinkled her brow. "A Vega, I think. Yes, definitely a Vega."

"A car? That doesn't make any sense."

"Nothing your fiancée said this afternoon made much sense, Cole. Perhaps..." She let the word linger as she coyly wet her lips. "You should look around a little more before you do anything hasty. I think we could have some fun together."

Fun. He liked fun. Especially with a woman like Ingrid. She was beautiful and bright—everything a man could want. If you overlooked her propensity for blackmail.

"We could order a pitcher of margaritas," she suggested, studying him through long, thick lashes. "From room service."

He vaguely wondered why he wasn't jumping at her offer. Ingrid Tate was sexy. Uncomplicated. Physically flawless.

Not like Annie. She certainly wasn't perfect. She had that tiny chip on her bottom tooth. A policy against sex before marriage. A fiancé.

Definitely not his type. Even if her kiss did make him dizzy.

"Cole?" Ingrid's impatient tone startled him out of his reverie.

"Sorry," he muttered, unable to work up any enthusiasm for Ingrid's invitation. Maybe he needed to solve this case first. Then he'd have Annie out of his system.

By the time he'd finally convinced Ingrid he was rejecting her very generous offer, Cole was ten minutes late for the appointed meeting with Annie's pen pal. He arrived at the front desk, out of breath, to face an uncooperative night clerk.

"Can you check again, please?" he asked. "I'm supposed to meet a man named Halsey. Roy Halsey."

The rail-thin male clerk didn't even look up from his filing. "I already told you, he's not here."

"Look again, Todd," Cole said, glancing at his name tag. "I'm not leaving here until you do."

Todd's nostrils flared. "Fine. Mr. Halsey did leave a message here. But I believe it's addressed to a woman." He held an envelope out of reach but close enough for Cole to read. "As you can see, it says Annie."

"That's me," Cole improvised. "My name's Anatole. Everybody calls me Annie."

Todd smirked. "No kidding. A guy named Annie. I

bet you had a wonderful childhood with a name like that.''

"Yeah,'' Cole said, grabbing the envelope. "Me and a boy named Sue hung out together a lot.'' He took a couple of steps, then turned. "Can you describe Mr. Halsey for me?''

The clerk arched a brow. "Describe him?''

Cole shrugged. "It's been a long time since I've seen good old Roy. I just wondered if I'd still recognize him.''

"He'd be hard to miss,'' Todd said with a derisive snort. "He's got bright red hair and buck teeth.''

"Anything else?''

"Freckles. Lots of freckles.''

Annie hadn't mentioned anything about freckles when she'd described Roy. Or buck teeth. Which either meant she didn't care or Roy had pulled the old switch-eroo. Entice her with a picture of a cowboy Casanova, then hope he could win her over in person. Cole hurried to a deserted alcove, tearing open the letter as he walked.

"It's a damn questionnaire,'' he muttered, looking in disbelief at the paper in his hands. Neatly typed in black ink was a series of questions, followed by directions to return the completed survey to the Regency. His jaw sagged as he read the questions.

Do you have a history of mental illness in your family? Can you two-step? Do you speak a second language?

This was beyond bizarre. This was just plain creepy. Why the cat-and-mouse game? Why the questionnaire? Why no phone number where she could contact him in case she was in trouble?

Cole knew the answer. Because Roy Halsey wasn't

just some lonely cowboy looking for a bride. This man planned and calculated every move he made. And he wasn't going to show his hand until he was ready.

Maybe if Annie saw this questionnaire she'd finally realize how crazy it was to marry a perfect stranger. Or maybe she'd fill it out and hope she scored high enough to become Mrs. Roy Halsey.

He sighed, rubbing one hand over the nape of his neck. He couldn't tell her anything. Not yet. Not until he knew the real story behind Roy. He'd have Ethel check the Colorado phone directories tomorrow for the name. Contact his buddy in the Denver police to see if Halsey had a record. Plan a stakeout at the Regency in case Roy returned.

He checked his watch. Eight-twenty. Still plenty of time left in the evening to run to the office and start the search. He needed to figure out the situation before it got completely out of control.

He needed to figure out Annie.

ANNIE LAY as still as a department-store mannequin in the big iron bed. Cole had given her the biggest bedroom on the second floor of his house, furnished with an antique cherry highboy and matching dresser. Decorative moldings enhanced the high ceiling, and the wooden floor creaked and groaned. Just like the rest of the big, old house. It seemed an odd choice for a bachelor, but judging from the tour he'd given her earlier, Cole obviously relished the challenge of remodeling this old place.

Not that he was home long enough to enjoy it. She refused to look at the digital clock on her nightstand again. It was already long after midnight. She'd spent the evening composing a list of editors who might be interested in Vega's story. Then she'd sketched a rough outline. But for some reason she'd been unable to concentrate, and had spent the rest of the evening staring out the living room window. Now she stared up at the bedroom ceiling, unable to succumb to her bone-deep exhaustion.

At last she heard the brief roar of the Blazer's engine in the garage. Heard the front door open. Heard the creak of old floorboards as he made his way quietly to the master bedroom on the first floor.

She turned onto her side, tugging the faded blue log-cabin quilt up to her neck. His five-hour meeting with Miss August must have gone well. Maybe Ingrid had wanted more from him than money. Maybe he was attracted to tall, blond and buxom.

She sighed, rolling onto her back. Why did she always have to be drawn to the wrong guy? It was great for her career but it wreaked havoc on her love life. In the past, the challenges and adventures that naturally came along with the job of an investigative journalist had been enough for her. But now...now she was engaged to Roy.

Annie had initially planned for her engagement to be a ruse. To stall him while she stayed at his ranch until it was safe to go out into the world again. She'd never met a real cowboy before, much less dated one.

What if Roy was the man for her?

His letters were always warm and funny. She'd sent him her picture a month ago. Of course, she'd known what he looked like from the magazine. He had a nice smile. Very nice teeth. And he wore glasses, which made him seem a little vulnerable.

He reminded her of Bill, her mother's fourth husband and Annie's favorite stepfather. Bill had been a newspaper man and taught her how to go after a story. He'd also advised her to work freelance so she could hang on to both her integrity and her enthusiasm. The last time she'd seen Bill had been nine years ago, at her college graduation. Her mother had moved on to husband number five by then.

She sighed again, rolling onto her stomach. Nine years ago she'd been full of hopes and dreams and idealism. She hadn't planned her life to turn out this way. Her career was exciting but financially unpredictable. Some months she barely sold enough stories to pay the rent. Her love life was almost nonexistent if you didn't count her three fiancés.

What had happened to her girlhood dreams of children and a husband and love that lasted a lifetime? Why couldn't she be more like her older sister, Teresa, who had a happy marriage and a hefty mortgage on a two-story house in Fort Lee?

Annie rolled onto her side. Maybe Roy would be the answer to all those dreams. Maybe her luck with men had changed. Although if Quinn did find her, she wouldn't have to worry about any more lousy relationships in her life. Maybe she could be reincarnated as a black widow spider. Have great sex, then kill the guy before he did something stupid.

But she wanted more than great sex. She wanted someone to confide in. Someone who laughed with her. Someone who cared about her.

Someone who kissed like Cole Rafferty.

She groaned into her pillow and flipped onto her back. She never should have kissed him. Even if it was the most sizzling, sensuous kiss of her life.

Her potentially short life.

She could have died happy right there in his arms.

Well, okay, she didn't really want to die in his arms. Not when he was probably checking his watch behind her back so he wouldn't miss his date with Ingrid. He certainly hadn't cared enough to follow her when she'd run out of the kitchen after that kiss.

Annie frowned at the moonbeams streaked across the tiled ceiling. Running away was becoming a bad habit with her. She needed to forget about that kiss. That one brief, we're-only-doing-this-because-Rex-is-watching kiss. It obviously meant nothing to Cole. He was using her to keep his father from interfering in his love life.

Just like she was using him.

Fine. No problem. This arrangement was only temporary, and she could certainly handle a simple infatuation. Besides, living with Cole should provide her with some interesting revelations. Once she saw all his faults and flaws, the attraction would be over. A man can't hide his true character twenty-four hours a day.

Annie sat up and punched her pillow, her fist sinking into the downy goose feathers with a satisfying whoosh. She did it again. Then she plopped down and planned her strategy.

Cole wanted the fiancée from hell. Fine. He got her.

4

"WE'VE GOT a problem," Cole announced as he entered the kitchen the next morning.

"We certainly do," Annie said, her voice still heavy with sleep. She closed the refrigerator door and turned to face him, squinting at the bright sunlight streaming through the window. Through bleary eyes she saw he wore nothing but an old T-shirt and a pair of cutoffs. She came to the depressing conclusion that the less he wore, the better he looked. Not an image she could handle first thing in the morning.

"You look awful," he said, moving toward her.

"Thanks," she replied, wishing she'd gotten dressed or at least combed her hair. "I'm not a morning person."

"I guess not. Maybe you need something to eat."

"That's the problem, Cole. There's no food in this house. I need food before I can begin to function."

He frowned in confusion as he strode past her to the refrigerator. "I have food. I stopped at the grocery store on my way home last night." He opened the refrigerator. "See, there's all kinds of food in here."

Annie stifled a yawn as she stumbled to the kitchen table and sat down. "I mean real food."

He pulled a package of sausage burritos out of the freezer. "What do you call this?"

She groaned and laid her head on the table. "I call

it disgusting. Don't you have any of the four food groups? Dairy? Fruit? Vegetables? Coffee?"

"Hey, if you need caffeine, I've got a whole case of Pepsi in here."

"I know. It's right next to the leftover pizza."

"Now that's what I call a perfect breakfast," he said, pulling out a can of soda and the pizza and setting it in front of her. "Eat up. You'll feel much better."

She sat up and stared at Cole's version of breakfast. How was it possible he could look so good and eat so badly? How could she possibly survive the next few days on this kind of diet? Then she remembered she might not survive at all if Quinn found her. As long as she was living dangerously, she might as well enjoy it. She popped the tab on the can of soda and took a long swallow.

Cole joined her across the table. "Now, to the real problem."

"Finding Roy?"

"No, Ethel."

Annie looked up from her congealed pizza. "Ethel is missing?"

He sighed. "If only I could be so lucky. No, Ethel's right here in Denver, and tonight she'll be right here in this house. Dad's bringing her over for dinner."

"Can we have real food for dinner?" she asked hopefully. "I can make a meal that knocks their socks off."

"That would be a disaster."

"Why? I'm a great cook!"

"That's what I'm afraid of. Dad will be so impressed with your cooking he'll overlook all your faults."

She frowned. "What faults?"

"The ones that make him believe you're the last woman I should marry."

She took a sip of soda. "I thought the infection went over well."

"Maybe." He picked up his pizza. "But I think you overdid it with that bit about Vinnie and the knife. Try to be a little less imaginative."

"How do you know it's not true?"

That stopped him in mid-bite. He chewed, swallowed, then looked at her. "Is it?"

She shrugged. "Part of it. I did have a boyfriend named Vinnie, and there was a knife involved. Or rather, several knives."

"Several?"

"He was a knife thrower for a circus. I was doing a story on him when—" Annie shut her mouth, wishing she'd bitten her tongue instead of that slice of pepperoni. She'd let herself get distracted by a handsome face again and completely lost her concentration.

"So you're a reporter," Cole surmised, reaching for another slice of pizza.

"I never said that," Annie replied, scrambling to come up with an explanation for her slip.

He grinned. "You're forgetting about my razor sharp detective skills."

"They're easy to forget since my fiancé is still missing."

"Ouch. Are you always this much fun in the morning?"

"I'm just a little stressed right now. I'll try to improve my mood by dinner tonight."

"No, it's perfect. If I had known how well you were going to adapt to this part, I would have invited Dad over for breakfast instead of dinner."

"We fiancées from hell aim to please."

"Good. Just don't take it personally when I insult your cooking tonight. Or better yet, do take it personally. Then we can have a big fight at the dinner table. That should show Dad how wrong we are for each other." He sighed. "As long as Ethel doesn't interfere."

"Afraid she'll see through our charade?"

He nodded. "If you think I'm good at nosing out the truth—"

"I never said that."

"—then you should see Ethel at work," Cole continued as if she hadn't spoken. "The woman is a pit bull. And she knows we only met yesterday. One word to Dad, and this whole fake engagement goes up in smoke."

"You mean your father would believe her over his own son?"

Cole grinned. "Ethel's ratted on me from the time I put a toad in the office watercooler when I eight. She's like the wicked stepmother I've never had."

"What about your real mother?" Annie asked, her reporter instincts kicking in. She regretted the question as soon as she saw the flicker of pain cross his face. "I'm sorry. Now I'm the one being nosy."

He shrugged, then tipped his soda can and took a long drink. "No problem. My mother divorced Dad while I was living in Ohio. He was working fourteen-hour days, and she got tired of being alone all the time. She lives in Taos now with her new husband."

"Poor Rex."

Cole sighed. "He never saw it coming. I think that bothered him more than anything. He took it as a bad reflection on his detective skills rather than his husband skills.''

''So is that why you never want to marry?'' she asked quietly, one finger circling the rim of her soda can.

''Me?'' He smiled. ''I don't have any husband skills. Which is what I intend to prove at dinner tonight. Now if we can only convince Ethel that our engagement is real.''

''Don't worry about Ethel,'' Annie assured him. ''I'll figure out something to tell her.''

WHEN THEIR dinner guests arrived, Annie grabbed Ethel and pulled her into the kitchen on the pretext of helping prepare the dinner. ''We have to talk.''

Ethel pursed her lips. ''I should say so. I couldn't believe it when Rex told me you and Cole were engaged. You just met yesterday!''

''Our engagement is a scam,'' Annie whispered.

Ethel folded her arms. ''I knew it! What kind of shenanigans is that boy up to now?''

Hearing the deep voices of the men in the next room, Annie drew Ethel into the walk-in pantry and closed the door behind them for privacy. She faced Ethel. ''It's not Cole's fault. He's just trying to help me.''

Ethel's brow furrowed. ''What do you mean?''

Annie leaned against a shelf full of Little Debbie snack cakes. ''I can't explain unless you promise not to say anything about this to Rex.''

Ethel shook her head. ''I don't know... I could never lie to Rex.''

''Even if it's for his own protection?''

Ethel's eyes widened. ''Are you actually in danger?''

Annie hesitated, then nodded. She couldn't tell Ethel everything, but her instincts told her she could trust the older woman. And her instincts were never wrong. Her instincts about women, anyway.

"I can't go into any details," Annie whispered. "But this fake engagement is Cole's way of protecting me. It's only temporary. I won't be here more than a few days, a week at the most."

Ethel clucked her tongue. "I knew something was wrong when you came into the office yesterday, but I had no idea it was this serious. And I still don't understand why Rex can't be told the truth."

"If Rex knew about my case, he might want to get involved. It's just too dangerous."

"If it's that dangerous, maybe you should go to the police."

Annie shook her head. "Cole is the only one who can help me. And he used to be a policeman, right?"

"One of the best," Ethel replied, a note of pride in her voice. "Cole may be a rascal, but he's a good man at heart. He takes after Rex."

"They're both intelligent men," Annie affirmed.

"Self-confident," Ethel added.

"Sometimes a little high-handed."

"Messy, too." Ethel smiled. "They both leave cookie crumbs on the desk."

Annie grinned. "Don't forget opinionated."

"Sometimes downright pigheaded," Ethel declared.

"Let's not forget handsome," Annie conceded, "and sexy."

Ethel closed her eyes and sighed as she leaned against the pantry door. "Rex Rafferty is the sexiest man I've ever known. Sometimes I wish…" Her voice trailed off and her cheeks grew pink. She stood up straight and cleared her throat. "Oh, my, what am I saying?"

Annie took a step closer to her. "I think you're saying you're in love with Rex."

Ethel's cheeks turned crimson. "That's outrageous!"

"But is it true?"

"Well...I suppose it is true," Ethel admitted in a whisper. "Although I'm much too old to be in love with anyone."

"Now that's what I call outrageous. You're never too old to fall in love. Have you told him?"

Ethel's eyes widened in horror. "Of course not! How could you even imagine such a thing? I could never tell Rex that I—"

"That you're madly in love with him," Annie said with a smile.

Ethel placed a hand over her heart. "He'd be shocked. Horrified. We worked together for thirty-five years, and he's never once..."

"That doesn't necessarily mean he's not interested. Some men just need a little encouragement."

Doubt wavered in Ethel's green eyes. "What kind of encouragement?"

Annie shrugged. "I don't know. I'm not exactly an expert on love." She stepped back to look Ethel over from head to toe. "Rex probably still sees you as his secretary. Neat. Efficient. Reliable. Maybe he needs to see you as a woman."

Ethel scowled. "I've been right under his nose for more than three decades. If he doesn't know I'm a woman by now, there's not much hope for us."

"He brought you here tonight as his date. That's a good first step."

Ethel rolled her eyes. "I've been his stand-in date ever since his divorce, and he's never even kissed me. I just don't think he's attracted to me." She reached a hand to her silver hair, patting the neatly pinned bun. "I've been thinking of dyeing my hair."

"I think the color is lovely," Annie interjected. "But maybe you could try a looser, more relaxed style."

"What about my clothes?" Ethel asked, looking at her mud-brown dress. "A woman my age would look just plain silly in those trendy outfits in all the stores."

"One of the magazines I used to work for had an article that recommended pastels for women over sixty." Annie studied Ethel's fresh-scrubbed face. "Some light makeup, too. Just go to any cosmetics counter and they'll fix you right up."

"I don't know," Ethel said, looking skeptical. "That's all just window dressing. I'll still just be good old dependable Ethel. I thought maybe after his wife left him..." She shook her head. "This is silly. I should realize by now that he's just not interested. I've done everything but stand on my head for that man."

Annie nibbled her lower lip. She didn't want to give Ethel false hope, but didn't love deserve a chance? Especially since Rex and Ethel seemed made for each other. "Maybe that's the problem."

Ethel looked at her. "What do you mean?"

"I mean it sounds like you've always been there for Rex. Supporting him and encouraging him and ready to do his beck and call. Maybe he's taken you for granted."

Ethel sighed. "And now it's too late."

"Not necessarily. I may not be an expert on romance, but my mother taught me a few of her secrets."

"Is she an expert?"

"Six marriages and counting."

Ethel's eyes widened. "Six?"

"She's an expert at catching men, not keeping them."

"So how do I catch one?"

"Sometimes Mom uses honey." Annie reached to the top shelf of the pantry, pulled down a slim bottle, then handed it to Ethel. "And sometimes she uses this."

Ethel frowned at the label. "Vinegar?"

Annie nodded. "You've been sweet to Rex long enough. Maybe now it's time to add a little unexpected flavor to your relationship."

"SMILE FOR the camera," Rex said as he peered through the viewfinder of his thirty-five-millimeter Kodak.

Cole smiled tightly as he held Annie on his lap, right where his dad had insisted she pose for these ridiculous pictures. They sat in the dining room with dinner waiting on the table, the less than tantalizing aromas drifting from the serving dishes. The camera flashed, and he blinked at the bright light.

"Am I too heavy?" she asked, shifting on his lap.

"No," he said, struggling to maintain his composure. "You're fine. Just please…hold still."

"Don't be so tense," she whispered, "the dinner will be fine."

Dinner? How could he possibly think about dinner at a time like this? Annie nestled close to him, her body warm and supple and her silky hair brushing against his cheek. He closed his eyes and stifled a groan as she moved restlessly.

"Dad, enough pictures," he said at last, shifting uncomfortably in the high-back chair. "You're going to run out of film."

Rex chuckled. "All right, I guess I have enough pictures of Annie's first dinner for family posterity."

Annie slid off his lap and stood up. "Speaking of dinner, it's going to get cold if we don't get started."

Cole took slow, even breaths while his father put away the camera. His heart was almost beating at a normal pace by the time they seated themselves at the old oak table.

"I hope everybody's hungry," Annie said cheerfully as she served up dinner. Cole's overly generous portion landed with an unappetizing thunk on his plate. She'd certainly taken his request for an atrocious meal seriously. He just hoped she didn't take his insults seriously.

"So what exactly is this?" he asked, cautiously spearing his food with a fork.

"It's an old family recipe," Annie replied before taking a sip from her wineglass.

"Which family? The Borgias?" Cole looked at the glob of food on his plate, trying to identify it. The dark green color reminded him of spinach, but it was too stringy. And it had an unusual odor that reminded him of that wedge of Limburger cheese that had been in his refrigerator since last summer.

"Is there cheese in here?" he asked, poking at it.

"That's for me to know and you to find out," she replied playfully.

"I'm afraid I won't find out until they pump my stomach."

Annie laughed, then turned to Rex. "Your son has the best sense of humor. I just find it irresistible."

Rex smiled thinly, then looked with longing at the crisp Caesar salad heaped on Annie's and Ethel's plates. "Aren't you ladies going to try any of this...special recipe?"

"We're watching our waistlines," Annie said primly. "Ethel wants to stay in shape for a rumba contest at the VFW hall, and I want to stay in shape for Cole." She blew him a kiss.

Rex looked at his former secretary. "I didn't know you liked to dance, Ethel."

"Yes, Rex. I do." She picked up her wineglass and drained it in one long gulp, then looked at Rex. "There are a lot of things you don't know about me."

Cole looked around the table, wondering how to shift the conversation to Annie's unsuitability as his wife. Then he looked at his plate. He wasn't positive, but he thought he saw his food move. "I really don't think I can eat any more," he said, pushing his plate away.

"You haven't eaten even one bite," Annie complained. "Are you trying to embarrass me in front of your family?"

This was more like it. He feigned a glare in Annie's direction. "I'm a meat and potatoes man. This...stuff isn't exactly what I had in mind for dinner tonight."

The silence was palpable. Annie slowly put down her fork as her gaze lifted to meet his. The mischievous gleam in her eyes made him bite back a smile.

"I'm just trying to improve your eating habits, darling. And I might as well tell you now that I've decided we are going to become vegetarians."

Rex cleared his throat. "Now, Annie, I admire your concern for my son's health, but a body can't survive on a bunch of leaves and roots. Right, Ethel?'' He looked to his former secretary for approbation.

"Of course, Rex," Ethel murmured, toying with her salad.

Annie cleared her throat. "Ethel, would you like some vinegar for your salad?"

"Oh," Ethel mumbled, as she hastily put down her fork. "Yes, Annie, thank you." But she ignored the bottle Annie set next to her plate and turned her full attention to Rex. "Actually, leaves and roots happen to be very nutritious."

Rex chuckled. "Don't tell me you like all that bird food, Ethel."

"Well, no…I mean, yes, it's actually very good for you. A few vitamins and minerals certainly wouldn't hurt you or Cole."

Cole looked warily at the goop on his plate. "Are you sure about that?"

Ethel sniffed. "You haven't even tasted it yet. Don't be as closed-minded as your father."

Rex stared at her. "Closed-minded? You think I'm closed-minded?"

Ethel blushed. "That's not exactly what I meant."

Annie leaned toward Ethel. "Pass the vinegar, please."

Ethel handed her the bottle, then took a deep breath as she turned to Rex. "Although sometimes you ignore new and exciting…opportunities just because…"

Rex put down his fork and folded his arms. "Because?"

Ethel stared at her plate as the words spilled out of her mouth. "Because you're comfortable with your routine and think you're too old to change."

Cole couldn't believe it. He'd never seen Ethel disagree with his father. About anything. Now it was as if she was purposely trying to annoy him. Perplexed, he looked at Annie and saw the corners of her mouth curve in a smile. Something smelled a little rotten here, and it wasn't just the food on his plate.

Rex sat in stunned silence, staring at Ethel.

So much for hoping his father would find Annie unsuitable wife material. Rex was too shocked by Ethel's behavior to notice the disastrous dinner. Maybe it was time for Cole to show his father just how stubborn Annie could be.

He cleared his throat to get his father's attention, then turned to Annie. "We are not becoming vegetarians."

"Yes, we are," Annie countered, her blue eyes glittering. His pulse kicked up a notch as she licked her pink lips. He almost smiled when he saw the competitive gleam in her gaze. She wanted to win this battle, even if it was only for show.

Cole folded his arms. "In fact, I've just decided to give up vegetables. I'm going to become a meatagarian."

"A meatagarian?" she echoed, pressing her lips tightly together as amusement danced in her eyes.

He nodded. "That's right. From this moment on, I won't allow another salad green, spinach leaf or garbanzo bean to touch my lips."

She leaned forward, her gaze falling to his mouth. "Then I hope you have a deep affection for hamburger, because I won't be touching your lips, either."

He pretended to waver at her threat. At least, he sort of pretended. Her words brought a sudden flashback of their kiss in the kitchen last night. She'd felt so good in his arms. And that kiss! His breathing hitched as he thought about it. His gaze moved to her lips. He was very aware of the way the tip of her tongue flitted out to moisten them. He could kiss her again. Tonight. Now, if he wanted. Apologize, then make up in front of their audience. They were supposed to be in love, after all. What more natural way to show their affection?

Cole threw his napkin on his plate, then pushed his chair back from the table.

"Hold it there, son," Rex said, holding out one hand. "No need to walk out in a huff."

"I'm not," he began, annoyed by his father's interference. He didn't want to walk out, he only wanted to kiss Annie senseless. But Rex wasn't paying attention to him. He turned to Annie, his face grave.

"I know you mean well, Annie," Rex began. "But my son isn't the kind of man to be led around by the nose. Rafferty men have always been strong-minded, independent—"

"Stubborn as mules," Ethel said under her breath.

Rex looked at her in surprise. "Did you say something, Ethel?"

Ethel looked up from her salad, her cheeks flushed a becoming pink. "I think Annie is right." She turned to Cole and narrowed her gaze. "Goodness knows the boy can't feed himself properly. He's been a cholesterol junkie since the day he was old enough to drive himself to Chuckie's Chicken Shack. Annie and her vegetables may be just what he needs."

Cole sank down in his chair, his stomach growling. "Maybe I will try a little of that Caesar salad," he said, with a hopeful look at Annie's plate. "Just as a compromise."

Rex shook his head. "Compromise is death. You

need to let her know who is going to wear the pants in the family, son.''

"Oh, Rex!" Ethel exclaimed, tossing her napkin onto the table. "This is the nineties, and women have been wearing pants for the last thirty years." She poured herself another glass of wine and said under her breath, "Why am I surprised you didn't notice?"

Cole didn't understand how his faux fight with Annie had turned into a battle between his father and Ethel. In the last thirty-four years, he'd never even seen her stand up to him like this.

"A man can't have a woman telling him what to do," Rex insisted.

Ethel squared her shoulders. "And a woman can't just stand by while the man she loves acts like a—a nincompoop because he's too stubborn to change."

"Are you calling my son a nincompoop?"

"It's not his fault," Ethel declared. "It runs in the family." She picked up her wineglass and drained it in one long swallow.

"Ethel, I think you've had enough to drink." Rex moved the wine bottle out of her reach.

"And I think you don't have any right to tell me what to do."

"I'm your boss," he countered.

"Ex-boss!"

"If you two don't mind," Cole cut in, "Annie and I are trying to have our own fight."

Ethel gave him one of her looks. The same one she'd given him twenty-five years ago, after he'd put grasshoppers in her purse. "Cole Rafferty, you know this girl only has your best interests at heart. And you started this entire argument by insulting her cooking."

Annie dabbed her eyes with her napkin. "I just wanted to make a good impression."

Cole rolled his eyes as he saw his father visibly soften, forgetting that he'd fallen for her waterworks, too.

"It's the effort that counts," Rex said, reaching over to pat Annie's hand. "You'll do better next time."

Cole gritted his teeth. He didn't want to go through this again. He wanted Rex encouraging them to break the engagement, not encouraging Dr. Annie Frankenstein to go back to her kitchen laboratory. But it was too late to repair the damage.

Annie dried her eyes and looked up with a bright smile. "Who's ready for dessert?"

"WHAT JUST HAPPENED here?" Cole asked, as he helped Annie carry the dirty dishes into the kitchen. Their guests had left ten minutes ago, barely speaking to each other. He still didn't understand Ethel's attitude or why it seemed to bother his dad so much. Rex should be worried sick about bringing Annie into the Rafferty family. Instead, he'd snapped more pictures of her serving that gelatinous mess she called dessert.

"Our dinner party was a disaster," Annie announced cheerfully, scraping leftovers into the trash can. "That should make you happy." Then she frowned. "I just hope your dad doesn't suffer too much. He ate all of his dessert just to make me feel better."

He sighed. "Don't worry, my dad has a cast-iron stomach. In fact, I think our plan might have backfired. My mom was a lousy cook, too, and I think your cooking made him feel nostalgic instead of nauseous." He began loading the sink with soiled dishes. "That's not what I meant, anyway. What happened to Ethel?"

"Love."

He turned to face her. "Excuse me?"

She rolled her eyes. "Ethel is in love. Is that so hard to believe?"

"Ethel? In love?" Cole couldn't even imagine that possibility. Ethel had been a fixture at Rafferty Investigations forever. Even after all these years he knew almost nothing about her personal life. It reminded him of his shock when he was eight years old and saw his third grade teacher walking her dog with curlers in her hair, like she was a real person. Ethel loved her Dictaphone and her billing charts, but a man? Impossible. He looked at Annie. "With who?"

She looked at him in amazement. "With Rex, of course."

Cole laughed. Annie Jones might be one of the smartest women he'd ever met, but she obviously didn't know about love. Which might explain why she was willing to wed a perfect stranger. "That's ridiculous. I've never even seen her so much as flirt with him before. I don't think she even knows how to flirt."

"She doesn't." Annie squirted dish soap into the stainless steel sink, then turned on the hot water. "But I told her we'd work on it."

"We?"

"Think about it, Cole. If Rex is involved with Ethel, he won't have time to interfere in your life. Isn't that what you want?"

"Well…yes. Of course that's what I want. But he's known Ethel forever, and there haven't been any sparks between them."

"There were certainly some sparks tonight." Annie turned off the tap and began washing dishes.

Cole studied her. "You put her up to this, didn't you?"

"I might have given her a suggestion or two."

"Such as?"

"Now, Cole, I can't tell you all my secrets."

He folded his arms. "So far, you haven't told me any of your secrets. And you've definitely got secrets, lady."

She tipped up her chin. "I thought we were talking about Rex and Ethel. I think they make a cute couple."

"I think you're trying to change the subject."

Annie turned to face him. "You already know everything about me you need to know, Cole. After all, this…arrangement is only temporary. As soon as you find Roy, I'll be out of your life for good."

"What if I don't find him?"

She swallowed. "That's not an option."

"But it is a possibility. Even I can admit it." He could also tell her he'd already found Roy, or at least gotten a strong lead. But he had her on the ropes, and his curiosity overcame his sense of duty. Annie Jones intrigued him. He wanted to know everything about her. Then maybe he could find a way to free himself of this strange fascination she held for him.

"If you can't find Roy," she said, her voice unnaturally quiet, "then I guess I'll have to resort to Plan B."

"What's Plan B?"

She sighed, rinsing a dish under the tap water. "I'll tell you as soon as I figure it out."

He moved a step closer to her. "Why don't you just tell me everything now, Annie? What's the real deal with Roy?"

She blinked at him. "I already told you—he wants to marry me."

"The question is why do you want to marry him?"

She didn't say anything for a long moment, her hands submerged in the soapy water. "I guess it's for the same reason you *don't* want to marry."

That took him by surprise. "And what reason is that?"

"Fear. I'm afraid I'm running out of time. And you're afraid, too."

He snorted. "Are you a reporter or a pop psychologist?"

"Right now, I seem to be the only dishwasher," she said, with a pointed look at the wet plates in the dish rack.

He picked up a dish towel and started drying the dishes. "Okay, so tell me what I'm afraid of."

"That's easy. Commitment. Maturity. Responsibility."

"Is this multiple choice or do I get to fill in the blank?"

She laughed as she reached for another dish. "Oh, please, fill in the blank. I love to hear men's reasons for avoiding matrimony. They're so creative."

"In the first place," he began, trying to ignore the sensations her laughter created in the pit of his stomach, "I'm not afraid of anything."

"You looked positively petrified when I brought out the dessert. And you didn't eat a bite."

"That was self-preservation. Not fear."

"So you're not afraid of anything?" she challenged. "How about rattlesnakes? Bombs? Guns?"

"I have a healthy respect for all three," he said.

"Healthy enough to keep my distance. But that's not the same as fear."

She looked thoughtful for a moment. "But you're afraid of marriage?"

"I'm not afraid of it," he said firmly, then he smiled. "I have a healthy respect for marriage. Healthy enough—"

"—to keep your distance," she finished for him. "Very funny, Cole. But that's not a reason."

He picked another plate out of the dish rack, frustrated by the way the conversation had veered from Annie's secrets to his personal life. He'd never shared his feelings about marriage, or his reasons for avoiding it so ardently. But maybe if he spilled some of his secrets, Annie would finally open up to him.

"Okay, here's a reason," he said. "I don't like divorce."

She blinked. "Well, nobody does. That's like saying you're against war. That's not a reason."

"It's a great reason," he countered, irritated at her casual dismissal. "You can't have a divorce without a marriage. I simply believe in taking preventive measures." His gaze fell on the large portion of dessert left in the serving dish. "Like preventing botulism by avoiding certain foods."

She wiped a handful of silverware with the dishcloth. "You mean, you're avoiding marriage, love, a family, on the off chance that it might end in a divorce?"

"Yes."

She shook her head. "That's so cowardly."

He turned toward her, stung. "I call it smart. I worked on a police force, remember. I've seen plenty of the aftermath of divorce. Stalkings, poverty, kids involved in a nasty tug-of-war. It's not pretty." He tossed the dish towel over his shoulder. "And in my opinion, it's not worth it."

"I'm not arguing with you about divorce. It's too common and it's too easy. But not all marriages end that way."

"You're right," he said dryly, "some end with one spouse blowing the other away."

She picked up another handful of silverware. "You're such a pessimist."

"And you're a dreamer." He leaned one hip against the kitchen counter. Time to go on the offensive. "Only your dream of the perfect marriage is going to turn into a nightmare if Roy turns out to be a jerk...or worse."

"Well, as soon as you find him, I'll find out everything I need to know about my husband-to-be."

"And live happily ever after?" Cole asked doubtfully.

She didn't look at him, her gaze intent on the soapy white bubbles in the sink. "That's my plan."

More questions burned in the back of his throat, but he could tell by the stubborn set of her jaw that she didn't plan to elaborate. It reinforced his earlier instincts. Annie was keeping something from him. Something important.

Leaving the wineglasses to air dry in the dish rack, he turned on his heel and walked out of the kitchen. For some reason, he couldn't concentrate with Annie around, and he needed to focus on this case. Especially since his own client didn't trust him. It was obvious that Annie Jones intended to keep her secrets all to herself.

Too bad she didn't realize Cole knew all sorts of ways to make secrets—and fiancés—come out of hiding.

5

THE NEXT THREE DAYS passed so peacefully Annie began to get nervous. She slid farther into the big claw-
foot bathtub, letting the thick white bubbles engulf her.
This was the fourth bubble bath she'd taken since she'd
moved in with Cole. A welcome reprieve after the tension of the last few months undercover as Vega's fiancée. Those months almost seemed like a dream…or
a nightmare.

By the time she'd finally gotten her hands on his
private journal, he'd gotten wise to her. He'd sent her
a warning by beating up her photographer. A warning
she'd heard loud and clear. So she'd grabbed his journal and made a run for it. That journal had traveled
with her to Colorado and was now secreted under the
mattress in her bedroom. It contained everything she
needed to nail Quinn Vega.

Now she just needed to stay alive long enough to do
it.

As soon as she was safely tucked away at Roy's
ranch, she could finish writing her story. She'd already
pulled together a rough draft. Now came the more te-
dious job of weaving all the complex details into a
smooth and comprehensive exposé. Maybe when
Quinn's illegal activities were made public, she'd be
able to come out of hiding. Then she could get her life
back. Her friends and family in Newark wouldn't miss

her yet—they were used to her taking off to parts unknown for a story. But how long would Vega hold a grudge? She might have to hide from him for months. Years. She closed her eyes, dreading that possibility.

Annie pushed those unpleasant thoughts out of her mind, letting the steamy, fragrant water lap against her bare shoulders. She leaned her head against the inflatable bath pillow and breathed a soft sigh. She felt almost decadent, lolling around on a weekday afternoon like a spoiled princess while Cole was working so hard on her case.

Or was he?

She opened her eyes and frowned at the brown water spots on the ceiling. He claimed to be working on her case exclusively, yet he hadn't come up with even one lead. Just how hard was it to find a cowboy in Colorado? She'd done her own share of investigating as a reporter, and she knew there were numerous ways to track down a missing person. Did he know more than he was telling her? Or was he just a lousy detective?

A knock on the door startled her. She slid down in the hot, sudsy water when she remembered that the lock on the bathroom door was broken. "Who is it?"

"Me." Cole's deep voice drifted through the door. "I'm sorry to bother you, but there's a guy downstairs who would like to meet you."

Annie swallowed. *Roy.* So much for her lousy detective theory. Cole had finally found her fiancé. Fiancé number two, anyway. Heaven help her if he ever crossed paths with fiancé number one. Cole probably wouldn't enjoy it much, either. Quinn Vega had a vicious jealous streak.

"Annie?" he called, when she didn't say anything. "Are you all right?"

"Fine," she replied, her voice strained. "I'll be right out." This was it. No more phony engagement. No more bubble baths. No more Cole. Her heart skipped a beat. Suddenly her plan to hide out at Roy's ranch didn't seem quite so perfect.

"Annie?"

"Coming." She took a deep breath. "Get a grip," she muttered to herself, then rose and climbed out of the bathtub. She toweled herself dry and combed her wet, stringy curls with her fingers. She slipped into her underwear, then donned a denim dress and a pair of leather sandals. After wiping the steam off the bathroom mirror, she gave herself a quick once-over.

"Ready or not, Roy," she murmured to her reflection, "here I come."

Cole stood in the second-floor hallway, waiting for her. "You smell good."

"Thanks," she said, self-conscious beneath his warm gaze. "It's the raspberry bubble bath I bought yesterday...with your money." She swallowed, suddenly realizing how much she owed this man. And after today she'd probably never see him again.

"I don't know how to thank you, Cole," she began. "For this dress, all the clothes you bought for me, letting me stay here...everything." To her surprise and chagrin, tears stung her eyes. "I don't know what I would have done without you."

"Hey." He stepped forward, gently brushing one lone teardrop off her cheek with his fingertips. "What's this?"

She emitted a shaky laugh, stepping away from his touch. "Nothing. Just a little homesick, I guess."

His brow furrowed in concern. "Is that all?"

"Of course that's all," she replied, not quite certain

of her emotions. Was it missing Newark that bothered her? Or the prospect of missing Cole?

Annie mentally shook herself. She hadn't known Cole long enough to miss him. Certainly not long enough to discover his flaws. And the men in Annie's life always had flaws.

Like Phillippe, she thought wryly. He'd swept her off her feet several years ago in Paris, where she'd been an intern for CNN-International. After only ten days, he'd proposed marriage. When she'd regretfully informed him that she wasn't in love, he told her not to worry. He only wanted a green card, not a real wife. Her subsequent story on green card marriages had garnered accolades from her colleagues and even a prestigious award.

So maybe it was better to leave Cole now, before she discovered the worst.

"Would you rather meet him later?" Cole asked, obviously confused by her behavior. "I can tell him to come back."

"No. I'm fine," she assured him. "So where is he?"

"Downstairs." Cole stepped away from her. "Sorry I didn't give you any warning."

"No problem," she said, trying to sound cheerful. Confident. A woman in complete control of her life. "Lead the way."

He headed down the stairs, and Annie had the exquisite pleasure of studying him from behind. She liked his loose-hipped stride and the snug fit of his denim jeans. She liked the way his chambray shirt stretched across his shoulders and the way his dark brown hair curled around the collar. Annie closed her eyes, trying to imprint the image in her mind. Unfortunately, she bumped into him instead, her eyes flying open as her nose impacted against his solid shoulder blade.

"Hey." He reached out to steady her. "What's your hurry?"

"No hurry," she replied, as they reached the living room. "I'm just anxious to meet..." Her voice trailed off as her gaze fell on the man standing next to the mahogany coffee table.

He was average height, but with a stocky build that was all muscle. His dark hair was short and neatly cut, accentuating the sharp angles of his face. He was as intimidating as he was attractive.

But he wasn't Roy.

"This is Sergeant Mateo Alvarez with the Denver police department," Cole said. "Matt, this is Annie Jones."

"Nice to meet you, Miss Jones." Mateo smiled as he shook her hand, his shrewd, dark eyes assessing her.

The police? Annie took a deep, calming breath. The chances of this policeman being on Vega's payroll were practically nil. After all, Quinn couldn't possibly corrupt every cop in the country.

"Have a seat, Matt," Cole said, drawing Annie onto the blue-and-beige-check sofa beside him.

Although the living room's freshly painted ecru walls still remained bare, old and new furniture combined to give the room a cozy atmosphere. Sergeant Alvarez looked right at home as he sprawled on the beige corduroy love seat.

"What are you doing here?" Annie asked bluntly. She realized she was being rude, but she needed to get her bearings. Had Quinn filed a missing person's report? Had Mateo Alvarez somehow traced her here?

"Cole asked me to stop by," Mateo replied.

Annie turned to Cole. "Why?"

"I just realized we never reported your stolen purse," he said, looking puzzled by her reaction. "Matt's a good friend of mine. I thought he might be able to locate it for you."

Her purse? He'd scared her half to death just to find her stupid purse? She thought about strangling him, but that probably wouldn't be too smart in front of the cop.

Cole turned to Alvarez. "I know it's a long shot, Matt, but it's got all her money, her credit cards and her driver's license."

My identity. A shiver raced up her spine. If Alvarez located her purse, he'd realize she wasn't Annie Jones. Then he'd tell Cole.

Matt pulled a small notepad and a stubby pencil from his shirt pocket. "When did the theft take place?"

"About a week ago," she replied, deliberately vague.

"It was six days ago," Cole said in clarification. "At the Denver Airport."

Sergeant Alvarez jotted the information on his notepad. "Can you describe the purse snatcher?"

Annie could describe the young woman right down to the green streaks in her blond hair. She had a petite build and wide-set eyes. A jagged red scar stood out above her right eyebrow.

"He was a tall man," she improvised, "with black hair and a beard. That's all I can remember. It's kind of a blur."

Sergeant Alvarez leaned forward, his gaze intent on her face. "I'm sure it was very traumatic for you."

On a scale of recent traumatic events in her life, the purse snatching had registered about a one and a half. But she only smiled tightly and nodded.

He glanced at Cole, then made another note. "Well, I can't make you any promises, but I'll do my best to locate your purse."

"Thank you," she murmured, desperately hoping he failed.

"Matt's got great resources," Cole said. "If he can't find it, nobody can."

She sincerely hoped that included Quinn. At least if Vega tried to trace her through her credit cards, he'd find a felon instead of his fiancée. Still, that would get him as far as Denver. And that was much too close.

Matt flipped his notepad shut. "You both need to know that even if we do locate the purse, chances are the money and credit cards will be long gone."

"Of course," Annie replied. "I've already given them up for lost." She stood. "If you'll excuse me, I have to go dry my hair. If it dries naturally, I frighten small children."

Both men laughed, but she had the uneasy feeling Alvarez knew she'd been lying through her teeth about the purse snatcher. She escaped up the stairs and into her bedroom, shutting the door firmly behind her.

Maybe it was time to come up with Plan B.

"So WHAT do you think?" Cole asked after Annie had left the room. Matt was a good friend and an even better cop. He reminded Cole of his old partner, Nick Chamberlin. Both men had great instincts and the brains to back them up.

"She's a knockout." Matt leaned back, stretching his legs in front of him. "But a little edgy. What's her story?"

Good question. Cole had known Annie almost a week and still knew little about her. He knew she liked her popcorn with lots of butter but no salt. That she teared up at sappy phone commercials on television. And that she liked to take bubble baths. "She has a few...personal problems." That was vague enough to be intriguing, and he saw the spark of curiosity in Matt's eyes.

"Nothing serious, I hope."

Cole shrugged. Could you call marrying a perfect stranger serious? Desperate? Crazy? "I'm trying to help her straighten things out." *And come to her senses.*

"So how did you two meet?"

Cole smiled. "She showed up in my office and had a case I couldn't refuse."

"I think you mean a face you couldn't refuse." Matt chuckled. "You forget how well I know you, Rafferty. You've always had great taste in women."

"Annie isn't like any woman I've known before," he said truthfully. "I still haven't learned all her secrets." The mystery surrounding her had intrigued him at first. Now other things intrigued him. Like her smile. The violet depths of her eyes. The way she looked after one of those bubble baths. He hadn't been able to resist touching her. And then he almost hadn't been able to stop.

"Well, it sounds like you'll have a lifetime to discover all her secrets. I hear congratulations are in order."

Cole looked at him in surprise. "You've heard about our...engagement?"

Matt nodded. "I read about it in this morning's newspaper."

"What?" Cole shot off the sofa and strode to the front door. He pulled the *Denver Post* out of the box and twisted off the rubber band. Then he rifled through the pages until he reached the society section. "Well, I'll be...."

"Came as a surprise to me, too," Matt said with a wry smile. "Cole Rafferty a married man. Who would have believed it?"

Cole was still trying to believe his eyes. But there it was in black and white. Their engagement picture. For all the world to see.

His father had done it again.

He studied the photo Rex had taken at dinner the other night for family posterity—and newspaper publication. Annie looked radiant as she smiled at him. And Cole looked...he looked like a lovesick fool. He stifled a groan. Did he always look that dopey around her?

He folded up the page with their picture and stuffed it in his shirt pocket. Annie had enough to worry about without seeing their engagement in the *Post*. Maybe he could get the newspaper to print a retraction.

Matt heaved a long sigh. "I just can't help but think of all those women who will be heartbroken when they see that announcement. Of course, I'll be more than happy to provide counseling and consolation. Just send 'em my way, Rafferty."

"Sure thing." Cole tossed the rest of the newspaper on the coffee table. Then a thought occurred to him. "Hey, if I'm lucky, maybe Roy will see this and get the hint."

Matt arched a brow. "Who's Roy?"

Cole clapped him on the shoulder. "That's a good question. One I intend to answer."

Mateo stood up and headed toward the door. "Well, if you need any help, call someone else." He shook his head. "We're swamped down at the department. Sure you won't consider going back into police work, Rafferty? Even on a part-time basis?"

A week ago, Cole might have considered the possibility. But now he had Annie. "I'll keep it in mind. I've got my hands full at the moment."

Mateo swept a quick glance up the stairs. "You certainly do."

BY MIDNIGHT, Annie had reached a decision. She didn't like it. In fact, she wasn't certain she could even go through with it. But she couldn't think of a better alternative.

Annie had to ask her father for money.

The glow of the streetlights cast long shadows in the big kitchen. She stood next to the wall phone, her long flannel nightgown brushing the tops of her bare feet. Her hand rested on the telephone receiver as her pride wrestled with her desperation. Contacting George Bonacci was definitely a last resort. Her mother was honeymooning in Italy with husband number six. Her sister didn't have the kind of money she needed. Besides, they'd both worry about her if she called them up in the middle of the night, desperate and destitute.

Her father had never worried about her. After her parents' divorce, when Annie was three years old, she'd rarely seen him. An estate attorney in New York City, he'd sent child support payments instead of birthday cards. Attended a state bar conference instead of her high school graduation. George Bonacci had been the first man she'd learned *not* to depend on.

Now she had to turn to him for help. She couldn't stay with Cole any longer. Not when he affected her this way. He made her laugh. Made her feel safe. Made her want to kiss him again. She was falling for him, and she couldn't stand the thought of another disillusionment. Not when her life was already in a shambles.

Annie gritted her teeth, picked up the receiver and dialed her father's home telephone number. She'd keep their conversation short and sweet, just long enough to ask George to wire her a loan. All she needed was enough money to hole up in a cheap motel room until she found Roy. Since she'd never mentioned her father to Vega, he wouldn't be able to trace her through him.

She'd just worked up her nerve when an automated voice on the other end of the line announced that the number she'd dialed had been disconnected.

"Damn," Annie muttered, hanging up the receiver. Her father had either moved or changed his telephone number without telling her. She was disappointed, but not at all surprised.

"Now what?" She stared at the telephone, frustrated and completely out of ideas. If only she could confide in someone. If only... Annie swallowed and picked up the receiver. One person knew about her predicament. With a shaky finger, she dialed the number.

"Can't sleep?" a deep voice intoned behind her.

Annie jumped, her heart racing as she slammed the receiver down. "Cole! You scared me."

"Sorry." He walked into the kitchen, his blue bathrobe cinched loosely around his waist. He leaned against the kitchen counter, the lapel of his robe gaping open far enough to reveal the silky dark hair on his broad chest. "So who were you calling?"

She swallowed, her mind racing for a reasonable explanation. "I...was calling for pizza. But they don't deliver this late."

He stared at the telephone for a long moment, then

turned his dark-eyed gaze to her. "You're hungry? After that fantastic gourmet dinner I cooked for you tonight?"

She smiled in spite of herself. "I don't think fish sticks is officially classified as gourmet food."

"It's the sauce that makes it special," he countered. "I just wish they put more of it in those little plastic packages."

"Someday I'll make you real food," she replied, glad that he'd bought her pizza story.

"You want real food?"

He pushed away from the counter and grasped her shoulders, steering her toward a chair. "I'll make you a midnight snack that will knock your socks off."

"I'm not wearing socks," she said, as she sat down.

"I noticed." He turned abruptly and began pulling food out of the cupboards.

Annie watched Cole as he worked, an odd feeling of contentment stealing over her. She leaned back in her chair, letting the warmth and comfort of the big, old kitchen envelop her. Tomorrow would be soon enough to track down her father or come up with a different plan. For now, she was going to forget about her father and Vega and finding Roy. She was going to put her problems aside long enough to enjoy a midnight snack with a man who seemed almost too good to be true.

"Here you go," he said, setting a plate before her. "My pièce de résistance."

Annie stared at her plate. "It looks like a graham cracker sandwich."

He smiled. "It's a s'more."

"A what?"

"A s'more." He sat across the table from her before taking a s'more for himself.

She gingerly picked up the warm s'more. "What's in here?"

"Ambrosia." He took a bite of his s'more, then closed his eyes with a soft moan of appreciation.

Annie followed his example, tentatively nibbling at one corner of her s'more. To her surprise, a delicious blend of warm chocolate and gooey marshmallow melted in her mouth. "This is wonderful!"

He grinned. "I told you so."

She devoured her s'more, then picked up another one. "Where did you find the recipe for this?"

"There is no recipe, it's a camp classic."

"We never had anything like this at my camp," she said, licking her fingers.

He picked up a second s'more. "You went to camp?"

She nodded. "Step-daddy number three didn't like my sister and I hanging around all the time, so he paid for four full summers at Camp Carson in the Poconos."

"Sounds rough."

"Actually, it was wonderful. I love to camp."

"Me, too," he said, sounding surprised. "But your stepfather sounds like a jerk."

"That's why Mom divorced him."

Cole took a bite, then swallowed. "So exactly how many times has your mom been divorced?"

"Five."

He shook his head. "What a nightmare."

"I agree it's a little excessive," she began.

"A little? It makes me think the words *happily ever after* really do belong in a fairy tale. My parents' marriage ended in divorce, Matt Alvarez and his wife split up two years ago—''

"Oh, come on, Cole," she interjected. "Don't you know anyone who is happily married?"

He shrugged as he licked marshmallow off his thumb. "My old partner, Nick, back in Ohio. He and his wife, Lucy, just had twin girls. They seem pretty happy."

"See?" she said, glad to have proved her point. A man like Cole shouldn't spend the rest of his life alone. He needed a family to fill up this big house. A woman who loved and cherished him. Someone to eat s'mores with him in the middle of the night. Annie put down her half-eaten s'more, suddenly losing her appetite.

"One example of marital bliss isn't going to make me a believer," he said, unaware of the small smudge of melted chocolate on his upper lip.

Annie's mouth watered at the sight. What would he do if she got up right now, walked over to him and licked it off?

She swallowed hard. "Are you a serial killer?"

He choked on his s'more. "What?" he gasped, when he finally recovered his breath.

"Or a con man? Did you leave Ohio because a swindle went sour?"

He stared at her. "What are you talking about?"

She leaned forward, her forearms resting on the table as she studied him. He was kind and gorgeous and sexy. The longer she knew him, the better she liked him. Which meant there had to be something seriously wrong with this man. She needed to figure it out before her past repeated itself. "Are you connected to a drug cartel?"

He put down his s'more. "Are you serious?"

"Completely," she replied. "I know you used to be a cop. Were you kicked off the force?"

"Of course not! I left voluntarily."

"Why?"

He leaned back in his chair and folded his arms. "Not that it's any of your business, but I wasn't thrilled with my life in Ohio. I had an exciting career, great friends, a nice condo...."

"But?" she prodded.

"But...I don't know." He raked his fingers through his hair, making it stand up on end. "For some reason, it wasn't enough. So I moved back, bought this house and took over Rafferty Investigations. But something is still missing."

"What do you want, Cole?" she asked softly.

He looked into her eyes, and her heart began racing in her chest. "Right now, I want to solve this case."

Annie stood up, her knees shaky. She had her answer. "Then I'd better let you get some sleep. Thank you for the s'mores."

Cole dabbed at his mouth with a paper napkin as he rose, wiping away the chocolate and her fantasy. "Good night, Annie."

"Good night, Cole." She turned and headed for the stairs. If she was smart, she'd be telling him goodbye.

THE NEXT DAY, Cole hunkered down in a suede chair behind a huge pink marble pillar in the Regency Hotel lobby. Now all he had to do was sit back and wait for the rat to take the bait.

Not that he knew for certain Roy Halsey was a rat, although he certainly was as stealthy as one. According to the front desk clerk, a man had stopped in every day for the past week to see if there were any messages for

Roy Halsey. Roy obviously wanted a response to his bizarre questionnaire.

Today, Cole intended to give it to him.

He opened the folder in his lap and looked at the information inside. After a thorough search he'd found that Roy really did exist, residing on a ranch in the foothills near Golden, Colorado.

It was a prosperous ranch, according to Cole's sources. He'd also discovered that Roy led a perfectly normal life. No arrests. No apparent psychological problems. No harem of mail-order brides stashed away in the cellar.

So why the disappearing act? Why the unlisted telephone number? Why the odd questionnaire?

Today was the day Cole planned to find out the answers to all his questions. No more delays. No more distractions. No more midnight snacks with a delectable woman.

A deceptive delectable woman.

Annie had lied to him. Again. After she'd left the kitchen last night, Cole did what he'd been itching to do since he'd caught her on the telephone and she'd spilled that lame pizza delivery story. He'd picked up the receiver and pressed the redial button.

The voice on the other end surprised him. "St. James Hospital. May I help you?"

"What city is this?" Cole had asked.

The hospital operator didn't say anything for a long moment. "We're in Newark, sir. Would you like me to connect you to the psychiatric ward?"

Cole had slowly hung up. Annie had called a hospital? After midnight? In Newark? Several possible explanations came to mind. Someone in her family was sick. She had a friend working as a doctor or nurse on staff. She'd dialed the wrong number. That one was a stretch, but none of them explained her reason for keeping the call a secret. Or the fact that she still didn't trust him.

What exactly did Annie Jones have to hide?

Or rather the woman who called herself Annie. The one who kept her secrets so well. His mind drifted to what he did know about her. The curve of her cheek, the silkiness of her skin, the taste of her mouth.

He mentally shook himself. If Roy showed up— when Roy showed up, Cole could finally discover if this guy deserved a woman like Annie. Even if it meant staking out here for the next seventy-two hours straight. He looked at his watch, then leaned back to watch the people milling about the hotel lobby.

His gaze suddenly focused on a black felt cowboy hat bobbing through the crowd. A bowlegged cowboy in faded blue jeans approached the front desk. Cole sat up, his muscles tensing. When the desk clerk handed the man the familiar bright yellow envelope, Cole knew it had to be Roy.

He waited, his heart beating hard in his chest as he watched the man calmly place the envelope in the inside pocket of his black leather vest.

Time to make his move.

He stood up as Roy turned, giving Cole a perfect view of his face. Cole's mouth dropped open. Roy looked nothing like the man the hotel clerk had described. Nor how Annie had described him. This man had a bushy handlebar mustache. A long beak of a nose. And a leathery, lined face that couldn't put him a day under sixty. No red hair. No buck teeth. No freckles.

What the hell was going on?

Cole moved from behind the marble pillar, determined to find out. "Mr. Halsey?" he called across the wide lobby.

The cowboy looked up, the blood draining from his face. He took one look at Cole striding purposefully toward him, then whirled and made a run for it.

Cole was so surprised he stopped in his tracks, watching the man move through the crowded lobby to the front entrance. Then his adrenaline kicked in, and he ran after him. He gained on him and was almost within reach when a large body blocked his path.

"I wanna talk to you," growled a familiar voice.

Cole looked straight into Bruno's ruddy face. Then he saw the cowboy disappear through the front entrance. "Not now, Bruno," he said, trying to sidle around the burly security guard. "I need to meet someone. It's important."

"You're just trying to duck me," Bruno accused, clamping a beefy hand on Cole's shoulder. "And you're not going anywhere till you pay up in full."

Cole resisted the urge to fight his way to the front entrance. Bruno had at least fifty pounds on him and looked like he could lift a cement truck. He also had a gun. Besides, Halsey would be long gone by now, lost in the maze of cars in the parking lot.

With a sigh of disappointment, Cole shrugged Bruno's hand off his shoulder. "I don't owe you a dime."

"Ha. How about fifty dimes—I mean—" Bruno screwed up his forehead "—you owe me fifty bucks, and there are ten dimes in a dollar. That makes it…"

"Five hundred dimes?" Cole guessed.

"Yeah." Bruno held out his hand, palm up. "You owe me five hundred dimes."

"I left all my spare change at home," Cole quipped. "By the way, does the hotel know you're shaking down the guests?"

"In the first place, you're not a guest." Bruno's hand curled into a fist. "And in the second place, you welched on a deal. You were supposed to fork over two hundred bucks in exchange for that ring."

"Which I did. Just ask Ingrid."

"Ingrid says you only paid her a hundred. She's got a soft heart, so she let you get away with it. But not me. I want the rest of my money."

Cole shook his head. "I paid Ingrid the full two hundred. It sounds like she doesn't want to share."

"She ain't that smart."

Now that was the pot calling the kettle black. Cole shrugged. "Well, I can't prove it. I guess the next time someone blackmails me I'll have to ask for a receipt."

Bruno scowled at him. "I don't like you, Rafferty."

Cole brushed the imprint of Bruno's paws off his jacket. "And I don't like the service here. Now if you don't want me filing a complaint with your supervisor, I suggest you let me leave."

Bruno's scowled deepened, but he stepped aside. "Don't come back here again."

Cole sauntered toward the door. Bruno's menacing snarl didn't scare him. Well, it did, but he didn't have to worry. After the way Roy had run out of here, Cole doubted he'd ever set foot in the Regency Hotel again. Which meant he'd have to tell Annie he'd found her fiancé—and lost him.

Would she be angry? Hurt? Relieved? Cole's relief could almost be described as euphoric. He'd wanted to nab Roy, then prove to Annie that he wasn't husband material so she'd break the engagement. But he'd never been certain that Annie wouldn't ride off into the sunset with Cowboy Roy.

He started to whistle as he walked across the parking lot to his Blazer. Once he told her about Roy Halsey's bizarre behavior, Annie would surely give up on this crazy mail-order marriage idea once and for all.

6

ANNIE TURNED the nozzle of the garden hose and aimed the spray at the flowers she'd just planted on the south side of Cole's house. The spindly marigolds looked fragile and vulnerable. Just like she felt.

Because Quinn Vega was on her trail.

She'd called his office from a pay phone near the garden center earlier this afternoon, disguising her voice.

"Mr. Vega is out of town," the receptionist had told her. "On personal business."

When Annie had asked how long he planned to be gone, the reply had confirmed her worst fears. "Indefinitely."

Which could mean until she was definitely out of his life. She swallowed as her skin turned to gooseflesh. Maybe she was becoming paranoid. Overreacting. His office had only said he was out of town, not stalking his former fiancée.

Annie waved the hose back and forth, soaking the ground surrounding the flowers. "Calm down," she murmured under her breath. "Even if he traces you to Colorado, he doesn't know where to look. And even if he starts looking in Denver, it's a big city. It could take him days, weeks, months."

That thought reassured her until she remembered that all Quinn would have to do is show her picture to the

Denver police, and Sergeant Mateo Alvarez would tell him exactly where to find her.

Then she'd end up like Jared, her photographer. Or worse. Since Cole had interrupted her last night, she'd called the hospital today to check on Jared's condition. He was stable. But he didn't want to talk to her. Big surprise. He'd learned the hard way that any connection to Antonia Bonacci was not good for your health.

That was her last thought before she felt a big hand clasp her shoulder. She screamed, whirling away as she turned the hose on her attacker.

Cole.

Annie stepped back, her heart racing in her chest. Her breath came in deep gasps as the blinding panic slowly loosened its grip on her lungs. "What are you doing here?"

"It looks like I'm taking a shower," he replied, glancing at his soaked shirt. "And I do live here, remember? Guess you didn't hear me coming."

"You shouldn't sneak up on a person like that." She gripped the hose, hoping he couldn't see her hands shaking.

"Especially when they're holding a dangerous weapon."

She was not in a mood to joke about weapons. Then she saw the glint in his eyes as he glanced at the hose.

"Don't even think about it," she said, stepping away from him, the hose at the ready.

He held up both hands. "Okay, I surrender. We don't have time for a water fight, anyway." His smile faded. "We need to talk."

"So talk," she said, not liking his serious tone. What more could possibly go wrong in her life?

"Not here," he said, wringing out the front of his shirt with his hands. "Let's go inside."

"You go ahead and change into some dry clothes. I'll be there in a minute." She needed to regain her composure. First Cole had scared her to death, and now he stood right in front of her with that wet shirt molded to his powerful upper body.

He looked at the marigolds. "Nice flowers."

"Do you like them, Cole?" She really wanted him to like them. It made her feel better to know there would be something left of her after she'd gone. Maybe he'd even remember her when he looked at them.

"I think they're beautiful." But he wasn't looking at the flowers. She caught his gaze on her and fought an overwhelming urge to tell him everything. To fall into the safety of his arms. To stay there forever.

Annie turned to the flowers before she did something foolish. The blooms were looking a little soggy, but she kept spraying them until she heard Cole walk into the house.

She couldn't stay and put Cole in danger. She was on her own. She'd always been on her own. She should be used to it by now. If Cole missed her, he'd soon find some other woman to take her place. That personal ad still had them crawling out of the woodwork. Just yesterday, a woman had come to the door wearing nothing but a sheer negligee under her raincoat. Three days ago, another woman had cornered Cole in the produce section of the grocery store and made suggestive remarks about the zucchini. It still galled her to think about it.

Annie finally took pity on her drowning flowers and directed the spray toward a wilting lilac bush. That's when she spied another woman. This one sneaking in through the back gate with an overnight bag in her hand. Annie pressed her lips together. She'd had it with these female predators stalking Cole like he was the catch of the day. He belonged to Annie. Temporarily, anyway. And she had every intention of protecting her territory.

So she turned the hose on the woman.

The woman's bloodcurdling scream was like music to her ears. Annie suddenly felt much better.

After giving the woman a good, thorough soaking, she turned off the spray of ice-cold water. The woman stood there, shivering and sputtering as the water dripped off her.

"Now why don't you just get lost, lady," Annie suggested. "Cole's mine. *All mine.*" She tipped up her chin. "I'm his fiancée."

"That's what I was afraid of," the woman replied, wiping wet hair out of her eyes. "I'm his mother."

"WHAT IS MY MOTHER doing here?" Cole asked after Lenore had dripped her way through the house and into the bathroom. "And why is she wet?"

"I sort of sprayed her with the garden hose," Annie explained.

"You what?"

"She's not hurt, she's just wet."

He whistled low. "You're really taking this fiancée from hell role seriously, aren't you?"

"It was a mistake," Annie retorted. "I never would have doused her if I'd known she was your mother. I thought she was one of those women."

"What women?"

She rolled her eyes. "Oh, please, don't play dumb with me. I've seen them panting after you like bimbos in heat. When I saw another one hot on your trail, I decided to cool her off.''

Cole stared at her, a smile curving his lips. "Jealous?"

"Me? Jealous?" His smile widened as a hot blush flooded her cheeks. "Not in this lifetime."

"Admit it, Annie." Cole stepped closer to her as the wall clock chimed four times. "You want me all to yourself."

She looked into his deep brown eyes and swallowed hard. "You're delusional."

"Actually, I'm a detective. Which means I know how to gather clues and draw the most logical conclusion."

"What clues?" she spluttered.

"Hosing down perfect strangers, for one. You also tripped that woman at the mall yesterday."

"I didn't trip her," Annie said, lifting her chin. "She fell over my foot while she was trying to stuff her business card down your pants."

Cole regarded her with a smug smile. "What about the chicken?"

"I don't remember tripping any chickens."

"You made roast chicken with raisin dressing for dinner the other night after I told you it was my favorite meal."

"You had that chicken thawing in the kitchen sink all day long. I had to cook it so I could wash my hair."

"That's another thing." Before she could move, he took another step toward her and stretched out one hand to softly caress her errant curls. "You keep washing your hair with that raspberry stuff," he said in a low voice. "You know how much I like it."

Her breathing hitched. He stood so close to her she could see the pulse beating in his throat. "You do?"

He nodded as he gazed intently into her eyes. "I do. I like it a lot. It reminds me of Stella."

Annie blinked. "Stella? Who's Stella?"

"One of my old girlfriends. Her hair smelled like raspberries, too." He crinkled his brow. "Or maybe it was Alison? No." He shook his head as he stepped away from her. "It was Carlene. Definitely Carlene."

She ground her teeth. "Sounds like you need a Rolodex to keep track of them all."

He grinned. "See, you are jealous."

Annie gave him a shove. "And you're a conceited, egotistical jerk!"

Cole looked over her shoulder. "Hi, Mom."

Annie swallowed a groan as she turned to see Lenore standing in the doorway. She'd changed from her soaked clothing into a bright pink wind suit. A waterproof wind suit.

Lenore looked at her son. "This is the woman you're planning to marry?"

Cole walked over to kiss his mother's upturned cheek. "You look great."

"I look like a drowned cat," Lenore countered, as she ran one hand over the ash blond hair plastered against her head. "And you're changing the subject."

"Mom, this is Annie," Cole said, steering his mother toward the powder blue wing chair in the corner. "The love of my life."

Lenore sat stiffly in the chair. "The love of your life just called you an egotistical jerk."

"I didn't really mean it," Annie said as she sat on the sofa. "Just like I didn't mean to spray you with the hose, Mrs. Rafferty."

"My name is Mrs. Clemens now," Lenore clarified. Then she narrowed her eyes on Annie. "Why exactly did you spray me?"

"It's a long story, Mom." Cole sat next to Annie. "Why don't you tell me what you're doing here instead."

Lenore lifted one blond brow. "Didn't your father tell you I was coming?"

"He didn't say a word."

"Well, when I heard the news about your engagement, I just couldn't stay away. I had to see the girl who stole my son's heart." Lenore looked at Annie like she'd rather throw her in jail than welcome her into the family. "You're not quite what I expected, Annie."

"I really don't hose down perfect strangers every day. It's just that I've been a little stressed lately." To her surprise, Cole's warm hand closed around hers and gave it a reassuring squeeze. Or maybe it was a signal. Was she supposed to horrify his mother as well as his father? If so, she'd gotten off to a rousing start. Lenore's lips were pursed with disapproval at the sight of their clasped hands.

"Weddings are stressful," Lenore agreed. "That's why I'm here. I want to help. I hope you don't mind putting me up for a few days."

Cole glanced at Annie. "Gee, Mom, we're still getting used to the engagement. The wedding is a long way off. A very long way off."

"Good." Relief eased the taut lines on Lenore's face. "But you can't start planning too soon. In fact, I brought something for you." She reached into her damp canvas tote bag. "Fortunately, it didn't get ruined by all that water."

Annie wished she could say the same about Lenore's cashmere slacks. "You didn't have to buy us an engagement gift."

"I didn't." Lenore tapped a sheaf of papers together on her knees. "I brought a test."

"A test?" Cole and Annie chorused together.

"A compatibility test," Lenore replied, then turned to Annie. "I'm a marriage counselor. Didn't Cole tell you? After Rex and I divorced, I went back to college and got my degree."

"But we're not married, Mom."

"I know, dear. But I counsel engaged couples, too. In fact, I believe that's where counseling can do the most good."

"Just think of it as preventive treatment," Annie murmured under her breath.

"Marriage is a big step. I'm sure my son—" Lenore cleared her throat. "I mean, neither one of you want to make a mistake. Premarital counseling is a way of finding things out about each other that you don't already know. Secrets aren't good for a marriage."

Cole suddenly looked much more enthusiastic about the prospect. Annie swallowed hard, knowing too well that sometimes secrets were necessary.

Lenore stood up and handed each of them a copy of the test and a pencil. "You two go ahead and get started while I make a pot of coffee." She shivered. "I still can't seem to shake this chill."

"Your mother is never going to forgive me," Annie whispered after Lenore left the room.

Cole was bent over his test, busily filling in the blanks. "I'd say you're off her Christmas list."

Annie sighed as she turned her attention to the test. She wouldn't be anywhere near the Rafferty family at

Christmas, so why did Lenore's opinion matter so much? It was only natural for a mother to be protective of her son.

"Are you ready to compare answers?" Cole whispered, peeking over at her test.

Annie shielded her writing with one hand. "Are we supposed to cheat on a compatibility test?"

Cole grinned. "Only if we want to prove to everyone how incompatible we really are. And we'd better hurry. If Mom catches us cheating, I'll have to tell her you made me do it."

"Thanks a lot." Annie sat back. "All right, question one. How many kids do you want?"

"If I was ever going to marry, which I'm not, I'd want three kids."

She flipped her pencil around to erase her answer. "That's what I had down. I'll change it to six."

"That should be enough to scare any potential grandparent," Cole mused.

"Next question. Name your favorite kind of music."

"Jazz."

Annie frowned and began erasing again. "Me, too."

Cole glanced at his test. "How about favorite movie?"

"*Casablanca.*" Annie peeked over his shoulder. "What did you pick?"

"*The Maltese Falcon.* I'm a big Humphrey Bogart fan."

"Me, too." She grimaced. "This is a little scary."

Cole shrugged. "It's just coincidence. What do you have down for your dream vacation?"

She smiled. "You'll never guess."

"I put down camping."

Her smile faded. "Tell me you're kidding."

"How do you think I learned how to make s'mores?" he asked. "I love to camp."

She held up her test. "Ditto."

He laughed. "Hey, there's a great spot near Telluride. We could go there for our honeymoon."

For a moment she almost forgot they were pretending. It felt good to think about the future. A future without Vega and panic and fear. A future with Cole. She swallowed the lump in her throat. "Sure. Sounds great."

"All right, we'll both leave camping for question four. After all, we should have at least one thing in common. Now let's move on to the essay questions."

"Tell one thing you like about your future spouse," Annie read. "That's easy. I like the way you make me feel safe."

Cole didn't say anything. He just sat there, watching her, his Adam's apple bobbing in his throat.

"Now it's your turn."

"I can't think of anything."

Annie bit her lower lip. Could she blame him? She'd been evasive and dissembling from the moment they'd met. She tried to hide her disappointment, but Cole must have seen it.

"What I mean," he explained, "is that I can't think of just one thing. I like your smile. The color of your eyes. The way your hair smells. I like the way you talk and walk and make me crazy when you argue with me. I like everything about you."

She didn't deserve such glowing compliments, but they certainly made her feel better. "I'm not sure that will convince your mother we're incompatible."

He smiled. "Okay, I'll just put down that I like the way your hair smells."

"Sure you're not thinking of Carlene?"

"I was just making that up."

The telephone rang before she could challenge him on it.

"I'll get it," Lenore called from the kitchen. "You two keep working."

"Moving on to the next question," Annie said with a long sigh. "Tell one thing about your future spouse you'd like to change."

"That's a tough one." Cole tapped his pencil on his knee. "You go first."

"Thanks a lot." She thought for a moment. "Okay. I want you to take care of yourself."

"Hey, I'm in great shape," he protested, pounding his fist into his tight stomach.

"No argument there," she agreed. "But I want you to eat better. Take care of yourself—so we could grow old together."

"I'm not becoming a vegetarian," he said stubbornly.

She laughed at the disgruntled expression on his face. "Me, neither. Not after those great barbecued ribs you made the other night. But how about a few fruits and vegetables to balance out your diet?"

"I guess I could live with that," he agreed.

"Now it's your turn. What would you change about me?"

He gazed into her eyes. "I'd want you to trust me."

"I do trust you," she answered automatically.

He shifted closer to her on the sofa. She could smell the spicy scent of his aftershave and feel the warm strength of his body. "No, I mean really trust me. Something isn't right, Annie. You're afraid. If you had a gun instead of a hose earlier, I'd be a dead man."

"I think you're exaggerating," she said, not meeting his gaze. The urge to tell him everything was a physical ache in her throat. But this wasn't the time. Or the place. Not with his mother in the next room.

"You're hiding something from me."

Lenore walked into the living room. "How are you two doing?"

"We're finished," Cole said, and his tone made Annie wonder if he meant more than just the test. "Now all we need is your professional opinion, Mom."

Lenore sat down, cradling a steaming cup of coffee in her hands. "It will take me a while to assess your answers. But you both should know that a test can't predict the success or failure of a relationship. You must nurture your love. Treat it with respect and care and, most important of all, honesty. If you don't have trust between you, then you don't have anything worth keeping."

Annie suspected Lenore had overheard the last part of their conversation. She looked more relaxed, almost friendly. As if she knew Cole and Annie's engagement didn't stand a chance.

"So who was on the phone, Mom?" Cole asked after a long silence.

"Oh, I almost forgot. It was for you, Cole. Some guy named Roy. Roy Halsey. He wants to meet with you at the Regency Hotel tomorrow morning. Ten o'clock sharp."

"COLE, are you awake?" Annie called softly into the darkness. She stood at the base of the stairway, peering into the shadowy living room. Since the unoccupied bedrooms were in various stages of remodeling, Cole had given his mother the master bedroom and moved onto the sofa for the night.

The shape under the blanket moved, then half sat up. "Yeah. What time is it?"

"A little after one o'clock." She padded toward him, her bare toes sinking into the thick carpet. She had on her flannel nightgown, but goose bumps still prickled over her body. Maybe they were caused by the sight of Cole's broad, bare chest illuminated in the moonlight.

"Is something wrong?"

"We need to talk," she whispered, when she reached the sofa.

He pulled her down next to him, covering her exposed feet and ankles with the blanket. "So talk."

His voice sounded rough with sleep. His face was shadowed with dark whiskers. As the warmth of the blanket suffused her, she felt her body begin to relax. "I'm going to meet Roy tomorrow."

"No way."

"Cole, listen to me." She placed her hand on his arm, feeling the muscles tense beneath her touch. "We didn't have a chance to discuss it with your mother here."

"I think she likes you," he said out of the blue. "Even though you doused her with the hose and called me a jerk." He sighed. "You seem to have a way of growing on a person."

"I like her, too."

"I wonder what Dad will think when he finds out Mom is here." He lowered his voice to a husky whisper. "Do you know what Mom told me after dinner?" He didn't wait for her to reply. "She told me Ethel and

Dad would be perfect for each other. She said she's known Ethel has been in love with him for years.''

"You're changing the subject," Annie said, determined to make him listen to her. "We were talking about Roy."

"That subject is closed."

"I'm reopening it. I have to meet Roy tomorrow. That's why I came to Denver, remember?"

"I keep trying to forget it," he said firmly. "Marrying a perfect stranger isn't the answer to your problems, Annie."

"I didn't say I was going to marry him." She shifted her weight, trying to get more comfortable. "I just want to meet him."

"And then what? You two go off together to select a china pattern? You don't know anything about this guy, Annie. He's a nutcase. He dresses in disguise and..." Cole's voice trailed off.

"Wait just one minute," she said, slowly enunciating each word. "How do you know this? I thought your investigation was coming up empty."

He didn't say anything for one long moment. "I've had a break in the case."

"You found Roy?" she said, her voice rising. "And you didn't tell me?"

"Shh." Cole placed a finger over her lips. "I wanted to check him out before I told you."

"That wasn't part of our agreement," she answered. Her lips tingled from the touch of his finger. But she couldn't get over the fact that he'd kept this from her. What else did he know?

"I was acting in your best interests. Someone had to, since you weren't thinking clearly." He gently traced the curve of her cheek. "Now it's late. Why don't we—"

"I can't believe you kept this from me! Don't you realize what finding Roy means to me?"

He stared at her for a long moment. "I haven't a clue, Annie. Why don't you tell me?"

She swallowed. "Look, we're never going to agree on my reasons for accepting Roy's proposal, and I'm not up to another debate. You'll just have to trust that I know what's best for me."

"I'd rather you trusted me." He shifted closer to her, his weight sinking into the sofa cushion, spilling her next to him.

She placed both hands on his chest to keep from tumbling against him. His skin felt warm, his heartbeat strong and steady beneath her fingertips. She tried to pull away, tried to keep her distance because she couldn't think clearly when she was this close to Cole. But he clasped her shoulders to keep her from moving away from him. They were touching in too many places. He was so close, so tempting.

"Trust me, Annie."

She wanted to give in to the temptation to tell him everything. To let him protect her, shoulder all the burden. And he certainly had the shoulders to do it. Broad, strong, capable shoulders that she couldn't keep from touching. She ran her hands up his chest and over his shoulders and taut biceps.

"Trust me," he whispered again, leaning forward so his mouth was next to her ear. His warm breath curled all the way down to her toes. His rough whiskers scratched her cheek. She squeezed her eyes tightly shut, trying to block out all the sensations whirling through her body. She thought about Jared, laying in that hospital bed in Newark, battered and broken. That could be Cole.

She pulled away from him. "I can't," she whispered brokenly. "I don't want you involved."

He cupped her face in his strong, lean hands, his thumbs gently brushing over her cheeks. "You're too late."

Then he kissed her. It was a soft, melting kiss that almost undid her. It seemed only natural to lay back on the sofa. Only natural for Cole to stretch out on top of her, his weight a welcome burden. They fit perfectly together.

His kiss deepened, his mouth clinging to hers. His hands curled around hers, then brought them over her head in an illusion of surrender. But she was a willing captive to his embrace. She couldn't stop kissing him. He teased open her mouth with his tongue. Her lips parted, and they clung together. They kissed deeply, hungrily, as if each was afraid the other would break the sensuous truce.

Annie made soft, eager moans in her throat. His kiss was like a thirst she couldn't quench. She wanted more of him. She stroked her hands up and down the long length of his back, her fingernails lightly scoring his bare skin. He moaned and held her tighter.

He lifted his head. "Trust me," he whispered, then dropped soft, light kisses on her chin, her cheeks, her nose. "Trust me."

His fingers deftly unfastened the top button of her nightgown. "Trust me," he whispered, as he bent his head to nuzzle her neck. Another button. Too many buttons. She silently cursed her flannel nightgown. It was perfect for the crisp Colorado nights, but a hindrance for a night with Cole. But he wasn't letting mere buttons deter him. Another fell open. Then another. His lips followed the path of his fingers, a scorching trail that left her breathless.

She'd never trusted her instincts about men before, but she knew in her heart this was right. This was Cole.

Then he did the unthinkable. He stopped.

Annie opened her eyes. He gazed at her, his brown eyes full of desire. He hovered above her, tense, waiting.

"Yes," she breathed, pulling his head down for another bone-melting kiss. "Oh, yes, Cole." She threaded her fingers through his hair, hoping his mother was a sound sleeper. They kissed long and hard.

Cole lifted his head. "Annie." His voice sounded ragged. "I can't make love to another man's fiancée. Tell me you'll forget all about Roy. Promise me you won't meet him tomorrow. Or ever."

She swallowed a groan of frustration. This was blackmail. Only she knew Cole didn't see it that way. He had an ingrained sense of honor that was hard to find these days. Honor had made him take her case for free. Allowed her to live in his house without having to fight off his advances. Now that same honor wouldn't let him make love to her while she was engaged to another man. She loved him for it. No matter how irritating it was at the moment.

"You have lousy timing," she said, wrapping her arms around his waist. "But you're a great kisser. Kiss me again, Cole."

He did, his mouth moving over hers in a long, passionate kiss. A kiss that almost convinced her to forget about Roy and Vega and everything except the man she held in her arms. He had great body language. His mouth said *trust me*. His hands said *trust me*. His body said *trust me*.

Through the sensual haze enveloping her, she considered telling him everything. How easy it would be to confide all her secrets to him. Easy, but unwise. Cole still had the heart of a cop. He'd go to the police. Or, at the very least, tell Mateo Alvarez. Annie couldn't let that happen. She trusted Cole. But she'd learned the hard way that she couldn't trust anyone else.

He must have noticed the change in her because he lifted his head, his fingers gently caressing her cheek. "Annie?"

She sighed. She could kiss him again. Use her hands and her mouth to persuade him to forget all about his sense of honor and duty. But he wouldn't respect her for it. And more important, she wouldn't respect herself. She closed her eyes, wondering at her lousy luck with men. She'd finally found a good one, but she couldn't have him. Not even for one night.

"I'm sorry, Cole," she whispered.

He dropped his head on her shoulder. But he didn't say anything, didn't try to change her mind. He'd already unleashed all the heavy artillery. He was forced to retreat.

So why did Annie feel like the loser?

He pulled away from her, then sat on the sofa taking slow, deep breaths. At last he said, "I'm going with you tomorrow."

She swallowed and sat up, hastily buttoning her nightgown. "That's really not necessary."

"I'm not up to a debate about this," he said wearily. "Not now. I'm going with you."

She stood up, wrapping her arms around her waist. She hadn't noticed the chill in the air until now. "I'm sorry, Cole,'' she said, then took swift, shaky steps out of the room.

"Me, too," he said, so softly that she barely heard him.

COLE LAY on the sofa, holding the telephone receiver next to his ear. He was patiently counting the rings, determined to stay on the line until his call was answered.

Alvarez finally picked up. "Who the hell is calling me at three o'clock in the morning?"

"This is Cole Rafferty."

"Rafferty?" Alvarez emitted a snort of disgust. "You'd better be calling because you need a kidney or something equally important, or else I am hanging up."

"This is important. It's about Annie."

"Annie needs a kidney?"

"No, but a brain transplant might be in order," he said wryly. He didn't really mean it. Annie was perfect. His recent opportunity to find out just how perfect she really was had kept him on edge and wide-awake. He needed to do something to take his mind off her before he went crazy.

Alvarez chuckled. "You sound a little frustrated, Rafferty. Isn't the lady falling for your usual lines?"

She'd fallen right into his arms. But that didn't make Cole feel any better. He wanted her heart, too. Her trust. "Annie is a little stubborn," he admitted.

"Not to mention quite an accomplished little liar."

Cole stiffened. He tightened his fingers around the telephone receiver, wishing it was Alvarez's neck. "Care to elaborate?" he asked in a low growl.

"Hey, don't shoot the messenger. I just call 'em like

I see 'em. Remember that description your girlfriend gave us of the purse snatcher?''

"Yeah. A tall man with black hair and a beard."

"Try short, blond and female. One of the bag handlers at the airport witnessed the whole thing."

"Female?" He sat up. "The purse snatcher was a woman?"

That's right. The description your girlfriend gave was the exact opposite of the real perp. Interesting, huh?"

His mind raced to find a logical explanation. He couldn't think of one. "So when exactly were you planning to give me this information?"

"Hey, I just got off duty at midnight. I thought it could wait until morning. You're not getting married before then, are you?"

"No." Cole rubbed the bridge of his nose, wondering what to do next.

"Good," Alvarez replied. "In fact, you might want to rethink this whole engagement. I know it's none of my business, but it's pretty obvious what's going on here."

"You're right," Cole retorted. "It's none of your business."

"Hey, you're the one who called me, remember? In the middle of the night. So in return, I'm going to give you a little unsolicited advice. I'd think twice before tying the knot with this lady, Rafferty. She's got trouble written all over her."

"You don't know Annie like I do." Cole knew he sounded defensive, but he couldn't help it. She brought out some primitive protective instinct in him.

Alvarez snorted. "I know when someone lies to the cops they usually have a compelling reason. Like keeping their rear end out of jail. Just how well do you know your fiancée?''

Too well to get a decent night's sleep. He knew she looked incredibly sexy in a flannel nightgown. Kissed him with a fiery intensity that made his head spin. Maybe that was the problem. Was he letting his attraction to her affect his reason? He swallowed his pride and decided to ask for an objective opinion. ''So what's your take on this, Matt?''

Alvarez sighed. ''I don't think Annie Jones is her real name.''

Cole rolled his eyes. ''I know that much. I think her real name starts with a B.''

''Oh, that's helpful,'' Matt said wryly. ''You may want to find out the rest of it before you apply for the marriage license. You might also want to run her name through the computer at the department. I wouldn't be at all surprised if she has a record.''

He'd suspected himself that Annie might have a criminal past. Or worse, be a fugitive from justice. But it made his stomach twist into knots to hear Matt suspected the same thing.

''Maybe there's some other explanation.''

Matt sighed. ''You used to be a cop, Rafferty. All the signs are there. She didn't want us to find her purse because we'd probably find some form of identification. Or worse.''

''Worse?'' Cole asked.

''Drugs, contraband, stolen property,'' Matt said, a weary edge to his voice. ''The possibilities are endless.''

Stolen property. He thought of that three-carat diamond ring in her possession and stifled a groan. No wonder she didn't want to confide in him. She probably thought he'd turn her over to the cops.

Would he? It was a question he couldn't answer at three o'clock in the morning. Not with the memory of her imprinted so firmly on his mind and his body. He cut the telephone conversation short and hung up. Then he folded his hands under his head and stared at the ceiling.

He kept remembering the way Annie had whispered his name. The way she had kissed him. Could he fall that easily and that hard for a felon? Could she really fool him that completely?

He didn't know, and the worst part was that he didn't care. He wanted to go to her. To forget about all his questions, his reservations, his good intentions. He just wanted Annie.

If that was really her name.

He pulled the pillow over his head and groaned. It was going to be a very long night.

7

THE NEXT MORNING didn't improve Cole's mood. He and Annie stood outside Room 315 at the Regency Hotel, the room Roy had designated for the meeting.

"Cole, for the last time, I'm going in there alone!"

"No, you're not." He glared at her, frustrated by her stubbornness and his lack of sleep. Now was not the time or the place for another argument. Soft classical music was piped discreetly into the hallway. The thick pink carpet muted Annie's footsteps as she paced impatiently back and forth.

She stopped in front of him and planted her hands on her hips. "I can handle this all by myself."

"I didn't even want you to come this far. Roy is expecting me, not you. So just stay out here."

"You can't tell me what to do, Cole." Sparks flashed in her violet-blue eyes. She looked flushed and furious, and he had to exercise all his willpower to keep from kissing her.

She took a deep breath. "Now, I'm going in there alone. I really think it's for the best."

He took a step closer to her. "I think it's completely nuts. Look, you hired me to handle this case. Why don't you stay here while I go in to meet Roy? He called me, remember?"

"He proposed to me."

"Thanks for the reminder," Cole said dryly. "It

slipped my mind." Neither one had spoken a word
about what had happened last night. Or rather, didn't
happen. He hadn't slept a wink, so he was tired and
cranky. Annie didn't look rested, either. She'd been
jumpy and distracted all morning. Maybe that was only
natural. A case of bridal jitters. After all, she was about
to meet the man of her dreams. The man who would
whisk her away from all her problems. From him.

Annie tried one more time. "Let's not argue about
this anymore."

"Agreed. Let's just go in and find out what kind of
crackpot you've agreed to marry."

Annie lifted her chin. "Cole, you're fired."

The lack of conviction in her voice almost made him
smile. "You can't fire me."

"I just did!"

"Firing someone implies hiring them. No money has
exchanged hands here. Except for the all the money
I've dropped bribing Bruno. So, in effect, you owe
me."

"I don't understand you," she exclaimed, throwing
her hands up in the air.

"Well, then we have one more thing in common,"
he replied, his voice rising, "because I don't understand you, either." He clenched his jaw, forcing himself to calm down and appeal to her reason. "You don't
know anything about the man waiting behind that door.
It's not safe for you to go in there alone."

She obviously wasn't ready to listen to reason.
"Look, we had a bargain. According to our agreement,
as soon as Roy is found, our fake engagement is off."

He folded his arms. "Since you haven't technically
met Roy yet, our fake engagement is still on. Now, as
your phony fiancé, I have an obligation to look out for

you. That's why I'm not allowing you to go in there without me.''

"But my *real* fiancé is in there." Her shoulders sagged, and a worried frown creased her brow. "How will it look if I come waltzing in with another man?"

He emitted a sigh of exasperation. "We've been living together for the past two weeks. You didn't worry about appearances then."

"That was different. I was desperate. Now…"

"Now you have Roy." Cole's mouth was set in a stubborn line. He hadn't even the met the guy, and he already had an overwhelming urge to punch him in the face.

She glanced at her watch. "I'm fifteen minutes late."

"Let's hope good old Roy isn't a stickler about punctuality, or else he might go thumbing through the yellow pages for a new bride."

"This is not helping," she muttered, then scowled at him. "All right. You can come with me. But don't say one word. Let me do all the talking."

"Fine," he said, willing to compromise on that point. If it was necessary, he'd let his fists do the talking for him.

Annie stepped in front of the door to Room 315, her hand visibly shaking as she reached up to knock. Cole wanted to hold her in his arms. Comfort her. But she didn't want him, he reminded himself. She only wanted Roy.

The door swung open. Cole took an instinctive step toward Annie, ready to protect her from the maniac inside.

Only the maniac was a woman.

"Come in, come in," she said, a wide smile wreath-

ing her round, lined face. She looked about sixty, her
gray hair pulled into a neat braid. She had apple green
eyes, which matched the color of her Western shirt,
and faded blue jeans tucked into a pair of weathered
cowboy boots.

Cole saw Annie's mouth fall open in surprise. A
surge of hope shot through him. Maybe this was all a
mistake. Maybe Roy was a transvestite. Maybe they
had the wrong room.

Annie obviously had the same thought. She reared
back to read the number on the door. Then she turned
to the woman, who was eyeing her up and down and
nodding in approval.

"I'm looking for Roy Halsey," Annie said, her gaze
flitting over the hotel room.

"Then you've come to the right place," the woman
replied. "Come on in. My name's Hildy, and I ordered
up hot coffee and some of them fancy rolls."

Cole followed Annie inside. The room was every bit
as ornate and ostentatious as the rest of the Regency
Hotel. The king-size bed was draped with a ivory cov-
erlet made of silk and lace. Heavy mahogany furniture
was polished to a high sheen. Finely detailed oil paint-
ings hung on the walls. Halsey might be elusive, but
he was obviously wealthy if he could afford these luxurious accommodations.

Annie stopped in the middle of the room, looking
around as if she expected Roy to pop out of from under
the bed or the closet. "Hildy, my name is—"

"Annie," Hildy interrupted. "I recognized you from
the picture."

"Roy showed you my picture?"

Hildy nodded. "I've seen it at least a dozen times,
but you're even prettier in person." She circled Annie,

making small murmurs of satisfaction. "Just look at those hips."

Annie looked down in dismay. "What's wrong with them?"

"Not a thing," Hildy assured her. "They're nice and wide. Perfect for birthing Roy's babies."

Annie's mouth fell open. "Babies?"

Hildy nodded. "We've got a working ranch, and it's time for Roy to start making some little cowhands of his own. You look strong enough to drop one every spring."

Annie glanced uncertainly at Cole. He smiled at her, then helped himself to a glazed cruller from the platter. He hadn't eaten a bite of the big breakfast his mother had fixed this morning, but his appetite was suddenly coming back.

Annie had picked at her breakfast, too, but she ignored the pastries, her gaze fixed on Hildy. "Roy was supposed to be here today."

Hildy sighed as she rolled on the heels of her cowboy boots. "I know, but the cattle got out again last night, and he's still rounding them all up. Do you ride, Annie? We can always use an extra hand."

Annie's eyes widened. "Ride what?"

"Well, horses, of course."

Cole took the last bite of his doughnut, then licked the sweet glaze off his fingers. Annie didn't look too happy about the fact that Cowboy Roy was off rounding up cows instead of his bride. Cole, on the other hand, couldn't be happier.

"Uh, no." Annie cleared her throat. "Do you work for Roy?"

Hildy slapped her thigh. "That's a doozy. No, actually Roy works for me. I should have introduced myself. I'm Hildy Halsey, Roy's mother. He lives with me out at the ranch."

Cole grabbed another doughnut. Roy and Annie...and Mom Halsey. All one big happy family.

Only Annie didn't look too thrilled by the prospect. She sank into a wing chair. "Does anyone else live there?"

"Oh, there's about ten of us counting the ranch hands," Hildy replied, scratching behind her ear. "I'm sure looking forward to turning my kitchen over to you. Those boys eat enough grub to fill up the Grand Canyon."

Annie fidgeted in her chair. "About Roy..."

"He'll be so tickled when he sees you, Annie. We'd better plan an early wedding so your father doesn't have to load up the shotgun. I thought June might be a good month."

"June isn't very far away," Annie said weakly.

"My boy isn't one to dilly-dally once he ropes his gal," Hildy informed her. "But you'll see that for yourself when I take you back to the ranch with me."

Cole choked on his third doughnut. He grabbed a cup of coffee, the hot liquid scalding his throat.

Annie gave him a distracted look. "Are you all right?"

"I'm fine," he gasped, putting down the coffee cup.

Hildy looked at Cole, a frown wrinkling her tanned brow. "So who's your sidekick?"

Annie jumped in before he could reply. "This is Cole Rafferty. He's my—"

"Therapist," Cole interjected. He ignored Annie's glare as he turned to Hildy. "We thought it might be a good idea to do a little premarital counseling."

Hildy scowled. "Horse hooey. Roy's not even here."

"Exactly," Cole said. "And I have to admit I find that very troubling, Mrs. Halsey. It indicates a certain lack of...enthusiasm."

"Cole," Annie warned under her breath.

He ignored her, his attention on Hildy. "Maybe you can tell us a little bit about your son. Does he have trouble meeting women? Does he fantasize a lot? Hear voices?"

Hildy bristled. "My son isn't crazy, Doctor."

Annie rolled her eyes. "He's not a doctor."

Hildy ignored her, obviously offended by Cole's insinuation. "I'll admit my boy's not perfect. He might tip the bottle now and then, but Annie here looks like just the woman to dry him out."

Cole shrugged. "I'm just trying to understand why a man with Roy's obvious charms would have to advertise himself in a magazine to find a wife."

Hildy raised her chin. "I happen to think it's very romantic. Why, back in the pioneer days it wasn't unusual at all to conduct a courtship by mail. And if you think Roy can't find a gal any other way, then you're mistaken, Dr. Rafferty."

Cole could see Hildy meant every word. But that didn't explain why Roy hadn't let anyone catch him yet. He was one slippery cowboy.

"I believe it," Annie said, coming to her fiancé's defense. "He looked very handsome in his picture."

Hildy visibly relaxed, her face softening into a chagrined smile. "Sorry I got my dander up. Guess it's only natural you'd have questions about Roy since you've never even laid eyes on him."

Cole folded his hands on his lap, trying to look

Freudian. "Then I'm certain you can understand why I can't allow my patient to go the ranch at this time. She and Roy should meet in a neutral environment."

"I really don't think that's necessary," Annie said through clenched teeth.

"I think it is," Cole said firmly. He expected her to argue with him, but she kept her mouth shut. She was probably afraid he'd do something even more outrageous than posing as her therapist. Like tell Hildy he was her fiancé. And he would, if it became necessary. He reached into his pocket, then handed Hildy a business card. "Here's my card. Please have your son contact me as soon as possible."

Hildy's disappointment was obvious as she took the card from him. "Sounds like a bunch of nonsense to me. But I'll have Roy hightail it into town. He can't wait to lasso his bride."

"THAT WAS completely uncalled for!" Annie exclaimed as she hurried toward the elevator. She wanted to get away from him. To have a chance to think without his infuriating logic and sinewy body to confuse and distract her. This morning, she'd convinced herself to leave Cole behind and follow through with her plan. Now she was right back where she started, and she didn't know if she'd have the strength to go through all this again.

Cole easily matched her furious stride. "You don't think it's a little strange that Roy sent his mother to meet you?"

She stabbed the elevator button with her index finger. "Hildy seems very devoted to him."

Cole snorted. "And I'm sure Roy's very attached to her. Have you ever seen the movie *Psycho?*"

She whirled to face him. "Will you stop trying to scare me away from Roy! It isn't going to work."

"Then what will work? You must have some reservations. Otherwise, you would have gone to the ranch with Hildy."

Annie turned to stare in stony silence at the elevator doors. When they finally opened, she marched inside the empty compartment. "For your information, I'm going home to pack." Home. She swallowed. She'd only spent a short time at Cole's, yet she was already calling it home. Although it wasn't just the house that had imprinted itself on her heart. It was Cole.

He followed her inside.

"Sounds like a delay tactic to me."

He couldn't be more wrong. Annie pressed the lobby button, and the elevator doors slid closed. She should have packed this morning, but she'd been too apprehensive to think straight. Too busy telling herself she didn't have any choice. She had to leave. She'd imposed on Cole long enough.

But before she left, she needed to retrieve Vega's journal from underneath her mattress. Annie closed her eyes, imagining what might happen if she left it there for Cole to find. He'd contact Vega and ask all sorts of uncomfortable questions. And Quinn would answer them with his .357 Magnum.

The elevator lurched into motion. Cole stood rigid beside her, the tension emanating from him almost palpable.

"So you're not going to change your mind?" he asked, staring straight ahead.

"No."

"Then I guess I'll have to change it for you." He reached out to push the stop button on the elevator's control panel. The car lurched to a halt. Cole turned to her, his body blocking the control panel.

"What do you think you're doing?" she exclaimed.

"Holding you hostage until you come to your senses."

This was the last place she wanted to be. Trapped in an elevator with him. Alone. She swallowed and took a step back. "The hotel won't let the elevator stay out of order for that long. They'll bring in a technician to fix it. We'll be out of here soon."

"Maybe. But we'll be in here long enough for you to give me an explanation. Be honest with me for once, Annie." His voice softened. "You owe me that much."

Annie started to deny it, then realized he was right. He'd let a perfect stranger into his home. Taken her case free. Fed her and clothed her and kept her safe. And she'd repaid him with secrets and lies. She was so tired of hiding the truth. So tired of running away. Part of her almost wished he could keep her in this elevator forever. Safe from Vega and his henchmen. Just the two of them.

She sighed. In a few hours she'd be out of his life, on her way to the ranch with Roy. What would it really hurt to confide in him now?

"It's a long story," she began.

He folded his arms and leaned against the back wall of the elevator. "I'm not going anywhere. So you might as well start at the beginning."

She slid down until she was seated on the pristine gold carpet. The walls were carpeted, too, with thick gold braid trim in the corners. This elevator was more stylish than her apartment in Newark.

Annie pulled her knees to her chin and wrapped her

arms around them. "I've always had bad luck with men."

He arched a brow. "You have two fiancés at the moment. I've recently met several women who would kill for that kind of luck."

"Except that one of my fiancés has gone into hiding and the other doesn't believe in marriage."

Cole didn't say anything. Obviously his opinion about marriage hadn't changed.

"Anyway," she continued, an odd weariness stealing over her, "this bad luck I've had with men somehow turns into good luck for my career. You were right before, Cole. I am a reporter. An investigative journalist, actually."

"An investigator?" One corner of his mouth tipped up in a smile. "So we have something else in common."

She nodded. "We both like mysteries and we both like to be our own boss. I do mostly freelance work. My stories have appeared in the *New York Times*, the *Boston Globe, Newsweek* magazine, just to name a few."

"I'm impressed. You must be good."

She sighed. "I'm very good at finding the right story and the wrong man. I let my instincts be my guide. I must have inherited my instincts about men from my mother."

A smile of satisfaction settled on his face. "So Roy is just another newspaper story. You never had any intention of marrying him."

"You're right. I never meant to marry Roy...at first." She moistened dry lips. "I found him in that magazine and was intrigued by the idea of mail-order romance. So I started corresponding with him. He wrote sweet, funny letters. I liked him. I decided to forgo my exposé and just keep corresponding with Roy. Besides, I had a much bigger story brewing. One that fell right into my lap. Or rather, I fell right into his lap."

A muscle flickered in Cole's jaw. "You met another guy?"

"Yep, and landed the biggest story of my career. Only..." Her voice trailed off. Her throat was tight. It was too easy to remember the chill she'd felt the first time she'd read Vega's journal. The panic that had led her to Denver.

He slid onto the floor next to her. "What happened?"

"I almost killed a man."

Cole didn't say anything for a long moment. "Did you cook for him?"

Annie laughed, snapping the tension in the elevator car. "For your information, I'm a fantastic cook. I can make a cannoli that would make you cry."

"My eyes watered quite a bit when I ate that pudding stuff you whipped up for dessert at our dinner party."

"Only a good cook could make something taste so bad."

"Guess I'll have to take your word for it." He reached for her hand, and his broad fingers curled around hers. "So who did you almost kill?"

Annie took a deep breath. "A photographer. His name is Jared Costello, and he's one of the best in the business. He's twenty-seven and has a wife and a new baby."

She turned to him. "I didn't need the photos. I had all the information I needed for my story—names and dates and everything. I uncovered the largest money-laundering business in New Jersey. But I got greedy—I wanted pictures, too."

"Wait a minute. How exactly did you get this information?"

"I went...undercover." She couldn't bring herself to tell Cole she'd posed as Vega's fiancée. At the time, she'd thought the end would justify the means. Now it seemed like a cheap trick. Almost tawdry.

Had Jared ended up in the hospital because she'd played Vega for a fool? Broken his heart? Although, the more she'd learned about Vega, the more certain she'd been that the man didn't have a heart. But he did have his pride and a massive ego. Vega must have been livid when he discovered his fiancée had betrayed him.

Cole squeezed her hand. "It's not your fault."

She wished she could believe him. "Yes, it is. I sent Jared there on a ruse of getting some publicity shots. I shouldn't have taken the risk. They broke both of Jared's legs. That's when I knew the story was out of control."

"So what did you do?"

"I accepted Roy's marriage proposal and bought a one-way ticket to Colorado. His timing was perfect. I thought it was the answer to all my problems." But she realized the truth. She was using Roy. Just as she was using Cole. Both men could be at risk because of her. They could end up like Jared. Or worse. She'd been so worried about saving her own skin, she hadn't considered the consequences. Even worse, she'd used her bad luck with men as an excuse for her selfish behavior.

"I'm a mess," she muttered, wondering how her life had gotten so out of control.

"I think you're beautiful," Cole replied, pulling her into his arms. "And brave and resourceful and sexy."

"Cole, I—" she began, but he silenced her with a kiss. It was a hard, possessing kiss that caught her by surprise. She found herself pressed against the floor, his hands on her shoulders, his mouth everywhere. His urgency called to her, making her want to live only for this moment. For this man.

She arched her neck as his lips trailed down her throat. Cole Rafferty had the ability to make her forget everything. Even her own name.

Then she realized he didn't *know* her name.

"Cole," she said huskily, threading her fingers through his hair and gently pulling his head up. "My name isn't Annie Jones."

"I know."

She blinked at him in surprise. "You know?"

He smiled, propping himself on one elbow. "Give me a little credit. I'm a private investigator. I realized the moment you came into my office that you weren't playing straight with me."

"But you still took my case?"

"Unlike you, I've got great instincts. And at this moment, I'm really glad I listened to them." He trailed one finger down her cheek as he gazed into her eyes. "So may I ask exactly whom I have the pleasure of kissing?"

She smiled. "My name is Annie Bonacci. Antonia Kathleen Bonacci."

"Kathleen?" he echoed, his brow crinkling.

She laughed. "My father is Italian, but my mother is Irish."

"Well, it's a pleasure to finally meet you. Now shut up and kiss me, Antonia Kathleen Bonacci."

She did as he asked, reveling in the strength of his embrace. It felt so good to confide in him at last. To share her burdens with someone. She wished she could tell him about the journal. But she knew him well enough to know he wouldn't let it rest. He'd want Vega behind bars—want to make certain she was safe.

Maybe she was safe. Quinn hadn't tracked her down yet. Maybe her trail was cold. The thought of that thrilled her almost as much as the feel of Cole's hands on her body. Then she couldn't think about anything but him.

"You're not going to marry, Roy," Cole said, his breathing ragged. It was a statement, not a question. "Say it, Annie."

"I'm not going to marry Roy."

He rewarded her with another kiss, deeper and more passionate than the one before. She moaned low in her throat, so tempted to let him carry her away on waves of desire. But she couldn't let him distract her from the problems that remained. She had made this mess. It was up to her to clean it up.

"What about Hildy? How will I tell Roy?"

He grinned. "You don't have to tell them anything. They say a picture is worth a thousand words."

She struggled to sit up. "What are you talking about?"

"This." He reached into his pocket for his wallet, then pulled out a folded piece of newsprint. He opened it and handed it to her.

Annie couldn't believe her eyes. It was an engagement announcement. And under the picture were the words Jones-Rafferty Nuptials in bold print. Her name might be wrong, but her picture was there for everyone to see.

"When did this happen?" She could barely get the words out.

He shrugged. "A few days ago. It was another one of Dad's brilliant ideas. Although this one actually did help me. I haven't had any propositions since."

A few days ago. The words pounded at her brain until a headache began throbbing in her right temple. So much for hoping the trail was cold. It was now red-hot. And if she didn't make a run for it they were both going to get burned.

Cole's lips covered hers, then he raised his head. "I know this is going to sound corny, but I feel the earth move when I kiss you."

Annie opened her eyes. "It's the elevator. They've started it up again." Her stomach dropped at the sudden motion. Or maybe it was the knowledge that Quinn could be in Denver at this very moment.

They got to their feet as the elevator made its descent. Annie barely got her clothes adjusted and her hair tamped down when the elevator doors opened. Bruno stood right outside, his hand on the gun at his belt.

He took one look at Cole and narrowed his eyes. "I should have known. This is going to cost you, Rafferty. Big time."

By the time Cole had paid Bruno's outrageous bribe to forget about the hijacked elevator, Annie's shock at seeing the engagement picture had worn off. On the ride to Cole's house, she realized she wasn't the only one in trouble this time. If Quinn couldn't find her, he'd go after Cole. She had to tell Cole everything.

Maybe they could go on the lam together.

"You've been awfully quiet," Cole said, as they

pulled into the driveway. He looked at her, his brown eyes full of concern. "Are you all right?"

"I'm fine," she said, her throat dry. "But there's something else I need to tell you."

"Shoot."

She closed her eyes at the image that word conjured up. "Let's wait until we get inside."

They walked up the steps, Cole's hand resting possessively on her hip. "So what do you have to tell me that's so important?" he asked, unlocking the door.

Annie didn't want to tell him anything until he was sitting down. She stepped inside, then nearly fell over when a chorus of voices greeted them.

"Surprise!"

8

"IT'S A SURPRISE PARTY," Cole said numbly, staring at the crowd of familiar faces. He saw aunts, uncles, cousins, friends and business associates. Balloons and colored streamers dangled from the ceiling. A poster-size color reprint of Annie and Cole's engagement picture hung on one wall.

Annie stood in silence next to him. She looked pale and a little shaky. She'd almost jumped out of her shoes when they'd opened the door and been blasted with the sound of voices shouting in unison. He still had the imprint of her fingernails on his forearm.

Rex moved toward the door, his face lit up with a broad smile. "We sure fooled both of you." He threw one arm over Cole's shoulder and wrapped the other around Annie. "Ladies and gentlemen," he announced. "I'd like to present the happy couple. Cole and his bride-to-be, Miss Annie Jones."

Everyone hooted and applauded. Cole saw his mother passing around a tray of drinks and encouraging the guests to help themselves to the buffet table.

"Dad, what is all this?" Cole sputtered.

"It's your surprise engagement party," Rex replied. "Your mother and I planned it. We thought it would be a perfect opportunity to introduce Annie to everyone." Rex gave Annie's shoulders a squeeze. "And I'm sure they'll like her as much as we do."

So much for his plan to make Annie his fiancée from hell. His dad liked her. His mother liked her. He liked her. Cole mentally kicked himself. *Admit it, Rafferty, you more than like her. She's gotten completely under your skin.*

"We've got cake," Rex announced, pulling them into the center of the living room, "and sandwiches and punch. And some sort of vegetarian dip Ethel brought that's really pretty good."

"Where is Ethel?" Annie asked, the first words she'd spoken since they'd arrived. No doubt she felt a little lost in this sea of unfamiliar faces.

Rex frowned as he scanned the room. "I'm not sure. Maybe in the kitchen. I know she's around here someplace."

Cole's mother walked up to them, raising herself up to kiss her son's cheek. "Surprised?"

"I'm stunned." That was an understatement. He couldn't believe his father and mother had joined forces to plan this party. Their divorce had been fairly amicable, as divorces went. His father had been hurt, his mother ready to move on with her life. As far as he knew they hadn't even talked to each for over eight years. Until now. They'd put aside their differences to plan this surprise party.

For him.

He felt like a heel. Nothing was working out like he'd planned. He'd planned to feign hurt and disillusionment when his engagement to Annie was broken. Now he realized how much his broken engagement would hurt his parents. He'd planned to help Annie see how foolish it was to marry a perfect stranger. But even though she'd agreed not to marry Roy, she still looked nervous and apprehensive.

Cole put his arm around her waist and drew her to him. "Are you all right?"

"We need to talk," she whispered, her breath warm against his ear.

"Later," he promised. He knew what she wanted to discuss. Now that the case of the missing bridegroom was solved, they could call off their so-called engagement. The only problem was that he wasn't ready to let go of the fantasy yet. If Annie was still his fiancée he had every right to caress the silky curls of her hair. Keep his arm firmly about her. Brush his lips over her brow.

Cole pulled away and looking into her beautiful violet-blue eyes. "Would it be too much trouble to pretend we're in love just a little longer? At least until the party is over."

She answered him by rising on her toes and placing a gentle kiss on his lips. He pulled her closer, his hands at her slender waist. She moaned softly at the contact and pressed her hands against his chest, then slowly slid them over his shoulders and around his neck and deepened the kiss.

Cole forgot about their audience until he heard the sounds of laughter and applause. He broke the kiss, then grasped her hand and gave it a gentle squeeze to show his appreciation.

She gazed at him. "I don't have to pretend, Cole."

Before he could begin to comprehend her words, Uncle Leo walked up to them and started telling one of his jokes. Usually Cole actively avoided Uncle Leo at family gatherings, because once he got started telling his corny jokes, he didn't stop. But it was too late. Leo had them cornered.

All Cole could do was hold Annie's hand and won-

der if he was hallucinating. Or if she'd just told him
she loved him.

ANNIE STOLE AWAY from the party shortly after Mateo
Alvarez approached them to offer his congratulations.
He still made her feel a little uncomfortable, although
he seemed friendly enough. Everyone at the party had
been so kind. And so anxious to meet her. She smiled
as she mounted the stairs to her bedroom, remembering
some of the more quirky members of Cole's family.
She'd met so many people, she couldn't remember half
their names.

Not that it mattered. She wouldn't be sticking around
long enough to see them again. She had to leave Denver. The sooner, the better. And she had to convince
Cole to go with her.

Not just because she'd put his life in danger. Not
just because Quinn Vega was an extremely jealous man
who, if he thought Cole was her lover, would shoot
first and ask questions later.

But because she loved Cole.

Annie walked into her bedroom, closed the door and
leaned against it. She closed her eyes, savoring this
brand-new startling discovery.

She loved Cole Rafferty.

He'd looked stunned when she'd told him. But not
dismayed. She hoped that was a good sign. But she
didn't have time to worry about it. Moving quickly,
she went to the bed, pulled her duffel bag from underneath and began packing her meager belongings. She'd
tell Cole all about Vega as soon as the party was over.
Then she'd help him pack so they could make a quick
getaway.

Maybe they could camp out in the mountains.

She reached under the mattress for the source of all the recent trouble in her life. Quinn's journal looked harmless enough with its red leather cover and gold-edged pages. But inside was enough damaging information to put Quinn behind bars for good. She'd almost finished writing her exposé on Quinn Vega and it was dynamite. But her story would be worthless without the journal to substantiate her allegations.

She'd just stuffed it into the duffel bag when she heard a noise. Annie tensed, pricking up her ears. There it was again. A soft, muffled sound of distress. It sounded like it was coming from the bathroom.

Annie moved into the hallway and stopped in front of the bathroom door. She tapped lightly and waited. There was no answer.

Her hand curled around the doorknob. She was certain she'd heard someone. Thanks to the broken lock on the door, she could find out exactly who that someone was.

She cracked open the door and saw a woman sitting fully clothed in the empty bathtub. "Ethel?"

"Go away," Ethel ordered, dabbing a tissue at her nose.

Annie ignored her and walked into the bathroom. "I'm not going anywhere until I find out what on earth is the matter."

"Oh, nothing much," Ethel replied with a bitter laugh. "I've just come to the mortifying conclusion that I'm a complete numskull."

"That's ridiculous," Annie said, seating herself on the edge of the porcelain tub.

"It's true." Ethel dabbed at her red-rimmed eyes. "How else can you explain the fact that I'm crying over a man at my age?"

"This is about Rex?"

"Who else? That handsome, sexy idiot who has made it perfectly clear he's not interested in me."

"Oh, no," Annie exclaimed in dismay. "He said that?"

Ethel grabbed another tissue out of the box. "Of course not. Rex would never come out and say it. But actions speak louder than words, and there's been absolutely no action." She sniffed. "If you know what I mean."

Annie nibbled on her lower lip, wondering how to advise Ethel. She looked wonderful with her new hairdo, the soft gray curls framing her face. Her makeup was perfect, and her stylish new clothes nicely emphasized her trim figure.

"He's called me every night for the past week," Ethel continued. "So I foolishly built my hopes up that he felt something for me. Last night we talked until almost two in the morning."

Annie arched a brow. This didn't sound like a disinterested man to her. Maybe he just needed a little shove in the right direction. If Rex was anything like Cole, his sense of honor might prevent him taking advantage of a woman who used to be in his employ, just as Cole had regarded her as off-limits while she was engaged to another man.

"I think you should jump him," Annie announced.

Ethel's eyes widened. She put down her tissue. "What did you say?"

"Jump him," Annie repeated. "Get him alone somewhere and show him exactly how you feel."

"But what if he doesn't like it?" Ethel asked, looking horrified at the prospect.

"What if he does?" Annie countered.

While Ethel considered that possibility, Annie heard Cole calling her. She rose, then handed Ethel a washcloth. "Wash your face, then go and find Rex. At least you'll know where you stand."

Ethel took the washcloth. "Maybe. I'll have to give it some thought. One thing is for sure, I'm through being a complete ninny about this."

"Annie, are you up there?" Cole's voice sounded strident.

"Coming," she called, then hurried out of the bathroom. She met him in the middle of the stairway. "What is it?"

"There's someone here who wants to meet you," he replied, a muscle flickering in his jaw.

Was that all? The way he'd been bellowing her name, she'd figured the house was on fire. She started down the stairs. "Who is it?"

"Your fiancé."

"My WHAT?" Annie stopped abruptly on the bottom step. Her gaze fell on the man standing in the center of the room. He was a tall man, well over six feet from the top of his brown felt hat to the tip of his cowboy boots.

"Roy?" she asked, stunned to find the man from *Mountain Men* magazine standing in Cole's living room. She wasn't the only one, judging by the puzzled expressions on the faces around her.

"Annie?" Roy's expression reflected the surprise in his voice.

Cole stepped in front of her. "How did you find her?"

"With this." Roy held up Cole's business card, imprinted with his office and home addresses. "Mom told me if I found you, I'd find Annie."

"Just what exactly do you want, Halsey?" Cole asked.

Roy tipped his cowboy hat. "I came to fetch my fiancée. I hear she's been looking for me."

Rex shouldered his way through the crowd surrounding them. "What's going on here?"

"That's a damn good question," Roy replied, glancing around the living room. "Looks like I walked in on a party."

"It's my son's engagement party." Rex scowled. "Who are you?"

Roy rolled on his heels. "I'm Annie's fiancé."

"That's impossible!" Rex's bewildered glare moved from Roy to Cole and Annie, then to Roy again. "She's engaged to my son."

Roy folded his lanky arms. "Then I expect she's got some explaining to do."

That was an understatement. Everyone turned to stare at her, waiting. Annie licked her lips, wondering how to explain this little mix-up. "Uh, maybe we should go somewhere more private."

Roy propped one booted foot on a chair. "I'm plenty comfortable right here, sweet cakes. Now, are we engaged or not?"

She swallowed. "Not. Not anymore, that is."

Roy blinked at her in surprise. "What?"

Annie hurried to explain before she lost her nerve. "I'm sorry, Roy. I loved all your letters, and I'm sure you're a very sweet guy, but..." Her voice trailed off. *But I'm in love with Cole.*

His jaw dropped. "I don't believe it."

"It's true," Annie gently insisted. She had no idea

her rejection would be so traumatic for him. "I'm so sorry for any inconvenience I've caused you and your mother. I'm sure you're a very nice man."

Roy sank onto one of the folding chairs and tugged at the collar of his chambray shirt. "I feel like I'm being slow roasted over a hot branding flame."

Cole shoved a cold beer into his hand. "Maybe this will help."

Roy tipped up the beer and guzzled it. Then he wiped the back of his hand across his mouth. "Much obliged. Now I'd like to hear the whole story, sweet cakes. From the beginning."

Annie sat next to him. "You already know most of it. You replied to my letter right away and asked me to send you a picture of myself. We started exchanging letters once a week, then in March, you proposed and invited me for a premarital visit to your ranch. Only I couldn't find you after I arrived in Denver."

Roy dropped his head in his hands and groaned. Annie bit her lip, hoping he wasn't about to cry.

Cole must have sensed Roy's distress, too. He pushed another beer into his hands and slapped him on the shoulder. "Buck up, Roy. You'll get over her."

Annie laid one hand on his arm. "I'm so sorry. I didn't realize you'd take it this hard. I know I had no right to lead you on." Her gaze settled on Cole, and her heart contracted. "Maybe if things had worked out differently…"

"It doesn't matter," Roy said, his voice flat. He lifted his head. "I'm a doomed man."

His tone had an ominous ring. Annie's regret turned to fear. Certainly he wouldn't do anything rash over a woman he'd never met before. Would he? "Roy, don't be silly," she said, her voice harsher than she intended. "I'm not that great a catch."

"Annie's right," Cole said cheerfully. "She'd probably make you miserable. She cooked up a dinner that wasn't even edible. She's barely civilized in the morning. She doesn't take orders well. She uses my razor to shave her legs. And she wants to become a vegetarian."

That litany of complaints should have been enough to scare any cowboy back to the ranch. But Roy only looked more dejected.

She patted his arm. "I'm sure another woman will come along, and you'll forget all about me."

"That's what I'm afraid of," he exclaimed. "Another woman coming along. Then another. Then another. She won't give up until she has me roped and branded." He drained another bottle of beer.

"Who?" Annie and Cole chorused.

"My mother." Roy groaned. "I wondered why she was so hell-bent on me meeting up with you. Especially since I was convinced Annie was some sort of crazy stalker."

Annie blanched. "Why would you think that?"

"Because I never responded to any of your letters, but they just kept coming. The next thing I know you're on your way to Colorado to marry me!" He took another long swallow of beer. "Don't you see? My mother must have been writing those letters, then signing my name to them. She cooked up this whole crazy scheme!"

Nobody said anything for a long moment. Then Cole grinned. "Hildy put your picture in that magazine."

"That's right," Roy said on a long sigh. "Along with a caption that read, Lonely, handsome cowboy seeks loving wife to keep him warm at night. Do you have any idea how many women replied to that nonsense?''

Cole glanced toward his father. "I think I can guess."

Rex cleared his throat, his cheeks ruddy. "I think I'll go make sure we have enough ice." He backed out of the room. The other guests began to mingle once it was evident there wasn't going to be a fight over Annie.

"I still don't understand," Annie said, confused and relieved at the same time. "Are you saying you don't want to marry me?"

Roy chucked her under the chin. "It's nothing personal, sweet cakes. I don't want to marry anybody. But that doesn't stop my mother, the world's busiest matchmaker." A muscle flickered in his jaw. "First she puts my picture in that magazine. Then she starts writing letters and signing my name. She even proposed for me!"

"That's not all she's doing," Cole said.

Roy looked at him. "What do you mean?"

"She's sending out a questionnaire, filled with some of the most bizarre questions I've ever seen." His mouth tipped in a smile. "Although now that I realize they were written by your mother, they make a little more sense."

Annie frowned. "You never told me about a questionnaire."

"That's because I was protecting you."

"From what? A multiple-choice question? I hired you as a private investigator, not a bodyguard. All you were supposed to do was find Roy."

"And here he is." Cole motioned toward their unexpected guest.

Roy looked between the two of them. "You mean you not only stuck around for two weeks but actually hired someone to track me down?"

A blush crept up Annie's cheeks. "I was very anxious to meet you."

"But you found Rafferty instead."

Her eyes met Cole's, and her heart melted at the expression on his face. "That's right," she said softly.

Cole handed the cowboy another beer. "I still have one question. Who were the other Roys?"

Roy froze, his beer can in midair. He slowly lowered it. "What other Roys?"

"The men who came to the Regency Hotel and left the messages for Annie. Each time it was a different man. One had red hair and freckles. Another was bow-legged and had a bushy handlebar mustache."

Roy's eyes narrowed. "Those rattlesnakes. I should have known they'd side with her."

"Who are they?" Annie asked, curious and thankful that Roy wasn't devastated without her. On the contrary, he seemed thrilled that she'd dumped him.

"Ranch hands. Mom must have hoped they could find Annie and bring her back to the ranch before she got away."

"So you never knew I was looking for you?" Annie asked.

Roy snorted. "Oh, I knew, all right, I just didn't know Mom was behind it all. I couldn't believe a woman would be crazy enough to come after me when I hadn't given her any encouragement. That's why I ran in the other direction. I just got back from Durango two days ago, hoping you'd given up."

He took another long swallow of beer. "But Mom still wouldn't let it alone. When I refused to meet with you and your therapist, she threatened to bring you out to the ranch herself." He reached into his shirt pocket. "So I came to give you something."

"An engagement ring?" Annie guessed, expecting the worse.

"A bus ticket," Roy replied, handing her an envelope. "Straight back to New Jersey."

Now she knew why he'd crashed the party. He didn't want to wed her, he wanted to get rid of her. She realized she'd been so preoccupied with Roy she'd forgotten all about Vega. And wasted precious time. She needed to talk to Cole.

Cole must have read her mind, because he suddenly stood up. "Well, I'm glad we've got that settled." He snatched the bus ticket from her hand and handed it to Roy. "Annie and I had better go mingle. You're welcome to stay and enjoy the party, Roy. There's more beer in the fridge."

"Thanks," Roy said, tipping up his bottle in a salute. Then he smiled at Annie. "And may I say that if I was ever crazy enough to send for a mail-order bride, I'd want her to be just like you."

Annie thanked him, taking it as a compliment. Then she walked off hand-in-hand with Cole. But instead of mingling, Cole led her through the French doors to the patio. It was quiet and secluded, the guests preferring to stay near the beer and the food.

To the west, the sun was setting over the mountains. The vibrant rainbow of colors streaking through the snowcapped peaks almost took her breath away. A cool breeze drifted through the trees, a welcome relief after the warm, stuffy living room.

Cole turned to face her. "Alone at last."

"I'm glad you brought me out here. I have something to say to you."

"Me, too."

She chickened out at the last moment. "You go first. Mine is going to take a while."

"Mine will only take three words." He placed his hands on her waist and pulled her close. "I love you."

9

ANNIE STARED into Cole's brown eyes, stunned into speechlessness. Had she heard him right? It seemed too incredible. Too wonderful. "Can you say that again?"

"I'll show you, instead," he said, his voice low and husky. Then he kissed her, his lips moving hungrily over hers. She kissed him while her mind raced. But she couldn't think clearly when she was this close to him. All she could do was feel. Feel the welcome pressure of his body against hers. His strong arms around her. His lips and his tongue melding with hers.

He finally ended the kiss, his forehead pressed against hers. "Stay with me, Annie. I want us for real this time. I want you."

Annie's knees started to shake. Cole loved her. This couldn't be happening. She'd never had good luck with men. This must be some kind of mistake. "Are you absolutely sure?"

"Yes," he said with a smile. "Because I can't imagine living without you."

She noticed he avoided the M word like the plague, but she didn't care. If this was the closest Cole Rafferty could come to a commitment, she'd welcome it with her arms wide-open. Maybe someday... No, she wouldn't worry about someday. She'd take her life the way she'd lived it for the last few terrifying months— one day at a time.

He kissed her again, long and hard. "So what do you say, Annie?"

She didn't get a chance to say anything, because Rex stepped onto the patio. His short, silver hair looked rumpled, as if someone had run their fingers through it.

"Sorry to interrupt," Rex said, shoving his hands in his pockets. It wasn't cold outside, but he looked uncomfortable.

Cole pulled Annie in front of him so her back was pressed against his broad chest. He wrapped his arms around her waist, his chin resting on her shoulder. "Can you give us just a few minutes, Dad? We know we're supposed to be the guests of honor, but we've got something important to discuss. It won't take long."

Annie smiled. Not long at all. Just long enough to tell Cole she loved him, too.

Rex cleared his throat. "Annie's wanted inside."

"At the moment, she's wanted out here," Cole replied, nuzzling her neck.

"There's someone here to see her."

"Who?" Annie asked, snuggling into the warmth of Cole's embrace.

"Your fiancé," Rex replied stiffly.

"I'm her fiancé," Cole murmured, his lips moving along her jawline.

Rex folded his arms across his chest, his eyes narrowing. "Her *other* fiancé."

Annie forced herself to pay attention. "You mean Roy?"

"No, I mean *another* fiancé." He pointed toward the house, the living room visible through the glass in the French doors. "Fiancé number three."

Annie's gaze fell on the newest arrival to the party, and Cole stiffened behind her. Awareness hit her like a bucket of cold water.

Quinn Vega had finally found her.

"ANNIE, DARLING," Quinn exclaimed, rushing toward her as she walked numbly into the living room. He looked as handsome as ever, his Armani suit perfectly tailored to fit his tall, lean body. His dark hair was sleek, and his chiseled face was accentuated by a pair of steel gray eyes. Compared to Cole he seemed almost too polished, too flashy. She found it hard to believe she'd been attracted to him—until she'd discovered the rotten core within the dangerously handsome man.

Quinn enfolded her in his arms. "I thought I'd never find you." He pulled her close against him. Close enough for her to feel the bulge of the handgun he had concealed beneath his suit coat. The steel butt of the gun dug into her ribs. She got his message loud and clear.

Quinn reeked of the cloying aftershave he always wore. She gulped a breath of air, her lungs constricting with the combination of his viselike hold and her panic. At last he let her go. She stumbled to find Cole standing right behind her.

He glared at Vega. "Who the hell are you?"

Quinn held out his hand. "Vega. Quinn Vega. I'm Annie's fiancé."

"That's impossible." Cole bit the words out, ignoring Quinn's outstretched hand. "I'm her fiancé."

Annie closed her eyes. This was a nightmare. Unfortunately, she wasn't going to wake up. She opened her eyes to see Roy approach, a beer bottle dangling from one hand. He had a silly grin on his face.

"Hey, I'm her fiancé, too," Roy said, clapping Vega on the back. "Maybe we should form a club." He turned to Annie. "Just how many guys did you find in that catalogue?"

Vega's thick black eyebrows drew together. "What catalogue?"

"It's called *Mountain Men,*" Roy explained after taking another swig of beer. "A woman can browse through the available men, then pick the one she wants. Annie picked me."

"Then she picked me," Cole said, the muscle knotting in his jaw.

"But she picked me first," Quinn asserted.

Someone in the crowd of partygoers emitted a tipsy giggle and said, "Will the real fiancé please step forward?"

Rex Rafferty stood shoulder-to-shoulder with Cole, his mouth pressed in a thin line. "Annie, I think you owe my son an explanation. I think you owe us all an explanation."

Before Annie could say a word, Vega snaked his arm around her waist. "I think I can explain," he said smoothly. "You see, Annie has always been a little…high-strung. Impulsive. We had a big blowup, which I can now admit was all my fault. But I was too stubborn to admit it then, and she threatened to do something crazy." He shook his head. "Although ordering a husband from a catalogue is something I never expected."

"Join the club," Roy muttered, reaching for another beer.

"But I forgive you," Vega said, pulling her closer. Annie tried not to cringe at the sensation of his hot breath on her neck. "I know you've been under a lot of stress lately, what with the accident and all."

"Accident?" Cole echoed, his hands clenched at his side.

Vega nodded. "A photographer she works with got mugged. He was on assignment in a rough part of town. It really shook her up. She wouldn't even talk to me about it. His name is Costello. Jared Costello. He's doing all right now." Vega shook his head. "Guess he learned his lesson the hard way—stay out of places you don't belong."

Annie tried to slip out of his grasp, but he held her firmly against him and smiled at her. "I'm so glad I finally found you. Things will be different between us from now on, darling. I promise."

His words held an edge of malice, and she suppressed a shiver. Vega intended to make her pay for betraying him.

"Wait a minute," Cole said, his gaze on Annie. She swallowed at the look of confusion on his face. The hope that still lingered in his eyes. "What about us, Annie?"

She dug her nails into her palms. She wanted more than anything to run into Cole's arms. To tell him she loved him. To tell him everything. She closed her eyes, imagining Quinn's reaction. Cole didn't know how dangerous Quinn Vega could be. That gun hidden under his suit coat wasn't for show. He used it. He enjoyed using it. She swallowed hard and opened her eyes.

Better to break Cole's heart and save his life.

"I've got cheese puffs," Lenore called, as she walked into the living room carrying a full tray of hors d'oeuvres. She blinked in surprise at the tense group standing in the center of the living room. "Oh, my. A new arrival."

"It's another one of Annie's fiancé's," Rex muttered, an angry flush mottling his cheeks. "We're up to three now, and counting." He narrowed his eyes. "I always knew there was something funny about her."

Lenore pressed her lips together. "In my premarital counseling classes we call this a sign." She set down the tray, then stood stiffly next to her son. "A sign that this girl is all wrong for you."

Annie looked at Cole, flanked by his irate parents. She'd given him just what he'd wanted—the fiancée from hell. Only he didn't look too happy about her performance. She couldn't look at Rex. Or Lenore. Or the cheese puffs. Her stomach twisted into a tight knot, and for a moment she thought she might be sick. Or she could faint. Cause a distraction, then try to make a run for it. Only, Vega's men could be right outside the door. Even worse, Cole might try to interfere. She couldn't let him get hurt. She couldn't entangle Rex and Lenore and Ethel in her mess.

She took a deep breath. She only had one option. She had to get Vega away from the Raffertys as soon as possible. Before she caused any more damage.

"Well, what's it going to be, Annie?" Cole spoke softly, but she could hear the sharp edge in his tone. "Me...or Vega?"

She felt Quinn tense beside her. Everyone was staring at her. She swallowed, her throat tight and dry. But she was able to get the words out.

"I choose Quinn."

REX WALKED into Annie's bedroom and handed Cole a frosty bottle of beer. "You're better off without her."

"So tell me something I don't know." Cole bit the words out, gazing stonily at the hole he'd just made in the drywall with his fist. Destroying his house wouldn't bring Annie back. He didn't want Annie back. Not after the way she'd played him like a violin.

His hand curled around the beer bottle as he surveyed the room. Annie's robe still hung on the door. Her canvas duffel bag sat open on the bed. Her hairbrush and comb still lay on the dresser.

But Annie was gone.

"Good riddance," Cole muttered, then tipped back his beer. He still couldn't believe it. One minute he was kissing her, the next minute her fiancé shows up to whisk her away. Fiancé number one, that is. Her real fiancé.

Quinn Vega. The guy sounded like a slick used car salesman. He looked like one, too, with his fancy suit and beady eyes. Roy was a better catch than Vega. And Cole was a better man than either of them.

Only Annie obviously didn't think so.

Rex sat on the bed next to him, clapping his hand on Cole's knee. "I know this is rough on you, son. Ethel's getting rid of all the guests. And your mother is driving Roy home." He shook his head. "That guy about drank his body weight in beer."

"I'll drink to that," Cole said, taking another swig from his bottle.

"Damn." Rex swore softly under his breath. "This is all my fault. I never should have pushed you into finding a girl and settling down."

Cole didn't want to tell him he'd never had any intention of settling down. Annie had been a ruse. A trick designed to teach his father a lesson. Only it had backfired on him. "Dad, believe me. I only have myself to blame."

"No, I'm at fault, too. I've been alone too long and wanted some grandchildren to fill up my days. But you need to live your own life. Give yourself time to get over her. Don't rush into another relationship."

Just the words he'd wanted to hear—two weeks ago. Cole closed his eyes. It seemed his plan was a brilliant success. Annie truly was the fiancée from hell.

She had chosen Vega. Then she'd walked out of Cole's life without so much as a backward glance. She didn't even take her meager belongings. It was almost as if she couldn't get away from him fast enough.

"Take it from me," Rex continued, taking a long a swig of beer, "you don't want to get stuck with the wrong woman on the rebound."

Cole rubbed his temple, trying to ease the dull throbbing there. "What are you talking about, Dad? As far as I know, you haven't even dated since you and Mom divorced."

"That's right. Because I didn't want to get stuck with the wrong woman on the rebound. Besides, I had my work to keep me busy." Rex sighed. "But now that I'm not going to the office every day, I'm thinking maybe eight years is long enough to be alone."

Cole's stomach twisted into a tight ball. He'd been without Annie for less than an hour, and it already seemed like an eternity.

Rex drained his beer, then rose. "I guess it's time for me to stop worrying about your love life and start having one of my own."

Before Cole could reply, Ethel stuck her head in the door. "The guests are all gone," she said in a hushed voice usually reserved for hospital waiting rooms and mortuaries. "Why don't you boys go downstairs and let me clear out this room. You don't need any...unpleasant reminders."

"No," Cole snapped, then took a deep breath to regain control. His world had just turned upside down, and his head was still reeling. He didn't want to deal with anyone right now. He just wanted to get good and drunk and forget all about Antonia Kathleen Bonacci. Forget about her false kisses. Her deceptive smile. Her devious violet-blue eyes.

Forget about the way he'd fallen in love with her.

"Please," he said, his voice calm, "just leave me alone."

"Are you sure, Cole?" Rex asked, with a wary look at the battered drywall.

"Positive." He took another long swallow of beer. "Just go. I'll be fine."

Rex hesitated, then followed Ethel out the door and down the stairs.

Cole fell back on the bed, wondering if Annie had already forgotten about him. He rolled to one side and propped his head on his elbow. His gaze fell on the half-packed duffel bag.

He pulled out her flannel nightgown, burying his face in the soft folds of the fabric. Her scent still clung to it. He breathed deeply, then flung it to the floor. "You're pathetic, Rafferty."

He sat up, ready to throw everything that reminded him of Annie into the trash. The same place she'd just thrown their relationship. He made a grab for the duffel bag, and something inside it caught his eye. He pulled out a book bound in red leather, the word *Journal* stamped in gold leaf on the front.

Annie's journal. He opened the cover and saw the

word *private* written in bold black marker, with several exclamation points behind it. He snorted. That was like a green light to a private investigator. He hesitated, then tossed the journal aside.

He already knew more than he wanted to about Annie Bonacci.

"WHERE ARE YOU taking me?" Annie sat in the back seat of the black limo with Quinn, as far away from him as possible. She curled one hand around the door handle, ready to make a run for it at the first red light. Then she heard the click of the electric locks and knew the driver behind the dark glass had anticipated her escape plan.

Vega shook his head. "You're always asking questions, Antonia. It's really not an attractive trait in a woman. Too bad you didn't learn that sooner."

"Maybe you should publish a book of manners for mobsters." Annie buried her shaky hands in her lap. "You could fill it with all the handy do's and don'ts for wives and girlfriends. Don't ask too many questions. Do carry an extra round of bullets in your purse. Don't complain about who dragged wet cement into the house. You know, helpful stuff like that."

Vega chuckled. "That's what I like about you, Antonia. You could always make me laugh. Of course, I wasn't laughing when I found out you stole my journal." He turned toward her, his eyes dark and deadly. "Where is it?"

She swallowed, realizing she'd walked out of Cole's house without her clothes or her toothbrush or that incriminating journal. "I lost it."

Quinn leaned toward her, his voice low and harsh.

"Now that isn't the least bit funny. I don't think it's true, either. Want to try again?"

She closed her eyes, hoping that Cole didn't come across it. More likely he'd burn it in a bonfire with everything else she owned. It was just what she deserved after the way she'd treated him. At least then he would be safe. "I left it at my apartment in Newark."

Quinn grasped her chin and squeezed it tightly between his broad fingers. "Nice try, Antonia, but we both know that's a lie. My boys tore that place apart but they didn't find my journal. Which means you must have it with you."

She swallowed hard as she held out her empty hands. "It's not here."

He smiled. A thin, cold smile that gave her the chills. "Then it must be with that Rafferty fellow." He let go of her. "Your...fiancé."

"He wasn't really my fiancé, exactly." Her chin throbbed but she knew better than to let Vega see her pain. Or her fear.

"Then what is he, exactly?"

"A private eye. I hired him to find Roy."

"Ah, yes. Your other fiancé." He leaned back in the butter-soft leather seat. "You have been a busy girl since you left New Jersey. Tell me, will there be any other fiancés popping out of the woodwork?"

She shook her head. Tiny goose bumps prickled her skin from the cold air blowing out of the vents. She rubbed her hands over her bare arms, trying to warm them.

"Good," Vega replied. "Call me old-fashioned, but I believe three fiancés are two too many. I want you all to myself."

Her throat constricted. "What are you saying?"

"That our engagement is still on, my dear." He ran his tongue slowly over his thin lips. "At least until you hand over that journal. That's the price of your freedom, Antonia. Otherwise, I can promise you that you'll live unhappily ever after."

10

COLE TURNED the last page of the journal, his mouth hanging open at the revelations he'd just read. Unable to resist discovering all her secrets, Cole had decided to read the journal. It had only taken him a couple of pages to realize the journal belonged to Vega, not Annie. By then he'd been mesmerized by the incidents recorded on the pages. He also realized something else.

He was a complete idiot.

Or a lousy detective. Probably both. Annie hadn't been overcome with passion when Vega arrived, she'd been paralyzed with fear. He held the journal with both hands and whacked himself on the forehead with it.

Why didn't he pick up on the clues sooner? Annie had been on the run from Vega. She'd told him she'd gone undercover to get her story. She just failed to mention she'd gone undercover as Vega's fiancée. The guy must be furious.

Cole closed his eyes as he imagined her facing that danger alone. Then he realized he was wasting precious time and sprang to his feet. He ran out of the room and pounded down the staircase two steps at a time. He had to find her. He had to save her from that megalomaniac. Just the thought of Annie in Vega's slimy hands made him want to hit something. Or someone.

He rounded the banister, pulled open the closet door

and reached inside for his gun holster. His hand hit something soft and warm. Something that moved.

Cole jumped back as a startled shriek emanated from inside the closet. "What the hell?"

He watched in disbelief as a hairy hand shoved aside the curtain of coats hanging inside. Rex scowled at him from the shadowed recesses of the deep closet.

"What do you think you're doing?" Rex barked.

Cole blanched. "What am I doing? What are you doing in my closet?" Then he saw another face and a familiar fluff of soft gray curls. "Ethel?"

"Hello, Mr. Rafferty," Ethel said, her arms twined around Rex's neck and her cheeks flushed a deep pink.

Cole's mouth fell open. "Are you two making out in my closet?"

Rex pulled Ethel closer to him. "Yes. Didn't I just tell you that I planned to start having a love life of my own?"

"Well, yeah, but I didn't know you meant to start in the next five minutes."

Ethel tipped her chin. "It's my fault. I jumped him from behind."

Rex grinned as he gazed into her eyes. "And I got the best surprise of my life." He reached for the closet door handle. "Now if you'll excuse us..."

"Wait a minute," Cole interjected, holding the door to keep his father from closing it. The shock of finding Rex and Ethel together had faded, and his adrenaline was pumping. "I need my gun. I'm going after Annie."

Ethel wrenched herself from Rex's arms. "Cole, no! I know how much you love her, but violence won't solve anything. Rex, do something!"

Before Cole could explain, Rex jumped out of the closet and grabbed him.

"Let's tie him up," Ethel suggested, dodging coat hangers, "until he comes to his senses."

Rex looked at Cole. "Do you have any rope?"

Cole rolled his eyes. "Even if I did, I wouldn't tell you. Now listen to me, I'm running out of time. Annie's in trouble."

Rex frowned. "You got her pregnant?"

Cole clamped his jaw to keep from howling in frustration. "No, not that kind of trouble. It's Vega. The man belongs behind bars. Annie was doing a story to put him there when all hell broke loose. She was on the run from him, but he tracked her down here." He struggled out of Rex's grasp. "Now she's in his clutches, and I've got to save her."

Rex looked at Ethel, then back to Cole. "Are you drunk, son?"

"Of course not." He took a deep, calming breath. "Look, if you don't believe me, it's all documented in Vega's journal upstairs. Get it, then call the police."

He lunged for his holster, but Rex stepped in front of him. "Where do you think you're going?"

"To find Annie."

Rex frowned. "Do you even know where to look?"

Cole raked his hand through his hair. "No. I'll check the airport first, then the bus stations—"

The telephone rang. Cole jumped for it, hoping Annie had found a way to escape. He kept reminding himself that she could take care of herself. Annie was the most gutsy, resourceful woman he'd ever met.

He picked up the receiver. "Annie?"

"Cole?" said a soft, feminine voice on the other end of the line. "This is Ingrid."

The disappointment hit him like a fist in his chest. "Ingrid who?"

"Ingrid Tate. From the Regency Hotel."

His hand reached for the disconnect button. "Look, I don't have time to talk right now."

"It's about your fiancée."

His hand halted. "Annie? What about her?"

He could hear Ingrid sigh. "I'm not sure how to tell you this."

"Fast, Ingrid. Say it fast."

"She's two-timing you, Cole. I saw her with my own eyes. I knew she was the wrong woman for you from the moment we met."

Cole's hand tightened on the receiver. "You saw her? When?"

"Just a little while ago. She was with another man, and they looked quite chummy. He couldn't keep his hands off her."

"Where?" Cole choked the word out.

"Well, he had one hand on her arm and another around her waist."

He clenched his teeth with impatience. "No, I mean where did you see them?"

"Here," she replied, sounding startled by his brusque tone, "at the Regency. They just checked into one of our most expensive suites."

"I'll be right there."

"I was hoping you'd say that," Ingrid replied. "But I don't get off duty until eight. How about if we meet at my place? I know we could have a good time together." She lowered her voice to a seductive purr. "I'll make you forget all about her."

Cole knew without a doubt that was impossible. "Ingrid, you're wonderful, but Annie's the only girl for me.''

''But she's with another man!''

Cole hung up the phone. ''Not for long.''

ANNIE PACED back and forth across the dusky rose carpet in the spacious suite at the Regency Hotel. Vega had left her without a word of explanation, placing the burly chauffeur as a guard outside the door. She had no idea where Quinn had gone or when he would be back. To make matters worse, her imagination had kicked in.

What would he do to her? Drop her out of his private jet at thirty thousand feet? Dump her in the Hudson River once they got to Jersey? Suffocate her with his toxic cologne? She didn't believe for a moment that he planned to continue their engagement. Vega liked to play mind games. Lull his victims into a false sense of security, then wreak his revenge.

She walked to the window and peered out. Twelve stories, and no drainpipe. Scratch that idea. She resumed pacing. If only this place had a laundry chute. Then she could career her way to safety and hope there was a cart full of laundry at the bottom to soften her landing. But there was no chute. No working telephone, either. Vega had ripped the cord out of the wall before he left. As far as she could tell, there wasn't any way out of this five-star prison.

She sat on the bed and buried her head in her hands. At least Cole was safe. Shocked, hurt and probably mad as hell, but safe. She thought about the last time he'd kissed her. How wonderful and right she'd felt in his arms. Until Vega arrived, bringing her bad luck with men right along with him.

She sat up. Maybe it was time to stop blaming fate and start making her own luck. She couldn't give up now, especially since she'd finally found a man worth fighting for.

Annie squared her shoulders. She'd gotten away from Vega before, and she could certainly outsmart that cretin standing guard outside. She stood, took a deep breath, then strode to the door. To her surprise, it was unlocked.

The cretin stood at least six-five and didn't look at all happy to see her standing in the doorway.

"Get back inside," he growled.

She forced a smile. "Hi. I'm Annie. What's your name?"

His face hardened. "Benedick."

"Benedick?" She cleared her throat. "Really? That's quite...unusual. I like it."

His wide shoulders relaxed a fraction. "My mother named me after her favorite character in *Much Ado About Nothing*. She loved Shakespeare." He folded his arms and leaned against the doorway. "I always preferred his tragedies myself, like *Macbeth* and *King Lear*."

Shakespeare? Okay, so maybe he wasn't a cretin. But he was still blocking her escape route.

"*The Taming of the Shrew* is my favorite." Annie motioned toward the suite. "Why don't you come inside, Benedick? You must be bored standing around out here."

He wavered for a moment, then set his jaw. "The boss pays me very well for just standing around."

She glanced at her watch. "Just as well. I'm already running a little late." She breezed past him.

"Hold it!" He captured her arm with one beefy paw. "Where do you think you're going?"

She blinked innocently at him. "To dinner. Quinn asked me to meet him at the restaurant downstairs at seven o'clock." She leaned forward and whispered, "If you let go of my arm, I'll bring back a doggie bag."

But Benedick didn't loosen his grip. "You're not going anywhere, lady. I've got strict orders. Nobody goes in or out."

Annie's widened her eyes. "But that doesn't apply to me. I'm Quinn's fiancée. And Quinn is not going to be happy sitting down there in that restaurant all by himself.

Benedick hesitated. "Nope," he finally said. "I got my orders. You stay here."

The elevator chimed, the doors slid open and an elderly couple walked out. Annie used the distraction to make a break for it. She aimed a sharp kick at his kneecap and wrenched her arm free as he let out a grunt of pain. But she only made it halfway to the elevator when a thick, hairy forearm wrapped around her waist.

"Put me down!" she shrieked, her legs flailing in the air as Benedick hauled her to the room. Annie elbowed him in the ribs, but he didn't even flinch. He dumped her inside the room without a word, then closed the door, leaving her alone once again.

She pounded her fist against the door and screamed for help. But she knew it was useless. All the rooms at the Regency were soundproof. Why couldn't Quinn have held her captive at a Motel 6?

Annie turned her back to the door, then slid down it until she sat on the floor. So much for outsmarting Benedick. Time to come up with a new plan. Maybe she could write an SOS message on toilet paper and hang it out the window. Or overflow the bathtub until the water leaked into the room below and maintenance came to investigate.

A knock at the door startled her out of her reverie. Her heart began to pound. Vega. Then she realized he wouldn't knock on his own hotel room door.

"Who is it?" she called out.

"Room service."

Her stomach growled. Maybe she could think better after a seven-course gourmet meal. She opened the door. And gave a soft cry.

"Cole!"

He rolled the cart inside, his gaze scanning the room. "Is Vega here?"

She shook her head, too stunned to speak. He pulled her into his arms. Annie closed her eyes as they held each other tight. A flurry of emotions assailed her. Joy. Relief. Terror. She'd thought she might never see him again. Never hold him again. And that had scared her even more than Vega and his deadly threats. She swallowed hard as she clung to Cole, wondering how he'd found her. Wondering how she could make him leave before Quinn returned.

"Thank God you're all right," he murmured, his warm breath curling in her ear. "I thought...never mind what I thought."

She pulled back far enough to look up into his face. "I can only imagine what you thought of me, Cole. I lied to you from the first moment we met."

He cupped her face in his hands and began dropping tender kisses on her face as she tried to explain.

"I accepted Quinn's proposal to get a story," she said, as his lips brushed over one eyebrow, then the other. "I accepted Roy's proposal so I could find a safe

haven to write the story." She closed her eyes as he
rained kisses on her nose and chin and one corner of
her mouth. She couldn't let him distract her. She
couldn't let there be any more secrets between them.
"I used you, Cole. Because I was scared and broke and
desperate. But I never thought Vega would invade your
home or your family. I was an idiot..." Her voice
cracked and she couldn't go on. Not when he held her
so sweetly in his arms.

"Don't talk that way about the woman I love," he
admonished, leaning his forehead against hers. "I used
you, too. I knew you were desperate. Hell, I took advantage of that fact to get what I wanted."

"The fiancée from hell," she said, suppressing a
hysterical bubble of laughter in her throat. "I was certainly perfect for the part."

He caressed the length of her cheek with his knuckles. "All I know is you're perfect for me."

She looked into his deep brown eyes and saw the
truth of his words. Her heart did a triple somersault in
her chest. "You still...want me?"

"I never stopped wanting you." Then he kissed her,
a long, deep, possessive kiss that proved it to her more
thoroughly than words ever could. At last he lifted his
head and smiled. "Which is why I turned into a jealous, brainless jerk when I thought you wanted Vega.
Then I read his journal and realized the truth."

Vega. The name alone caused a cold chill to run
through her. "So you know how dangerous he can
be?"

Cole nodded, a muscle knotting his jaw. "I still can't
believe I let you walk out the door with him."

"And I can't believe you found me." She couldn't

stop touching him, couldn't believe he was really here. "How did you get past Benedick?"

One corner of his mouth quirked up in a smile. "You mean that Neanderthal outside your door?"

She nodded, still stunned by his unexpected arrival.

"Oh, that was easy. I brought my own Neanderthal. Bruno took care of him for me."

"Bruno?"

Cole whistled low. "That guy has a mean right hook. Remind me never to get on his bad side."

"I think it's too late for that," Annie replied, her knees weak with relief. "But how did you ever get him to help you?"

"The usual way. Cold, hard cash. I've almost paid him enough to cover his daughter's orthodontia bill. He told me she'll be sending me a thank-you note."

Then he pulled her close and kissed her again. "I would have given everything I owned to find you."

"Oh, Cole, I'm so sorry I didn't trust you," she whispered. "I'm sorry I ever got you involved in this mess."

"I'm just sorry I didn't figure it out sooner."

She pushed him toward the door. "We can apologize to each other in the car. Let's get out of here before Quinn comes back."

"Hey, don't worry," he said, wrapping his arms around her and pulling her to a halt. "Bruno will handle Vega. And the police are on the way. You're safe now."

As soon as he said the words, the door opened and Quinn Vega stepped in the room. He blinked in astonishment at Cole, then at Annie. The next moment he had a gun in his hand. "I see we have company."

Annie's breath caught in her throat as Cole stepped

quickly in front of her, shielding her from the lethal barrel of the .357 Magnum. His back formed a solid barrier, blocking her from Vega's view. But she'd already glimpsed the malevolent glitter in Quinn's dark eyes.

"Give it up, Vega," Cole said coolly. "The police will be here soon."

Quinn sneered. "If they're as easily bribed as that clown of a security guard, I don't have to worry."

"Why, that double-crossing..." Cole muttered under his breath.

Quinn kept his gun aimed at Cole. "I know just how you feel. I wasn't too happy when I found out Annie double-crossed me. But we can commiserate later. Right now I'd like to make you a deal."

Annie stood behind Cole, her hands on his broad shoulders. She could feel the tension in his muscles, could see his gaze trained on the gun. He was ready to strike as soon as Vega gave him the opportunity. She eased out from behind his back, determined to help him. It was her fault they were in this predicament. She should have told him the truth from the beginning.

"Save your deals for the D.A.," Cole said. "You'll have better luck if you're not charged with attempted murder."

Vega smiled. "Don't worry about me, Rafferty. Quinn Vega always gets what he wants. To make it very simple, I want the journal. Give it to me, and I'll let Annie go."

It was a blatant lie. Quinn Vega never let a betrayal go unpunished. But maybe she could use the journal to barter for Cole's life. "I'll give you the journal," Annie interjected, "on one condition."

Quinn smiled. "You're hardly in any position to name conditions, my dear."

He had a point. Still, she'd do anything to keep Cole safe. "My condition is you let Cole retrieve the journal and leave it for you at the front desk."

Quinn arched a brow. "And you'll stay here with me as...collateral?"

She swallowed and nodded.

"Annie," Cole said under his breath.

"Fine." Quinn glanced at the Rolex on his wrist, then turned to Cole. "I'll give you thirty minutes. But if you bring the police back with you, she's a dead woman."

Annie looked at Cole, seeing the indecision on his face. *Where were the cops?* Cole couldn't move with that gun aimed at his chest. But Vega couldn't cover them both. She inched toward the room service cart, hoping to find a weapon to help even the odds against them.

"You're nuts if you think I'm leaving Annie alone here with you," Cole said.

Vega just smiled. "Twenty-nine minutes."

Annie backed up against the cart, wishing for once Cole wasn't so damn noble. He didn't deserve to die over her. "Please go, Cole."

He ignored her, his gaze fixed on Vega. "I love Annie. I'm not leaving her."

Vega's eyes narrowed. This probably wasn't the best time for Cole to declare his love for her, but her heart swelled just same. This wonderful, brave, sexy man loved her. At that moment, Annie Bonacci knew she was the luckiest woman in the world.

Now if only her luck would hold.

She glanced surreptitiously at the cart and her hopes

fell. No knife. Not even a fork. Stabbing Vega with the silver spoon resting on top of the cart didn't seem like the best defense. Neither did the silver tureen full of soup.

Then it hit her. Boiling hot soup might be just what she needed to disarm him. Especially if Vega didn't see it coming. If he did.... Annie suppressed the shiver of apprehension that snaked down her spine.

"I love you, too, Cole," she said softly, realizing she might not have another chance to say it.

"How romantic," Vega sneered. "I suppose this means you want to die together." He pulled back the hammer on his gun. "I'll be very happy to oblige you."

That was her cue. She grabbed one handle of the silver soup tureen and hurled it like a discus at Vega. He turned toward her just as the tureen glanced off his shoulder, the creamy white soup splashing him full in the face.

Soup splattered everywhere. "Damn," she muttered, feeling the rain of cold, wet drops on her face. "Chilled soup. Just my luck."

Vega coughed and sputtered, wiping the thick, milky soup out of his eyes. That gave Cole just enough time to jump him. They both hit the floor, the gun waving wildly in Vega's hand. A shot went off, blowing a hole through the large plate glass window.

Annie stood helplessly by while they rolled back and forth over the soup-stained carpet. When they rolled near her, she drew her foot back and kicked the gun out of Vega's hand. It skittered across the floor.

Cole pinned Vega at last, his chest heaving as he wedged his forearm against Vega's thick neck.

"I can't breathe," Vega gasped, his eyes bulging.

"Good," Cole muttered, then reached into his jacket pocket and pulled out a pair of hot pink handcuffs. With the flawless precision of long practice, he flipped Vega onto his stomach, and wrenched both arms behind his back, cuffing his wrists together.

"Where did you get those?" Annie asked, still staring at the pink handcuffs.

Cole got slowly up off the floor, brushing small chunks of creamy potatoes off his knees. "Some woman who read that personal ad sent them to me, along with several creative suggestions on how to use them."

She smiled as she walked into his arms. "I see you chose the traditional method."

He shrugged as he pulled her closer. "I guess I'm just an old-fashioned guy. I prefer my women ready and willing."

"Women?" Annie echoed. "Plural?"

He grinned. "Not anymore. There's only one woman for me." He leaned his face close to hers. "Is she ready and willing?"

She showed him just how willing by kissing him until they were both breathless. The sparks arcing between them made Annie oblivious to everything, even Vega's indignant sputters and curses.

At long last they broke the kiss as a shower of tiny droplets rained over them. The both turned to see Vega's vain attempts to rise to his knees. The slimy vichyssoise puddled beneath him made it impossible, causing him to belly flop back onto the carpet and sending a fine spray of soup into the air.

Cole wiped a milky droplet from Annie's forehead. "I suppose we should go call for help."

But help had already arrived.

"What the hell is going on in my hotel?" Ingrid exclaimed, standing in the open doorway. She wore a white Lycra jumpsuit and heavy gold jewelry. She picked up the gun lying on the carpet, gingerly holding the handle between her thumb and forefinger.

"Shoot him!" Vega gargled from his trussed position on the floor.

Ingrid's limpid blue eyes narrowed on Annie. "I'd rather shoot her. Unfortunately, shooting the guests is against hotel policy."

"I can explain," Annie said, her knees weak with relief. She felt giddy and so wonderfully alive.

Ingrid arched one blond brow. "Then explain why the couple in the next room complained that there was an orgy going on up here. Explain why Bruno is flashing hundred dollar bills all over the place. And last but not least, please explain why there is an extremely attractive unconscious man lying in the hallway."

Annie swallowed.

"It's a long story."

"Then explain why that man—" she pointed to Vega "—claimed he was your fiancé."

"That's an even longer story. But I'm sure it will all come out at his trial."

Ingrid rolled her eyes, then looked at Cole. "The woman runs away from you, lies to you, then almost gets you killed. How long are you going to let her treat you this way?"

Cole grinned at Annie. "For the rest of my life."

"I CAN'T BELIEVE this day has finally arrived," Cole whispered in Annie's ear. They stood on the edge of the dance floor, holding each other and gently swaying to the beat of the big band music emanating from the speakers.

"Are you excited?"

"You bet. I've dreamed of this day for so long." He sighed wistfully. "Ethel's retirement party."

Annie poked him playfully in the ribs. "You're going to miss her. Admit it, Rafferty."

"Well, maybe a little." Then he brightened. "Hey, they're playing our song." He pulled her to the center of the dance floor as the lyrics of "It Had to Be You" drifted out of the speakers.

"Since when is this our song?" Annie asked, wrapping her arms around him. Sometimes she still couldn't believe he was real. And all hers. They hadn't spent even one day apart since nailing Vega a month ago.

"I requested it," he said with a smile. "I thought it might make nice background music when I ask you a certain question. We've been so busy sending Vega to prison forever and planning Dad and Ethel's wedding, but I can't wait any longer."

He twirled her once, then dipped her. Annie draped backward over his forearm, her head spinning as she looked at the crystal chandeliers. He pulled her upright.

She let go of him, her throat tight. "What question?"

He went down on one knee, clasping her hand as he gazed into her eyes. "Antonia Kathleen Bonacci, will you marry me?"

She laughed as she pulled him to his feet. "I thought you didn't believe in marriage."

"I don't believe in divorce. There's a big difference. So whether it's for better or worse, it's going to be forever."

"Are you serious?" she asked softly.

Cole stepped toward her, his love shining in his deep brown eyes. "I've never been more serious. I love you, Annie. I want to love and honor and cherish you for the rest of my life. I want you for my wife."

Her vision blurred. "Oh, Cole."

He took a deep breath. "What do you say, Annie?"

She didn't even hesitate. "Yes. On one condition."

"What?" he asked, wrapping his hands around her waist and drawing her close to him.

"No engagement. I've had my fill of fiancés. Let's elope."

He grinned. "Deal. Is tonight too soon for you?"

"Not soon enough," she breathed, unnerved by the desire arcing between them.

"I've been a fool, Annie," he said huskily. "I thought avoiding marriage would keep me from getting hurt. But I never hurt so much as when I thought I'd lost you. My heart always knew you were the only woman for me, but I was just too thickheaded to see it."

"And I was too convinced of my bad luck with men to realize I simply hadn't found the right one. Now that I've got you, I'll never let you go."

"I'm not going anywhere," he vowed, then kissed her in the middle of the dance floor as the music reverberated around them. A kiss filled with more love and passion and promise than she'd ever imagined.

"Hey, you two." Rex chortled as he danced by with Ethel. "Save a little something for the honeymoon."

Cole turned to slap Rex on the back. "Gee, Dad, I was about to give you the same advice. You're not as young as you used to be. You'll need to pace yourself."

Ethel's cheeks turned a bright pink. "I still can't believe I'm going to be a bride at my age."

Cole leaned over to kiss her cheek. "Welcome to the family, Ethel. Now tell me what you did with my net."

"Net?" Ethel echoed. "What net?"

"The basketball net that hangs on the door of my office. It's gone."

"Oh, that net," she said, with a mischievous gleam in her eyes. "I threw it away, since you won't be needing it anymore." She looked at Rex. "Shall we tell him?"

"Tell me what?" Cole asked, his brow crinkled.

Rex grinned. "Ethel and I are giving you full control of Rafferty Investigations. We newlyweds won't have time to meddle in your business anymore."

Cole's mouth curved into a slow smile. "Full control?"

Rex nodded. "That's right. The business is all yours, son. You'll have free rein to run it any way you want."

"I don't know what to say," he sputtered, as Rex and Ethel danced away.

"Say you'll let me in on some juicy cases so I can get a good story," Annie suggested. "I happen to think a detective and an investigative journalist make perfect bedfellows."

"I couldn't agree more." He pulled her into his arms. "In fact, I've already got a case for us to crack."

She smiled as they swayed to the music. "What is it?"

"Racketeering at the Regency Hotel. We'll have to go undercover in the honeymoon suite for several days."

"And nights?" Annie asked hopefully.

"Definitely. We'll have to act like we're madly in love with each other. In fact, to be really believable, we'll have to spend all our time together in bed." His dark eyes smoldered. "Are you up to the challenge?"

"You know I'll do anything to get a story," she said huskily.

Cole drew her closer to him. "I'm counting on it."

"But what happens when we solve the case?"

He feigned a sigh of disappointment. "Then the honeymoon is over."

Annie pressed her body against him and whispered, "Promise you won't solve it too fast, Cole."

He moaned deep in his throat. "Lady, you picked the slowest private detective in Denver."

JENNIFER DREW

Taming Luke

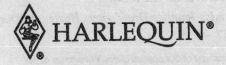

HARLEQUIN®

TORONTO • NEW YORK • LONDON
AMSTERDAM • PARIS • SYDNEY • HAMBURG
STOCKHOLM • ATHENS • TOKYO • MILAN • MADRID
PRAGUE • WARSAW • BUDAPEST • AUCKLAND

What woman can resist a good challenge? Especially one as yummy as Luke Stanton? But not only did Luke give our beleaguered heroine fits, he gave us a hard time, too.

Luke became such a bad boy, even we couldn't control him! What's a mother-daughter duo to do? (Jennifer Drew is our pseudonym for the writing duo of Barbara Andrews and Pam Hanson.) We asked Pam's second-grader, Erik, what he would do with a wild man who misbehaved? His answer was simple. "Put him in a cage."

So we did...!

Enjoy your trip to Arizona (Erik's birthplace), where a beauty vs. the beast matchup sizzles under the Southwestern sun!

—Jennifer Drew

Books by Jennifer Drew

SILHOUETTE YOURS TRULY
DEAR MR. RIGHT
THE PRINCE AND THE BOGUS BRIDE
THE BAD-GIRL BRIDE

SILHOUETTE ROMANCE
1040—TURN BACK THE NIGHT

Don't miss Jennifer Drew's next Harlequin Duets in January 2000!

For Erik,
who knew exactly what to do
with a "wild man" who got out of hand.

early, too.

1

MAYBE SHE was hallucinating.

Jane Grant stopped, rubbed her eyes and let out a low whistle. She wasn't hallucinating. Her always unpredictable boss, Rupert Cox, had added a statue of a Greek god under the cascade of sparkling water in front of the Phoenix headquarters of his sporting goods company.

She'd always loved the high-pressure jet of water, glowing like liquid gold as it caught the early-morning sun and fell into the surrounding pool. A water god was the perfect touch on this August day, his face raised as gleaming water splashed over a body so perfect it made her gasp in admiration. Even from a distance she saw the power in the arms raised to clutch his head and the chiseled grace of the naked torso. If only real men looked like that!

She hurried toward the statue, eager for a closer look before she rushed up to the top-floor offices where she was assistant to the CEO's executive secretary, Miss Polk. Once upon a time she'd wanted to work in a museum surrounded by beautiful things, but little girls had to grow up. It wasn't so bad being a well-paid peon, even if her eccentric boss did like to begin his workday at the crack of dawn, sometimes prompting Miss Polk to ask that Jane come in early, too.

"Oh, no!"

The statue moved.

She froze, hoping she'd only imagined it. Momentary relief that no one had heard her shriek turned to apprehension. There wasn't a security guard in sight, and most employees wouldn't come to work for another hour.

The male version of Galatea, Pygmalion's perfect creation, turned his back to the spray and brushed water from his face with the edges of his hands, then slicked back a long mane of wet hair.

He was taking a shower in Rupert Cox's prized fountain! How could he? Didn't he care if he got into big trouble?

"Oh, this is too much!"

She was too agitated to be afraid of the trespasser. Where did he get the nerve to use a beautiful ornamental fountain as his personal tub? If Mr. Cox saw him... She didn't even want to think of her employer throwing a fit and having another heart attack.

She charged toward the intruder, knowing she had to do something but not sure what.

"You can't do that here!" she shouted from the pavement beside the pool.

He couldn't hear her over the splashing of water.

"Hey, you can't take a shower here!"

Desperate now—as assistant to Mr. Cox's executive secretary she had to take action—she stepped up onto the marble rim of the pool and yelled as loudly as she could.

"You can't use the fountain that way!"

Finally he turned and walked slowly in her direction, as naked as a man could be without getting arrested. The scrap of cloth clinging wetly to his groin was more a pouch than actual underwear; water was dripping from it and trickling down his thighs. His skin was golden tan everywhere she dared look, and water beaded on one chocolate-drop nipple as he raised his arms again to squeeze more water from his hair.

"This fountain belongs to the Cox Corporation. You can't bathe in it!" She tried to sound as intimidating as Miss Polk, but her voice wavered before she could give him an ultimatum.

"I'm not bathing. See, no soap." He held out open palms and looked her over from head to toe, not even trying to be subtle.

She was squirming inside her skin, his steady gaze making her feel as exposed as he was. Worse, she felt like an idiot. It wasn't fair! He was the bare-chested trespasser, and she was doing him a favor by not screaming for help.

He started toward her, moving with unhurried casualness, his long, tanned feet visible now on the slippery aqua tiles lining the bottom of the pool.

"Look, if you're homeless, if you need a place to stay, I have a little money you can have, and a friend of mine volunteers at a mission—"

"Thanks, anyway. A bedroll is enough for me," he said, gesturing toward a knapsack and rumpled sleeping bag on the other side of the pavement.

"You don't understand. You can't camp out on Cox property."

"Oh?" He stopped a few feet away and looked her over again with deep-set blue eyes that shattered the last of her poise.

"You have to leave now."

"Is this Cox a tyrant?" he asked.

"Yes—no...not exactly...."

She tried to back off the rim of the pool, not realizing how treacherous wet marble could be.

Incredibly, he moved faster than she fell. Instead of plunging forward and landing on her face in the shallow water, she was swept clear of the sharp-edged rim and caught in his powerful wet arms. She instinctively clutched at shoulders as firm and smooth as well-worn saddle leather, then regretted touching him.

"Let go of me!"

"Steady now. Get your footing. The bottom's a bit slick." He had a slight accent, too indistinct to pin down but definitely foreign.

"I can manage."

She tried backing away, but her left foot slipped, thrusting her leg awkwardly between the damp, hairy limbs she was trying to avoid. His thighs closed around hers, preventing a fall but throwing her into a panic.

"Easy does it. I'm not going to hurt you."

Maybe it was his accent; his voice was oddly soothing in a sexy, deep-throated way. For whatever reason, she calmed down for an instant, letting him catch her off guard. He grabbed under her arms and lifted all five foot nine inches of her over the rim of the pool. She stood dumbfounded in the puddle dripping from her legs, shifting uneasily from one soggy foot to the other.

"You can't sleep here, either," she mumbled, looking over her shoulder at his makeshift bed but thinking about his adorable little navel tucked in a nest of fine hairs that thickened at the edge of his practically nonexistent bikini.

Things like this didn't happen to Jane Grant, twenty-six-year-old office worker, substitute mother to her sister, Kim, since their parents' death in a car accident nearly five years ago. Her life was mundane with a capital *M* and would stay that way until Kim finished college three years from now and qualified for a teaching certificate. Jane wasn't the kind of girl who splashed around in fountains with nearly naked men, especially not hunks who made the Greek gods look like sissies.

"It seems I'm guilty of trespassing," he said cheerfully.

She didn't need to look at him to know he was grinning.

"I have to get to work," she said, retreating cautiously.

She glanced down at her neat two-inch bone pumps, pretty sure the discount footwear would dry into stiff, toe-pinching discards. Her cream-colored panty hose were soaked to the knees, but at least her pastel green suit had escaped all but a few splashes on the skirt—and wet handprints where the creature from the company pool had grabbed her.

"Sorry if I delayed you," he said. "Didn't expect anyone to be coming to work so early."

He sounded courteous enough, but she detected a twinge of amusement—maybe even irony—in everything he said. Was he enjoying himself at her expense?

"I'm going into that building," she said, needlessly pointing at the large pseudo-Spanish office complex with light sand-colored walls and ornate cast-iron balconies not intended to be used. "You have approximately three minutes to disappear before security boots you out of here."

He only smiled more broadly.

"Some of the guards are bigger than you. A lot bigger," she added.

His skeptical grin made her feel like a kid yelling threats at a playground bully.

"Thank you for the warning."

He sauntered over to his gear and bent to roll up the bed.

She didn't want to do it, but her eyes had a will of their own.

She watched.

Good grief! He was a masterpiece! His shoulders and back rippled with muscles under skin as smooth as burnished copper. His waist was lean and his hips narrower than the breadth of his chest. She'd always poked fun at her friends when they rhapsodized over men's behinds, but the Greek god's was world-class: full, round, muscular, undulating just enough as he walked to make her moisten her lips with the tip of her tongue.

And his legs! She was a connoisseur of men's legs. She was tall enough to appreciate height, but most of the men who towered over her had skinny sticks or chunky tree-trunk appendages. The fountain-bather's limbs were perfectly proportioned, gloriously tanned like the rest of him except for shoe lines at the backs of his ankles. It wasn't hard to imagine legs like his wrapped around hers.

She must be losing her mind! Policing the grounds wasn't her job, and Miss Polk treated tardiness as one of the seven deadly sins. She had to go—now. She pictured Miss Polk. The woman she reported to was a walking caricature of a career woman from another era: short and scrawny, but big-busted with unfashionable tortoiseshell glasses and salt-and-pepper hair pulled into a severe bun. She lived in dark suits and probably owned several hundred white blouses, all of which looked as if they had to be ironed. She wore sensible stubby-heeled shoes and sometimes pinned a watch on her lapel to compare the time with that on her large, mannish wristwatch. She intimidated everyone but her immediate and only superior, Rupert Cox. Miss Polk would know how to handle a vagrant who showered under the company fountain.

Jane tried to ignore the squishing in her shoes as she hurried toward the building, not even indulging in another look at the hunk. With a little luck, she might be sent on an errand to the far reaches of the building where she could slip off her pumps and let them dry. Even though she had a title—Assistant to the Executive Secretary—she did any odd job too minor for Miss Polk's personal attention, anything from buying retirement gifts to making travel arrangements. She liked the variety of her tasks, even though she sometimes found Miss Polk's heavy-handed supervision irksome.

But where else could she find a job that paid well enough to support both she and her sister and help with Kim's tuition? Her sister worked hard at a variety of part-time jobs, but as a student her earnings were limited.

When Jane reached the office three minutes late, Miss Polk didn't even glance at her watch. She looked flushed and flustered, making Jane wonder if the Cox Corporation was on the brink of bankruptcy.

In her five years with the company, two as Miss Polk's assistant, she'd never seen her boss pink-cheeked and distracted.

"Oh, yes, Jane, I forgot you were coming in early," the older woman said. "I guess you can busy yourself at your desk for a while."

Busy herself at her desk? For this she'd gotten up at an unholy hour, steamed her eyes open in a hot shower, drank three cups of coffee to keep them open and thought of getting a night job as she drove to work? Something was radically wrong, but she knew better than to ply Miss Polk with questions. She didn't want her head to be the first to fall into a basket under a downsizing guillotine.

By ten o'clock Jane had done everything that needed doing and was pretending to reorganize her desk. Her pencils were all razor-sharp, her paper was lined up with military precision and her shoes had stiffened into torture devices. There was nothing left to do but surf the Net on her computer and wonder why Miss Polk kept popping in and out of Mr. Cox's office as though it had a revolving door.

"Jane, Mr. Cox wants to see you in his office," her supervisor said, again slipping through a small opening that didn't allow Jane to see into the opulent interior of the CEO's inner sanctum.

Jane's heart skipped a beat, and she rose to comply with leaden dread. She rarely went into Rupert Cox's private office, and then only to accompany her supervisor and take notes. In fact, weeks might pass without a glimpse of the corporate magnate. He had a private elevator opening into his office and rarely showed himself in the outer office. He never, ever, asked for her by name.

She forced herself to smile, hoping her face wouldn't freeze into an idiotic grin. Looking straight ahead, all she saw was the huge mahogany desk, the surface as smooth and shiny as glass, and the telescope Mr. Cox used to survey the grounds, one of his many eccentric habits.

"Join us over here, please, Jane," his voice boomed.

If Rupert Cox ever lost his financial empire, he could recoup his losses playing movie villains. He had a deep, compelling voice that gave her goose bumps whenever he directly addressed her, which was blessedly seldom.

His office had the floor space of a two-bedroom apartment, one side lavishly furnished with period furniture, including sofas and chairs upholstered in what he called bawdy-house red brocade. There, unceremoniously sprawled on a Victorian love seat, with his feet propped on the surface of a carved and polished ebony table, was the last man she ever expected to see again: the Greek god.

"We won't need you anymore for now, Miss Polk," Cox commanded.

The executive secretary moved slowly toward the door, her whole body stiff with disapproval. Jane wanted to beg the woman not to desert her, but Cox himself was escorting Jane to a chair, his hand firm on her upper arm.

"Jane, I'd like to formally introduce you to my grandson, Luke Stanton-Azrat. Stanton is his father's name. Azrat is a name some African tribe tacked on."

"An honorary name I choose to keep," he said,

standing and acknowledging her with a nod, but staring so intently she thought of X-ray vision.

He was even more dangerously disturbing with clothes than without—not that what he was wearing could be called office attire. His khaki shorts left most of his thighs bare, and he'd apparently ripped the sleeves off a shirt the same color. His feet didn't look slender now in chunky ankle boots with heavy gray socks folded down over the tops. His hair had dried to a sandy-brown with sunbleached streaks of gold. And he seemed taller standing here in the office, at least six-two.

"You're from Africa, then," she said because some comment seemed to be expected from her. What was there to say to a stranger after she'd seen him practically naked?

"I see you've dried off quite well," the grandson said, not responding to her comment. "Sorry to be the cause of your drenching."

"Thank you."

What on earth was she thanking him for?

"Don't be uncomfortable on my account," he said with a sheepish grin as he resumed his seat. "Grandfather saw your valiant effort to eject a savage from his fountain." He gestured at the high-power telescope sitting on a tripod overlooking the front grounds.

"Damn cheeky, Luke," Mr. Cox said with no ill will. In fact, he seemed to be amused by his grandson's prank. "Of course, you'll have to shape up after this. Not act like you're wallowing in some blasted watering hole."

His grandson didn't look intimidated, but Jane felt two inches high with a feather for a backbone.

She was sitting precariously on the edge of an antique chair, the upholstered seat too slippery and rounded to accommodate her bottom in comfort.

His grandson was still examining her with hooded eyes, managing to look totally at home on a piece of furniture designed for a five-foot woman in hoop skirts.

Not for the first time, she wondered why she'd been summoned to the lion's den.

LUKE KNEW what was coming and sympathized with the woman even as he tried to hide his amusement. Judging by her reaction to his early-morning dip, he expected her to go ballistic.

"I'm not a young man," Rupert was saying, sucking in his gut and throwing back his still-broad shoulders in an attempt to belie his statement. "As you know, Jane, I had a heart attack last year, and I've had to give a lot of thought to the possibility of retiring."

Jane. Janie. Luke liked a nice simple name.

"You may also know my only child—my daughter—preceded me in death a few years ago. Now, Jane, Luke is, so to speak, an orphan and my only direct descendant. That also makes him my heir."

Rupert tended to use a person's name a lot when he wanted something. Luke made a mental note of this technique. Even though he had no intention of staying in the States longer than the six weeks he'd rashly promised, he had a deep curiosity about this stranger who was his only living relative.

"I want to be very up front with you, Jane. My daughter eloped to Africa with Peter Stanton very much against my wishes. I had a suitable young man all picked out for her, but she wanted to defy me. The marriage lasted only a very short time, then she returned home for a while and later married a Dutch banker, settling down in Amsterdam. Unfortunately, she wasn't able to have more children.''

Luke felt a tinge of familiar anger. He was glad his mother had left him in Africa, but his father had never completely recovered from her desertion. Luke had loved growing up in rough-and-tumble camps while his engineer father worked in Africa, but Dad had grown increasingly morose and reckless, especially after Luke went to England for his degrees in engineering and began his own career. Heavy drinking and a disregard for his own safety had contributed to the bridge-building accident that took his father's life only a year ago. Luke hadn't sought out his grandfather earlier because it would have been a betrayal of his father's wishes.

Maybe if his father had lived, Luke wouldn't have been curious enough about the grandfather he'd never met to answer the man's summons. And it had been a summons, not an invitation, Luke realized.

He'd said no in seven different languages at least a hundred times, but his grandfather was still determined to make him into a company head. When would Rupert believe he wasn't there for a job and didn't need an inheritance? Maybe when Luke figured out why he'd come to visit a man who sent inappropriate Christmas and birthday gifts to a grandson he didn't even know.

All he'd promised was to stick around for six weeks. He didn't know what the devil Rupert expected to accomplish by throwing this pretty secretary at him. Did the old man really think her perky breasts and ripe pink lips would make him forget Africa? His grandfather wasn't the first big chief to sacrifice a virgin to get his way, but Luke could guarantee it wouldn't work.

Now *there* was an intriguing question: Was she a virgin? Certainly she seemed innocent enough in her short but prim business suit. She was a looker, all right, with hazel-green eyes, creamy skin and sable hair pulled back except for the strands that framed her gorgeous face. Her full lower lip had the soft, swollen look of a woman who's been well kissed, but she hadn't dared look him over in the pool the way an experienced woman would. His guess was she was a sensual woman who didn't know what she wanted—yet.

"I want you to be my grandson's tutor, Jane," Rupert said, finally getting to the point.

"His *what?* Mr. Cox, I don't understand! What can I possibly teach your grandson?"

Luke had to bite his tongue to keep from making a few suggestions that would nullify his grandfather's efforts and let Jane off the hook. His grandfather could certainly be persuasive, but how much of his warmth and charm was genuine? And how serious was his heart condition? Another reason Luke had agreed to come was that he thought it might be his only chance to get to know the man who had so bitterly opposed his parents' marriage. His father had taught him a lot about the world, but not much about himself or the past. Now Rupert was coercing an incredibly beautiful girl into a job she obviously didn't want. Luke just shook his head, wondering if coming at all had been a mistake.

"It's very simple, Jane. Before I hand over the

reins of the company to Luke, he needs to learn how we do things in America. In short, I want you to civilize my grandson. Even though he was educated in England, he's spent too much time in the bush.'' He looked at Luke. ''No more stunts like prancing around naked in the fountain.''

''Not quite naked,'' Luke said mildly.

''But why me? I'm not an etiquette expert.'' She sounded desperate.

''You handled the situation in the pool beautifully. Sent the young rascal scampering for his clothes. I saw it all through my telescope.''

''You give me too much credit! Please, Mr. Cox, I'm really not qualified to—''

''According to Miss Polk, you're very well qualified. I expect you to move up the ladder here. But of course, I also expect you to take on any assignment that comes your way. There's no room for slackers in this organization.''

The threat was so obvious, her face paled. Luke's first instinct was to leap to her defense, but he decided his opinion wouldn't sway a man as determined as Rupert. Luke hadn't been able to convince him he had no interest in running a company that made golf clubs and other toys for adults. He was an engineer and a bridge builder, and damned if he'd get calluses on his butt from sitting in an office all day.

Rupert couldn't change his mind, but the older man was trying hard. He'd even managed, in a weak moment when Luke was still concerned about his grandfather's health, to extract the promise that Luke would take over the company *if* he decided to stay in the country.

No way was that going to happen, not even if Rupert threw a dozen sexy secretaries his way.

"Now, do we understand each other, Jane?"

"Yes, sir."

For a minute Luke thought she'd tell his grandfather where he could put the assignment. She didn't, but who was he to pass judgment? Maybe she really needed the job.

"Splendid, splendid."

Rupert sucked in his gut again and slicked back his full mane of silver hair, reminding Luke of an aging wolf who was still fighting to lead the pack. The man was too accustomed to riding roughshod over people and getting his own way. Old resentments surfaced, but so did regrets. Luke knew he was going to enjoy besting the wily corporation head, but part of him wanted to know more about his long-lost relative, his mother's only living parent.

"Think of *Pygmalion*. You do know that play, don't you, Jane?" Rupert asked.

"The flower girl who was made into a lady by—"

"Yes, yes, that's it," Rupert said. "All you need to do is polish Luke's rough edges, show him how we do things here. You have thirty days, then I have some plans for him. I'll have Miss Polk arrange for you to use my vacation home in Sedona. You'll have an unlimited expense account to spruce him up—buy some decent clothes, among other things."

"You expect me to—"

"Stay in Sedona. No distractions there. This is no forty-hour-a-week assignment, but you'll be extremely well rewarded. You can expect a sizable bonus based on how well you do."

"It's not the money. It's, it's—"

"It's settled. Miss Polk will make the arrangements and answer any questions you may have."

"I'm still going home in six weeks," Luke said under his breath as his grandfather ushered Jane out of his office. It would take more than sacrificing a virgin to put him behind Rupert's desk.

2

"TELL ME MORE about this Greek god," Kim insisted, adding her own red tank top to the pile waiting to go into her sister's suitcase.

"He's a wild man! I'd rather try to tame a gorilla."

"He sounds fascinating."

"You know I never wear red," Jane said, noticing the bright garment and seizing on it to change the subject.

"You should. It makes you come alive."

"The last time I checked, I was definitely breathing." She usually wasn't sarcastic, but Kim was treating the whole thing as a lark. It wasn't *her* job hanging by a thread.

"Are you afraid of him?"

Leave it to her sister not to pull any punches.

"No, not afraid, but he's so…so—"

"Masculine? Macho? Untamed?" Kim put the red top into the suitcase along with her own yellow bikini. Jane was too agitated to protest.

"Smug. That's it—smug. You should see his smirk."

"I'd love to. I'll go with you and help."

"There's an idea." Jane considered it, but she'd been a substitute mother too long to let her sister walk into trouble with her. "Unfortunately, you have classes starting pretty soon and a new job at the Steak House.''

"My loss! How long do you expect to be gone?"

"I have thirty days to do the job."

"You'll be staying alone with Jungle Boy for a whole month?"

"No! No, no, no! Miss Polk guaranteed we wouldn't be the only ones there. A couple live there and take care of the place, and company execs are scheduled to come in two- and three-day shifts to teach him the business. I'll just be his..."

"Nanny?"

Jane laughed for the first time since Rupert Cox had dropped the bombshell on her.

"That's as good a title as any. I have to ride herd on a man who showers in public fountains."

"Wish I'd seen that."

"Well, I wish I hadn't. Then I wouldn't be in this mess."

Also, she wouldn't be speculating how he kept the little pouch from falling off. Maybe it was some trick he'd learned in Africa.

"Maybe you can finish in less time," Kim suggested optimistically. "Although I don't think I'd want to. What's so terrible about staying in Mr. Cox's fancy Sedona hideaway?"

"Being blackmailed into it."

She couldn't sacrifice her career to get out of the assignment. It was that simple. And complicated. Her chances of getting another job as good as the one she had were nil if Cox fired her. And she'd promised her mother, in her heart, that she'd take care of Kim. That meant helping with tuition as well as paying the rent, and her salary and benefits at the Cox Corporation were excellent for someone with only a two-year associate's degree in business.

"Look at it as an opportunity to meet new people—male people especially. Chances are there'll be a whole parade of neat guys coming to the house," Kim said.

Kim's curly-haired, dimpled cuteness was a magnet to the opposite sex, and she was always urging her big sister to be more aggressive, to go after men who attracted her, and to date more to get into circulation.

"Button-down business types, the same ones I see every day at work."

Even talking to her sister, Jane couldn't stop thinking about bronzed skin glowing in the morning sun and muscles rippling under golden spray. She knew why her dating life was so abysmal. She'd always been intrigued by adventurous, bigger-than-life men who intimidated her so much she shied away. She wasn't the kind of woman who rode on the back of a motorcycle or hung around dives to attract rodeo riders, but pale-skinned business types bored her.

"I can understand why you're a charter member of the born-again virgins," Kim teased. "The only man you ever slept with was Bryan, and he was more interested in himself than he was in you."

Jane tossed Mr. Hopper, her shabby stuffed kangaroo, at her sister and missed. Kim sure had her number: The small group of friends she hung with did spend a lot of time griping about their practically nonexistent sex lives and wondering if they'd ever sleep with a real he-man—or even have a decent first date.

Being single was complicated enough without putting her personal life on hold to civilize a drop-dead gorgeous wild man.

"Anyway, no one can blame you if the guy is totally incorrigible."

"Failure is not an option," she said, quoting Miss Polk who frequently repeated Cox's favorite trite maxim.

"What have you got to lose?" Kim asked.

"My job," Jane said dryly.

"Let me get this straight. You're off to spend a month tutoring a virile hunk who oozes sexuality from every pore. He has a body worth giving up chocolate for and a dreamy face, but you don't want to go because he's too self-confident."

"Smug and cocky."

"Because he plays by his own rules, not anyone else's?"

"He thinks he can do whatever he wants regardless of how other people feel about it."

"Are you sure you're not just scared silly of having a close encounter of the romantic kind?"

"Don't you think about anything but men?" Jane asked.

She knew her question was unfair. Kim worked hard and got excellent grades. But Jane wasn't in the mood to be analyzed by her cheeky little sister. And she wasn't reassured by Kim's sly smile.

THE SLEEK RED leased Ferrari was a bit of all right, making Luke smile to himself as he negotiated the switchback roads to Sedona with the skilled touch of a professional race driver. In fact, he'd driven in a few races but didn't like the lifestyle of a pro: constantly traveling and staying in crowded, constraining cities. He belonged in Africa, doing what his father had done. No doubt his grandfather had learned about his love for fast cars by having him investigated. It was one more lure to bring him into his grandfather's business.

"It won't work, Rupert," he said aloud, wishing he hadn't felt compelled to come to Arizona to meet his only relative. True, he felt a wary fascination, wondering how much of his own character came from his maternal grandfather, but it was much too late to form any kind of bond.

The elder man had promised, as a condition of Luke prolonging his visit, not to interfere if he decided to leave in six weeks. He was going back to Africa to do what he loved best, and a company of mercenaries wouldn't be able to drag him back into his grandfather's net.

"Sly old devil," he said with a trace of affection.

Not only had he found his grandfather looking robust in spite of his heart problem, but Luke seriously doubted the man would ever willingly give up the power of his position as CEO. He might make his grandson a figurehead, but he'd still be there, pulling strings. It didn't matter. Luke had his life mapped out, and it didn't include Rupert's company.

Jane was a wrinkle he hadn't expected, though. Was she in on the plan or had Rupert decided to use her on the spur of the moment? Him and his bloody spyglass!

He wouldn't put it past the old reprobate to find the sexiest woman around and disguise her as a prim-and-proper career girl. Who better to get inside his head and report back to Rupert?

No, she was probably just what she seemed: an

employee roped into teaching him some manners—
American-style manners, that is. She hadn't been acting when she ordered him out of the fountain. He'd
shocked the pants off her—or rather, he wished he
had. He wouldn't mind cavorting on the front lawn
or anywhere else with her. She was the genuine article, all right, and too gorgeous for her own good—
or his.

He was still disappointed that she'd insisted on
driving her own car instead of riding to Sedona with
him. Looks aside, he wanted to pump her about his
grandfather, and it sounded as though there would be
lots of watching eyes and curious ears when he got
to the house.

He expected plush digs, but the red rocks of Sedona were so spectacular under the hot August sun,
he wouldn't mind camping out with his bedroll. The
landscape was a deep orange-red like burning coals,
but the town itself was plagued with tourists who
didn't have enough sense to take a siesta on such a
hot afternoon.

Just off Highway 89-A, he approached his grandfather's hideaway. The house had adobe walls and
heavy Spanish tiles on the roof, but it also had a
security gate with a uniformed guard on duty.

"Is Miss Grant here yet?" Luke asked, stopping
even though the guard had motioned him ahead as
soon as he recognized the car.

"Yes, sir. She got here a couple of hours ago driving a white compact—"

"Much obliged," Luke said, not needing a full
report.

She was expecting a wild man. He decided not to
disappoint her. It wasn't going to be easy, treating

her like a primary-school teacher, especially since he'd spent his early years being tutored in construction camps, but the last thing he needed was to get involved.

"Bloody hell," he said, knowing how complicated his stay would be if he let himself do any of the things he could so easily imagine doing with Miss Jane Grant. A man could make some silly decisions with those long, shapely legs wrapped around him. It was much safer to make sure she wouldn't want anything to do with him.

Leaving the car in the circular driveway, he quietly eased the door shut, leaving his socks and shoes in the boot along with his shirt, wallet and watch. He used the magnetized holder to hide the keys under the fender. He debated whether to strip off his walking shorts, but settled for pushing them low on his hips.

He'd asked Polk enough questions about the place to know the lay of the land. Nice old girl, Polk, he thought, idly wondering whether her loyalty to Granddad went beyond the office. Rupert must have some hold on her, the way she scampered around, knocking herself out for the old man's every whim. Of course, there was no understanding females. If he'd read Jane's eyes right, she wanted to tell Rupert to go soak his head in his own pool.

But she was here, ordered to undo the habits of years spent in road-building camps, running with native kids and generally raising hell when his father was too busy to pay attention, which had been most of the time.

"Good luck, honey." He grinned, thoroughly enjoying himself for the first time since coming to the States.

He made his way barefoot to the rear of the sprawling adobe house, pleased to see that Rupert had landscaped the place with rocks and cacti instead of trying to transform the desert into a phony version of Versailles. The environmentalists in Phoenix were probably ready to lynch him for his water-wasting fountain.

He found Jane doing exactly what any wage slave chained to a desk most of the time would do when suddenly thrown into the lap of luxury: idling by the pool.

Even at four o'clock, the sun was blistering hot, and she had sense enough to stretch out on a lounger shaded by a big umbrella. He stopped, still concealed by the corner of the house, and decided his memory hadn't played tricks on him. She was stunning.

Better still, she was alone and sprawled out without artifice: a modern-day Eve in a bright yellow bikini, one knee drawn up and serving as a prop for a magazine she was reading.

He'd recognize her legs anywhere: long, smooth, shapely. He speculated how it would feel to rub sunscreen from her cute little toes to the sleek fullness of her thighs, parted now with only a narrow bit of cloth between them that sparked his imagination like a torch set to dry kindling. Which was why he needed to make sure she'd never let him, even if it meant scaring her a little with his wild ways.

His luck couldn't be better. She looked heavy-lidded and languid, only moments from falling asleep. What he really wanted to do was wait until the magazine fell, a sign she'd lapsed into dreams, and wake her with a kiss.

Bad idea! Too personal. He didn't want her to scurry back to Phoenix. The next tutor his grandfather sent might not be so much to his liking.

He let out a fiendish howl.

It was a war whoop owing more to Native Americans than Zulu warriors, but it definitely got her attention.

She shrieked.

He ran toward her, but veered off at the last second, plunging feetfirst into the pool.

He swam, slicing through the tepid water with powerful strokes, performing for her but immensely enjoying every lap for the release it gave him. Rupert had maneuvered him into a six-week stay, hoping to entice him into making it permanent. The best way to get through his "etiquette" lessons was to treat them as a game, he decided, feeling less constrained than he had in Phoenix.

After ten fast laps, he looked over to the concrete apron of the pool and saw what he'd hoped to see: slender ankles and shapely calves.

"You're not funny!" she said, bending forward so her words carried to him loud and clear. "You startled me, but it was a trick a ten-year-old would pull. If you think I'm going to run back to Phoenix because of your silly stunts, you're in for a surprise, Mr. Stanton-Azrat."

He was impressed. She remembered the name he'd made up to seem more alien to his grandfather. He wondered if she'd noticed any similarity between his so-called tribal name and a rodent's behind.

Swimming over to tread water near her feet, he looked up and grinned guilelessly.

"Sorry I acted like a crazed wildebeest scenting water. I just had to go for it."

"Do wildebeest shriek like a bad movie version of Geronimo?"

She was sharp, this one, but he had a few more tricks up his pant leg.

"Join me," he invited.

"No, thanks."

"Our whole relationship is water-based."

"We don't have a relationship. I'm your instructor."

"And none too pleased about it," he surmised.

"It's part of my job to do whatever comes along. I like my job, and I need to keep it."

"Point taken."

He watched, timing his move for the exact moment when she turned to walk away.

If she hadn't been so mad at him for scaring her, she might have seen it coming. His arms rose out of the water, circled her hips and brought her plunging backward into the water.

She came up sputtering in his arms, pounding her fists on his shoulders, angry enough to spit nails.

"You have no right to do that!"

"Sorry, love. I felt sorry for you, standing there in the hot sun, when you could be cooling off in the pool."

"Don't call me that! I'm Miss Grant to you."

"If that's what you want me to call you, Janie, I'll give it a shot. Miss Grant—"

She splashed hard, sending a wave of water breaking over his head before remembering he was a modern-day Poseidon. Niagara Falls could come rushing down on his head, and he wouldn't care.

"Don't start what you can't finish, Janie."

He dived, and she tried to climb out of the pool, managing to get her arms and one knee over the edge before he struck.

She expected to be pulled back and ducked. Instead, he pulled himself up beside her, pinned her hips down with his arm, lifted her leg beside the other, and kissed the back of her knee. Not once or twice, but repeatedly. She squirmed and squealed until she realized that was exactly what he wanted. He didn't stop until she stopped struggling.

"My favorite flavor—coconut oil." He rose effortlessly and offered her his hand.

There was no graceful way to get from her stomach to her feet. She ignored his hand and scampered to her hands and knees, outraged when he put his arm around her waist and lifted her to a standing position.

"Don't ever do that again!"

"Help you up?"

"Half drown me! Fondle me!"

"I suppose I should've asked if you can swim, but I don't understand the fondling part."

"Oh, yes you do! You—"

"Just being playful, love. No offense intended."

"Don't let it happen again. And don't call me love!"

Luke watched her stalk to the house and disappear through the sliding glass door that opened onto the pool area. What the devil was he going to do with her for a month?

"Seduce her, you idiot," he said aloud, even as his inner voice vehemently warned against it.

Not that he wasn't prepared to. When he went back to working with a construction crew in Africa, the opportunity for fooling around would be rarer than unicorn horns. He had promised himself to have some fun on this jaunt his grandfather had suckered him into making. But Jane was a nice girl—pretty but no party girl. He didn't want any emotional ties to confuse him into staying a day longer than he'd promised himself. And he didn't want to leave any broken hearts behind, a problem that had caused him some complications during his brief stint as a race car driver.

He should just ignore her, but there wasn't much chance of that if she made more appearances in that yellow bikini. He was going to lose some sleep, remembering the way the narrow strips of cloth clung wetly to her spectacular breasts and cute bottom. Plus, it was her duty to civilize him, whatever she thought that meant.

There was only one way to play it safe—to play the part of Tarzan.

3

HER NAVY DRESS was missing! Jane searched the clothes the housekeeper had hung in the closet, but it was obvious Kim had slipped it out of the garment bag when she wasn't looking.

Jane loved that dress, even if her sister did call it the date dampener. Now, when she really needed something high-necked, loose-fitting and long, she was staring at Kim's white halter dress, a shorter, skimpier version of a movie-star classic.

"That little sneak," Jane muttered, but it wasn't her sister's wardrobe games that had her two seconds away from bolting.

How on earth could she have any influence on a man so rambunctious and uninhibited and sexy and—

Her cheeks got hot just thinking of lying on the hard wet concrete while a man she barely knew had kissed the backs of her knees.

He was a wild man! And for the next month he was *her* wild man unless she wanted to hit the unemployment line—not exactly an attractive option.

She fumed at the unfairness of being drafted as keeper to her boss's renegade relative. How was she going to get through this?

"By not playing Luke Stanton-Azrat's game," she

told herself with quiet determination, yanking a pair
of beige linen slacks from a hanger.

At least Kim had let her bring a bulky white cotton
cardigan for cool nights. Buttoned to the neck over
a tank top, it would send a message as well as the
navy dress—or even better since it would be obvious
she was only wearing it on such a hot night to dis-
courage his even hotter intentions.

LUKE WANDERED through the downstairs rooms, admiring the house a little more than he wanted to admit. He liked the rough plastered wall tinted the color
of desert sand, the gleaming hardwood floors and the
Navajo rugs in black, red, yellow and turquoise.
There were giant earthenware pots with broad-leaved
plants, black leather couches and chairs, comfortably
indented from long use, and heavy carved wooden
tables with lamps and odd bits that looked like prized
possessions, not some decorator's arty idea of accessories. The caretaker's wife, Wilma, kept everything
polished like a new sports car, but the place still
managed to look as though a man enjoyed living
here.

He slumped down in an overstuffed chair and let
one bare leg hang over an arm, wondering how much
longer it would be before his own personal Ms. Manners came down the iron spiral stairs. Had he over-
done the wild-man bit? He hadn't meant to scare
her—just put a comfortable amount of space between
them. Who knew a little kiss on the back of her knee
would taste like a tropical drink and have the impact
of a stick of dynamite?

He waited, wondering what he'd do if she didn't

show. His first impulse was to carry a dinner tray to her room and apologize.

Nope, too civilized. Better to figure out a way to induce her to come down.

He came up blank, but it didn't matter. The soft click of heels carried down to him. Jane slowly descended the open stairway, hanging on to the railing and keeping her eyes on the steps.

For several heart-stopping moments his eyes followed her progress, taking in the grace of her movements and the way her dark sable hair framed her face. As for her sensational legs, he could only remember them as he'd seen them at the pool. She'd wrapped herself up like a mummy, swathed in bulky clothes from neck to ankles.

"Aren't you going to be too warm in that sweater?" He rose slowly and stood by the chair, wondering how close she'd dare get to him.

"Not at all." Her airy tone didn't fool him. "It'll get cool after the sun goes down."

"That won't be for several hours. You must be planning to linger a long time over dinner." He did enjoy baiting her, not that he thought it was especially laudable.

"Hardly." Her tone brought the temperature down a few degrees. "Is that your idea of dressing for dinner?"

"This is the only coat I brought. Sorry about the wrinkles." He pretended to examine the many creases in his white linen jacket.

"I meant the trousers you're *not* wearing. Do you always wear those...things?"

She was looking a little pink in the cheeks.

"You don't like 'em?" He hitched his thumbs into

the waistband of the old bush shorts he'd hacked shorter with his Swiss army knife just for this occasion.

"They're inappropriate." She was staring over his left shoulder, feigning indifference.

I don't think so, love, he thought with a trace of genuine amusement.

"I'm wearing a tie." He tried to sound penitent, holding out the tip of the old striped school tie he'd worn as a kid.

"Most men wear one with a shirt," she pointed out.

What am I letting him do to me? she asked herself. She sounded like a critical old maid. Why should she care if he looked like a cartoon wild man? All she had to do was ignore him as much as possible for six weeks—forty-two days. How long was that in hours? Minutes?

"I'm not most men, Jane."

Was that a threat or a warning she heard in his voice? Neither was necessary. She was as wary of him as she would be a tiger that escaped from the zoo. Only in this case, Rupert Cox had made her a very unwilling animal trainer.

"If you two would like to go out to the patio, dinner is all ready," Mrs. Horning said from a doorway on the far side of the room.

"You're a sweetheart, Wilma. I'm so hungry, I could eat half a rhino," Luke said, basking in the approval radiating from the housekeeper.

Jane crossed the caretaker's wife off her very short list of potential allies. Would her husband, Willard, be taken in by Luke's rakish charm, too? Jane had the uncomfortable feeling Luke was playing a game, and she didn't know the rules.

Jane led the way to the recreation room, past the ornate antique billiard table, and through the sliding glass door to the pool area.

"Not this patio, Janie," Luke said, stepping out beside her. "Here, follow me. I had Wilma set the table on the west patio."

"I'd rather you didn't call me that."

"Whatever you like, love. If it's Miss Grant you want, it's Miss Grant you'll get."

"Just plain Jane will be fine."

Even in her sensible inch-and-a-half heels, she was hard-pressed to keep up with his long, lanky strides. And didn't she feel awkward, trailing behind a man who was all legs from the hem of his rumpled jacket to the strap of his sandals! She nearly collided with him when he turned abruptly.

"Plain Jane won't do at all," he said, deliberately twisting her meaning. "Pretty Jane, maybe, or Pouty Jane."

"I'm not pouty!" She automatically covered her lips with two fingers, self-conscious because she did have a habit of pursing her lips when she was thinking hard.

"You're not put out about Rupert making you my guardian?"

She hesitated. "It is unfair. I work hard being at Miss Polk's beck and call. There's no reason for me to be here."

"Me, neither." He grinned and shrugged his shoulders. "We're both dancing to the same tune."

"Not quite. I'm just trying to hang on to my job

until my sister finishes college. You'll take over the company someday.''

"It'll never happen. Come on, let's find our dinner, and you can tell me about the pretty sister you left at home.''

He put an arm around her shoulders and guided her along a path of round, ruddy-colored tiles. She stiffened under his touch, even though her bulky knit sweater made it as impersonal as a handshake.

The sun was still a fiery orb in the sky, affording no letup in the summer heat. Who knew cotton could be so warm?

When they rounded the corner to the west end of the big stucco house, she could see where the plateau dropped off sharply, allowing an unobstructed view of the famous red rocks of Sedona. It seemed more like a movie setting than real life.

The patio itself had just enough space for a small redwood table shaded by a green-and-gray-striped umbrella. Sitting knee-to-knee, four people could share the table, but Jane felt crowded when Luke seated her on a heavy wooden chair with bright flowered cushions and took his place across from her. His knee brushed hers when he slid the chair close to the table, and his mumbled, "Sorry," did nothing to relax her.

Their places were set with an intimidating number of gleaming silver forks and heavy geometric-patterned china dishes in shades of turquoise and orange. The table was covered by a pale beige linen cloth, with the matching napkins monogrammed *R.C.* A slender-lipped bottle was sitting in a silver cooler filled with ice.

"Wine with a cork," Luke mused, picking up a

corkscrew opener and examining the mechanism.
"My guess is, I'm supposed to decant and pour."

If he knew enough to do that, why did he need
etiquette lessons from her? Now, if he'd cracked the
bottle across the table and taken a swig, she could
offer some useful advice—like try not to cut yourself
on the jagged edge.

Instead, she refrained from commenting and put
the elegant linen napkin on her lap, forgetting to
shake it open. Luke stood and tackled the cork, his
narrow tie only partially covering a golden-haired,
deeply tanned chest. In the wardrobe department, she
decided he definitely needed help!

She didn't know where to focus her eyes. Fortunately, Willard pushed through the door at the end
of the house, carrying a silver tray.

"Fresh prawns," he said cheerfully. "My wife
won't tolerate skimpy frozen shrimp."

"Looks first-rate," Luke said, admiring the big
pink prawns served in a crystal dish set in a larger
dish of crushed ice.

"Has to be for Mr. Cox," Willard agreed, resting
his hands on the front of the white apron covering
his rotund, Santa-style belly.

"Very nice, thank you," Jane agreed, a little
miffed because Luke was much more at ease with
servants and fancy dining than she was. What on
earth was she supposed to teach him?

She felt more and more like part of a plot to keep
Rupert's grandson entertained.

Worse, she was hot enough for spontaneous com-
bustion. Her face had to be pinker than the prawns,
and the sweater was sticking to her shoulder blades
like a wet rug. She tried to push up her sleeves in-

conspicuously as Willard was leaving, but Luke was too sharp-eyed.

"Are you sure you don't want to slip out of that sweater, Janie? Looks to me like we're about three hours from a cooldown."

He grabbed a giant prawn with his fingers, dunked it in spicy red sauce and made it disappear, tail and all, in one big bite.

She picked up the delicate silver cocktail fork at the outer end of the lineup of flatware on her left and tapped it lightly on the edge of the ice dish. He ignored her subtle hint, stuffing a second prawn in his mouth and chewing with gusto while she watched, fork suspended, as his lips moved without restraint.

"Try one," he invited, pushing the tail out of his mouth with the tip of his tongue and planting it beside the first in the mound of ice.

"Don't tell me you don't use forks in Africa!"

"Depends on whether I'm feasting on grubs from under a fallen log or dining with a politico who needs softening up to grant the right permits."

She dropped the fork, wondering whether she was going to faint from heat or squeamishness.

"Only pulling your leg, Janie."

He stood quickly, worried he'd gone too far this time. Either she was shocked silly by the thought of eating grubs, which he had tried and found not especially to his liking, or she had heat prostration from bundling up like an Arctic explorer.

"Here, have a drink. You don't look so good."

He stood, picked up her untasted wine and held it against her lips until she downed a few good swallows.

"That's enough!"

No thanks there.

"You're burning up," he said, touching her cheek with the backs of his fingers. "You'd better peel the sweater off before you pass out. It's hotter than I expected when I told Wilma we'd eat outside."

Stepping behind her, he reached down and undid the row of pearly buttons on her cardigan. She wasn't, both to his relief and disappointment, wearing one of those lacy little brassieres with tantalizing peepholes. A tank top was sticking to her like a second skin, damply outlining the lushness of her breasts. She was a sight to give a man an appetite, and not for dinner.

"Don't do that!" she protested when the deed was already done, pushing his hands away and wrapping the sweater around her like protective armor.

"Just trying to help." He moved into her range of vision and held out his hands palms up, trying to show his good intentions. "I thought for a minute you were going to pass out."

"I'm fine—just a little dehydrated. All I need is some water."

Still holding the sweater shut with one hand, she grabbed a water goblet and drank, noisily swallowing until she drained it.

"Seems we have company," he said, catching a glimpse of a little green creature scurrying around the rear legs of his chair.

The lizard was fast, but Luke was faster. He reached down and captured it by the tail, exhibiting his prize on his palm with the delight of a schoolboy tormenting his teacher.

"He's a cute one," he chuckled, holding it closer to her.

Her little shriek was soft but satisfying.

"He won't hurt you. With all this food, we can spare him a little nibble."

He retrieved one of the prawn tails and laid it on the ground along with the lizard, but the beastie scurried away, too terrified to investigate the treat.

"If you think you're going to get rid of me with dumb stunts…"

He sat down, leaving the chair some distance from the table so he could stretch his legs and lean back comfortably.

"Is that what you think I'm trying to do?"

Putting space between them was good; scaring her off wasn't. It occurred to him that if Jane bolted, Rupert might send Miss Polk to take her place, and he didn't think the iron maiden would be nearly as entertaining.

"Either that or you're naturally boorish."

"Ouch, that hurts," he complained. Oddly enough it did. "Will you take off that Arctic survival wear, relax and enjoy a nice dinner if I promise to behave?"

"Depends on what your idea of behaving is."

"I'll begin by apologizing for the bit at the pool."

"That's a start."

He noticed she wasn't discarding the sweater.

"I'll call you Miss Grant and use every fork in the lineup."

"Oh, finish your prawns," she said with an exasperated sigh.

He hid a smile behind his napkin when she slipped her arms out of the sweater and let it bunch up behind her rigid back. Except for an occasional glance at her chest, he got through the rest of the dinner in good form.

Their conversation revealed that they had one thing in common: They were both orphans. Jane talked willingly enough about her sister, but by the time they finished off the meal with fresh raspberries in a swirl of chocolate sauce, he was pretty sure the only layer she'd peeled off was the sweater. Without being obvious, she was keeping him at arm's length, telling him only things she would tell any stranger. There was more to her than he could begin to guess, but it was probably best if he didn't probe for soft spots.

"Now what?" he asked after Wilma carted off the last of the meal, leaving them with snifters of brandy she was ignoring. "Miss Polk was clear that I get my orders from you. What's on the docket for tomorrow?"

"A little shopping trip."

"I don't shop." That was one piece of nonsense he wanted to squelch right away. "Buy whatever you like. While you do, I'm going to do some hiking, take a look around."

"You have to shop."

Half a bottle of wine had certainly stiffened her spine, but the resolution on her face only made her more delectable. Her tank top had dried, but that did nothing to diminish the appeal of her tantalizing breasts.

"I don't think so," he said firmly. "No shopping."

If she knew him better, she'd know it was time to sound the retreat. Or maybe she had more grit than sense.

"You can't wear jungle-boy outfits to all the meetings on your agenda. Miss Polk has you scheduled—"

"Jungle *boy?*"

"You know what I mean."

"Don't make the mistake of thinking you're my nanny," he said with real seriousness.

"I was given an assignment," she said stiffly. "I don't want it, but I can't afford to lose my job. If you're going to thwart me—"

"Not thwart," he said in a mellower voice. "I just don't shop."

"I can't buy clothes for you. You'll have to be measured—consulted."

"You've consulted me. I like to be comfortable—period."

"Please don't do this to me!" She grabbed the brandy snifter with both hands and tipped it to her mouth.

"It's strong," he started to warn her.

He'd suspected she was no drinker, and her sputtering cough confirmed it. He thought of putting her over his shoulder and patting her like a baby, but his saner self won out. He watched while she gulped water, wishing he wasn't so fascinated by the bobbing of her breasts.

"This is the worst night of my life!" she wailed theatrically.

It could get worse, he thought, beginning to wish she'd put the sweater back on.

"Maybe we can make a deal," he offered, against his own better judgment.

"What kind of deal?" Her words were muffled by the napkin she was pressing against her full pink lips.

"I'll go shopping if..."

He tried to think of something so outrageous, she'd be sure to turn him down. It was going to be a long six weeks if he let her lead him around like a puppy on a leash. Rupert's plans be damned! He wanted to go camping in the mountains while he had the chance to see some of America's Southwest. He didn't expect to ever return to the region.

"If what?" She sounded more skeptical than hopeful—with good reason.

"If you tuck me in." He wasn't sure why he came up with that, but he expected it to be enough to scare her off.

"You mean..." She looked as if she'd just swallowed that little lizard and didn't know what to do about it.

"A proper tuck-in. The kind any good nanny does, since you seem to fancy yourself one. Fluff my pillow, check the covers, tell me a bedtime story."

"You're being ridiculous!"

"Oh, I have to warn you. I never wear jammies. Here's my proposition—I'll go to one store for one tuck."

"Only one shop?"

She couldn't seriously be considering his challenge! No woman alive would be content going into just one clothing store.

"I won't budge on that—only one. And the tuck is done when I say it is."

She sat statue-still. He'd expected her to storm off, maybe dash the last bit of brandy in his face. She was making him edgy—and it took a lot to put him off balance.

"Done."

"You agree to my offer?" He'd misread her and didn't much like it.

"Yes."

"And I'll only go to one shop—one."

"Yes, I understand the concept of one. What time will you be retiring, Master Luke?"

"Let's see." Every instinct he had told him to back down, cancel this nonsense before he outfoxed himself. "I'd like to finish unpacking my gear, check out the news on the telly, get undressed—you wouldn't count that as part of the tuck and help me, would you?"

"It's not part of the tuck. Tell me a time." Her tone was cold enough to give a man frostbite.

"Eleven will do nicely," he said.

She glided away without another word while he sat twirling his brandy snifter and wishing he'd gone straight to Swaziland after his last job instead of satisfying his curiosity about his grandfather. Building a few railroad bridges seemed like a cinch compared to outguessing a woman. Of course, there was always the hope she might change her mind.

Yes, that was probably her strategy: get him all lathered up, then pull a no-show.

He sat brooding for a long time, not enchanted by sunset on the red rocks of Sedona and definitely not looking forward to eleven o'clock. Why had he made such a ridiculous offer?

"You expected her to turn it down, that's why," he muttered, idly wondering what she'd wear to tuck him in.

The more he thought about it, the more likely it seemed she wouldn't come, so he relaxed.

A little.

4

HE WAS TRYING to get rid of her.

It was the only possible explanation.

Jane paced the small balcony outside her bedroom window, turning every seven steps when she ran out of space. She felt like some poor squirrel trapped on one of those diabolical miniature treadmills, expending a great amount of energy without any possibility of making headway.

How could she tuck a grown man into bed? Next he'd want her to give him a bath! It was all part of his scheme to send her scampering for home.

If he didn't like his grandfather's plan to polish his rough edges, why didn't he refuse to stay here? He said he didn't want anything to do with the company, so why go through this charade? Why put *her* through it?

She probably surprised him by agreeing to the tuck-in. Most likely he'd only made the offer because he was sure she would nix it.

"Well, two can play his game," she muttered, walking toward the light spilling through the glass door to the bedroom and checking her wristwatch for the hundredth time.

She wasn't even sure which room was Luke's. Mrs. Horning had pointed it out in an offhand way, but there were at least eight bedrooms including hers on the upper floor of the house. Unfortunately, there weren't other guests yet, and the Hornings had an apartment over the garage. She was all alone with a man who was either a genuine beast or a trickster.

Allowing only two minutes to find the right room, she smoothed her wrinkled slacks and reluctantly slipped back into the heavy sweater, buttoning every button as though her life—make that, her virtue—depended on it.

Finding his room turned out to be easy. She'd forgotten the carpeting in the upstairs hallway. Guests could move silently from room to room, but not without leaving footprints in the thick pearly-white plush, newly vacuumed by the housekeeper. His long steps were as easy to follow as tracks in the snow.

She knocked softly, her last hope of reprieve shattered when he immediately called out, "Come in."

After being in her room, elegant with a ruffle-draped four-poster bed and a mirrored dressing table, she was totally surprised by his. It was a shambles.

"Are you trying to get the housekeeper to quit, too?" she asked, taking in the bed stripped to the mattress cover and the haphazard piles of bedding on the floor.

"That mattress is too soft," he complained, impatiently shaking out a king-size yellow sheet and trying to spread it in the area between the foot of the bed and the double door of the closet.

"Why don't you ask for a room with a firmer mattress?"

"I'm settled in here. The floor will do nicely once you get me properly tucked in."

"I can't even get to you. Your stuff's everywhere."

She recognized the battered backpack he'd had in Phoenix, and on top of one of the piles of discarded clothing, was the embarrassingly familiar scrap of what had served as his fountain-dipping attire.

"My laundry," he explained needlessly, pushing aside a heap with his foot.

He was still wearing the hacked-off bush shorts, for which she supposed she should be grateful, but his jacket, tie and sandals were scattered like disaster debris.

She kept her eyes focused on the floor.

"You can start by helping me with this sheet," he said irritably. "It's big enough for a circus tent."

"I'm surprised a hardy adventurer like you needs a sheet."

"Synthetic carpets aren't fit for humans. I'd rather sleep on sand." He scrubbed his knuckles over his rib cage, letting her know the prospect of sleeping on the luxurious plush was enough to make him itch.

"You might try folding the sheet in half," she suggested dryly.

"Take an end," he ordered, flipping the sheet in her direction.

She did, but only because she hoped a little house-keeping help would count as tucking in.

"You're a great little sheet tamer," he said as she spread it with almost no help from him.

He grabbed several thick pillows from a mound on the floor and threw them on his makeshift bed.

"I'll just slip out of these—" he turned his back and unsnapped the top of his shorts "—and you can do the tucking with the other sheet."

"No! Don't you dare!"

"You agreed to—"

"No way."

"Our deal's off, then?"

She bit her lower lip, torn between exasperation and amusement. His performance as an uninhibited wild man was convincing, but she strongly suspected he was doing it to make her back down. What he didn't realize was that she'd been Kim's surrogate mother through her sister's difficult teen years. She could be stubborn when she thought she was right. More than her job was involved now. Darned if she'd let Luke Stanton-Azrat bully or embarrass her into quitting.

"Lie down," she said in what she hoped was a stern, no-nonsense voice.

"Yes, ma'am."

His expression was bland as he hit the floor with one graceful flop and stretched out on his back, cushioning his head on the mound of pillows.

"This is your tuck," she said, making the top sheet from the bed billow over him before it floated down to cover him from head to feet.

"It's not a shroud, love," he said as his head emerged from under it.

"You've been tucked in. Good night."

"Not so fast, Miss Grant. You're not done yet."

He wiggled around under the cloth, then tossed aside his shorts and a scrap of black she tried to avoid seeing.

"Now fold the edges of my sheet like a good nanny. You wouldn't want my toes poking out and getting cold, would you?"

"You're carrying this too far."

"How long will the shopping take?"

"Oh, all right, but freeze—don't move a muscle."

She dropped to her knees and started folding the two sheets together along the edges, making a neat rectangle of his makeshift bed. In spite of her admonition, he stirred enough to make her uncomfortably aware of the contours of his body under the thin covering.

"There," she said when she'd finished, feeling out of breath even though she hadn't exerted herself.

"Nicely done. Now for my story."

"Oh no, I've had enough. I'm done."

His expression was somber, but she was sure he was laughing at her behind those deep blue, unreadable eyes.

"Not till I've had a bedtime story. It isn't a proper tuck-in without one."

"All right, I'll tell you a story," she said through gritted teeth. "Once upon a time there was a prince—"

"A handsome prince?"

"He thought he was hot stuff, but he was really just self-centered and spoiled."

"Self-centered, eh? That sounds harsh."

"I'm telling the story. You're supposed to listen."

"Yes, ma'am."

"The prince thought it was great fun to play tricks on people, especially people who didn't dare fight back."

"He sounds despicable."

She wanted to give him a withering look, but meeting his gaze was too unsettling.

"One day his father, the king—"

"Not his grandfather?"

"This is a fairy tale, not a biography," she said impatiently, boosting herself up to sit on the edge of the bed and put more distance between them. "One day the king got a new slave girl—"

"A smashing beauty?"

"If you like. The prince did some trivial thing to ingratiate himself with the king, so the king gave him the slave girl on one condition."

"Always a condition in these tales," he complained.

"The prince had to be kind to her always."

"That shouldn't have been too hard."

"It wouldn't be for most people, but the prince liked to have everything his own way."

"Something bad is going to happen to this prince, isn't it?" He was grinning now.

"The prince thought he could get away with anything, so he made the slave girl—"

"Do all kinds of nasty things?"

"Stop interrupting! He made her work from dawn to dark with hardly any food, and the king found out."

"The prince is in for it now."

"So the king decided to make the slave girl into a princess and the prince into her slave. That's the end of the story."

"There's no happy ending?"

"For her there was."

"No, not unless she won the heart of the prince."

"It's my story, and the princess sent her new slave to row boats or work in the mines or something."

"What a hard-hearted woman."

"Now you're tucked in. I've kept my part of the deal."

"Have you now?"

He sat up, the sheet falling alarmingly low on his

torso. She started sliding along the edge of the bed to leave without stepping on his sheets, but he caught her foot and pulled off her shoe.

"Luke, don't be silly. Give me my shoe."

"The end of your story needs something—a romantic touch."

"Let go of my foot!"

He ignored her protest and bent his head over her toes, softly pressing his lips against the top of her foot before he slid her shoe back on.

She bolted into the hall, slamming his door behind her.

Her door was the kind that locked by pushing in the handle on the inside, but there was no way to confirm that the mechanism worked. She locked and unlocked the door three times before deciding the flimsy hardware was no defense against Luke if he really wanted to come in. She was being silly. He liked to tease, but he wasn't a threat—to anything but her peace of mind.

Underneath the firmly stretched nylon of her stocking, her foot tingled.

Tomorrow she was going home.

"I'M GOING HOME," Jane said the next morning, passing up the breakfast buffet, but latching on to a cup of coffee as though it were a lifeline.

"Bad idea, love. You've nothing to gain and everything to lose by retreating," Luke said, looking up from his heavily laden plate.

"I'll regain my self-respect," she said, pretending to sip the scalding hot coffee so she wouldn't have to meet his gaze.

"You haven't lost it. I'm the one who's behaved like an ass."

He hadn't intended to apologize. For some odd reason, she seemed to bring out his finer sensibilities.

"Staying is pointless. It's nothing but a big game to you," she insisted.

"Not entirely." He didn't know where to begin or how to explain his curiosity about his grandfather when he didn't understand it himself. "Tell you what. We'll go shopping and—"

"In one store," she dryly reminded him.

"That should be enough," he said blandly. "If I'm not a lamb the whole trip, I'll help you pack."

"You won't dress like the king of the jungle or swing from any chandeliers?"

He deserved her skepticism, but it smarted a bit.

"I promise to be a model shopper. I'm in your hands."

"I have a list of things you're supposed to buy."

"Courtesy of the redoubtable Miss Polk?"

"She's very efficient."

Jane's defense of her boss was pretty lukewarm, Luke decided, but loyalty was an admirable trait, whatever form it took. He found the thought of Janie sticking up for him oddly pleasing—and highly unlikely.

"Where are we going?" he asked, hoping it involved a nice long drive back to Phoenix with Jane beside him.

"There's a very nice shopping center here in Sedona, the Plaza de la Sol. Mr. Cox gets most of his suits made by a tailor there."

"And Miss Polk thinks he'll suit me properly?"

"I've seen your schedule. You need some real

clothes. And Miss Polk is adamant that you get a haircut soon. Next week, for instance, the lieutenant governor will be here and—"

"I capitulate. I'm yours to costume for whatever charade my grandfather has planned."

"Will you actually wear the new clothes after we pick them out?"

"You're too pretty to be so cynical, love."

"Stop calling me love! Will you wear them?"

"I will wear whatever you—personally—lay out for me."

She made a little snorting noise. Apparently his cooperative attitude didn't totally ring true with her.

"We leave in twenty minutes. It's nine thirty-two," she said, apparently expecting him to synchronize watches. "I'll drive."

Now, that was cruel, he thought. One of the places he really liked to be in control was behind the wheel of a vehicle.

"No need for you to use your car," he said cheerfully. "Granddad loaned me some great wheels."

She gave him a withering look. "Be outside in nineteen minutes."

CONTROLLING THE BEAST in Luke Stanton-Azrat was draining. The fifteen-minute drive felt like a half day's trek over uncharted territory. Her little compact was crowded with Luke scrunched into the passenger seat, and his arm brushed hers every time she had to make a turn. She had to wonder if it was accidental.

Miss Polk's directions were, of course, perfect. Jane not only found the Plaza de la Sol without any trouble, but she had a good idea where to find Javiar's, the exclusive menswear establishment, where the senior partner was waiting for them.

Jane regretted having to rush past all the wonderful shops, among them galleries featuring Southwestern art and Native American crafts, jewelry stores with displays of silver, turquoise, onyx and other gemstones, the Christmas shop, a toy shop catering to the child in everyone, and a fragrant-candle boutique.

But she was eager to hurry through the shady tiled plaza graced by a small fountain with water tinkling through an upraised pitcher held by a concrete cupid. It wasn't hard to imagine Luke stopping to cool his feet in the coin-littered pool surrounding it.

Determined as she was to get him to the tailor's without incident, she couldn't resist stopping at a glassblower's stall. The man was making a whimsical little creature, blowing through a pipe and twisting nimbly to form a fragile swan.

"Isn't that beautiful!" she exclaimed, almost forgetting Luke for a moment. "I wish I could make something like that."

"I'll get it for you," Luke offered.

"No. Thank you, anyway. I just like to watch glassblowers. When I was little, I wanted to work in a museum—be surrounded by beautiful things. Not a very practical career goal."

"Miss Polk definitely wouldn't approve."

"No, she probably wouldn't. Look, there's Javiar's." It was located on the balcony level, sandwiched between a leather goods shop and a store that seemed to sell nothing but beads. She was eager to end their conversation and get this ordeal over with.

"Mr. Cox's assistant made an appointment for

us," she said when they joined a reedy young man in a charcoal suit.

"Of course, Miss Grant," he said before she could mention her name. "And Mr. Stanton."

"Stanton-Azrat," Luke said, giving his extra name an odd little inflection that roused Jane's suspicions again.

The proprietor, Mr. Javiar himself, bustled out to greet them. Small and impeccably dressed in a greenish-gray silk-blend suit, he gave the impression he was used to catering to royalty. Luke was definitely going to get the crown-prince treatment.

Three early-bird tourists, forty-plus women overdressed for Arizona but probably at home in East Coast designer showrooms, were pretending to examine hand-loomed neckties while they watched Luke saunter to a small cubicle. He was followed by Mr. Javiar, wielding a cloth tape measure, and his assistant, who carried a clipboard to write down measurements.

Jane hung back, pretending to check out some silk shirts under glass.

"There's one I definitely would like," the plumpest of the tourists said with a dignified giggle.

Jane knew darn well they weren't talking about ties.

The dressing room was too crowded to properly shut the curtain. Jane groaned inwardly when she caught a glimpse of Luke's torso, bare to the navel with a jade amulet in the shape of an arrowhead hanging on a leather cord between his spectacular pecs. One of the tourists was openly staring, slack-jawed in admiration.

"Waist thirty-three and a quarter," Mr. Javiar said

crisply. "Now elevate your left arm, please, Mr. Stanton-Azrat." He made the name sound dignified.

The tape flicked around Luke's hips as though it had a life of its own, and Jane annoyed herself by wondering how much room they allowed for expansion in that particular area. She took a deep breath and decided that, for once, Kim was right. She did need to work on her social life. What she needed was a sweet, sane, reliable man to ward off fantasies about wild ones.

Covering her mouth to conceal a yawn as she imagined dating some nice junior executive, Jane was startled by a female shriek, and horrified when Luke raced past her, a half-sewn shirt clinging to his shoulders like sails on a ship.

He'd bolted!

Okay, he didn't want new clothes, but this was ridiculous. Javiar scurried after him, muttering about expensive silk. His assistant trailed, whipping the tape measure around his hand as though trying to tame it.

Jane stepped out on the balcony just in time to see Luke grab a vine from a plant clinging decoratively to the wrought-iron railing and leap off into space.

"Oh no!"

She raced over to look, expecting to see him lying in a crumpled heap on the red tiles below.

Instead, he was tackling a wiry bald man in a red shirt, and grabbing something from him.

"He got my purse back," one of the tourists cried out, nearly toppling over the railing herself in her excitement.

Jane grabbed the back of her chartreuse-and-black

flowered tunic until the tourist steadied herself, but the woman was too excited to notice.

"Marvelle, he got it back!" She was bouncing with enthusiasm.

Luke hauled the purse snatcher to his feet as the plaza's security guards rushed over to take charge of what turned out to be a shaved-head juvenile, as muscular as Luke but definitely not in his league.

From then on, it was all Luke's show. He was becomingly modest, but still able to milk maximum admiration from the eastern tourists and a crowd of admirers that included the pale-faced tailor's assistant. Mr. Javiar retrieved the shirt remnants, but was hard-pressed to keep a stiff upper lip as his shop began to resemble backstage after a rock concert.

Jane was torn between admiring Luke's heroics and wishing the earth would swallow her up. Against her better judgment, she was impressed by his deed but appalled by the hopelessness of trying to change him to his grandfather's—and Miss Polk's—specifications. He was a man who molded *himself,* and had a great deal of fun in the process.

A security guard took statements. The female tourists fawned over their hero. Half the people in the plaza seemed to be crowded into the shop, all of them babbling with excitement. Luke finally put on his shirt, neglecting to button it.

Jane wanted to congratulate him, but the urge to strangle him was stronger. For a couple of minutes, she thought the brittle-but-well-preserved victim would persuade Luke to accept a reward: lunch, at least.

Jane cornered Mr. Javiar, sympathetic when she

saw his crisp white shirt had wilted, making his neck look scrawny and his chest concave.

"I never expected anything like this," he said in a haughty voice that made her wonder why people who cater to the rich tend to be more pompous than their clients.

"Do you have all the measurements you need?" she asked.

"Yes, but we didn't begin to look at fabrics...." He had a stricken look.

"This is what Mr. Cox wants." She handed him the computer-generated list she'd kept hidden from Luke, hoping to order what Miss Polk called a suitable wardrobe without taking all the choices from him.

"This is—" he finished lip-reading the list "—overwhelming. We need to go over styles, coordinate the accessories, consult on—"

"No, we don't. Mr. Stanton—" she couldn't bring herself to say Azrat without cracking up "—Mr. Stanton needs everything on this list ASAP. If you can't tailor everything yourself to his specifications, we'll settle for off-the-rack. I trust your judgment."

"But, Miss—"

"How long will it take?"

"Six suits, three jackets, formal wear..." He was tallying the list, consternation turning to a highly refined glee. "Say four weeks."

"Four days."

"That's impossible! Even if I employ temporary help—"

"Charge it all to Mr. Rupert's account. He'll be very pleased if his grandson makes a good impression at some very important meetings."

"Four days." His thin lips curled around his words, and he whipped out a gleaming white handkerchief, probably never before used for anything as mundane as wiping away sweat, and dabbed his high forehead. "I'll have to take shortcuts. Mr. Cox never wears anything off a rack. And there will have to be fittings. That's essential for the Javiar look."

"Use a model the same size. His grandson isn't particular." That was the biggest understatement of her life. "Oh, and there's one change. Add Jockey shorts to the list. Two dozen pairs, nice thick hundred percent cotton."

What had she become? She took a downright malicious pleasure in making sure Luke would have practical new underwear—forget those silky black things. She wished she could!

"Sorry the shopping trip was such a fiasco, Janie," Luke said when he had finally torn himself away from the admiring throng. "Tell you what, we'll try again tomorrow."

"No need."

"You're not going home because of the purse snatcher?"

She'd forgotten all about leaving, but she wasn't sure why. Maybe it was the headiness of authority, making such a big—make that, expensive—decision on her own. Miss Polk expected her to guide and suggest. She'd cut to the chase and done the job with precious little help from Luke, other than providing a body for the tailor's measuring tape.

"No, I finalized all the details, that's all," she said, deciding to mention his newly ordered wardrobe later.

"Can I buy you lunch?" He sounded almost penitent.

"Mrs. Horning is expecting us. She's baking scones."

He was quiet all the way to the car. For a moment she thought he was going to open the door for her, then he patted the deep pockets of his khaki shorts, seemingly not finding something.

"Think I forgot something," he said. "Would you mind waiting just a minute?"

"No, but—"

Alone, Jane tried to imagine what he could have left behind.

BACK AT THE MANSION, lunch was so calm and normal, Jane departed the patio table near the pool feeling too sleepy to function.

"I'm going to take a nap," she told Luke.

"Good idea, love."

"Jane," she corrected with little hope of influencing him in any way whatsoever.

Her room was deliciously cool after another meal outdoors in the sweltering heat. Luke had charmed Wilma and seemed determined to spend as little time as possible confined by walls.

She slipped off her shoes and started to turn back the heavy ivory spread when she saw something on the pillow. It was a small black box with gold lettering on the cover.

Almost as puzzled as she was curious, she lifted the cover and took out a small object wrapped in tissue. In a moment she was holding the exquisite handblown glass swan in her palm.

5

JANE FELT vaguely guilty for sleeping so late. She was, after all, here to do a job, and a restless night was no excuse to lie in bed until after nine. She showered and dressed in record time, putting on white shorts and a pink shirt without giving it much thought.

She knew how a real nanny must feel: What did her charge get into while she was sleeping? Heading toward the kitchen for her morning coffee, she stopped in Mr. Cox's small but well-equipped office and retrieved a thick sheaf of papers and the latest fax—Luke's homework for the day. He was going to love reading through annual reports, sales figures and labor contracts. What kind of bargain could she strike to win his cooperation? And how was she going to achieve Miss Polk's blunt directive: Get his hair cut.

Right.

Anyway, she liked it long.

She stuck the papers in a manila folder and continued toward the kitchen, feeling a little sorry for herself. She'd gone from being a well-paid errand girl to playing baby-sitter for a wild man. She had as much job satisfaction as a highway worker holding a Slow sign.

"Get those filthy things out of my kitchen!"

Jane walked unnoticed into the room as Mrs. Horning read the riot act to Luke in a strident voice.

"They can't hurt you," Luke said, looking as dumbfounded as Jane felt. "They're just the—"

"I know what they are, and I draw the line at having such things in my kitchen. Get them out!"

"Get what out?" Jane asked timidly, half expecting to see tarantulas scurrying across the floor, her own worst-case scenario.

"I did a bit of hiking in the hills this morning. Came across a dead rattler, run over on a back road," Luke explained. "I have a friend in Botswana who'd give his eyeteeth for rattles like these." He held out his hand to let her inspect his trophies. "Had no idea anyone would object. No poison in the tail."

Mrs. Horning was holding a wooden spoon as though it were a bayonet, but managed to speak more calmly. "Your foreign ways are your business, I'm sure, but I'm terrified of snakes. I want no part of one round me."

"I'm sorry, love. Won't happen again. I'm no hunter anyway. I believe any creature has a right to stay in its natural environment."

He gave Jane a penetrating look she chose to ignore. She wasn't going to leap to his defense; she didn't like his grisly souvenirs any better than the housekeeper did.

"A man has to know where he belongs, too," he said in a somber voice just loud enough for Jane to hear. He went past her and disappeared before she could say anything.

After a few more minutes of sputtering and fretting, Mrs. Horning poured Jane a big mug of coffee fragrant with vanilla and let her escape to the table by the pool. Before sitting down, Jane checked the seats of chairs, the potted plants and the ground around the table. She was a native of Arizona; she knew there were creatures that she'd rather not confront. Leave it to Luke to shatter the imaginary line between "out there" and "in here."

She was still clutching the folder of papers he was supposed to study. This definitely wasn't the day to worry about haircuts.

As it turned out, she didn't have an opportunity to worry about anything Luke did that day. She was left totally to her own devices, hard-pressed to explain where he was when Miss Polk made her daily call to check on him. At least Jane could report that the wardrobe problem was under control.

When he didn't show up for dinner, she started worrying seriously. His car was there; so were his personal possessions, in considerably better order than the last time she'd seen them. She felt like a sneak, looking in his room to check on him, but like it or not, she was responsible for him. She went to bed, hoping this was just another example of his outrageous behavior.

Of course, there was always the possibility he was out saving another damsel in distress from a petty thief. She didn't like that thought at all. Not at all. Not that she thought he was in danger from common criminals, just from his fawning admirers.

Jane didn't fall asleep that night until she heard the telltale sound of Luke's door being opened and closed. She tried to tell herself it was a relief not to have to tuck him in.

It didn't work.

THE MORNING SUN streaming through the windows did nothing to improve Luke's foul mood. Yesterday's climb hadn't been steep enough, nor the terrain rugged enough, to clear his mind the way he'd hoped. One day of exploring hadn't provided him any more insight into his grandfather or his own reasons for being here.

In fact, it had been dangerous. Not physically, of course—he could handle that kind of challenge. The real peril came from letting Jane inside his head. His gut feeling was that Rupert was using her as bait to keep him in the country permanently. Was the old man doing it without her knowledge or consent? Luke was inclined to believe her innocence was real, not feigned, but that made the attraction he was feeling even more hazardous.

He finished dressing, lacing up his heavy boots for another day of tramping the hills. No doubt Miss Polk had prepared an agenda for him to follow, but she—make that Rupert—wasn't going to pull his strings. If the old man had things to tell him, let him do it in person. Somehow Luke had gotten the impression when they first met that he'd be spending the thirty days getting to know his grandfather, not being groomed by strangers for a job he didn't want.

What was this stay in Sedona, some kind of initiation rite Rupert had engineered to make him worthy of running the company? Luke had no intention of jumping through hoops for anyone. He was tempted to call the whole thing off.

Trouble was, the old devil would probably sack Janie if he left now. Of course, she was a sharp cookie; she could get another job. But would he ever get another chance to understand his grandfather's indifference to him?

This was an odd way to get acquainted with his only living relative, Luke thought sourly, staying in a house with only hired help.

Part of him hoped his would-be nanny would still be sleeping, so he could leave without confronting her. Another increasingly insistent part perked up at the thought of seeing her.

"Janie, love," he said to himself, "you've certainly complicated this little fact-finding mission of mine."

JANE WAS DETERMINED not to allow Luke to sneak out on her again. She set her alarm to ring at the crack of dawn and managed to get downstairs, carrying the manila folder even before Mrs. Horning arrived. If she'd correctly read the tracks on the frequently vacuumed carpeting, Luke hadn't left his room yet.

She started the coffee, made toast from a loaf of whole wheat and smeared it with honey. No skipping breakfast today. She was going to need fuel for maximum energy. No way was Luke-the-Azrat going to evade her or his responsibilities. She'd dressed in denim shorts, running shoes, a short-sleeved blue oxford-cloth shirt and a cotton cap. Wherever he tried to go, she was ready to follow.

"You're up early, Miss Grant."

He managed to enter the kitchen quietly enough to startle her even though she'd been expecting him.

"What are we going to do today?" Her tone said she wasn't in the mood for any of his nonsense.

"Don't know that I've ever had honey like that."

He poked his finger into the carton of spun honey and sucked it with appreciative noises.

"I'll make some toast for you." She moved the honey out of his immediate reach. "It's not nice to stick your fingers into food."

"Three or four eggs lightly over and a rasher of bacon would be smashing," he said, sitting on one of the plank-seat chairs beside a long bleached-wood table.

"I'm not..." She started to say "the cook," but decided it would be a good idea to feed him. She could talk about what he was supposed to do while he was occupied with breakfast. "I'm not very good at fried eggs. I usually break the yolks."

"No problem."

He locked his hands behind his head and stretched out his long, muscular, golden-brown legs. He was wearing battered high-top shoes with heavy socks turned down to cover the top laces. The footgear didn't bode well for a day spent poring over dull business documents.

Actually the breakfast was one of her better culinary efforts: four perfect eggs, the edges brown from the bacon drippings she used to fry them, a plate of crisp, thin-sliced bacon, coffee that tasted almost as good as it smelled and a tall glass of home-squeezed orange juice that Mrs. Horning had left in a pitcher in the fridge.

"Who'd suspect you can cook," Luke said, munching a piece of bacon he'd picked up with his fingers and dipped in yolk.

"Please use a fork when your grandfather's people are here," she begged.

He looked up, grinned and picked up the utensil in question.

"You're absolutely right, Janie. It's boorish of me. And you certainly are one of Rupert's people."

"I didn't mean me." She reached over, snatched a strip of bacon from his plate with her fingers and munched it noisily. Why should she be stuck trying to teach him manners he should have learned from his mother—if his mother had stayed with him. She felt an immense sadness, knowing how she still missed her own mom.

"About today, it's urgent you at least look at these reports before any company execs get here." She pushed the thick folder in his direction.

He flicked open the cover and shuffled through the papers, continuing to eat.

"They look pretty dry. Will there be a quiz?"

"I wouldn't be surprised if Miss Polk stays up all night writing one," she said. "If you flunk, I flunk, too."

"Hardly seems fair." He rested his arms on the table and gazed at her.

"It's business," she said weakly, looking down at her empty coffee cup. "You know, no one is making you go through with this."

"No one can."

"If you really don't intend to go into your grandfather's business, why bother staying here?" Why make *me* stay here, she implied.

"He's my only relative. I thought he might show up at his summer home."

She had no idea where Rupert Cox lived in the Phoenix area. Not gossiping about her boss was another of Miss Polk's admirable but annoying traits.

"I have a few questions for him, and I won't find the answers in this." He pushed the folder away.

"Maybe just an hour—"

"I've taken a fancy to your red rocks. There's a trail I want to follow...."

"I'm going with you, then."

"Isn't that taking your responsibilities a little too seriously?"

"We'll pack a lunch. You have to take a break to eat. You can look through these then." She pushed the pages back toward him.

"You're so set on this, you'll trail along after me in the blazing hot sun?"

"I'll wear a hat, carry plenty of water. Don't think for one minute I can't keep up."

"You can't, not if I've a mind to leave you behind."

"If that's what you want to do, do it. I'm going."

He shrugged, not exactly a show of enthusiasm. Mrs. Horning came in then, still a little cool toward Luke for bringing the snake rattles into her kitchen but willing enough to put together a picnic for them.

"Meet me by the front door in twenty minutes," Luke ordered.

"How do I know you won't leave without me?"

"Janie, you've got to stop being so skeptical. If I say I'll do something, I do it. I give you my word I'll wait for you."

She believed him. Whatever character flaws he had, dishonesty didn't seem to be one of them.

True to his word, he was waiting for her twenty minutes later, an old khaki backpack sitting on the floor by the main entrance.

"Borrowed it from Willard," he said. "If you're

dead set on lugging those papers, you can stick them in my kit. You'll have your work cut out just keeping up without carrying a load.''

''I belonged to the hiking club in high school,'' she said, miffed by his assumption that she wasn't up to the challenge. ''We went on field trips in the mountains and down into the Grand Canyon. You won't have to slow down for me.''

His grin was aggravating. If this Neanderthal thought he had a monopoly on stamina, he'd better enjoy eating her dust.

AFTER SEVERAL HOURS of walking, Jane was still keeping up. She had spunk, he had to give her that. He'd pretty well gotten the lay of the land yesterday, and he'd deliberately picked a route that involved the maximum uphill hiking. Part of him wanted her to beg off when the going was rough. Unfortunately, his feelings about her were so mixed, he was enjoying her company immensely. She was witty when she wasn't worried about answering to Miss Polk, energetic enough to keep up with him, and so beautiful with her dark hair tied in a ponytail and bobbing out from under her little hat that he found himself inventing reasons to take her hand or guide her by the arm or fall back and watch the way her calves and buttocks flexed when she climbed.

Worse, he let his imagination run amok, looking for flat rocks and level areas where— Where nothing was going to happen because he was leaving and going back to his natural environment. A man could lose his heart to beauty—in the wilderness of Arizona or in the eyes of a beautiful woman—but Luke couldn't let either be a snare.

HER CALVES WERE TIGHT and achy. Keeping up with Luke was no leisurely stroll, and she hadn't done any serious hiking in a long time. She could handle the discomfort; pride alone would carry her along in spite of it. What was really tough was being with Luke and having him think of her as an adversary, his grandfather's monitor or spy. She found herself wanting to get closer to him. What was under his sometimes breezy, sometimes brash exterior? Why was he staying in Arizona when he didn't seem to have any kind of relationship with his grandfather? Was he really indifferent to the company? Or was she being a fool, reading more into his character than was sensible? Maybe that was it. Her track record with men was abysmal. Relationships without a future were her specialty.

"You okay, love?" He turned and offered his hand to boost her up a steep incline.

"Just fine, thank you."

His fingers were long and hard, gripping her wrist with pressure just short of hurting. She loved strong hands, especially when they were gentle.

"There's a plateau up ahead, a good place for a rest if you're ready for lunch."

"If you're hungry..." She didn't want him to stop because he thought she needed to rest.

"I'm always hungry." He said it in a way that made her doubt he was talking about food.

"All right, we'll stop, then."

The sunbaked, rocky ground was too hot for comfort, but Luke found a small patch of shade and spread a square of checkered cloth. Sitting side by side with his hip wedged against hers, they could hardly avoid touching. They wolfed down sandwiches and shared tea still cool in a thermos.

"Do you mind if I take a power nap, just ten minutes or so?" he asked. "Does wonders for the stamina."

"I thought you'd look through some of these documents while we're resting."

Miss Polk's dreary reports seemed trivial compared to the vivid burnt-orange rock formations and the limitless azure canopy of the sky. She wished her job wasn't on the line, prompting her to act like Miss Polk's clone.

"Give me ten minutes, and I'll give them my full attention," he drawled sleepily.

He stretched out on his back, pulled the visor of his cap over his face, and was either asleep instantly or pretending to be.

She looked at her watch, realizing she had to stay awake to time his nap, or they both might suffer from bad sunburns. The shade barely extended to his shoulders, and his legs already had a ruddy glow under his deep tan.

Minutes passed. Her lids grew heavy. She couldn't imagine anything more pleasant than cushioning her head on his chest and dropping off to sleep.

The heat was fast sapping the last of her energy. Twice her eyes shut, her head bobbing forward to recall her to consciousness. She curled up, using Luke's shoulder as a pillow, not intending to sleep, only rest for a minute.

"WAKE UP, sleepyhead!"

She sat up with a start, realizing what she'd done. "I'm sorry. I got so sleepy."

"No problem. You only dozed a few minutes. Just the thing to recharge your batteries."

She crawled over to the backpack on her hands and knees, drank from a water bottle and extracted the manila folder.

He looked with distaste at the first paper she handed him. "You're not going to hold me to it and make me read this now, are you? You've got to be kidding."

"The sales force will be here Tuesday. Fortunately the lieutenant governor canceled. Wednesday you'll meet the plant manager and—"

"Right."

He handled the document with much the same disdain Mrs. Horning had for snake rattles. Pushing his sunglasses up on the bridge of his nose, he read a line or two.

"This has nothing to do with me."

He tossed the paper back toward her, but it floated downward to the path they'd recently followed.

"I'll get it," she cried out.

She scrambled down, not worrying about the steepness of the incline in her eagerness to retrieve the paper.

Luke called after her, "Jane, let it go! Let me..."

Her left foot started sliding, throwing her onto her back. She couldn't dig her heels into sheer rock, and there was nothing to grasp, no way to stop her downward plunge. She cried out, knowing there was a dropoff below the path, but carried toward it by her own momentum. The sun was blinding, and she couldn't see any way to save herself.

Then she was shadowed by Luke's form leaping past her, and she came to a stop in his arms, braced against him, his body a barrier between her and the dropoff.

"Oh, Luke. Oh!"

"You're okay. Not even a close one. Easy now."

His arms were around her, her cheek pressed against his shoulder, her legs too shaky to support her weight. Her heart was racing, but it only took a moment to realize it wasn't all from fear. She wrapped her arms around Luke's waist, unabashedly clinging, feeling the sturdy columns of his legs hard against hers and his sunbaked cheek caressing her forehead. Sometime soon she was going to start hurting, her back and legs bruised by the fall, but for the moment she was engulfed by pleasurable sensations, loving where she was.

"I have you," he said softly.

He tipped her chin, brushing his lips across her forehead, then stood so still she could feel the beating of his heart.

His lips moved slowly down to the tip of her nose, then pressed against the sensitive bow above her lips. She flattened her hands against his back, wanting him close, wanting...

His kiss was so gentle, she was almost afraid she was imagining it. His lips grazed hers like the tickling of a feather, then he stepped back, effortlessly breaking her hold on his waist and putting an arm's length between them.

"You gave me a scare." He didn't sound lighthearted.

"Me, too. Sorry."

"My fault. I shouldn't have let you bring the damn reports. I had no intention of reading them. Miss Polk can..." He took a deep breath. "Maybe we should head back."

She nodded, but she wasn't at all eager to leave this enchanted place.

6

WHAT WAS IT about a kiss that made everything seem upside down and wrong side out?

Jane sat on the edge of the bed, bare toes dug into the plush carpeting, and tried to analyze how she felt about facing Luke over breakfast. Dread? No, not that, even though she was sometimes guilty of letting him intimidate her. Embarrassment? Be serious! She'd been kissed lots of times—vigorous teeth-rattlers, sloppy wet open-mouthers, tongue-to-tongue teasers. Luke's chaste little peck had probably been his way of showing relief that he didn't have to climb down the dropoff to retrieve her lifeless body.

Still, she was tempted to skip breakfast and hole up in her room until he went off somewhere to entertain himself.

Not one of her better ideas! The first contingent of company execs would arrive this evening, and she wasn't—*Luke* wasn't—ready for them. The tailor had promised to deliver at least one presentable outfit by this afternoon, but she still had to get Luke to a barber and coach him on what his grandfather expected.

A simple solution did exist: quit her job. If she couldn't get a well-paying new one right away, she could do temporary work. Thanks to her sister's new job, they could survive without Kim giving up school.

Who was she kidding? This wasn't just about her job anymore. Luke was getting inside her head, wreaking havoc with her emotions. All she had to do was close her eyes to remember the pleasing scent of his sunbaked skin or feel the tickle of his breath on her eyelids.

In less than a month, he'd do what all the desirable men in her life always did: walk away. He'd go back to Africa and life in the wilds, living in construction camps with no room in his life for permanent ties.

She might as well try to do her job and save her career, such as it was, even though she had a better chance of producing a pink-striped giraffe by tonight than a slicked-up, civilized Luke. Groaning loudly, she forced herself to start dressing for breakfast with her boss's beastly grandson.

LUKE BELIEVED in keeping his word, but his promise to stay thirty days was more taxing than he could have imagined. Rupert had baited his hook well. Jane was definitely getting under his skin. If he had any sense at all, he'd be on the next plane out. His plans didn't include falling for a gorgeous American, and he didn't want the complications of getting closer to her.

His grandfather was supposed to arrive in Sedona this evening with some of his minions. Maybe the two of them would have a chance to talk about something besides the company's sports equipment. Or maybe not. Was he making a big mistake, trying to satisfy his curiosity about his mother's father? He'd gotten along fine for years without this family tie.

Maybe he should have left things as they were. He'd waited too long to get acquainted with his grandfather, but before his father's death, it had seemed disloyal to seek out the man who'd vehemently opposed his parents' marriage.

Luke walked naked to the oversize dresser in his room and pulled open the top drawer, amused again by the stacks of pristine white briefs his little keeper had ordered for him. When it came to clothing, his philosophy was simple: less is best. But since Jane was so set on containing his male parts in a sheath of pima cotton, he might as well have some fun obliging her—and in the process annoy her enough to make her forget about his serious slip. Kissing her.

When she'd fallen, his common sense took a header over the cliff. He could still smell the flowery fragrance of her hair and taste the sweetness of her mouth. He should have seduced her then and there and gotten her out of his system, but he'd been afraid—yes, that was the word, afraid. He was already infatuated; he might totally lose it if his fantasies were realized.

He had to put distance between them, and ticking her off seemed the surest way to do it. He slipped into a pair of the new Jockey shorts, pulled on a cutoff tank top that ended above his midriff and padded barefoot down to breakfast.

"Morning, Janie."

She was standing with a cup of coffee, staring out the dining-room window.

"Good morn—"

She froze when she saw him, and he did his best to imitate a fashion model, twirling slowly to give her a good rear view. Women seemed to like a chap's bum, a mystery to him since the fairer sex came equipped with softer, rounder ones of their own.

"Good morning," she said stiffly, averting her eyes but not before she'd seen enough to rattle her. "Mrs. Horning is making muffins. They'll be ready in a bit, just enough time for you to get dressed."

She was playing it cool. He liked that in a woman, but he was counting on his outrageous behavior to make her forget his blunder in kissing her.

"They're a proper fit, don't you think?" He snapped the elastic waistband for emphasis.

"If you say so. I want to thank you for rescuing me. If you hadn't caught me—"

"The least I could do." He sat at the far end of the table, ignoring her suggestion to get dressed and watching intently while she sat on a chair as far from him as possible.

"There was a fax." Her tone was chilly enough to give him goose bumps. "Your grandfather is tied up and won't be able to get here this evening."

"Bloody hell!" The older man was playing games, and Luke was furious at himself for feeling disappointed.

"The others are still coming, so you really have to study the reports today," she said. "And Miss Polk is livid that you haven't gotten a haircut yet."

"None of her concern," Luke muttered, but his anger was focused on his self-important grandfather. What was so bloody important that he didn't have the courtesy to show up?

"I'm sorry you're disappointed," Jane said.

"No skin off my hide," he snapped, standing so abruptly he knocked over the chair.

"He has a lot of responsibilities," Jane said, making a weak stab at defending her employer. "Why don't you give him a call?"

"No way in hell."

He stalked away, feeling ludicrous in the sissy-boy underwear and embarrassed by his dumb stunt. Jane showed real class, considering his boorish behavior, but he couldn't stomach listening to her make excuses for Rupert's behavior. And damned if he'd get his hair cut! What was she planning to do, play Delilah to his Samson? He imagined a naked Jane chasing him with barber's shears, but it wasn't enough to restore his good humor.

He walked past the phone in the living room just as it let out a shrill peal. No way was he going to answer it. There was no one on this continent he wanted to talk to.

Jane caught it on the fourth ring, but by then he was halfway up the spiral steps, intending to dump the whole pile of lily-white undies on Willard and let the caretaker keep or dispose of them. He'd had enough of Miss Jane Grant trying to dress him like a corporation stooge.

He only half heard what she was saying on the phone, but it didn't seem to be a business call. There was concern in her voice, and he only had to hear a few sentences to know something bad had happened.

"Are you telling me everything?" she asked, an edge of panic in her voice. "No—yes—well, call me the minute you're through with the doctor."

"What's wrong?" Luke called down.

"My sister is in the emergency room. I'm more worried about what she didn't tell me than what she did. She fell rock climbing. Says it's only her ankle, but..."

"I'll take you to her. Give me two minutes."

"I can't possibly go to Phoenix now." She started pacing, trying to convince herself, not him. "What timing! I have to see that you get your hair cut, and there's all those reports you're supposed to read before tonight."

"Your sister is more important."

"Kim was adamant about me not coming, but..."

"I'll drive you there. Bring along the reports. I promise not to throw them out the window."

Her lower lip was quivering, and he wanted to offer the kind of comfort that involved taking her in his arms. Instead, he backed away and hoped his smile looked encouraging.

"She promised to call me as soon as she knew anything," Jane said, trying to reassure herself.

"We're going. Do you think we should tell one of the Hornings?"

He sent her to look for the housekeeper while he dashed up to his room, peeled off the constraining briefs and pulled on a pair of faded blue shorts. In less than five minutes he had the Ferrari outside the front entrance waiting for Jane. She didn't forget the stack of papers he was supposed to read.

"I shouldn't go. I shouldn't let you take me."

Impatient because he couldn't let himself take her in his arms and murmur comforting words, he ordered her to buckle up.

"We'll be there in no time. Leave it to me."

He didn't actually burn rubber pulling out of the driveway, but Jane left her stomach behind when they started down the twisting roads.

"You don't have to speed!"

She was a hypocrite, she knew, admonishing him

for driving too fast when she loved the way the sleek sports car held the road. Her pulse raced. Wind whipped hair around her face and made her feel like a kid on a carnival ride. Her fears about Kim were momentarily forgotten as she watched Luke's long, bare legs and powerful arms master the vehicle, taking curves with heart-stopping ease.

They didn't talk much, but he reached over and covered her hand with his.

"I've driven professionally. You don't need to worry about getting there in one piece," he said.

She didn't need reassurances about his driving. He was the only man she'd met who made an automobile seem like an extension of his own prowess. She wanted to blame the insistent tingle running through her on anxiety about Kim, but she couldn't fool herself. Her sensible, sane self knew Luke was driving too fast, but riding beside him in an open car was a terrific turn-on.

By the time they left the hills behind and hit the flat desert north of Phoenix, the Ferrari was chewing up the landscape, flouting Arizona's liberal speed limit. She expected to hear a siren behind them, but the man led a charmed life.

"Why did you quit racing?" she shouted over the wind.

"I wanted something concrete to show for my life, more than prize money and trophies. When I put up a bridge, I expect it to last for centuries."

She was beginning to understand why he'd never be satisfied in a business that made recreational equipment. He'd given her something to think about besides Kim's rock-climbing accident, but once they were close to Mercy Hospital, the frustration of crawling through Phoenix's urban traffic intensified her anxiety for her sister. It would be just like Kim to make light of some horrendous injury. Just the fact that she'd bothered to call meant it had to be serious.

Luke dropped her off at the emergency-room entrance, telling her he'd come to the waiting area after he parked the car.

"My sister is here," Jane told a chubby, pink-faced woman on duty behind the reception desk. "Kim Grant. She fell rock climbing."

"We see a lot of that," the woman said. "Beats me why anyone wants to climb sheer rock to get nowhere. I'd be scared to death of scorpions—snakes, too, but I loathe scorpions. My uncle was bitten once. I remember him telling us kids—"

"Can I see my sister?" Jane interrupted, knowing the friendly Arizona way of doing things might keep her there listening to chitchat for an aeon, not that the woman didn't mean well.

"Go right on back," she said, gesturing. "Someone will point you in the right direction."

She didn't need help locating the partly curtained cubicle where Kim was sitting on an elevated slab, one leg encased in a complicated-looking contrivance. Her sister was telling an animated version of her life history to a lanky young man in hospital garb.

"I don't get much time off," he said after a good laugh, "but I know how to make good use of what I do get. If you're free next Saturday, maybe we could go out."

Jane coughed for attention, but Kim ignored her until she firmed up the date.

"This is my sister, Jane," she said, introducing the resident as Dr. Tom.

"What happened? Are you in pain?" Jane asked.

"Jake said we were going to do an easy climb," Kim explained after her latest conquest sauntered away. "Easy my foot!"

"Why were you climbing so early in the morning? It's not your style."

"Actually I fell yesterday afternoon, but I didn't want to spoil things for the others, so I took some aspirins from the first-aid kit, and Jake wrapped my ankle. We were camping out, but it hurt so much I couldn't sleep all night."

"You should've come to the hospital right after it happened!"

"Well, Tom said it's only a simple fracture, but I have to use crutches for six weeks, and it's going to hurt a lot after the shot wears off. Why can't they give shots in a more dignified place? I told you there was no need to come, but I am glad to see you."

"You told me practically nothing! I've been worried sick. Luke drove like a maniac to get me here."

"He's with you? I'm dying to meet a real wild man. Bring him in."

"Don't worry about Luke. Do you have to stay here?"

"Only until a nurse brings me a prescription for pain pills and some crutches. Good thing I had a lot of practice using them when I hurt my knee."

"Did your friend stick around?"

"Jake left to take the others home. I thought he might come back, but he's not Mr. Reliable. You didn't see him, did you? Big shoulders, no neck. He played football for ASU until he flunked out. No matter. He's history, anyway. I'd rather leave before he gets back. Tell me all about this savage beast you're taming.''

What could Jane say about him? He was an incorrigible, maddening, impossible man, and he made her insides melt.

"I ordered new Jockey shorts for him, and he wore a pair to breakfast,'' she said impulsively, running one of his stunts past her sister.

"You mean..."

"No pants."

"Wow! Tell me more."

"He doesn't like having me ride herd on him. I don't care for it much myself, but a job is a job.''

"Speaking of jobs, I'm just sick I won't be able to work for several weeks. I can get to class all right on crutches, but no way can I wait tables just yet. Jane, I'm so sorry to put all the responsibility back on you.''

"Don't worry. We'll get by. I'll get my things and come home.''

"No! I'll be perfectly fine alone. You know I'm good on crutches. It would be a disaster if you got fired just to look after me. Anyway, Melinda is going to move in for a while.''

Kim was right. Without her sister's income, Jane was trapped. She couldn't leave the company until she had another job lined up, and there was no way to hunt for one while she was stuck in Sedona.

At least Kim's injury didn't sound terribly serious. Luke had been right, though. She'd had to see for herself.

Dr. Tom returned with the prescription, some pill

samples, crutches, a wheelchair and lots of soothing advice.

Silly me, Jane thought, to think Kim needs attention from me. She could go to a wake and leave with a great new boyfriend, unlike her sister, who'd made a career of falling for bad prospects.

Dr. Tom insisted on wheeling Kim out to the waiting room, making a decidedly big fuss over his patient. Jane looked around for Luke, suddenly realizing a Ferrari built for two wouldn't accommodate the three of them.

She spotted Luke sitting in a corner, a pair of gold wire-rimmed glasses perched on his nose, poring over the sheaf of papers she'd pessimistically brought along. She'd never seen him in glasses, and the contrast between his scholarly concentration and sinewy, suntanned muscles rocked her.

"Luke, this is my sister, Kim."

He stood without scattering the papers on his knees, smiled like a movie heartthrob and reached out to shake Kim's hand.

"My pleasure," her sister said, glancing sideways at Jane with a look of unbridled enthusiasm.

Jane gave him a quick account of Kim's condition and directions to their place. He agreed to see something of the city and come for her in two hours so she'd have time to get Kim settled.

"He's the one," Kim said when Luke left.

"He's too old for you."

"Not me, silly. You! Go for it, Jane!"

"It's not that simple. He's going back to Africa."

She knew it would be futile trying to convince Kim she wasn't interested. She couldn't even convince herself.

"You've always wanted to travel."

"He'll be living in construction camps out in the jungle or the bush or whatever."

"Would you rather live in a duplex in Sun City or a tent in paradise? Maybe he could build a tree house. Imagine making love in a leafy bower on an animal-skin rug. It gives me shivers thinking of the possibilities."

"What was in that shot they gave you?" Jane asked dryly.

She called a taxi, and it arrived to take them home. Kim wouldn't stop talking about Luke, asking questions that made Jane squirm. When her sister asked if Luke had kissed her yet, Jane almost wished Kim had fractured her jaw instead of her ankle.

Back at the apartment Jane settled Kim on the thrift-store couch covered by a red, white and yellow flowered chintz slipcover they'd made together. She changed sheets on both beds, washed some dishes and cleared away debris that might trip her sister as she hopped through the place on crutches.

"There's enough food so you won't starve," she told her sister. "I'll leave some cash so Melinda can go to the store if you need anything."

"Thanks, but you're the one who's starving." Kim's voice sounded slurred from the painkiller she'd taken, but she was still focused on her favorite topic: Jane's love live—or lack thereof.

"Don't say it," Jane warned.

"Starving for love. Really, Jane, this one is a winner. All that golden hair, bulging muscles and coppery skin. You'd never get cold at night cuddled up with him."

"This is Arizona. I only get cold when you set the air-conditioning too low."

"You've got to get out of that born-again virgins club. If I didn't know about Bryan, I'd think you'd never—"

"Don't think! And stop giving me a sales pitch about Luke Stanton-Azrat. He's made it clear his lifestyle isn't compatible with a wife and family. All I want from him is a tiny bit of cooperation—enough to stop his grandfather from firing me. When I leave the Cox Corporation, I want to hand my resignation to Miss Polk."

"Has she been to Sedona?"

"No, but her spirit haunts the place via fax."

Jane checked her watch, wishing she had her own car. Why had she let Luke rush to the rescue? She didn't need or want a big strong man to solve her problems.

When he did arrive, forty-seven minutes late, Kim was so groggy from painkillers, she was hard-pressed to tell him Jane's whole life history in the half hour he stayed drinking herbal tea, prepared by Jane at her sister's insistence.

"Jane is quite a woman," Luke said, grinning and getting into the tell-all-about-Jane spirit. "She did a capital job fixing me up with a corporate wardrobe. You should see the stack of—"

"Luke," Jane said, "we really have to get back. People are coming just to meet you."

"Sorry, love," he said to Kim, leaning over and kissing her forehead. "When your sister's right, she's right. Can't have a circus without the clown."

Kim giggled. She thought everything Luke said was hilarious.

"Take care now," he said warmly. "If you need anything, just give us a call. We can be here in two shakes of a lion's tail. Make that a monkey's. Papa lion is the laziest creature on earth. Does nothing but eat, sleep and—"

"Luke, we have to leave!" Jane interrupted.

"...keep the females happy."

"Should I call you Daddy Lion?" Kim teased, keeping her lids propped open by never taking her eyes off Luke.

"When will Melinda be here?" Jane asked, standing by the door but still reluctant to leave her sister alone.

"I've told you twice." Sometimes Kim could be a brat. "She gets off work at five."

"Meanwhile, you get some rest," Luke said, patting her shoulder.

Jane said goodbye and walked out to the parking area just in time to snatch up several pages of confidential reports as they blew out of the Ferrari. Luke had tossed the pile on the passenger seat without returning the sheets to their large manila folder. The pile was considerably reduced from what she'd given him. Insider information was probably floating all over Phoenix, and she had a pretty good idea who would be blamed if any got into the wrong hands.

"You're littering with sensitive company documents," she said as soon as he got close to the car. "Your grandfather will—"

He walked up to her, put both hands on her shoulders and loudly smacked his lips against hers. As a kiss, it was close to a nine; as a way of shutting her up, it was playing dirty.

"Don't do that!"

"I already have. Give up, Janie. I read the blasted things. There's nothing in them that interests me. I apologize for littering, but not for thinking they're garbage."

He picked up the pile, jogged over to the side of the building where the Dumpster was partially concealed by a brick wall, and deposited the lot in the trash.

She was afraid to object. His new method of silencing her was too hard on basic body chemistry. Her hormones were doing a rumba south of her navel.

The last thing she needed was to be scooped up by the golden gorilla and dumped into the passenger seat, but that was exactly what happened.

"You have no right to—"

"Buckle up, love. We've got a date with some clock punchers."

"Don't drive so fast this time. We'll get there in time."

"Glad to hear it. Afraid I was late getting to your place. I wanted to see the botanical gardens, and there was more there than I expected. Never saw so many cactus—cacti—and quite a crop of Homo sapiens, too. Most endangered species on the planet, but they haven't realized it yet."

"I'll put it on tomorrow's list of worries."

"Your sister will be fine. Plucky kid. A shame she'll be off work. Means you're pretty much stuck for the duration."

"The duration?"

"Of my visit to your fair land. I am leaving when I've done my time."

She'd be glad to see him go—or would she?

He honked at a motorist who tried to switch lanes by cutting him off. Jane always gave pickup trucks with gun racks the right-of-way, but Luke streaked ahead, letting them eat his dust, figuratively speaking.

The freeway out of town was clogged with rush-hour traffic, but Luke always found an opening, leading the pack without being an exhibitionist or endangering anyone.

The revolution of the wheels hummed through her, vibrating from the soles of her feet. She wanted to put her hand on Luke's thigh and feel the surge of the engine pulsing through him.

Wanted to, but didn't.

Flings weren't her style. Besides, he was strictly a temp on the mating scene, no matter how nice it would feel to rub her leg against his golden-haired calf or let her fingers wander over his lean, sun-browned midsection and chest. He had the kind of torso that had made Victorian matrons flock to museums to gape at chiseled marble statues.

She was hot and thirsty. Closing her eyes, she imagined sparkling water, an azure pool with a classical nude statue, face raised to the spray. The statue moved and became Luke, poetry in flesh, fully aroused and waiting for someone, for her....

Something nudged her arm.

"Sorry to wake you, Janie, but the engine is overheating. Probably happened when we were stuck in traffic without moving for twenty minutes. I need to get some water for the radiator."

"Oh, I didn't know." She was glad her face was red and hot from the late-afternoon sun so Luke couldn't tell she was blushing. He'd interrupted her dream at a crucial moment; she could still feel the statue-come-to-life slipping between her bare thighs and—

"This is as far as we go until it cools," he said, sounding pretty cheerful for a guy whose car was acting up on a desert highway. "Good luck for us, though. If that sign is right, we're only half a mile from a petrol station."

She looked up at a sand-scoured sign set well back from the road on private land: Jackrabbit Acres.

"That's not a good place, Luke. Not a good place at all."

"We're fresh out of choices. Anyway, how bad can it be?"

"Think bikers' hangout, chains, switchblades, blood."

"Sounds colorful. Come on. It's not the Sahara, but I don't want to leave you out here in this heat."

"August in the desert is no place for a picnic," she said, reluctantly getting out to trudge along the highway beside him.

Luke took her hand, staying on the traffic side.

People didn't perspire in the Arizona desert; they dehydrated. Jane's mouth was cottony, and her lips felt rough from dryness. Before they'd gone half the distance, she felt light-headed and slightly disoriented, as though this was part of her dream.

"You all right, Janie?" Luke stopped and touched her cheek with the backs of his fingers. "Bloody fool! Me, not you. I thought being a native, you were immune to the heat."

"I live in air-conditioned splendor," she said, giggling for no reason.

"Here's just the thing."

He pulled a large red bandanna from the back pocket of his shorts and folded it to make a head covering for her.

"Hang on. We'll get some fluid into you pronto."

Jackrabbit Acres had modernized the gas pumps, but nothing else. The combination saloon, general store and all-round hangout was a long wooden building bleached silver by fifty years or more of blowing sand. A porch with dusty board railings ran the length of the place. A weathered wooden bench offered some blessed shade, but a trio of bikers had pretty much taken it over, sprawled out guzzling beer and cussing the heat, warm brews and each other. One with shaggy, greasy blond hair and a filthy black sweatband seemed to be the leader. All three wore creased black leather pants and high boots. One was wearing a denim jacket, but the other two wore vests on bare upper torsos covered by crude tattoos and sweaty, matted hair.

Jane tugged on Luke's hand, hoping he'd skirt around them and follow a battered sign that said Deliveries in the Rear. Instead, he barged right up to the ugliest and biggest of the trio.

"A hog just like that passed me ten, fifteen minutes ago," Luke said, pointing at one of the motorcycles parked a few yards away. "Great machine. I was doing ninety, and the bugger made me eat dust."

The ferret-faced biker was leering at Jane with bleary, red-rimmed eyes. She was too light-headed to do anything but cower by Luke's side and wish the earth would swallow her up.

Luke talked the talk. Even Mr. Rodent-Face

stopped ogling her and expressed an opinion about camshafts and pipes.

"Be a good race if you could catch him," Luke suggested. "I don't know how, though. Same machine, twenty-minute start."

The dirty blonde swore and spat, and the three bikers tossed their cans aside, mounted their bikes and took off in a storm of dust and exhaust.

"Do you think they'll catch him?" she asked.

"Not likely." Luke grinned at her.

"You made that up."

"Too hot to take on all three of them," he drawled lazily. "Sit here. I'll get something to cool us off."

She leaned her head back against the splintery board wall, closed her eyes and wondered where she'd get the energy to walk back to the car. Luke could pick her up here, but she didn't want to deal with any more bikers on her own. She definitely didn't know the lingo.

"The owner's filling a gallon jug for the car," Luke told her when he came back. "These sodas aren't too cold, but we can cool down another way."

She took a can of cola from him and looked skeptically at the battered pie tin he was carrying.

"Ice cubes. The old boy parted with them for a price. Lean back and close your eyes."

"Why?" She took a big swallow of cola and did as he asked when he didn't offer an explanation.

"Let yourself relax," he said softly. "Just trust me."

Did she have a choice?

He lifted her right hand and cupped it in his palm, then slid a cube over her sensitive inner wrist. After the initial icy shock, her skin numbed and absorbed the wonderful, cooling dampness.

"It really works," she said with drowsy amazement.

"No talking."

He slid another cube over her inner elbow, making her shiver with pleasure, then did the same to her other wrist and arm.

"Mmm."

The cubes were slippery now, and he ran one over her forehead and cheeks, then down to the V-shaped neckline of her lemon-yellow cotton knit top.

"I'm cool now, really cool," she gasped, guessing what he had in mind next.

The cube slid down to the hollow between her breasts, small and slippery but still cold enough to make her cringe.

"Enough," she begged, but he was already sliding a fresh ice cube over the back of her knee.

She had too much imagination. She couldn't help wondering how an icy trail up her thigh and over her pelvis would feel, his cold fingers creating magic on overheated flesh.

"Oh!" Her moan came from way down deep and embarrassed her enough to break the spell. "I'm as cool now as I care to be."

She gulped more soda to cover her agitation.

"I'm not."

"You expect me to—"

"Turnabout is fair play."

"But it's your game."

"You're cool and comfortable now."

"Oh, all right." She didn't try to sound gracious.

"Wherever you like," he said, pushing the pan of

rapidly melting ice cubes in her direction, stretching out his legs and resting his head against the wall.

She picked up a slippery cube and lifted his hand. His fingers curled when she stroked his wrist with the fragment of ice, and she knew why he groaned with satisfaction.

She looked over her shoulder, relieved there were no other customers at the moment, and fished another cube from the water forming on the bottom of the pan. She was enjoying this more than she wanted to admit.

The contrast between the ice and the heat of his forehead gave her odd little shivers.

"There," she said when she finished sliding a piece over his throat. "You must be cooler now."

"Not quite," he whispered in a husky, spine-tingling voice. "There's still a lot of me to cool down."

His shorts had a single button above the suspiciously bulging zipper, she noticed, as a noisy pickup truck pulled off the highway, heading down the bumpy gravel road to Jackrabbit Acres. She scooped up the slippery remains of the cubes in one palm, quickly undid the button that held the waistband taut against his torso and pushed wet ice pieces under the zipper.

He jumped up, slivers of ice falling to the ground from the legs of his shorts.

She was too embarrassed to look at him. Her trick had backfired badly. He'd shed his nice new briefs. She'd touched all man instead.

She started tramping back to the car without him, fuming about his uncivilized ways. What kind of man went around not wearing underwear?

When he caught up, carrying the plastic milk jug of water, she was sitting in the car, eyes closed, pretending to sleep so she wouldn't have to look at him or talk to him.

"I owe you one," he said softly after he closed the hood and sat beside her to start the engine.

She had no doubt he'd pay her back.

7

SHE WAS FEIGNING sleep, and it suited him to let her. He was still amused—and thankful—for her prank. It had brought him to his senses, but she didn't need to know that. Far from cooling him down, it had had the opposite effect. He'd wanted to follow the trickles of melted ice on her skin with his tongue. He'd ached to retrieve the slivers of ice between her breasts.

He'd even been tempted to see if Jackrabbit Acres had rooms to rent by the hour. Fortunately, the cascade of wet ice had brought him to his senses. She wasn't a one-night-stand kind of woman; he couldn't get intimate without hurting her, and he liked her too much to allow that to happen. Intellectually she knew he would be leaving, but women got funny ideas in the afterglow of sex.

What would he do with Jane in the camps? True, a few engineers tried bringing their wives with them, but it never worked out. His own parents were proof of that. Even the spunky ones who could handle the primitive living conditions—and his mother hadn't been one of them—succumbed to boredom. Bridge builders worked from dawn to dark with only a short break to escape the noon heat. There was no social life for a woman, no amenities and little contact with family, friends or the world at large.

It's not for you, Janie, he thought, feeling an odd tightening in his midsection when he glanced over and saw her long, spiky lashes flicker and the moist pink tip of her tongue touch her lower lip.

"Awake, are you?" He couldn't resist any longer. He enjoyed talking to her almost as much as he'd liked planting a hard kiss on her parted lips.

"We should get there with a half hour to spare to get cleaned up," she said.

"You look fine the way you are, and I'm not about to prepare for a spit-and-polish inspection by a bunch of suits."

He even liked the way she pouted, her lips more kissable when they were slightly puckered. He wasn't very happy about his wild-man stunts, though. Everything he'd done to make himself look bad had put distance between them, but he wasn't comfortable knowing she didn't entirely trust him.

You don't have a place for her in your life, so it doesn't matter, he told himself without conviction.

He spotted trouble as soon as he pulled into the driveway in front of his grandfather's summer home: two Cadillacs, a Mercedes and a limo with a uniformed driver shining the windows. The company big guns had arrived early, probably another of Rupert's ploys to wear him down.

"Oh, dear," Jane said with real distress.

He gave her hand a reassuring pat, then swung himself out of the Ferarri without opening the door. His philosophy on taking his licks was to get it over with.

"Why don't you go around to the kitchen door?" he suggested. "No need for both of us to get dressed down."

"No, you were nice to drive me to Phoenix. It's my fault we weren't here when they arrived."

Arguing with her was like punching a wall of foam rubber: no pain and no gain. At least his grandfather wouldn't be here to give her a hard time. He did wonder, though, who was high enough in the company to rate a limo.

Luke led the way into the house, still wishing Jane would make herself scarce. He heard the tinkle of ice in glasses and the monotonous buzz of conversation before he saw the group standing around in the main room. Three men in dark suits and conservative neckties were trying to kill time, probably saying the same old things they always said to each other. Then he saw the fourth visitor, his silver-haired grandfather, sitting in a big leather armchair like a king holding court.

"Luke, where the devil have you been?" Rupert roared. "Horning said you had to chase down to Phoenix. Some kind of accident."

"That's my fault, Mr. Cox," Janie said, gamely stepping forward. "My sister fell rock climbing, and Luke drove me down to the hospital."

"We net two mil a year on gear for fool kids climbing rocks. Could do a lot more if—"

"Her sister will be all right," Luke interrupted, annoyed by his grandfather's obsession with business.

"Glad to hear it," he said automatically. "But you look like roadkill. Where're all the new duds I had Miss Grant buy for you? You look like you just got off a banana boat."

"Granddad, I thought you weren't going to come."

"Changed my mind," Rupert said brusquely.

The execs had managed to inch their way to a far corner, out of their boss's sight but still able to soak up every word for later analysis.

"You study all those papers I had Polk send?" the older man went on.

"Yes, sir. I'll be glad to sit down and discuss them after I've had a shower."

Rupert looked at a Swiss wristwatch with more dials than the cockpit of a 747 and grunted disapprovingly. "I'd like to hear what you think now."

Forgotten by the men, Jane was slowly backing away but hesitated when Luke plopped his dusty, sweaty, but still sexy body into a white chair. She knew he'd read at least some of the papers, but if her pupil flunked Mr. Cox's examination, she was the one at fault.

"What you need, sir," Luke said, "is to drop your least profitable lines and maximize promotional efforts where they can do the company the most good."

Luke had everyone's attention. Mr. Cox picked yes-men as his underlings. No one, with the possible exception of Miss Polk, ever made suggestions that weren't substantiated by several inches of computer printouts.

"As I see it," Luke went on, "the 'bigger-is-better' acquisitions of the eighties left you strapped for top-notch talent, so you made your management structure top-heavy."

The minions, top men in accounting, production and promotion, were closing in, sensing a threat to their domains. Jane was too dazzled by Luke's performance to enjoy their throat-clearing mumbles.

Luke was making intelligent comments, pinning down problems like a corporate raider about to pounce. For a man who didn't want anything to do with his grandfather's sporting goods empire, he was spouting facts and figures like an Ivy League MBA.

Luke glanced at Jane, as dusty as he was with her nose and knees sunburned and her hair windblown under the bandanna he'd tied on her head. He was out of his mind, making his grandfather think he cared a whit about desk-jockey issues. He was only doing it to blow smoke in Rupert's face and keep him from coming down hard on Janie. The older man had looked ready to fire her on the spot when they showed up looking like desert rats.

Luke quoted enough facts from the reports he'd filed in the Dumpster to make his grandfather believe he'd spent days poring over them, but he wished Jane would get her tail upstairs before Rupert noticed her again. The old man wasn't going to be impressed by a stack of pima cotton underpants, while Luke continued to wear the wardrobe he'd brought from Africa wadded up in a knapsack, which he fully intended to do.

"How would you cut down on top-heavy management?" his grandfather asked shrewdly. "Attrition?"

"Too slow. If you wait for the forty- and fifty-somethings to retire early, you won't have any vigorous young execs trained to breathe life into the company."

"Strong stand." Rupert looked impressed but unconvinced.

Damn! All he was doing was making his grandfather more determined than ever to involve him in

the company. It was bad enough he'd agreed to stay
six weeks. Now Rupert would pull out all the stops
to teach him the Cox way of managing a company
Luke never intended to head.

Luke kept talking, but his mind was on Jane. He
must be crazy, playing his grandfather's game just to
save her job. She wasn't his worry. He was compli-
cating his life even though he had every intention of
leaving the States without her. He wished he could
stop thinking about her, but he was burning to sample
that sweet, seductive mouth again and hold her in his
arms with nothing between them. It wasn't enough
just imagining the contours of her breasts; he needed
to hold them in his hands and taste them with his
mouth.

He wanted her; she wanted him, or would if he
really tried to seduce her. Why couldn't things between a man and a woman be simple and satisfying?

JANE WAS GRATEFUL to Luke for performing so well
for Mr. Cox, but surprised by his astute comments.
Was he wavering in his rejection of his grandfather's
offer to take over as CEO? She found that hard to
believe. He'd never be happy cooped up in an office
dealing with petty office politics, not to mention
wearing business suits and starched collars.

She retreated to her room, grateful for a chance to
shower and change into a sleeveless black crepe
dress, simple but dressy enough for dinner with the
sharp-dressed company men. Or did she dare skip the
meal? She was only hired help, but unfortunately, the
boss wanted her there.

She dawdled in her room, dreading the time when
she had to go downstairs. What was Luke up to? He

was an enigma, sending out signals she couldn't mistake even though he'd made it plain that anything between them was impossible. So why did it hurt knowing he'd soon walk out of her life forever?

She thought of inventing a headache as an excuse to miss the meal, but didn't. Much as she dreaded sitting down to dinner with Mr. Cox, Jane was too curious about Luke to beg off. She descended the spiral stairs, wary of calling attention to herself even though Luke had acquitted himself well in her opinion. He'd thrown down a gauntlet for the execs gathered there, challenging his grandfather to cut dead wood and modernize his operation.

The CEO didn't like changes unless he thought of them.

A nervous shiver tickled her spine as she walked into the room where the men were gathered.

Something was wrong. Luke and his grandfather were alone at the far end, walking a yard apart toward the front entrance.

Cox wasn't staying for dinner.

"Miss Grant." He summoned her with a bullhorn roar. "Didn't Miss Polk give you the name of my barber in Sedona?"

"Yes, sir, she did."

Then, turning to Luke, "See that you get your hair cut before Saturday," he ordered Luke. "It'll be a little get-together outside Sedona for some of my friends to meet you. People you need to know. I'll expect you to be there, too," he said, nodding at Jane.

Luke didn't respond, but Jane could see the tension in his squared shoulders and clenched hands.

His mouth was set in a tight line as he watched his grandfather walk over to the limo and get in.

If Luke wanted Rupert to stay, why didn't he ask him? Jane tried to convince herself that their relationship was none of her business, but she couldn't help wondering what had motivated Luke to come to the States in the first place. Why was he staying when there didn't seem to be any warmth between the two men? She still believed he wasn't interested in the company or his grandfather's fortune.

What was keeping him here?

He muttered something that made her ears burn and gave her a cold glance.

"Dinner should be ready," she said, falling back on an inane comment because she didn't know how to deal with the pain in Luke's eyes.

"Enjoy," he said rudely. "I'm not dressed for polite society."

He stalked out the front door, leaving her to face the hostile curiosity of the Cox execs.

"Will you be joining us—it's Miss Grant, isn't it?" the head of accounting asked.

Was she supposed to play hostess? Obviously these men thought so. They were practically standing in formation waiting for her to give the signal for the meal to begin. She looked at the open doorway and made a rash decision.

"Please go ahead without me, gentlemen. I won't be joining you for dinner."

She rushed out the door in pursuit of Luke. The Ferrari was still there, so he must have decided to walk off his anger or frustration or disappointment— whatever it was that simmered between him and his grandfather.

Following the neatly manicured footpath that wound around the house, she hurried to check out the rear patios, hoping Luke hadn't taken to the road. She wouldn't get far in her heels tracking him in the hills.

She found him in the pool.

Checking for discarded clothing before she got too close, she saw the contents of his pocket and his watch on a small metal table beside a lounge chair. His tank top was crumpled on the plastic cushion, but his shorts were nowhere in sight, making her hope he was swimming in them. She approached the pool with a somewhat easier mind, standing on the edge until he completed a lap and grabbed on to the rim inches from her feet.

"I'm sorry your grandfather didn't stay," she said.

"If you want to talk to me, come on in."

"I'm not in the habit of swimming in a dress," she said stiffly, trying to establish distance between them.

His hair was clinging to his head the way it had that morning under the company fountain. He had terrific bone structure, with high cheekbones and an aggressive jawline that went beyond handsome.

"Live recklessly for a change, if Rupert and his flunkies don't have you totally cowed. Take off your dress and dive in."

"How do you know I can swim?"

"You don't need to. I'll hold you up." His smile was infuriating.

"I'm supposed to trust you not to let me go under?"

A few minutes ago he'd looked miserably unhappy. Now he might as well beat his chest like a male gorilla, he was sending that kind of message.

Of course, he didn't think she'd do it. He was angry at his grandfather, and his release was to bait her.

She ambled over to the table, casually removed her watch and little gold earrings, then stepped out of her heels, worn without hose because her knees smarted from sunburn. With one quick zip, she let the dress fall to her ankles and stepped out of it.

Ignoring his low whistle, she stepped up to the edge of the pool in her ivory lace bra and panties and dived in. She did three fast laps before acknowledging him swimming beside her, practically matching her stroke for stroke.

"Where did you learn to swim like this, love?" he asked, trapping her between his arms when she paused at one end of the pool.

"Not in a jungle pond. My sister and I learned at the Y."

"You learned well."

He looked good wet—no, that was an understatement. He looked fantastic, drops of water beading on sun-bronzed skin, his hair streaming water over powerful shoulders and trickling down the silky hairs plastered on his chest. His nipples made her uncomfortable; she tried not to look at the hard, masculine points.

"You were angry when your grandfather left." She was putting him off by deliberately playing the heavy, calling him to account for his behavior.

"Let it be, Jane."

"If you're not happy with him, why not just leave?"

"It's not that simple."

He kicked away, swimming to the other end of the pool. She didn't follow; she'd seen the way he looked down at her breasts, damply encased in almost transparent fabric, and was sure he'd come back to her. Was she in the pool to better understand him or to have him hold her in his arms? She wasn't sure.

"I gave my word to stay in Sedona for thirty days. You know that," he said flatly, breaking water beside her, then immediately resuming his lap to the other end.

Well, she'd certainly been told. The only reason to stay in the pool was to watch him slice through the water with heart-stopping ease. And to avoid climbing out in her skimpy panties.

He did three more laps before he stopped beside her again.

"I can't thank you enough for driving me to the hospital. Kim really scared me when she called. She's all I have, and family is really important to me."

"Not to me."

"Luke, you don't mean that. You came all this way to get to know your grandfather."

"I've satisfied my curiosity about Rupert Cox. That's all it was. Curiosity."

"I don't think you have."

"Think whatever you like. I'm heading back when my time is up. Nothing can keep me here. I hope you understand that, Jane."

He wasn't just talking about his grandfather. He was warning her not to expect anything from him, not to feel anything for him.

He was too late.

"Are you up to a race?" he said. "My five laps to your three. Loser pays a penalty." His voice was light and teasing again.

"What penalty?"

"Winner's choice."

"I want you to get a haircut." She didn't, but she wasn't exactly in Rupert's good graces.

"Agreed—if you win."

"What do you want?"

"I'll think of something."

"Luke!"

"If you're afraid…"

"Of you? I don't think so. On your mark, get set—"

"Go."

To his credit, he gave her a second's head start, then swept past her, hardly rippling the water.

She wanted to win, needed to win, was counting on his extra laps to make it possible.

When he won by half a lap, she knew he'd been toying with her. He moved through the water like an Olympic champion, and a two-lap advantage wasn't enough.

"You knew you'd win." She was breathless and mad at herself for accepting a sucker bet.

"No, you made a contest of it."

She slapped the water, throwing spray on his face, but he only laughed it off, drawing her into the circle of his arms and treading water for both of them.

"Do you want to know what your penalty is?"

"I can hardly wait," she said dryly.

"What I'd really like is to have you spend the night with me."

"No!"

"Let me finish. That's not it. I'll settle for a nice kiss."

"Oh, all right." She'd secretly hoped the penalty would be pleasant to pay.

He reached down and cupped her skimpily clad bottom, drawing her so close his knee slid between her thighs.

"Just a kiss, you said."

She'd never been more ready and willing, but she hated herself for wanting a man who felt nothing but physical attraction for her. If he had any real feelings for her, they were so deeply buried they might never surface. She knew the deal: he was leaving. Alone. He hadn't left any room for negotiating.

"A kiss at a time and place of my choosing," he said firmly.

"This isn't it?"

She felt weak with disappointment, or maybe the swimming competition had drained all her energy.

"You'll know when the time comes," he promised.

HAIR, hair, hair! Jane wanted to scream. What was this obsession with cutting Luke's hair? He wasn't a marine recruit!

She crumpled the latest fax from Miss Polk and filed it in the wastebasket, suspecting her immediate supervisor was the one insisting on a makeover before Luke made his first official public appearance. If Rupert really was eager to have his grandson join the company, he should have enough sense not to make an issue over hair. Luke wasn't a servile peon like everyone else—herself included unfortunately.

Admittedly, barbers would starve if they waited for Luke's business, but Jane loved the wild-man look, the heavy sandy mane lightened by the sun and brushing his wide shoulders. It made him look unrestrained and untamed—and very, very sexy.

She hated this job. Just being in the same room with Luke made her edgy. Maybe a good clip job would take away some of his appeal, make him look more ordinary. She hadn't urged him to humor his grandfather in the past several days, but the party was tomorrow. She had nothing to lose by suggesting it—if she could find him. He'd gone off by car or on foot every morning since his grandfather's visit, once not even returning for dinner.

Whatever her boss expected her to accomplish

here, she was actually getting paid for lounging by the pool. Anyone who thought she had a soft job should try killing time as a vocation. It was considerably harder than real work.

She was in luck today; she caught up with Luke just as he was going out to his car.

"Are you in a hurry to go somewhere?" she asked, tagging along after him.

"Thought I'd go to the Grand Canyon and ride a mule to the bottom while I'm still in the area. Care to come along?"

"Done that, thanks. I started the trip feeling sorry for the mule and ended feeling sorry for me. The sun will be broiling hot, and mobs of tourists will have the same idea. Spring and fall are better times to go."

"Afraid I won't be here then. Maybe you know a better way to pass the time?"

Today he sounded more like the wild man she'd chased out of the fountain. The brooding, solitary Luke of the last few days was a little scary.

"I know a great little place in town—comfy chairs, soft music, personal attention...."

"Are you trying to con me, love?"

She shrugged her shoulders. "Thought it was worth a try. You're not going to a barbershop, are you?"

"Not unless you throw me over your shoulder and carry me there."

"Very funny. You're making my job awfully difficult, and Kim is counting on me."

"How is little sis?"

"Doing pretty well. All she talked about on the phone last night was her personal physician. Dr. Tom checks on her constantly. Well, have a nice day."

"Wait a sec, Janie. My itinerary isn't written in concrete. Do you have a better idea?"

"No, I'm not much of a tour guide."

"Keep me company, and I'll agree to a bush cut."

"Do you mean brush cut?" She was mildly horrified.

"No, a cut the way we do it in the bush. I sit still for five minutes, and you click the shears around my head."

"*Me* trim *you?* Be serious! I can't cut hair."

"I'm sure you can't, at least not like a professional, but a chimpanzee can be trained to use scissors."

"Thank you for the comparison." She wasn't as put off by his suggestion as she wanted him to think.

"Never saw a chimp with legs like yours. Why not give it a try?"

Why not indeed? She had to hang on to this job while Kim's ankle healed. If Luke trusted her close to him with a sharp instrument, why not give it a try?

He went upstairs to shampoo, while she borrowed scissors, a broom, dustpan and a tablecloth to drape around his shoulders from Mrs. Horning. When he was seated on the patio overlooking the pool, she secured the cloth with a wicked-looking safety pin.

"You and Sis have cut each other's hair, I imagine," he said, squirming a little while she made a center part with his comb.

"She wouldn't let me touch her crowning glory for a round-trip to Hawaii," Jane teased, making a tiny tentative snip.

"Ouch!"

"That didn't hurt," she said, wondering how to proceed.

The stylist who cut her hair sectioned it and used clips. She tried dividing it that way with her fingers, enjoying the closeness to Luke.

It made sense to her to start at the back and work around to the sides, but how much should she take off?

"Just a light trim," he warned ominously.

"Two inches?"

He shook his head, not doing anything for her concentration.

"At least one inch," she said firmly, doubting her employer would notice such a minor difference. But hair was part of a person's self-image; only the owner should decide how to wear it.

"It will take all day if you cut one piece at a time," he commented. "Or maybe you like being close to me?"

"No such thing!" she protested a little too vehemently.

She edged along first one side, then the other. His hair was nearly dry, warm and silky to the touch, but the ends crackled with life. The part she enjoyed most was checking for errant strands, letting his locks caress the sensitive skin between her fingers.

Now all she had to do was make sure the two sides were even. She stepped between his widely spread legs, combing to check for lopsidedness. His thighs felt hot against her bare legs, and she wished she'd vetoed his idea of doing this outside. She was close enough to get dizzy on the faintly herbal scent of shampoo mingled sensuously with the musky smell of hot skin. Taking a side strand in either hand, she checked for evenness—and dropped the scissors when he suddenly closed his thighs, capturing her between them.

"You've cut enough," he said, gazing at her under lids hooded against the sun. "Tell you what. I'll tie it back for the party. Just for you."

"Thanks a lot." Her gratitude was less than heartfelt. "Let me loose."

"I wonder."

"What?"

"Whether you should pay your penalty now." He circled her waist and rested his hands in the small of her back.

"The statute of limitations has run out," she said.

"I don't think so."

He was squeezing so insistently, she felt tipsy.

"I'm sure this state has laws about that." She was embarrassed at how weak her protest was.

"So does the Azrat tribe."

"Who are these Azrats?"

"Let me tell you a little secret."

He pulled her down on his lap and whispered in her ear.

"You didn't!" she said, giggling.

"Sad to say, I did. I made it up."

"Your grandfather must hate that name."

"He isn't too happy that his only heir is walking around with my father's name, either. That's why I spiced it up a bit."

"You just made the word up? It doesn't mean a thing?"

"It means, love, Africa is my home, and that's where I intend to live. Unless my grandfather accepts that, we're not going to be able to chuck all the baggage from the past."

"Do you want to?" She had to get away from him before she literally melted at his feet.

"I thought I did."

He stood, helping her to her feet, but didn't attempt to claim his kiss.

When he left, leaving her to sweep up hair and return the borrowed items, she tried to tell herself she was irritated because he didn't help to clean up.

But she knew her disappointment went much deeper, and much closer to her heart.

TO JANE'S SURPRISE, Luke didn't give her any static about going to the party the next night. He met her in the living room, on time and resplendent in new pale gray trousers and a tailored white shirt, the cotton so fine it was semitransparent. True to his word, his hair was neatly tied back with a leather thong.

"Very nice," he'd said in a low, sexy drawl, openly looking her over when she came downstairs in Kim's white halter dress. "Very nice indeed."

"It's my sister's," Jane said, sure she was blushing all the way to her toes at his reaction. "I didn't even realize she put it in my bag until I got here."

"Don't do that, love." He stepped close and brushed a tendril of dark hair from her cheek.

"Don't do what?"

"Don't be so self-deprecating. Don't give your sister credit. That dress is gorgeous because you're in it."

"Let's go," she said, knowing she should thank him for the compliment but unnerved by his mini-lecture.

Luke drove at a snail's pace, by his standards, so he wouldn't miss the palatial home hidden away in the hills on the outskirts of Sedona. When they got there, he gave the place high marks for ostentation with its ornate iron gate, impressive desert landscaping and stained-glass windows, but he could think of much better places to take Janie in her sensational backless dress. The white set off the sleek, lightly tanned skin of her back and arms, and the short, flared skirt whirled tantalizingly above long, shapely legs, making it hard to concentrate on anything else.

She was nervous about mingling with Rupert's snooty friends, and nothing he could say was likely to reassure her. He might do more harm than good if he said what he was thinking: every woman there was sure to envy her; she had the kind of inner radiance that comes along maybe once in a generation.

"If we're not having fun, we'll leave," he said instead.

"We can't do that! Your grandfather—"

"We'll play it by ear."

Somehow he'd get through this evening without confessing how he really felt about her. He'd thought of little else recently, but he couldn't make one plus one equal two. Following a hard hat into remote areas of Africa was no life for her. Taking over his grandfather's company was akin to a life sentence for him. They'd end up like his own parents had: apart and miserable.

His father had never recovered. His mother had built a new life, but her letters had told him how much she missed her son. Luke's loyalty to his father and love of Africa had made him refuse to join her after she remarried. To her credit, she understood and did the best she could to keep in touch. He regretted the separation, especially since her life had been so short, but this lingering pain made him even more determined not to pursue Jane.

He let a valet park the Ferrari, then put his hand under Jane's elbow and steeled himself to begin partying.

"You must be Rupert's grandson," a scrawny woman in a silvery, space-suit sort of jumpsuit said, descending on them as they walked under a two-ton chandelier into the main room at the front. "I'm Amelia Wellington."

"Call me Luke. This is my friend, Jane Grant," he said, almost able to see a cloud of perfume condensing around their hostess. He liked a nice subtle scent, but the natural fragrance of Jane's skin was more appealing to him than anything that came in an overpriced bottle.

"Miss Grant, a pleasure," the woman said with the automatic charm of someone who'd extended the same welcome a thousand times. "The buffet is set up poolside. You can go out those doors and to your right. Later, I'd just love to hear all about Africa, Luke."

As they walked toward the pool, the tiny frown on Jane's face made him even more reluctant to hobnob with Rupert's friends. In her scene-stealing dress, Jane wasn't going to be a success with the women, but he'd expected testosterone levels to shoot up like geysers when the men saw her. But, he soon discovered, not even lechery was enough to liven up the middle-aged and older crowd of successful bores. Janie never lacked for someone to make small talk with, but after a couple of hours her smile was almost as pasted on as their hostess's.

He managed to corner her when she was momentarily alone.

"I guess your grandfather couldn't make it," she said sympathetically.

"Doubt he ever intended to. It's the Azrat way of learning to swim. Throw the kid in the water and watch while he swims or goes under."

"You're no kid."

He was glad to see real warmth in her smile.

"And Rupert's no Azrat. He's just too smart to put up with a whole evening of dull chitchat," he said less sharply.

"The buffet was nice, especially the seafood," she said to change the subject.

"You ate one shrimp and half a cracker."

"I didn't know you were counting."

"I wasn't, but watching you is the only entertainment here. Do you think I've been sufficiently introduced into polite society?"

"Luke, it's not even dark. Mr. Wellington went on and on about how terrific the grounds look when the lights come on."

"What this affair needs is livening up," he said thoughtfully.

"Whatever you're thinking, don't. You said we'd leave if the party wasn't fun."

"It will be. Leave it to me, Janie."

He walked over to one of the white-jacketed waiters clearing away the buffet while she warily watched his every move. So far, nothing catastrophic. After a lengthy conversation Luke seemed to be returning to the other guests when he stopped by one of the tables and lifted a bright red-and-yellow-striped umbrella out of the well in the center. Before she could guess what he was planning, he separated the long pole, tossed aside the umbrella part and recruited two dazed waiters to hold the ends.

"Limbo, everyone!"

A boom box materialized, blasting away at enough decibels to bring the police if someone played it that loud in her neighborhood.

"The best sport takes the first turn," Luke announced, walking up to a woman with improbably black hair piled high on her head.

"I haven't done the limbo since I was a Girl Scout," she protested, looking for support from her bald, slightly paunchy husband, who definitely wasn't amused.

Luke took her hand, and she followed him over to the pole like one of the Pied Piper's victims.

"Show 'em, Maggie," one of the livelier men called out.

She threw her head back theatrically, wiggled hips encased in a midthigh white satin skirt and went under the pole with a spate of giggles.

The game was on. Jane watched with horror—and amusement—while their hostess gyrated her hips and wiggled under, followed by a plump, rusty-haired man who sent the bar flying.

"If there are more savages like him in the jungle, I'm definitely going to Africa on my next trip," a high-maintenance blonde said, coming up beside Jane as Luke finished his turn at the lowest level so far.

"One of the big thrills is a wildebeest ride," Luke said, overhearing the woman's comment and coming over.

"I love exotic rides," the woman purred.

Jane wanted to kick her cosmetically enhanced and aerobically conditioned rear end when Luke went down on one knee, his back toward the blonde, and ordered her to hop aboard. She did, pulling the thong out of his hair as he pranced around the pool with her on his shoulders, a rap beat blaring out of the boom box.

Jane backed away from the action, wanting to be part of it but too conscious of her role as Luke's keeper.

"Oh, boy," she muttered when limbo madness gave way to a conga line snaking between tables led, of course, by Wild-Man Azrat.

He was a rip-roaring success; she just wanted to go home. He dropped away from the revelers and came over to her, taking her hand and trying to get her to catch hold of the last person in the line.

"I'd really rather go home." She meant her real home, but for tonight she'd settle for her temporary quarters.

"Janie, love—"

"Stop calling me love!"

"Miss Jane Grant, the party is only starting to warm up," he said. "Please stay."

"If you won't leave, let me have the keys."

"Have you ever driven a Ferrari?"

She hadn't, and she couldn't imagine facing Mr. Cox if she got the slightest dent on a car like that.

"Never mind."

The blond jockey came over, no doubt hoping for another ride—and not necessarily around the pool.

"I'll get home on my own," Jane said.

"I'm leaving now," a dark-haired man with a bolo

tie and cowboy boots said. ''Be glad to drop you off.''

Never accept rides from strangers, she'd always been taught, but she'd seen her rescuer talking to practically everyone there. It was much more likely that she'd kill Luke than this stranger would turn out to be a serial killer.

Somewhat to her surprise, her benefactor didn't come on to her, didn't ask to be invited in for a nightcap and didn't even seem interested in talking.

Less than a half hour after he dropped her off, she discovered why.

She picked up the shrilly ringing phone reluctantly, afraid anyone calling late at night had to be the bearer of bad news.

This caller was bad news personified.

''Miss Grant, I don't like what I heard about the party. Some pretty important people were looking my grandson over—three board members were in attendance. His antics could make it damn near impossible to get him approved as the next CEO.''

''You weren't there. I mean, the party isn't even over, sir.''

''I got a full report on Luke's abominable behavior. I expected better guidance from you, young lady. You're seriously jeopardizing your future with this company.''

Why was she so gullible? The Good Samaritan who gave her a ride home must have been a spy for her boss!

''This is your last chance,'' he went on. ''Your job is to civilize my grandson and keep him in line. I expect you to be the one keeping tabs on him.''

She hung up, feeling two inches high. Miss Polk

was an amateur compared to her boss, when it came to chastising the hired help.

Jane was mad enough to throw a tantrum—if she knew how. Kim was the one who used to have healthy outlets like raging and screaming. She was practical Jane, always ready to be reasonable, logical and sensible. Luke probably thought she was dull, dull, dull. And she was, she thought, dragging herself to bed.

Finally, sometime after 2:00 a.m., she dozed off.

"WAKE UP, sleepyhead. This is becoming a habit."

His voice was soft and teasing. He'd retied his hair, but his shirt was hanging out, unbuttoned down the front.

"Your grandfather called me." Even asleep she'd stayed mad. "He had a spy at the party, not to mention three board members who would have to approve your appointment as CEO."

"Nice of him to warn us. He didn't fire you, did he?" He wasn't faking his concern.

"Not yet, and I'm going to quit anyway as soon as I can. Maybe if you apologize..."

"Apologize! To whom? For what? All I did was liven up a deadly dull affair. I'd rather hang out with a bunch of hyenas waiting for leftovers than go through the first part of that evening again."

"What a colorful way of putting it," she said dryly, getting out of bed to confront him. "You certainly seemed to be having a good time when I left."

"I make my own good times, but this isn't one of them, Jane. If you don't mind, I'm going to bed now."

"Don't let me stop you," she said.

"I don't suppose you want to tuck me in again?" he asked, his anger dissolving faster than the ice cubes at Jackrabbit Acres.

"What's in it for me?" She tried, but didn't succeed, in bantering with the same good humor he showed.

"That's really what it's all about, isn't it? What's in it for everybody—my grandfather, his board of directors, the company minions, Miss Polk. I'm just a pawn in Rupert's power ploys."

"Maybe you should go to bed," she said, hurt by his outburst.

"I didn't mean you, Jane. I saw Rupert blackmail you into being my keeper. But you don't have to stay with the company. I sure don't intend to hook up with it."

"Then why stay and play your grandfather's game?" she asked angrily.

"Damned if I know, unless it's this."

He pulled her against him and kissed her so emphatically she gasped. Reflex took over, and she wrapped her arms around him, ready for the next kiss and the next, returning them as his hands moved over her shoulders and back, hard and persuasive and exciting.

Things were moving too fast; she couldn't let down her guard and fall for a man who didn't have a place for her in his life—or his heart.

She pushed against his chest with her palms, knowing she couldn't break free unless he let her and half hoping he wouldn't.

"Sorry, I'm not interested," she lied in a husky, broken whisper.

"Neither am I."

He released her and moved swiftly away. She couldn't bear to watch his retreat.

9

SHE'D BEEN STAYING at Rupert Cox's elegant summer home for only two weeks, but it felt like two years. And her reason for being there was absurd: clean up his grandson's act. Much to her sorrow, she'd never met anyone less in need of transforming than Luke. Far from being the kind of bad boy who spelled disaster for long-term relationships, he was considerate, self-confident, intelligent and complex, nothing like the shallow men who had let her down in the past.

Worse, he was devastatingly attractive: tall, strong, distinctive and charismatic. She thought about him constantly, recognizing her emotion for what it was—love.

Who knew it could hurt so much to care for someone? He was the perfect man except for one small fact: his goal was to get back to Africa as soon as possible, a trip that didn't include her.

Would she go with him if he asked?

Maybe. Probably.

The way she felt now, she'd gladly live in a jungle tree house to be with him, but she knew herself too well to pretend they would live happily ever after. She'd miss Kim like crazy, and, worse, she'd feel guilty for breaking up their little family.

What Jane wanted most was a family of her own:

kids and a husband who would stay around to be a good father. Nothing Luke had said about his job or lifestyle suggested he'd ever be content in one place. The tree house didn't seem so romantic when she tried to imagine children in it.

Last night at the party, he'd gone too far. He'd made her look really ineffectual, at least in the eyes of Rupert's spy. But Luke was a full-grown, strong-minded man. How could anyone expect her coaching to make him executive material? She was trapped. Even if she hated her job—and she was beginning to—she wanted to leave it with the good recommendations she deserved.

Before she had a chance to go to breakfast, she got a phone call from Miss Polk.

"Really, Jane, Mr. Cox isn't at all happy. Do you need me to come replace you there?"

"No, I'm sure Luke was only trying to liven up the party."

Miss Polk cleared her throat skeptically.

"He was disappointed his grandfather wasn't there," Jane said.

She was curious herself why Mr. Cox wasn't spending more time with Luke.

"That's none of our affair."

Of course, she meant it was none of Jane's business.

No more fooling around, Azrat, Jane thought, after Miss Polk ended her lecture and hung up.

It was Luke's fault she was stuck in Sedona. The least he could do was cooperate. She psyched herself up to read him the riot act.

Practically foaming at the mouth in her eagerness to let him know what she thought of his stunts, she hurried to the dining room. Mrs. Horning was there, clearing the remains of Luke's breakfast.

"He's gone?" Jane asked without remembering to say good morning.

The housekeeper's confirmation was unnecessary as Jane heard the familiar sound of Luke's car retreating down the driveway.

LUKE DROVE without a destination, relying on the high-power Ferrari to distract his thoughts. He knew he was in deep trouble when driving didn't give him any pleasure. It was his grandfather's fault, of course, but he had grudging admiration, tinged with amusement, for the old man's cunning. How better to manipulate a reluctant heir apparent than assigning him a beautiful, desirable woman as his watchdog? The trouble was, Rupert's ploy had worked too well.

He'd done it again: pulled a dumb stunt to put her off. The party had been deadly dull; he wasn't sorry about livening it up. His regret was he hadn't danced with Jane, hadn't held her in his arms, hadn't made love to her.

He groaned and pulled off the road where parking was provided so people could stop and enjoy a sparkling stream. This early in the morning the site was deserted. He got out and sat on a big rock, skipping stones in the water, at a loss what to do about Jane.

Several hours later he arrived back at the house, no easier in his mind about her but still convinced a romantic relationship was a red flag for them.

"Hello," he said, finding her in the office scowling at a fax.

"These are for you."

She stood and thrust a wad of papers into his hand.

"Thank you."

He thought of depositing them in the waste bin, but she didn't look in the mood for theatrical gestures. In fact, she looked steamed.

"Don't smirk," she warned heatedly. "From now on I'm getting tough."

She was so earnest, so emphatic, so desirable, he wanted to take her in his arms and tell her to forget the nonsense about molding him to fit the corporate image. Instead, he did something bad. He laughed.

"I mean it, Luke. I still can't believe your grandfather had a spy at the party."

"The chap who drove you home?" he asked, feigning indifference when actually he'd been tormented by jealousy after she left, an exceedingly rare state of mind for him.

"Yes, and this morning Miss Polk was on her high horse."

"Uncomfortable position, always in a stew trying to control other people's lives," he observed mildly, wanting to wipe away the disapproval on her face with long, hot kisses.

"I wish you'd go back to your bridge building and get this over with!"

Her angry outburst only made him long to hold her in his arms even more. She was dressed in white shorts and a sleeveless pink top that paled beside the flush in her cheeks. He didn't want her to be upset, but what could he say that wouldn't mislead her?

"There's nothing I'd like more," he lied, knowing he loved the hot, arid beauty of this corner of the world almost as much as he loved his homeland.

"Then what's keeping you here?" she asked.

"I gave my word," he said dejectedly, hating his

rash promise to become CEO of the company if he decided to stay in the States.

"You're not keeping it! You're not even considering your grandfather's offer. Why don't you leave and stop—"

"Stop what?" he asked when she turned her back and seemed at a loss for words.

"Stop acting like an idiot! Behave yourself!"

There was no way to defend himself without telling her how he really felt. What he wanted to say was best said holding her against him, hugging her, punctuating words with long, sweet kisses.

"You might stop imitating Polk," he said instead as he walked away, leaving because he was as angry with himself as he was with her.

JANE HEARD the car roar away for a second time, and her throat ached with the effort of not crying. For just a moment she'd seen a warmth in his eyes that made her heart race, or maybe it was only wishful thinking on her part. Couldn't he see that she was his best chance for happiness, that they belonged together?

"You're an idiot," she said to herself, wondering why she didn't just leave, but knowing the reason had nothing to do with her job.

She waited with the patience of a charging rhino to see if Luke would return for dinner. By four in the afternoon she felt as if she'd been waiting a year.

She was in the office, trying to occupy herself by arranging paper clips and rubber bands in the desk drawer, when the phone rang.

"Janie." Luke's voice was oddly reserved. "I have to ask a big favor."

"Your humble servant has only to hear to obey," she said sarcastically. An afternoon of pacing and fretting had fueled her anger until she was ready to take him on with boxing gloves.

"I need you to post bail for me."

"Post bail?" She was so stunned, she forgot about being angry. "Why? Where are you?"

"I'm in jail in a place called Coppertown. Do you know it?"

"Yes, but why... What did you do?"

"Seems I was driving a bit fast. The local law officers took umbrage with my attitude. No sporting blood here. Didn't help that I have an international license. Did Polk have getting an Arizona license on your list or mine?"

He sounded so sheepish, she didn't rub it in that no one can get a driver's license for someone else.

"I'll have to call your grandfather to authorize bail money. Do you know how much it is?"

"No need to bother him." He sounded like a naughty little boy trying to avoid a spanking. "Just bring my traveler's checks. They're in the stand by the bed."

"If I do this, will you promise to behave and do everything I tell you for the rest of your visit?"

She thought it was worth a try, but there was dead silence on the other end of the line.

"Please let me talk to Willard," he requested in a strained voice.

"Oh, never mind. I'll come."

She couldn't let her boss's irascible grandson— and the man she loved—go to someone else for help. He'd probably fallen prey to a speed trap, but, judging by the rides she'd taken with him, she had no doubt about his guilt. It might be good for him to be locked up for the night. How bad could the Coppertown jail be?

She remembered an old movie she'd seen where a tourist was railroaded for an innocuous offense and sent to a chain gang on a prison farm. However unlikely it was that Luke would end up in orange coveralls and shackles, she couldn't help being worried about him.

The traveler's checks were easy to find, but the rest of her rescue mission hit a snag. Her car battery, left to bake under the hot summer sun without being driven enough to charge it, staged a major rebellion. It was soon clear she wasn't going anywhere in her car.

Willard was obliging, but he had a problem.

"My wife's mother is poorly. Miss Polk said to go ahead and run her down to Mesa for as long as she's needed there. I promised we'd leave as soon as supper is ready."

"I'm sorry about her mother," Jane said sympathetically. "If we leave right now, could you take me to Coppertown, then go to Mesa? There's no need for Wilma to fix dinner."

A few hours later the Hornings somewhat reluctantly left her on the dusty main street of an off-the-beaten-path tourist town. She'd had time to think about whether to bail out a man who thought he could flout all the rules.

She was within sight of the small brick building that served as police headquarters and, she surmised, also had holding cells for minor offenders, but she'd also noticed a number of tourist facilities on the way into town. Squaring her shoulders, she walked away from the jail and toward the nearest bed-and-breakfast. She was hungry, tired from a near-sleepless night and sick of playing nanny to Rupert Cox's rebellious grandson. Let him cool his heels.

The bed-and-breakfast had been a saloon and brothel in the rip-roaring days when mining flourished in the surrounding hills. The current owners had preserved the flavor of the Old West on the main floor, keeping the original bar and some tables in the front room while converting the rear into private living quarters. Upstairs, her room, reasonably priced because it was the off-season for tourists, was small but cozy with electrified replicas of gas lamps on the wall, a brass bedstead and a dresser with a pitcher and bowl for ornamental purposes, not for washing up as originally intended. The bathroom was down the hall, but the room was pleasant with colorful cotton-appliqué baskets embroidered on a cream-colored spread.

She wondered if Luke would have to sleep on an iron slab with no mattress.

He deserves it, she thought without much conviction, then consoled herself by walking down the street to a family-style restaurant in what had once been the town bank. She had a huge spinach salad with real bacon and fresh hot bread brought to the table on a little wooden cutting board. She wondered what prisoners in the town jail were fed, probably institutional fare like beans and franks or macaroni and cheese. She didn't like to think of Luke going hungry, but he didn't seem to be a fussy eater.

She went to bed really early, sinking down on the soft mattress and taking deep breaths to relax, but her mind wouldn't turn off. Luke deserved to stew in jail, but she couldn't erase the vision of a dank little cell with him huddled on an iron cot while rats scurried around his dinner tray on the cold concrete floor.

If he called his grandfather or Miss Polk, would one of them rescue him? Somehow, she doubted it. They'd probably want him to be punished a while. Was she acting like one of them, lying on a comfy, if overly soft, bed while Luke was in a miserable lockup, maybe sharing space with really mean criminals?

She rolled across the double bed, trying to find a good sleeping position, but she couldn't have been more wide-awake.

Darn it! She kept thinking about Luke driving her to the hospital after Kim's accident. He'd been compassionate and caring when she needed help. In fact, when he wasn't thwarting her every move and driving her crazy, he was one of the kindest, most considerate men she'd ever met.

Her eyes felt glued open; she was getting more exercise tossing and turning on the bed than she would in an aerobics workout. How long had she been trying to sleep? She looked at the light filtering through the window blinds; it wasn't even dark yet. No wonder she was wide-awake in spite of her fatigue.

"Oh, shoot!" she said aloud, finally giving in.

She felt too guilty to sleep. She couldn't leave Luke in jail. A few minutes later she was dressed and on her way to fetch him.

THE JAIL WASN'T quite the chamber of horrors she'd been imagining. The lone officer on duty was presiding over an orderly little office with the ambience of a drivers' licensing bureau. He went through a rear door and brought Luke, unchained and probably unrepentant, to the desk to sign traveler's checks for his release.

"What took you so long?" he asked her as the officer did some paperwork.

"Let's just get your car and leave." She wasn't ready for explanations.

"I'm sorry, ma'am. I'm not authorized to release the vehicle. You'll have to come back after eight tomorrow morning."

"But he paid the fine."

"Yes, ma'am, but you'll have to claim the vehicle in the morning."

He exaggerated his drawl, and she suspected he was enjoying his authority—the power to do nothing.

"Let's go," Luke said, taking her arm.

"But he has no right to—"

"We'll collect the car in the morning," Luke said firmly, leading her out to the pavement.

"They can't keep your car," she argued.

"Seems they can for now."

"You could thank me for coming," she said.

"Isn't it part of your job?"

"I should've left you in jail!"

"I thought you were going to. What took you so long?" he repeated.

"I wonder why I bothered coming at all."

"Where's your car?" He looked in all directions.

"In Sedona," she had to admit. "My battery is dead."

"How did you get here?"

"Mr. Horning. He had to go to Mesa because his wife's mother is sick."

"So we're stranded here. Why spring me? At least I had a place to sleep, albeit not five-star."

"I'm overwhelmed by your gratitude."

She'd been avoiding his gaze, but she looked up now to meet his eyes, weak with relief knowing he was all right. How was she going to feel when he went back to Africa to sleep in tents or huts or who-knew-what with marauding lions and awful crocodiles just waiting to make a meal of him?

"We'd better find a room, I guess," Luke said.

He put his arm around her shoulders, making her feel protected and cherished, an illusion she couldn't afford to enjoy. She pulled away, her emotions too fragile to risk getting any closer to a man who was going to leave.

"I have one at a bed-and-breakfast. Maybe you can get a room there, too."

"Let's give it a try," he said cheerfully.

It was a no-go, the owner informed them. All the other rooms were taken. If they wanted to share hers, it would be twelve dollars extra, including the breakfast.

"No, that won't—" Jane started to say as Luke was handing over the extra money.

"How will you list this on your expense account?" he teased, ignoring her protests about sharing a room. "You could call it a field trip."

"You could get a room somewhere else."

"Do you want me out on the dark streets in this wild frontier town?" he asked, grinning like a lottery winner.

She fumbled with the lock, then flounced into the room. It seemed smaller than when she'd left it.

"You can sleep on the floor," she informed him.

"No way, love. Synthetic carpets make me itch."

"Well, I'm not sleeping on the floor." She looked at the lone chair, straight-backed with only a thin cushion covering the wooden seat.

"We'll share the bed—platonically, of course," he said.

He sounded so matter-of-fact she wanted to shake him.

"When horses grow horns!"

"Then you'll have unicorns, won't you?" he asked with mild amusement. "Any chance of a shower?"

"Down the hall," she said crossly, trying to conceal the excitement pounding through her by being crabby.

"No need to wait up for me," he said, still maddeningly cheerful. "I'll just take the key. You won't use the dead bolt to lock me out, will you?"

She could imagine the scene he'd create: banging on the door, shouting witticisms, disturbing the whole place.

"I'll be sleeping when you get back," she said, pretending to be indifferent, as he left the room.

How could she sleep with him and not *sleep* with him? She couldn't do this. She absolutely couldn't do this.

He was fast, too fast. Before she could come up with a convincing reason for throwing him out, he was back.

"Luke, I don't want to sleep with you." She chose

the direct way, awkward as it was, because he might not want to do more than really sleep.

"I took a cold shower," he said glumly, still toweling his water-darkened hair.

To his credit, he'd redressed in his khaki shorts and body-hugging tank top, the cotton knit clinging damply to his chest. She would need a shower of frozen slush to eradicate what she was thinking.

"It's not the busy season for tourists. Maybe I can find a room somewhere else," she said.

"Bad idea, love. I won't have you walking the streets of a strange town by yourself."

"Then you go."

"No, we're rational, trustworthy adults. I give you my word I won't take advantage of the situation."

She knew how honorable he was when it came to keeping promises. She had to believe he'd keep his word about this, but could she trust herself?

"All right," she reluctantly agreed, suddenly seized by a compelling urge to brush her teeth. She grabbed the small bag she'd brought in case she decided to leave Luke in jail overnight and left the room.

When she returned, intending to sleep in the clothes she'd worn all day, Luke was in bed, sprawled out squarely in the middle, the sheet blanketing him up to his chin. She had her choice of six inches on his right or six inches on his left.

"There's no room for me," she whispered, hoping his closed eyes meant he was sleeping, although how she'd roll him over to make room for herself, she didn't know.

"Here, I'll get off your half."

He sat, letting the sheet fall, revealing his bare shoulders and chest.

"You're not wearing anything!"

"Don't look so horrified. You saw me in the pool."

"Tell me you're wearing your nice new—"

"The old ones suit me better."

She crawled into bed, wishing she hadn't asked. Especially she wished her imagination didn't work so well.

BY THE TIME the morning light was seeping through the blinds, Luke had to wonder if he'd gotten two hours' sleep. The bed felt stuffed with cotton balls and sloped downward in the center. He'd spent most of the night trying to cling to the far edge, exerting every ounce of self-control to keep his word. He'd never done anything harder in his life, lying there listening to Jane's soft breathing and aching to show her how he really felt.

Now, after a night of torture, he might still give himself away. She'd rolled against him—how could she not in this sorry excuse for a bed—and her warm form was pressed against his backside, liquid lightning shooting through him, testing his self-control to the max.

He felt her stir and held his breath, not wanting their contact to end even though it was making him miserable.

"You didn't stay on your side," she protested sleepily, waking up enough to realize she was on his side. "Oh, I'm sorry."

"The bed dips in the middle," he said magnanimously, suffering even more as she tried to wiggle away from him.

"I'll get up," she said.

She'd rolled away, but not far enough. The way he felt about her, he wasn't sure an ocean would put enough space between them to get her out of his head.

"It's still too early to get the car," he murmured.

"Sorry I crowded you."

"Come back, just for a while."

"Luke, it's not a good idea."

She wanted to; he could hear it in her soft tone and sense it in the way she stiffened, still only inches from him.

"We'll just lie here for a few minutes," he promised.

"That's what the boys used to say in high school," she protested weakly.

"Did you believe them?"

"I wanted to, but I didn't."

She wasn't talking about schoolboys in her past, he was sure.

He rolled on his side, snuggling against her fantastic backside, wishing she'd taken off her shorts. He draped one arm across her shoulders, not resting it there but trailing his arm downward, over her waist to her hip. Touching her thigh took his breath away. It was sleek and smooth and warm—everything he'd imagined and more.

Had he ever wanted any woman so badly? He had to inch away to keep from parting her between her thighs and ruining the magic that was building between them.

It was sheer torture, but at the same time it was

so deeply satisfying to hold her in his arms, he gladly honored his promise because it meant more time to love her with his heart.

She turned lazily onto her back, and he desperately wanted to put his hand under her rumpled shirt and caress her breasts, obviously freed from the constraints of a bra. He felt shaky just seeing her delicate nipples hardening under the soft cotton.

"Luke."

"What, Janie, love?"

She was quiet for so long, he thought she might have gone back to sleep.

"We should get up," she murmured at last.

"I know." He took her hand, bringing it to his bristly chin and touching the tips of her fingers with his tongue.

He closed his eyes and drew her little finger between his lips, gently suckling it. When she pulled it away, she rested her hand on his chest, touching his nipple with the moistened fingertip.

How was he going to live apart from her? He couldn't ruin her life the way his mother's had been ruined, and he couldn't stay without honoring his promise to take over his grandfather's company if he decided to live in the States.

He sat up abruptly, knowing they had to stop or he risked doing the unthinkable: hurting Jane.

10

JANE WAS SO CAUTIOUS driving the leased Ferrari, she let a battered pickup pulling a horse van pass her. Luke snorted his disapproval every time an old clunker cut in front of them, but he didn't criticize her driving. In fact, she was still amazed he hadn't given her any argument about not driving himself until he had an Arizona license.

Except for a few questions about Kim, he was quiet on the way home, and she wasn't up to small talk, except to say her sister was doing fine. Probably better than she was. She'd made a terrible mistake getting a room at the bed-and-breakfast, then letting Luke share it with her.

He'd held her in his arms and rejected her. He didn't want her. If he had, he would have found her the most willing partner possible.

She kept telling herself it was much better to find out now, rather than have him leave after making love, but there was a hollow ache where her heart used to be. She wanted him in her bed and in her life forever, not just one night.

Dummy, she admonished herself. *You never had a chance. He's the boss's wayward grandson. You're just his watchdog. Get on with your life!*

That meant getting on with her job, and her current assignment was a real stinker. She wanted to play the woman scorned and storm out of Luke's life. Unfortunately, or maybe fortunately, her pragmatic side insisted she do the stiff-upper-lip bit and hang on to her job until something better came along.

So she drove Luke into Sedona and waited while he took his driver's test. At least she had the satisfaction afterward of hearing him bluster because he'd missed four questions.

"You did get a license," she said mildly.

"That's not the point! The test must have been written by a chimpanzee. It didn't take into consideration road conditions or emergency situations. Take number eleven—"

"Do you want to drive home?" she interrupted, dangling the keys in front of his face.

"Then there was the one about turn signals," he fumed as he reached for the key ring.

She let him rant, realizing his anger was targeted at the bureaucratic test as a substitute for what was really bothering him. She sighed, knowing he was deliberately shutting her out.

THE NEXT FEW DAYS passed without incident. That alone was enough to make Jane nervous about what Luke might do next. At the house, he kept appointments with people from the company, not giving them any trouble. He didn't seem to mind talking to the production engineers and designers, but he said very little to her. He was withdrawn and often absent when he wasn't involved in business meetings.

Jane didn't get a single fax from Miss Polk for three days running, but she was sure Luke was far from "civilized." Maybe he was only biding his

time until he could honorably leave the country—
and her.

As crazy as he drove her with his antics, she
wasn't sure what to make of the new, subdued Luke.
Unfortunately, his outward changes didn't at all affect how she felt about the inner man. He was everything she'd ever wanted: wild and adventurous,
but gentle and caring.

Even if he did feel something for her, his life and
heart were halfway around the world. No matter how
much she loved him, there was no way she could
compete with that.

Plus, she had worries that had nothing to do with
what he did or didn't feel about her. His big public
debut was coming up. Rupert was throwing a soiree
to introduce his grandson to the company's principal
shareholders. The other party had only been a dress
rehearsal; this was the one that counted.

Now she knew how a shipbuilder must feel the
day his vessel was launched. Would Luke sink or
swim in his grandfather's eyes? As a precaution, she
spent her spare time reading help wanted ads in the
Phoenix Monitor.

The evening arrived as all dates with destiny do,
or so Jane thought as she put on her modest little
black dress for the second time since arriving in Sedona. She could go in her bathrobe for all the attention she was likely to attract. This was Luke's night;
a lot of people would be sizing him up, thinking of
profit and loss statements or stock prices. He was
meeting the money people, the ones who counted
most. She didn't have a clue what they'd think of
him.

One consolation was that the party was being held

at a prestigious resort tucked away among the red rocks of Sedona. She wouldn't have a long trip down the mountain with Luke, sitting by his side and wishing the ride could go on forever.

She was waiting near the bottom of the spiral stairs, hoping he was nearly ready so they wouldn't get a black mark for tardiness. She looked up when she heard his door, and her heartbeat accelerated as he came down the stairs.

His new silk-blend midnight blue tuxedo had looked dashing on the hanger, but on him it was dynamite. If she hadn't seen the scruffy Luke, she would have thought he was born to wear exquisitely styled formal wear. She silently thanked the tailor for producing such elegance without a fitting, but she knew the perfection was Luke more than the tux. He looked so splendid and refined, even his grandfather shouldn't mind his long hair held back by a narrow black ribbon.

"Do I pass muster?" he asked, grinning at the approval he saw on her face. He was wearing the monkey suit for Jane, and her expression when she saw it made even the stiff shirt worthwhile.

"You look wonderful!"

He loved the way she wasn't coy or reticent about expressing her feelings. In fact, he loved everything about her, not the least her ability to look both sexy and regal in her little black dress. He desperately longed to unzip the long back closure and kiss the creamy skin under it.

Since he'd held her in his arms after his jail stay, she hadn't been out of his thoughts. He wanted her so badly, the longing was a constant pain. Was it possible? Could he find a way for them to be together? He was weary of his grandfather's manipulations, but Jane was confusing his thought processes, clouding his judgment, making him wonder if he could ever get her out of his system.

They were walking toward the front door when the whine of the fax machine caught their attention.

"Ignore it," he advised, fed up with electronic micromanagement.

"I'd better not. It might be something I'm supposed to take to the party."

"I thought you were supposed to take me," he said dryly, but he accompanied her into the office.

He was the one to pick up the first sheet, frowning as he scanned it.

"What is it?"

"Good question," he said angrily. "My guess is, it's a copy of a press release."

She reached for it, but he didn't give her any of the three pages until he'd read them all.

"What the hell is this?" he demanded.

"I can't read through the back of the paper. At least show it to me."

She read the first page and looked up at him with beseeching eyes. "I didn't know anything about this."

"Aren't you going to congratulate the new CEO of Cox Corporation?" he asked, too furious at his grandfather's high-handed tactics to spare her his wrath.

"It says he's retiring. Did you know that?" she asked.

"Apparently I'm the last person to know a lot of things. How deep are you into this conspiracy?"

"I'm not! It's the first I've heard of it!"

"You can't possibly be as innocent as you seem," he said, lashing out.

"If you think—"

"If my grandfather thinks I'll be pressured by premature publicity, he still has a lot to learn. The only agreement I have with the old pirate is to stay six weeks. As far as I'm concerned, this tripe negates our deal whether it's been released to the press yet or not."

"What do you mean?"

"I mean, have a good time at the party. I'm not going!"

"Luke!"

She watched him storm out, then hurried after him to no avail.

Why, oh why, hadn't she thought to steal the man's car keys?

He was getting into the Ferrari when she burst through the door.

"Don't expect me to bail you out again!" she yelled.

He made a grand prix start and roared out of sight as despair washed over her.

Somehow she got to the party alone, her newly recharged battery performing better than the missing guest of honor. Considering Luke's state of mind, it was probably best if he headed straight for the airport.

How on earth was she going to tell his grandfather that Luke wouldn't be there?

Rupert Cox was holding court in the intimidating grand ballroom of the resort, surrounded by beautiful people who made Jane feel like one of Cinderella's stepsisters.

"Mr. Cox, can I speak to you, please?"

She must have looked as terrified as she felt. He took her arm and led her to a window alcove where she could deliver her message of doom in relative privacy.

"Sir, uh, well—"

"Spit it out, Miss Grant."

"Luke isn't coming, sir."

She'd never actually seen thunderclouds on a human face—until now.

"He'd better have a damn good reason."

She was going to be blamed no matter what excuse she gave. She jumped on the one least likely to result in her job being publicly terminated on the spot.

"He's feeling sick."

She was the one most likely to become ill.

Rupert wasn't pleased, but at least she'd given him a plausible excuse to relay to his guests. He wasn't going to can her on the spot.

He went to explain things, and she was planning her escape when the worst possible thing happened.

Luke showed up.

He walked toward the center of the huge room, conversations dying out in his wake. Gone was every hallmark of a civilized man. Clad in ragged shorts, he was bare-chested under a shabby khaki vest. He looked as though he'd been through a dust storm, his face framed by wild, windblown hair and his feet planted in dusty hiking boots worn without socks.

If she hadn't known how little time he'd had to shed his tux and get there, she would swear he'd been drinking heavily for a long time. But it was cold fury driving him, not alcohol.

Her boss's face was mottled red with anger and

indignation, and he didn't step forward to acknowl-
edge his grandson. Like everyone there, he watched
as Luke grabbed a goblet of champagne from a
waiter's tray, raised it toward his grandfather, swallowed hard and sent it crashing against a circular
platform where a small orchestra was providing
background music.

Two burly men in snug-fitting tuxes stepped forward, looking at Rupert for instructions.

"Throw him out," the CEO ordered.

Jane watched in horror as the security men
grabbed Luke's arms and marched him out, sullen
and unresisting. As she watched in shock, she heard
Rupert apologizing to his guests for the "homeless"
man's intrusion and explaining that his grandson had
been detained by illness.

"Please enjoy yourselves," he said heartily.
"We'll reschedule a party for my grandson when
he's feeling more himself."

"Should we call the police about the gate-
crasher?" some management type asked.

"No, just see that he stays out," Rupert ordered
gruffly.

Jane had had it, but she didn't move quickly
enough. The formidable older man was bearing down
on her, and there was no way to avoid him.

"Miss Grant, what do you know about this?"

She shook her head dumbly. No way was he going
to hear from her about Luke's reaction to the fax.
Stepping between Luke and his grandfather was the
surest way she knew of getting crushed.

"I have no idea," she fibbed weakly.

"Find out."

She wanted to hate her boss, but for a moment she

saw something in his face more touching than threat-
ening. He was genuinely hurt by Luke's behavior.

"I'll do what I can, sir."

Her career at Cox was history, her heart was
breaking and tears were building up like water behind a cracking dam. But old habits die hard. Luke
was her job, and she was going to go down fighting.

"Please do your best, Jane," Rupert called after
her.

She was outside starting her car before she realized
Mr. Cox had used her first name and actually said
please, but right now she couldn't think about anyone
but Luke. Where would he go? She only had one
good idea.

By the time she drove back to the house, parked
her car and took a shortcut through the house to reach
the pool, she was trembling with anger.

She found Luke furiously swimming laps in the
fading light of dusk, his clothes in a chair.

"How could you do that?" she shouted when he
sliced through the water near her.

"Did you enjoy the party?" he yelled back, turning and continuing to swim, forcing her to walk
alongside the pool in order to be heard.

"Come out right now," she demanded. "I have to
talk to you!"

"Do you?" He swam lazily to where she was
standing.

"What did you accomplish with that stunt?"

He emerged from the water, stark naked but seemingly totally at ease about it. She averted her eyes
and spotted a deflated vinyl mat used as a float in
the pool. Not seeing anything resembling a towel, she
grabbed it and threw it at him.

Smiling sardonically, he picked it up and held the floppy shield in front of him. He was ruining her life, jeopardizing her job and making her love him, but she couldn't help laughing at the makeshift loincloth.

"You can't run away from this." She wanted to say "me."

"No?" He kept his distance, water still trickling down his face.

"You may not care about your future, but you've jeopardized mine, too."

Why couldn't he see that she'd tell her boss to take a hike and work any job she could get if Luke would give the slightest indication he wanted her in his life. He was so caught up in worrying about his grandfather manipulating him, he didn't have enough sense to see happiness standing right in front of him: her.

"Do you have a message from Rupert?" he asked, bland words not quite concealing the cauldron of emotions seething just below the surface.

"Not from him, no, but maybe you're just as controlling as he is. The man wants to give you everything he's built in his life, and you keep pulling dumb stunts to put him off. Maybe you're just as heavy-handed as he is!"

She was shocked but not sorry she'd had enough nerve to challenge Luke this way. His angry expression was so like his grandfather's, she inwardly cringed but stood her ground.

"Maybe Miss Polk has competition for the job of head minion. What better way to move up in a company than by doing the boss's dirty work?"

"If that's what you think, I don't care!"

Why was he forcing her to lie when all she wanted to do was live in his orbit?

"Why don't you give up? You're not going to civilize me to Rupert's specifications."

"What will it take to get you to cooperate with me?"

"You want to make a deal?" The vinyl mat flopped against his naked thighs. "You want me to make you look good with the big boss?"

"Yes. You could start by pretending you're a gentleman instead of a savage," she snapped, her patience exhausted.

"All right. If you sleep with me."

His proposal—no, proposition—knocked the wind out of her.

"Did that already. At the bed-and-breakfast," she gasped, her throat tightening so she could hardly breathe.

She thought she'd die from the pain of wanting him and knowing he was going to walk out of her life no matter what she did—even give herself to him.

"Make love to me. That's my deal," he said more forcefully.

She was standing at the edge of a precipice. If she stepped off, would she fly or crash? She couldn't spend the rest of her life wishing she'd taken the chance.

"When and where?" she asked, determined to beat him at his own game.

"Here and now."

"Fine."

She hoped her voice sounded firm. Inside, she was shaking so hard her teeth should be rattling.

"Come here," he whispered.

She heard the vinyl mat slap the concrete, then she was in his arms without knowing which of them had moved.

His lips were cool from his swim as they closed over hers, kissing her so deeply she had to cling to his shoulders for support. She felt the grainy texture of his tongue and the ivory smoothness of his teeth as his lips moved, making the long, hard kiss an act of love.

He wanted her. Her body was electrified; her nerves were on fire. She forgot how she came to be in his embrace and returned his kisses with all her heart and soul. When he scooped her into his arms, it was a homecoming, the place where she longed to be forever.

She was lighter than he'd supposed, but the solid reality of her arms around his neck, her lips still locked on his, made him weak with longing. He raced through the house, both of them laughing in fits and starts as he navigated the spiral stairway hugging her against him.

He went to her room, hit the light switch with his elbow and lowered her to stand in front of him, her face softened by passion and even more beautiful than usual.

She was trying to see all of him without seeming to stare, a becoming modesty he found endearing. He saw happiness and anticipation on her face, along with a touch of awe that flattered him immensely. With downcast eyes, her lids were delicate flower petals, and her slightly parted lips were temptation incarnate. He hoped she wanted him at least a fraction as much as he wanted her.

"Trust me," he said with a stab of conscience because he was only thinking of the present, not what would follow when he left.

"Can I?"

She stood, unresisting as he unzipped her dress and lifted it over her head. Underneath she was wearing a black nylon slip, the lacy hem clinging to the fullness of her thighs.

Beneath the tan line on her chest, her breasts swelled over the confines of black lace. In his imagination he'd caressed them, kissed them, suckled until her nipples were hard under his tongue. The reality of actually touching her on top of her lingerie was far more wonderful. He felt undeserving but blessed. He kissed her with gratitude, then with love, engulfing her in his arms and never wanting to let go.

His body was sending him one message; his heart another. He needed to be inside her, but he wanted to be part of her forever. How could he possibly make love to her only once or only twice or only four times a day until he left? And he was leaving, of that he was sure.

He couldn't do it. If he made love to her now, he'd never be able to go.

He groaned, a primitive expression of anguish, and released her, stepping away, unable to look into her eyes.

"I'm sorry, Janie."

He left her standing there, too shocked to react, and strode through the house.

He was in love with her, but he couldn't let her follow him from camp to camp, becoming a shadowy presence as his mother had in the rough-and-tumble life at construction sites.

A rash promise was now ruining his life. If he stayed in the States, he was honor-bound to follow in his grandfather's footsteps and take over the company. He knew deep down in the depths of his soul that would destroy him. How could his love for Jane overcome the resentment he'd feel?

After years of indifference to family ties, his one link to his mother was strangling him. The irony was that Rupert hadn't tried to forge any kind of personal relationship with him. This was just another business deal, a way for an old man to ensure that his life's work would remain tied to him by blood.

Luke went back to the pool and swam until his shoulders burned from exertion and his legs felt too heavy to keep moving. Then he sat naked on the concrete apron, shivering through the cool hours before dawn until the midnight blue of the late-night sky faded into daybreak.

11

JANE KNEW it was the end.

Luke must think she'd lost all self-respect when she agreed to trade her love for his cooperation, but her job had nothing to do with her decision. She'd been willing to make love with no strings attached or on any terms he wanted, but still he'd rejected her. She would never forget standing nearly naked and needy while he walked away.

At first she'd cried, but her pain was too great to be washed away by tears. In the morning she'd had no idea how long she'd slept. The whole night had been a series of awakenings, always with a sense of being crushed by loss.

The next morning Luke was gone, his bedroom door standing wide-open and his belongings cleared out. Seeing the empty room, the bed neatly made even though Mrs. Horning was still in Mesa, drained the last of Jane's hope. Chalk up one whopper in the failed-relationships department, she thought sorrowfully.

At least she knew what Rupert Cox could do with his job and his ridiculous assignments. She and Kim had survived the misery and devastation of losing their mother; they could certainly get through some downtime on the job scene.

One thing she did deserve: a decent recommendation. She wasn't going to trust Miss Polk on this. She was going to the top to make her case, and she knew exactly where to approach the formidable CEO.

A luncheon for company bigwigs was on the agenda for today in the company's boardroom. Luke wouldn't be there, but she would. It was probably her last chance to tell her side of the story before she was booted out of her job. Rupert owed her a good recommendation; she wasn't going job hunting with a big black mark on her record, not after trying so hard to whip his grandson into what he perceived to be the ideal corporate image.

Attempting to mold Luke into something he could never be had been wrong from the beginning, and she should have had the guts to stand up to her boss much sooner. Her judgment had been clouded by love; she'd been willing to go along with anything to stay near Luke. Not to mention her obligation to support Kim.

She packed quickly, sick with dread at the prospect of facing Rupert, but absolutely determined not to slink away without protecting her job potential. That was Luke's style, not hers. He tried to solve his problems by disappearing whenever he didn't like a situation. Someone had to stand up to his grandfather, and she was the only candidate.

She drove to Phoenix and went right to the company, her empty stomach painfully knotted and her mind buzzing with the things she wanted to say to her manipulative boss.

She couldn't get to the boardroom without walking past the fountain. The sun shimmered on the cascading spray, and for one heart-stopping moment she saw a mirage of Luke standing under it. Then her eyes focused on the water, and her pulse slowed to normal. She was through with fairy-tale romance. It was time to look out for her own interests, and she could do it. All she had to do was present her case to the big boss and leave with her dignity intact, even if he told her to clean out her desk immediately.

The double doors to the inner sanctum of the movers and shakers were wide-open, and Jane could hear the buzz of conversation. Stepping with much trepidation into the unusually crowded room, she saw beyond the long, narrow meeting table that dominated the room to a side table set up as a buffet.

"Jane, here you are! Glad to see you." Rupert was beaming ear to ear, and he took her arm and led her into the room.

A cordial Rupert Cox was a surprise; a freshly shaved and shorn Luke, resplendent in a conservative pinstripe suit and burgundy silk tie, was a shock. He stood only a few feet away, charming a group of board members.

She stared, flabbergasted. He was articulate; he was gracious. Heaven help her, he was gorgeous. He was talking business as though the company was his life's work, his passion. Just when she thought the wild man had handed her one awful, final jolt, he was behaving like a to-the-manor-born CEO prospect. What exactly was he doing? And why? Why?

The current chief executive officer himself ushered her over to the buffet, a spread with enough platters and bowls of food for a catered wedding reception. She filled a plate as her boss urged her to try different items, but a few nibbles told her she wasn't up to food. As soon as he was distracted by one of his minions, she handed her plate off to one of the servers.

She wasn't going to get to say her piece to Rupert, not while he was working the room. Luke was avoiding her, not even looking in her direction, which was just as well. She was dying to know what he was pulling this time, but too afraid to confront him. The memory of their near-torrid night was branded on her consciousness; the pain of his rejection was like an open wound. She refused to nurture even the slightest hope that they might have a future together.

Illogically, she was sorry he'd finally gotten a real haircut. His hair still curled over his shirt collar, a lot longer than the current corporate norm but short enough to make him almost unrecognizable as the "homeless" man who'd crashed the party the previous evening.

He was up to something. Suspicion and curiosity kept her in the room even though her instinct for self-preservation urged her to flee.

She talked to people but only saw their mouths moving. It was impossible to concentrate on the words. Miss Polk even came over and congratulated her. Jane's stock seemed to be high; she felt as if she'd just been voted into an exclusive club, but it was one she didn't want to join. Finally she eased her way toward the doors, poised for flight.

And nearly collided with Luke as she started to race-walk down the corridor and away from the luncheon crowd.

"What do you think you're doing?" she asked in an angry but unplanned outburst as he blocked her way.

"Isn't this what you wanted?" he coolly asked.

"You're triumphant. You've tamed the savage beast and transformed him into a button-down-collar management type."

"It's not what I want, and neither do you. How did you pull this off, and why did you bother?" She gestured in the general direction of his stark-white shirt and elegant tie, but also meant his whole young-executive act.

"I'm only going along with the program. It's what you and Rupert both want, isn't it?"

His eyes, dark blue and searching, examined her face with such intensity she was forced to look down at his black wingtips, so different from the scruffy hiking boots he liked to wear.

"Your grandfather was ready to strangle you after your behavior last night, and I don't blame him. How did you explain coming in like a desert rat?"

"I told him it was a joke that backfired. And don't avoid looking at me, Janie. You helped to dress me for the occasion right down to my skin."

She wouldn't ask. She wouldn't even think about his cute round bottom and other spectacular attributes encased in the chaste white underpants she'd ordered for him. Whatever his game, he was playing dirty. She knew he was trying to get even with her for being another of his grandfather's flunkies. In a way, she didn't blame him, but it still hurt.

"Your grandfather is too smart to buy that it was a prank." Jane was incredulous. "The man is a captain of industry, and you want me to believe he fell for a phony story like that?"

"Sometimes people believe what they want to hear," he said dryly. "And sometimes they don't."

What had she said to him last night? Did she say

or do anything to reveal how much she loved him? She felt as though she was standing nearly naked in front of him again, only this time her emotions were being scrutinized, not her body.

"Are you really going to take over the company?" she asked as a smoke screen to avoid saying something she might later regret.

She had to start thinking of him as just another man-who-got-away, but forgetting him was going to be the hardest thing she'd ever done.

"If it's in the newspaper, it must be true," he said sarcastically.

"I didn't see the paper. Rupert really did release the news without your consent?"

"Or the board's. For some reason he let it slip past him, but says it wasn't intended for publication yet. His theory is that an insider doesn't want me as CEO, so the story was leaked to prejudice my chances. I don't know who I have to thank for jumping the gun."

"So you will take over. Did you plan to do it all along?"

He'd betrayed himself, and somehow that seemed even worse than rejecting her.

"I haven't lied about how I feel about desk jobs."

"You don't have to explain yourself to me," she said. "It's not my concern."

"I'm still leaving."

"Then why are you here?" She gestured at the boardroom, a beehive of activity at the end of the corridor.

"I wanted to be sure your future is secure."

"*My* future?"

Her future without him could only be bleak.

"You did your job well," he said without warmth. "You tamed me."

"Tamed." She repeated the word with silent anguish.

"Here you two are!" Rupert's voice boomed in the high-ceilinged corridor, and he was bearing down on them with a couple of minions in his wake. "Jane, I can't tell you how pleased I am. I couldn't have picked a better tutor for my grandson."

She could only stare at him in puzzlement and dumb misery.

"There will be a nice bonus for you, and you've earned a promotion. I'll let Miss Polk give you the particulars, but you won't be disappointed. Good work, Jane."

He patted her on the shoulder while Luke looked on with a scornful expression.

"Thank you, Mr. Cox, but I'm resigning."

No one was more surprised than she was, but she'd already made up her mind, and leaving the company still seemed her only option. She hadn't tamed Luke. She'd never wanted to change anything about him. All she'd done was try to carry out ill-conceived orders from Miss Polk to keep a job that had gone horribly wrong.

"You don't need to do that, Jane." Luke was the first to object.

"Yes, I'm afraid I do."

She'd made an unprofessional and unendurable mistake: she'd fallen in love with the boss's grandson.

She left, her heels echoing on the terrazzo floor. No one tried to stop her.

LUKE STOOD in a daze, watching Jane walk away. He felt as though he'd been hit in the midsection by a wrecking ball.

"What got into her?" his grandfather asked in a surprised tone that didn't demand an answer.

Luke didn't have one.

She was out of sight now, but the soft *tap-tap* of her heels still echoed in his head. He could hardly believe that only last night she'd been willing to make love with him for the sake of her career, and now she'd walked away from a promotion.

It had also been her submissiveness that he hadn't been able to handle. His ego didn't demand that she throw herself at him like a love-crazed teenager, but he wanted—needed—to have their lovemaking satisfy something more than his sex drive. He wanted to make love to her because he—

Luke realized his grandfather was watching him with a shrewd expression.

"She's quite a gal," Rupert said blandly.

"I guess," Luke agreed, angry at the older man for using Jane the way he had.

"Great legs."

Luke didn't want to discuss Jane's attributes with the man who'd used her as bait to lure him into the company.

"You and I have to talk," Luke said grimly.

JANE DIDN'T GO right home after quitting her job. She didn't want to face Kim until she could give her sister a good explanation about why she threw away her career, her promotion and probably her bonus. She especially didn't want to explain about Luke. The pain was so fresh and searing, she couldn't bear to tell her sister how Luke had rejected her. The situation would have been laughable if it hadn't hurt so much—both of them turned on, ready to do the deed, then he'd looked her over in all her semi-naked splendor and left.

Her eyes still clouded thinking about it. If she told Kim, she might bawl; sympathy would be her undoing.

"Jane, grow up!" she told herself bitterly. Happy endings were for storybooks. She had to focus on survival. Kim couldn't work on crutches, and the rent would come due just as it always did.

She drove around until it occurred to her she'd better save gas for getting to job interviews. Then she walked through a mall, but there was nothing in the stores to distract her, especially since even a new tube of lipstick was not in her budget at the moment. She had friends who found solace in whipping out a credit card and treating themselves to pretty things, but Jane was too practical for that kind of self-indulgence.

Finally she went home, and for the next two days pored over help wanted ads. Kim was unusually sensitive, not asking her questions or offering advice. It helped that she was still infatuated with her solicitous doctor, and Jane was glad. Kim was all grown-up and deserved a good relationship with a wonderful man.

As a stopgap measure, Jane signed up to do temp work, and there was a chance she'd get called to work a few days the following week. Somehow she and Kim would survive financially, but Jane knew her emotional recovery was a long way off. She'd fulfilled an impossible assignment, taming Luke, but it had cost her a job and her heart.

Two nights later she was working on a résumé, knowing nothing she wrote on it would help her get a good permanent position unless her former employer gave her a satisfactory reference. She dreaded talking to Miss Polk and hadn't done anything about asking for a letter of recommendation or cleaning out her desk.

Kim was out with her M.D. when the phone rang. Too lethargic to talk to anyone, Jane let the machine take a message.

"Jane, this is Luke Stanton."

As if she knew a dozen Lukes! But what had happened to Stanton-Azrat?

"When you get home," he continued in his machine-distorted, accented voice, "give me a call at 555-0729. Thanks, love."

She hated it when he used the word *love* without meaning the kind of love where people cared about each other and didn't hurt them.

"Oh, damn, damn, damn!" she said, erasing the message so Kim wouldn't hear it and decide to start giving advice to the lovelorn.

Jane had no intention of calling him, but his phone number kept running through her mind: 555-0729, 0729, 729, 29, 9. Where was he staying? Silly question. Probably at one of his grandfather's palatial homes.

Had he planned to step into his grandfather's shoes from the beginning? Was all his reluctance just a ploy to get better terms from Rupert? She didn't know what to think anymore. Whenever she thought about Luke—which was most of the time—she had

trouble getting past the big scene: him naked and
aroused; her pathetically eager; his abrupt change of
heart. Humiliation had new meaning.

The next evening her born-again-virgin friends
went to a movie to check out a new heartthrob who
was collecting rave reviews. Jane went along, feeling
a tad guilty about spending the money but reluctant
to sit home wondering if Luke would call again. The
exciting new star was a pallid blonde too young to
be interesting to her. In fact, she was afraid no man,
on celluloid or in person, would ever appeal to her
after knowing Luke. *Charisma* wasn't just a word to
her anymore.

Jane suspected the instant she got home that something was up. Kim had a coy, all-knowing expression
that suggested she was in the mood to play mind
games.

"Have a nice time?" Kim began innocently
enough.

"The movie wasn't bad," Jane said evasively.
"What have you been doing?"

"Oh, I read a couple of chapters for class. Being
on crutches should be good for my grades. Also the
phone rang so many times the receiver got hot."

"You're a popular girl," Jane said dryly, sure now
that Kim was stringing her along.

"Oh, by the way, Luke called. He really wants
you to call him back."

Jane didn't like the way her pulse started racing;
she hated being aware of her own heartbeat.

"I don't think so," she said more to herself than
Kim.

"You have to call him!"

Kim hopped on one foot over to the phone where

it lay on an end table and held the receiver out to her.

"Wouldn't it be easier to use your crutches?" Jane asked in the stern big-sister-knows-best voice she knew irritated her sister, hoping to defuse her determination that she call Luke.

"Call him, Jane. He's really eager to talk to you. Please?"

Instead of taking the phone, Jane walked into her room and left Kim holding it. Sure, Luke wanted to talk to her. He probably wanted to make some inane apology that would quiet his conscience and make her feel even worse than she did now. Or he wanted to say goodbye and wish her a nice life. She couldn't bear to hear that.

"Not on my nickel," Jane said, deciding she wouldn't talk to him no matter how insistent he was.

Unfortunately she did have a few things to pick up at the company, especially a picture of her mother and a cut-glass vase that had been her great-grandmother's, but she kept putting it off. Confronting Miss Polk would be bad enough, but how could she be sure Luke wouldn't be there? She couldn't imagine anything more awkward than running in to him at the office.

By Monday of the next week she had two job interviews scheduled for Thursday and Friday, but the temp job hadn't materialized. She was still on the list, but they didn't need her yet.

She came home in the late afternoon with three more job applications to fill out and barely enough energy to toss them on the kitchen table.

"You have a message," Kim said, zipping into the room, making crutches look like fun.

Jane held her breath, telling herself she didn't want it to be from Luke again but desperate to have some connection with him. She felt like half a person, functioning on the outside but numb inside.

"Miss Polk wants you to clean out your desk."

"I suppose I should go over there some day this week," she said without much enthusiasm.

"Not some day. Right away," Kim said sympathetically. "They've hired your replacement, and they'd like to have you do it this evening around ten. The security guard will take you up to the office."

"Why so late?" Jane asked, secretly relieved that she'd be able to go into the building at a time when she wouldn't meet anyone, especially not Luke.

"Mr. Cox has some ultraconfidential overseas conference call this evening. He doesn't want anyone in the office until he's finished," Kim explained, standing on one foot in front of the fridge and studying the contents as though she expected to find hidden treasure.

"Far be it from me to disturb him," Jane said bitterly. "He's only my own personal version of a natural disaster."

She hoped for the sake of her replacement that Rupert Cox didn't have any more sinfully sexy long-lost grandsons.

12

THE WALKWAY from the employees' parking lot to the administration building was well lit at night, the pinkish glow making it a bit eerie as Jane hurried toward her old workplace at exactly 10:00 p.m. She didn't mind being on the spacious grounds after dark, knowing security guards were on duty, but the area around the fountain made her uneasy. She approached it with trepidation, remembering this was where it had all begun.

Shadows played across the illuminated display, the water cascading upward day and night to dazzle any passersby who otherwise might not be impressed by the Cox complex. She supposed it was a kind of advertising statement, the same water endlessly recycled in a city that had blossomed in the desert.

Her eyes started playing tricks on her again. She caught a glimpse of movement, probably only the play of light on the spray. Still it gave her pause. A vagrant could be on the grounds, and she didn't know how far away the closest security guard was.

Should she run to her car? She hadn't bothered to change out of her casual white shorts, tank top and sandals, so she didn't have the disadvantage of heels and a skirt if someone chased her. Still, she was no sprinter; her best bet if threatened was probably a good ear-splitting scream. Should she keep heading toward the office complex or retreat while she could?

She would love to forget the whole thing, but the guard in the main lobby was expecting her. It would be cowardly to abandon her possessions, especially a photograph that meant so much to her, and she very much wanted to put everything about the Cox Corporation behind her.

She'd brought a canvas bag to carry her things. She slipped her purse into it, giving it some weight in case she had to use it to defend herself, although she didn't suppose it would do more than momentarily startle an attacker. She moved forward slowly, eyes riveted on the pool, ready to scream and flee if someone was hiding in it. Much as she'd like to turn tail and run, she didn't want to be embarrassed by a second request to clear her desk.

Imagination had nothing to do with what she suddenly saw. What on earth was Luke doing in the fountain?

She had a split second to make her decision: dash away to the parking lot, streak toward the building or confront him. This time the Greek god under the spray seemed to be fully clothed, at least by his standards. He was wearing dress slacks and one of his new, fine, white cotton shirts open at the throat, both sticking wetly to his torso.

"What on earth are you doing in there with your good clothes on?" she asked, incapable of walking past without satisfying her curiosity.

"Keeping cool while I wait for you."

"For me?" This was too much. "You can't be."

"I am."

He stood as still as a statue, water still raining down on him.

"I'm only here to clean out my desk."

Not, she thought, to frolic with a wild madman in her ex-boss's fountain.

"Miss Polk's orders," she added to give weight to her mission, not that she felt capable of putting one foot in front of the other under Luke's scrutiny.

"I doubt that," he said, walking out from under the spray but making no move to wring out his streaming hair or brush the water from his strong, handsome face. "Miss Polk is on her honeymoon."

"Honeymoon? That can't be—I mean, she called and left a message. I never dreamed—who did she marry? When—"

"She and my grandfather had a simple civil ceremony this afternoon. They're on their way to Paris for a few days."

"Miss Polk married to Mr. Cox?" She was so bemused, for a moment she almost forgot why she was there—but not for long.

"If Miss Polk didn't call me to come clear my desk, who did?"

"It didn't look like you were going to accept or return any of my calls, so I persuaded Kim to arrange for you to come here."

How could her own sister be so underhand? Of all the tricks Kim had ever pulled, this was the lowest.

"She had no right—"

"Don't blame your sister. I badly need to talk to you," he said in a quiet voice that sent shivers down her spine.

"I hope the guard will let me in," she said. "Now that I'm here, I really do need to pick up my things."

She was trying to ignore the pathetic way he was standing in ankle-deep water, looking half-drowned in what had been nice clothes. If he wanted to play jungle boy, his act was much better when he wore a loincloth—or whatever he called that little black pouch that barely covered his...

"You may not want to pack up your things just yet," he said.

"Of course I do."

She kept telling her feet to move, but they seemed to have taken root on the pavement.

"I meant it when I resigned," she said emphatically.

"There may be a nice position for you after the corporate restructuring," he said, taking a few steps closer until he was on the verge of stepping out of the pool of water surrounding the fountain.

"What restructuring?" she asked without enthusiasm, not wanting to hear that Luke had buckled under and accepted the job as CEO.

Or worse, that he'd deceived her from the beginning and had always intended to go along with his grandfather. If that were true, she'd made another horrible mistake about the character of a man, her worst ever because she might never get over Luke.

"Come on in and cool off," he invited her with outstretched arms. "I'll tell you all about it."

"No way. You come out here if you want to talk. You're ruining your new pants." She instinctively backed away, mistrusting herself, not Luke, if he came too close.

"I won't be needing them."

He stepped onto the rim of the pool, his bare feet making a little swishing noise.

"That must mean you're going back to Africa." Her throat was tight, but she couldn't let him know how she felt. Not when she knew he didn't feel the same way.

It didn't matter whether he took over his grandfather's job or hightailed it back to the bush. Either way, he was out of her life, so why did it hurt so much to know she was going to hear his decision now.

"Janie, love."

He'd never said her name that way, never called her "love" with so much warmth and longing.

He stepped down on the pavement and moved closer, letting her see that his rugged features were softened by passion. It was a look that didn't require words, but she didn't know what to make of it.

"You're..." She meant to say "really wet," but it was the moment for truth. "...the most special person I've ever known."

"I need you, Jane."

He took her in his arms, sighing deeply before his lips brushed tenderly against hers. His kiss was so sweet and satisfying, she lost herself in it, wanting it to last forever. She could feel the tickle of his breath on her cheek and hear the sensual murmur that welled up in his throat. The world around them ceased to exist as he dominated her senses and filled her heart with longing. She relaxed as he stroked her back and teased her lips apart with the tip of his tongue.

She loved the taste of his mouth, the texture of his tongue, the heady pleasure of being desired. She loved him.

He buried his hands in her hair, holding her head

while he nuzzled her nose and ear, his lips so gentle they tickled.

"We can't do this," he whispered.

She stiffened and pulled away, horrified by the possibility of another rejection.

"Jane—"

"You're a beast!"

She pushed hard against his chest with both hands, but moved him less than half a step.

"Go away! Never come near me again!"

"Janie!"

He caught her wrists, shackling them as surely as if he'd used handcuffs.

"Let me go, Azrat! I don't know what your game is, but I won't play it again!"

She struggled, but his grip remained firm without hurting her.

"You're angry because I left you that night."

He sounded calm and reasonable. That only made her more angry.

"I'm furious because you're an egotistical tease!"

"A tease?"

He did something too outrageous to be believed. He laughed.

"Janie, I didn't make love to you then because I was afraid I'd hurt you by going back to Africa. You have no idea how I hated walking away from you. You'll never guess how painful it was for me to want you like crazy and not be able to offer you a decent life without compromising everything I am."

"Right! And you're only being kind by doing it to me again!"

"I was trying to tell you we can't do what I want to do standing on the pavement under the lights."

He released her wrists and lifted one to his lips, softly kissing it.

"You tried to tell me that?"

Her anger and indignation drained, leaving her shaky and unsure. Blood was still pounding in her ears, and the area south of her navel was throbbing like an all-drum orchestra.

"I'm afraid you didn't quite succeed in civilizing me, darling, but I'm not an exhibitionist when it comes to making love."

In one quick movement he leaned down, grabbed her around the thighs and slung her over his shoulder.

"Put me down! Luke, put me down right now!"

She grabbed the tail of his shirt and hung on for dear life. If this was how a wild man treated his woman, she didn't know what to make of it. She was breathless with excitement.

"Put me down right now!"

His only response was a soft grunt.

"I'll scream! The security guards will hear!" She flailed at his back to no avail.

"I took care of them," he said smugly, if a bit breathlessly, taking quick strides toward the shadowy concealment between two rows of dark shrubs.

He lowered her feet to the ground with a relieved "oomph," and she lost her will to resist when he took her in his arms.

"I won't be a fool and let you go again," he said softly, shushing her with deep, hard kisses.

She caught her foot on something soft and tripped against him, all resistance to anything he wanted totally gone.

"My sleeping bag," he explained, going down on his knees and pulling her with him.

"You put it here! Why were you so sure I'd come?"

"I invoked the name of Miss Polk. How could you not obey?"

"She's not my boss anymore."

"Would you have come if your sister had told you I'd be waiting under the fountain?"

A kiss was her only answer.

His hair was damp but drying quickly, as all things did in Arizona's arid climate. She ran her fingers through it, combing the shortened strands with her fingers.

"I'm sorry you cut your hair."

"It will grow."

His voice was husky with passion, and she was afraid to believe this was happening.

But it was, and practical Jane was sent packing as Janie reached out for the buttons on his shirt.

Luke was edgy. Twice he'd come close to making love to Jane, and twice he'd backed away, hurting her and tormenting himself. He felt like a volcano about to erupt, but he wanted the night to be as memorable for her as it was sure to be for him.

Somehow, with fumbling on his part and nervous giggling on hers, they managed to strip off their clothes and hang them like stream-washed laundry on a bush. He zipped them into his worn but durable sleeping bag, not wanting little pests distracting them. He'd tried to think of everything: protection, warning away the security guards so she wouldn't be embarrassed, picking the only place of concealment on the grounds.

He knew what women liked; he'd had opportunities to learn. He just wasn't sure what would make Jane happy, and nothing was more important to him.

"Luke."

She whispered his name, and his heart swelled with love.

She was cradled against his chest, her tongue flicking against his throat, then she wiggled lower and caught his nipple between her teeth, teasing it while one soft hand made lazy circles on his stomach, moving a little bit lower each time.

All the things he'd dreamed of doing during long, restless nights alone were possible now, but the joy of being with her overwhelmed him. It didn't matter what they did together; it was what they meant to each other that counted. He gently stroked her breasts, so enchanted by the velvety smoothness and the pebbly flesh surrounding her erect nipples that all his urgency and apprehension was transformed into a deeply pleasurable arousal.

"We have all night," he whispered in her ear.

"Unzip me, sir," she said, poking her hand out of the sleeping bag to hunt for the zipper tab.

"Janie, you wouldn't...."

"Leave you? Not unless you're toying with my affections. I only want to open this bag."

She took a bloody long time with the zipper, kneeling, then leaning forward and crawling over his feet to flatten it.

"There, isn't this nicer?"

She rose up on her knees and stretched languidly, for one instant a temptress revealing her full breasts, then a bashful lover linking her fingers to conceal her femininity.

"Come here."

He half rose and patted the unfolded sleeping bag beside him, his voice sounding oddly muted in his own ears. "Please, Janie," he begged without shame.

She snuggled beside him, her left leg lying across his right, her hand resting between them.

His arsenal of sensual tricks had always seemed more than adequate, but how could he possibly please this woman as much as she deserved? He wanted her to melt with longing and climax repeatedly until she experienced all that he was feeling for her.

"Aren't you going to kiss me?" she asked shyly.

"You can count on it, love."

He kissed her softly at first then heatedly, filling her mouth with his tongue until her breath was as ragged as his. Straddling her hips, he lavished kisses on her shoulders, her breasts and the length of her torso, nuzzling her, his tongue finding her moistness.

"Now," she gasped, touching him with magical fingers.

Trembling with urgency, he held back, taking precautions, loving her with his whole being, joining his body to hers.

"Janie, I love you," he whispered, his release more satisfying than he could have imagined.

Holding her close, he fell asleep.

JANE AWOKE SLOWLY in the first light of dawn, remembering she'd fallen asleep still linked to Luke. His hand was heavy on her breast, and even though nights were always cool in the desert climate, his flesh against hers was overheated in the confines of the sleeping bag. But small discomforts were overshadowed by total awareness of the man cradled against her. She reached across his hip and lovingly patted his round, firm backside, then tickled the little hollow at the end of his spine until he groaned with pleasure and threw his leg across hers, locking her even closer against him. He awoke slowly, too, kissing her in all the little places he'd overlooked the night before, then parted her thighs and caressed her with the tip of his finger until she squirmed with pleasure and invited him to say good morning in the nicest possible way.

"People will be coming to work," she said some time later, drowsy with contentment. "Someone might see us through an opening in the bushes."

He'd unzipped the sleeping bag and was lying spread-eagle with her tucked against his side, her head cradled on his chest.

"Toss me my clothes," he said lazily.

"You mean I should get up, risk being seen and deliver them to you?"

"Be nice if you did," he teased.

"Give me one reason why I should be the one to get them."

"You're my woman."

"I'm what?" She yanked a cluster of chest hairs hard enough to get his full attention.

"Ow! My woman—if you want the job."

"I don't remember applying."

She leaned over him on one elbow, secretly admiring his lean, tan, bristly cheeks, just fleshy enough to nip with her teeth. But she didn't want to start anything—and he looked ready for anything she might have in mind—until they settled a few things. Quite a few things. Maybe getting dressed wasn't such a bad idea.

"I'll get them," she said, "but don't read anything into it. I'm only doing it for modesty's sake."

"Understood." He grinned sheepishly. "I only asked so I could watch your bottom wiggle when you walk over there."

"You're terrible!"

She scampered over to the bush, feeling so self-conscious she wanted to break off a branch and play Eve to his Adam. Gathering his clothes first, she noticed his conservative cotton briefs were conspicuously absent. She made a bundle of his trousers and shirt, then hid his skimpy black pouch in one of the pockets, hurling the wadded-up garments directly at him. She dressed herself behind the thickest part of the bush, relieved when she was clothed.

"Your nice clothes are a mess," she said, turning around to find that he was dressed. "I think the pants shrunk."

"I won't need them," he said.

He was going back to Africa. She'd known since the beginning, but that didn't make it any less painful. A night like last night probably only happened to one woman in a million. How could she go back to an ordinary life without him?

"You're leaving."

"Yes, I have some things to take care of, but I'm coming back."

"Here?"

"Come sit by me."

"Tell me the coming-back part first."

He got to his feet in one fluid movement and took both her hands, standing in front of her with a boyish grin.

"I knew when you quit your job you were nuts—

or crazy about me—to put up with my antics for the sake of keeping it, then tossing it away, promotion and all.''

"I really needed the job, but I guess I needed you more.''

"Oh, love, when I realize I nearly blew this..."

He kissed her. Kissed her again. The morning sun was liquid gold around their tiny patch of shade, and someone called out to another person on the walkway beyond their hideaway.

"You can't be CEO of the company," she said with alarm. "You'll hate it, Luke. And you can't break your promise to your grandfather, or you'll hate yourself.''

"Will you come with me to Africa?"

"Yes.''

It might not be right for her, but being separated from Luke would be so wrong.

"There are places I want to show you, people I want you to meet," he said with a dreamy expression on his face that made her insides feel like roasted marshmallows.

"I want to be part of your life no matter where you go, Luke.''

"Three or four weeks should be long enough. Do you want to get married here before we leave?"

"Married! Leave in three or four weeks?"

She had a funny, scared feeling, but Luke hugged her close and it went away.

"No, stay that long. I should be able to tie up all my business in that time.''

"You want to live here, then? Run the company?"

Relief mingled with a sick feeling for his sake. He was going to buckle under to his grandfather.

"Did I say that?"

He tilted her chin and smiled down on her, his sapphire blue eyes easily the most beautiful she'd ever seen.

"You promised your grandfather—"

"The trouble was," he said gravely, "I didn't like being blackmailed into staying. I wanted to get to know my only blood relative, but Rupert didn't seem to have any time for me. I was angry—mostly at myself for making that dumb promise to take over for him if I liked the States well enough to live here."

He stroked her hair, combing it with his fingers.

"I've never seen dark hair as fine as yours."

"Luke!"

She couldn't get mad at a man who made her feel like a goddess, but he was driving her crazy, leaking out bits of information instead of telling her the whole story.

"Sorry, love." He brushed a soft kiss on her cupid's bow and lovingly patted her backside. "I should tell you about my talk with Granddad."

"Please do."

"Here, sit down on the sleeping bag. I don't want anyone to see us before you hear the entire thing."

They sat side by side, the fingers of his left hand linked with her right.

"I had a long talk with Rupert."

Still, he hesitated.

"Yes, but what did you say?"

"I outlined some of the programs I plan to implement if I take over as CEO." He laughed softly. "I'm not one to run a sweatshop. I favor a relaxed workweek with flexible hours and on-site child care.

Also, company-sponsored wilderness retreats for employees, plus some production incentives like stock distributions.''

"He'll never agree to any of that."

"No? You should have heard what he had to say about my ideas on product diversification. And you've already heard what I think of all the dead wood in the upper echelon.''

"What was his reaction?"

She was breathless in anticipation, wondering if Luke had toe marks on his backside from being booted out.

"He decided he's been a little hasty about his decision to retire." Luke smiled broadly. "He isn't so sure I'm CEO material when he does step down."

"I don't understand any of this."

"We hashed things out bit by bit for several days. Turns out he wants his grandson in his life, and he thought the way to guarantee it was to hand over the company. Of course, he planned to stick around to give advice."

"He was using the business to hide his feelings?"

"Yes, and I behaved like an idiot to keep him at arm's length. Seems he was afraid I'd bolt if he came on too strong as the repentant granddad. My mother ran away because he was too heavy-handed and demanding. He didn't want that to happen with me, so he thought the best way was to tie me to him through company responsibilities."

"What about his sudden marriage to Miss Polk?"

Luke covered her knee with his hand, gently kneading but not answering.

"I know!" she said, stopping his hand on its upward trip so he didn't distract her from getting the whole picture. "Your grandfather married his other candidate for CEO. If not his grandson, then his wife would be his logical replacement."

"She's been his mistress and right-hand assistant for years," Luke said sheepishly. "I should've tumbled to it when she went off on the haircut crusade. It was a wifely thing, not what an executive secretary would insist her boss's wayward grandson do."

"You two wasted a lot of years," Jane said with new compassion for grandson and grandfather. "What will you do now?"

"Now that I'm all 'civilized'?"

"That's doubtful, but I'm glad you're not at odds with your grandfather anymore. Even though he can be overbearing, I think he's just a lonely man who misses his family."

"Tell me, Janie love," he said, taking her hand in his. "Why did you stick with the job when I was doing my best to drive you away? I know your sister needs help from you, but there was something more, wasn't there? Do you love me the way I love you?"

"I guess the answer is yes."

"You guess!"

He tumbled her onto her back and hovered over her, his grinning lips only inches away.

"I'd have to hear exactly how much that is," she said.

"You're going to hear, again and again and again. Jane Grant, I love you immensely, immeasurably, unceasingly."

He proved it with a kiss that made her tingle all the way to her toes.

"I have a confession to make," he said in a soft

voice. "Actually I've fallen in love twice since I've been here."

"Twice?" She had a sudden fear that he wasn't kidding.

"First with you." He kissed her softly and reached under her rumpled tank top to caress her breast. "Then with this beautiful desert country of yours. When we get back from our honeymoon—"

"Honeymoon?"

"How do you feel about a safari after I've taken care of my business? Show you something of my world before I come live in yours."

"I can't believe this is happening!" Her happiness was bubbling up and almost overwhelming her. "What are you going to do when we come back here?"

"Make love to you, build bridges, make love to you—it would be nice to try a proper bed."

"What about your grandfather's company?"

"There may be a place for me someday in the corporate structure, but meanwhile..."

His kiss told her all she needed to know about "meanwhile."

Celebrate **15** years with

HARLEQUIN®
Makes any time special ™

In celebration of Harlequin®'s golden anniversary

Enter to win a *dream!* You could win:

- A luxurious trip for two to
  The Renaissance Cottonwoods Resort
  in Scottsdale, Arizona, or

- A bouquet of flowers once a week for a year
  from **FTD**, or

- A $500 shopping spree, or

- A fabulous bath & body gift basket including
  K-Tel's *Romance and Candlelight* CD set.

Look for **WIN A DREAM** flash on
specially marked Harlequin® titles by
Penny Jordan, Dallas Schulze,
Anne Stuart and Kristine Rolofson
in October 1999*.

RENAISSANCE.
COTTONWOODS RESORT
SCOTTSDALE, ARIZONA

COMING NEXT MONTH

HARLEQUIN Duets™

#9

THE RANCHER GETS HITCHED by Cathie Linz

Best of the West

An MBA didn't exactly prepare beautiful, savvy Tracy Campbell
for life on a Colorado ranch, especially not as the housekeeper!
But how hard could it be to follow a recipe, she asked, until she
scraped the exploded casserole off the ceiling? Or learned what
a challenge twins could be. Or discovered how crazy a mule
headed, sexy rancher determined to stay away from city women
could make her. But even Zane couldn't deny the chemistry
between them....

AN AFFAIR OF CONVENIENCE by Marissa Hall

Mallory Reissen's schedule said it all: meeting, meeting, have
wild passionate sex with Cliff Young. Best friends, they agreed a
no-strings-attached affair was their solution to busy careers and
no time for dating. The problem was, once they'd concluded their
intimate negotiations, they wanted each other again and again.
But now their careers were getting in the way. Perhaps the only
solution was...marriage.

#10

BRIDE ON THE LOOSE by Renee Roszel

In one impulsive act, Dana Vanover jumped overboard, dumped
her fiancé and—for good measure—decided to lose her memory.
If no one knew who she was, it would be easier to shake her past.
Enter Sam Taylor, virile veterinarian and dangerous rescuer.
Around him, Dana was having trouble remembering to forget....

MARRIED AFTER BREAKFAST by Colleen Collins

Millionaire Dirk Harriman, wanting a taste of ordinary
America, got more than he expected when he rescued
beautiful and extraordinary Belle O'Leary. Belle was impulsive,
flamboyant, while he was rich and boring. Still the sexual sparks
sizzled between them. Was that why every time he tried to say
goodbye, it just didn't work out that way?

Do the Harlequin Duets™ Dating Quiz!

1) My ideal date would be:
a) a candlelight dinner at the most exclusive restaurant in town
b) dinner made by him even if it is burnt macaroni and cheese
c) a dinner made lovingly by me—to which he brings his mother and two ex-wives

2) If a woman came on to my ideal man, he would:
a) flirt back a little, but make it clear he's already taken
b) tell her to go away
c) bail me out of jail

3) The ideal setting for the perfect date would be:
a) a luxurious ocean resort with white sand, palm trees, picture-perfect sunsets
b) a desert island with just him and a few million mosquitoes
c) a stateroom on the *Titanic*

4) In his free time, my ideal man would most often choose to:
a) Watch sports on TV
b) Watch sports on TV
c) Watch sports on TV *(let's not kid ourselves, even ideal men will be men!)*

If you chose A most often: You are wonderful, talented and sexy. A near goddess, in fact, who will make beautiful music with just about any man you want. The only thing that could make you more perfect is reading Harlequin Duets™.

If you chose B most often: Others are jealous of your charm, wit, intelligence, good fashion sense and ability to eat whatever you want without gaining a pound. The only workout you need is a good evening with Harlequin Duets™.

If you chose C most often: Don't worry. Harlequin Duets™ to the rescue!

Experience the lighter side of love with Harlequin Duets™!

HARLEQUIN®
Makes any time special.™

Look us up on-line at: http://www.romance.net   HDQUIZ